Robert Clement Sconce, Sarah Susanna Sconce Bunbury

Life and Letters of Robert Clement Sconce

Vol. II.

Robert Clement Sconce, Sarah Susanna Sconce Bunbury

Life and Letters of Robert Clement Sconce
Vol. II.

ISBN/EAN: 9783337134686

Printed in Europe, USA, Canada, Australia, Japan

Cover: Foto ©Raphael Reischuk / pixelio.de

More available books at **www.hansebooks.com**

LIFE AND LETTERS

OF

ROBERT CLEMENT SCONCE,

Formerly Secretary to ADMIRAL SIR JOHN DUCKWORTH.

Compiled for his Grandchildren,

BY HIS DAUGHTER,

SARAH SUSANNA BUNBURY.

IN TWO VOLUMES.

VOL. II.

LONDON:

COX & WYMAN, PRINTERS, GREAT QUEEN STREET,

LINCOLN'S-INN FIELDS.

1861.

CONTENTS.

CHAPTER I.

[1836.]

CHAPTER II.

[1837.]

CHAPTER III.

[1838.]

CHAPTER IV.

[1839.]

CHAPTER V.

[1840.]

CHAPTER VI.

[1840.]

CHAPTER VII.

[1841.]

CHAPTER VIII.

[1841.]

CHAPTER IX.

[1842.]

CHAPTER X.

[1842.]

CHAPTER XI.

[1843.]

CHAPTER XII.

[1844.]

CHAPTER XIII.

[1845.]

CHAPTER XIV.

[1846.]

LIFE AND LETTERS,

&c.

CHAPTER I.

[1836.]

My Father's chief clerk, Mr. Law, died early in this year; and my Father took the entire charge of his large orphan family till arrangements could be made for sending them to an uncle in England, which was not for several months.

To Madame Reboul, in May, he writes:—

I have not written since the return of my children. You can fancy my joy in seeing *our* good little Bob again after such a long absence. He told you himself of his success in the object we had so much at heart, and received a most kind letter from you in return. I have loved to talk to him about you all: one of these days you will see him again, and he will tell you about *me*. I wish *I* had an equal chance of seeing you. I am not at all sure that you would know me, for I believe I have made more haste than most people do to grow old; but yet, except in *looks*, I don't know that you would find in me any great change; for when I am well, as I am now at last, and mean to continue, I am as active as ever, and addicted with as much ardour to all my old pursuits.

For a long time past I have been plunged deep in Bob's Greek, and am still going on with him, and shall not only continue to work for him while he is with me, but after he goes to college; since I can so save him a very large portion of his time.

By reading his books before he reads them, and noting and explaining all the difficulties, he reads and understands them in a quarter of the time they would otherwise require. You can fancy how much of this sort of work I have already done for him, by the estimate we have made, that, if my manuscripts were printed, they would fill three or four octavo volumes. In case I *should* one of these days print them, I will send you a copy of my work, handsomely bound, to lie as an ornament upon the marble tables,ª—a pretty *lady's* book, to be sure!—but then I must try and find time to illustrate it with some of the many sketches you know I have of classic scenes. If I had but time to do all I should like to do, I really might accomplish this; but though I believe nobody in all the world works harder, I never can find time for half I ought to do. I *never* do *anything* for mere amusement, but *ride* for health's sake, and read and write all the rest of the day.   *   *   *   *   You may fancy the many questions I had to ask Mr. Miège, and how glad I was to hear his exclamation, "Comme nous avons parlé de vous!" You know it was quite natural for me to like to hear that you were as curious to know all my concerns as I am to know yours, and that you are fond of talking of your old friend; but how much *gladder* should I be to hear you talk with my own ears!   *   *   *   *

If all my boys turn out like Bob, they may take care of themselves; but it is too much to hope that amongst a *number*, *all* will be remarkable for talent and industry. At all events, I will do all I can, as long as I am alive and well, to give them just what I have given him; and while they are young, their good Mamma will give all *her* help; for she is just as ardent as I am in desiring, above all things, for them, next to *good principles, learning.*

To Miss Fanshawe, about this time, he writes :—

It is a sad long time since I wrote to you or that dear Sister Harriet, who, with yourself, always make but one mingled impression in my memory, where you are both constantly retained with an interest that will quite certainly never diminish. Ten thousand thanks, my kind friend, for that letter you wrote to Mr. Baker on Bob's account. The answer, you know, you sent to me through *my friend,*[b] that oldest and dearest friend I have in the world, who is always doing, and has always been doing, all the kindness she possibly can to me; but yet pray don't think that I consider your part in this matter as done for *her* sake, because I know it was done quite equally for my own. I am quite sure that you had a sincere pleasure in interesting yourself for my boy; and I, too, was truly glad to see that a letter about my affairs was addressed to *you*, as having occupied yourself with them for my advantage.

One *likes,* you know, to be obliged by one's own real friends; for obligation then sits easily. You know how willingly I would do as much for you. You remember how cordial and unreserved our intercourse has been, and you are sure, that among my hopes and wishes, is the hope and the earnest wish, that the day may come when that intercourse will be renewed. Thank you again and again, for bespeaking Mr. Baker's good-will for my Boy. You know, he says he will make acquaintance with Bob when he goes to College, and I am quite sensible of the advantage to Bob of such countenance.   *   *   *   *   *

I can fancy you in your retirement amusing yourselves

---

many a winter's evening, in turning over your well-filled
journals of all your travels. What multitudes of interesting
materials you have accumulated to think and talk about all
the rest of your lives! If I could do as I pleased, I would
travel as much as you have travelled. In the last eight years
I have spent one fortnight out of Malta—a week of it upon
the sea, and the other week in Sicily, in a tour from Syracuse
to Messina with my girls. How we enjoyed it no one can
tell who has not lived for eight years in a narrow boundary
like ours, with eternal rocks and stones in one unvarying
prospect. My horse carries me in a morning's ride first to
one extremity and then to another (not both, though, in the
same morning) of our tiny country, and one fancies that no
privilege would be more enviable than that of going a
hundred miles straight on end without stopping! I believe if
I were in London and saw a stage-coach going out of town, I
should jump on the top of it (for I have been six months free
from rheumatism, and *can* jump), and be content to go in
whatever direction it happened to be going, just for the
pleasure of seeing the hedges run by—as you know they
seem to do.   *   *   *   *

To Mr. Sleeman, August 8th, 1836, he writes :—

MY DEAR SIR,—Heartily do I hope that since the last
letters passed between us, your home has been as happy a one
as mine; that it has been as little disturbed by sickness and
vexations from without, and so left to the unmixed enjoyment
of love and peace within. You have known, like me, the
comfort of a dear Son's return to your roof after a long
absence, and therefore you can imagine the comfort I have
had in my Boy's companionship for the last ten months.

It was natural for me to make the most of our time
together, and as his disposition in that respect is like my own,
we have been scarcely ever out of each other's sight, reading
together most of the day, and riding the rest of it; and
keeping each other always alert, whether in our arm-chairs or

our saddles. It has been my habit all my life, to open occasionally my Greek books; and long before he came, I had those that he would, I knew, require, constantly before me, picking out all their difficulties, and hunting for all the means that I could derive from Scholiasts and annotators to clear them away. An ardent disposition, a powerful motive, abundance of books, and an habitual liking for them, have thus enabled me to serve my Boy for a pioneer. A professional tutor would have made a much better road for him, but would not equally have cheered him on. He and I have poked our way, through brambles and over rocks, as rapidly *together* as he could have travelled over bowling-greens and gravel-walks with a Parr or a Porson *behind* him. Yet, even here, in Malta, we *had* these, or one of these worthies, Porson, and others like him; such as the good German Hermann, whom Parr called " his hero;" and they *have* " made our rough places plain." But, in another month, I shall lose my fellow-student, for he must be at Oxford in October, and I shall find a sad falling-off in the spirit of the next great man that falls into my hands, be he Homer or Shakspeare, Cobbett or Cervantes. Are you a Conservative? I am sure you are; for it seems the natural side for your profession. What *I* am I don't the least in the world know. I have always liked the *Whig* side best; but as things now are, there is no such party among the people. However, pray don't think I like *Cobbett* a bit better than you do, except that he seems to me the liveliest writer that ever handled our language.   *   *   *   *

But where is Bedford?" Among the many ships-of-war that visit us, I should rejoice to see him come here with his lieutenant's coat on. Promotion is difficult enough; but if your life is spared, you will, I have no doubt, see him a captain. You ought to have great interest in the navy; for your son should represent his uncle, who left no one of his own in the profession, and who had innumerable friends among its most distinguished members. He filled for many years a post in which he was able to gratify his kindly nature by doing kind offices to those who might now repay them to his nephew. Perhaps you have heard that I was the Commander-in-Chief's Secretary when he was Captain of the Fleet in the North Sea.

We were shut up together for nine months in the *Impregnable*, without once seeing the outside of the ship; and you can fancy the value of such a temper as his in such a society as that in which we lived. Sir W. Y—— was the essence of sourness; he and the Captain and First Lieutenant were not on speaking terms, though they dined daily at his table with us.

The officers, who were invited in their turn, never spoke but when the great man rarely addressed a few words to them. This was our condition within, and without were the billows buffeting us at our stormy anchorage in the open sea, some twenty miles from the land. Never could one be in a plight in which a good friend would be of more value than good Admiral Bedford was to me.

You know my Sister came out to us lately. Since I wrote last, another baby,[a] too, has been added to our numbers; so that I have now four boys and as many girls, and all collected under our roof. When will all be together again? Before Bob leaves college, Clement must go to school, and in England; for here there are several, but they are of such a sort that any measure of mischief may be learned there, but no good.

All of us, in cordial concert, salute you and yours.

Believe me, my dear Sir, yours, with great regard,

R. C. SCONCE.

Among the visitors to Malta this year were the Prince and Princess of Capua, of whom we saw a good deal. We

---

[a] My Father's fourth Son, William, was born in the April of this year.

first met them at the wedding of General Wood's daughter, when the Prince talked a great deal to my Father, and told him he remembered him at Naples some ten or twelve years before. The Prince and Princess begged my Father and his family to do them the favour to call on them, saying they desired only to be visited as private gentlefolks. The Prince spoke of his great liking for the English, which he said was shown by his choosing an English wife; and the Princess, on her part, said she could not form a better wish for the bride than that she might be as happy in her marriage as herself.

Another remarkable person, whom we saw a good deal of this year, was the Rev. Joseph Wolff, whom we esteemed much for his kindness of heart and remarkable simplicity of character, united to his piety and learning. The following quaint notes from him may cause a smile :—

" MY DEAR MR. SCONCE,—I make quite free with you, for you are such an excellent man; therefore I take the liberty of asking, whether you have a *ball*[c] after your *dinner* ; for, if so, I am sure that you will not be displeased at our going away after dinner, before the ball *commences;* for I have a *decided dislike to balls,* and had it, even when I was a Jew. I am sure that you will not be displeased with me by asking you this. I confess that I consider balls to be the *Devil's hot-house.* Yours most affectionately,

"JOSEPH WOLFF."

"SUEZ, 14th April, 1836.

" MY DEAR OLD SCONCE AND MRS. SCONCE,—Many, many thanks for your kindness towards my beloved wife; and I am sure that you will continue so to do.

---

[c] Our dear Father did not give *balls.* He occasionally took my Sister and me to balls and parties, and would have done so oftener, with the utmost cheerfulness, had we pressed it ; but we could not but feel how much he was out of his element in a ball-room (though he never showed weariness when with us), and were reluctant to take him from his library table by his fireside. We often had a share in an opera-box, and there also he accompanied us whenever we had no other proper escort.

"I have had opportunity hitherto to proclaim the name of Jesus Christ at Alexandria, Cairo, Suez, Tor, Mount Horeb, and Mount Sinai; and Boghos Youssuf Bey, as well as the Viceroy, were particularly kind and attentive to me. I returned last week from Mount Sinai, to which place I brought a number of Greek Bibles and Testaments, which I gave to the monks there.

"I sent the history of the convent, written in Greek, to Lady Georgiana, which she will be glad to lend to you for your perusal, and, if you please, for translating it; and if you and Mrs. Sconce and Sally[f] and your Son call on Lady Georgiana, she will give you, as well as to old Smith, of the manna of Mount Sinai, and of the dates, to taste. I intend to leave this for Jiddah, and go (D.V.) to Mosawah, Adwah, and Gondar—in the latter place Jews are; and from thence I intend to go to Shoah, where I will find again Jews. Fare-well; I am most affectionately to your whole house, yours,

"JOSEPH WOLFF. *Missionary*."

In September, my Brother left Malta to go to Oxford, and on the 1st of October my Father begins writing to him again:—

Much as we all miss you, and grieved as we are to lose you, you can imagine that we think a great deal more of your pain than our own. We have each other to love, and our quiet home to shelter us; while you are surrounded by strangers, and exposed first to the buffeting of the natural sea, and then to the metaphorical storms of life, which are apt to inflict a much greater suffering. As for the first trial, we have had the great comfort of hearing, by your letter from Gibraltar, that you passed happily through its first stage.

*   *   *   *   *   *

In every way in which it is possible for me to do anything

---

[f] Mr. Wolff had been our fellow-passenger from Falmouth to Malta.

towards the fulfilment of any of your wishes, you will always be quite certain that you can entirely depend upon your dear Papa. You can fancy, dear Bob, the dulness of my morning rides when I lost my companion. They were made still duller by the poor pony's dejection. He was immediately separated from his old associate Tunis; for we had no longer any work for him, and I sold him; and pony seems to have missed him both in the stable and on the road; for he has lost all his spirit, and instead of trying to run away, as he used, he crawls along most lazily. I believe I was almost as sorry as he was to lose poor Tunis after eight years' friendship with him. He was the surest-footed, best-tempered, sprightliest-going creature of his kind.   *   *   *

Our darling Fanny is not either better or worse, I think, than you left her.   *   *   *   *   *

I had not myself any hopes from the leeches or blister, and grieved for the pain inflicted upon my poor dear. However, leeches, you know, create small annoyance, and blisters affect some people more severely than others, and happily the suffering in her case was not great, and was made still less by her extraordinary fortitude and patience; for little quiet Fanny has these virtues, dear Bob, in as great perfection as many a big-boned blusterer in red or blue.   *   *   *

All the rest of us are just as you left us, except that I have advanced a long step further towards blindness. Not that I expect total darkness while I am yet above ground, but that I must be content to give my eyes ample rest, to seek occasionally other amusements than reading and drawing, and so endeavour to eke out my light to the last. I can't do better than pursue the course in which you initiated me, and so become a Philidor.

[He frequently played chess at this time, of an evening, chiefly with General Wood and Mr. Smith.]

I wanted to read Apollonius Rhodius, and had only got through the first book, when I found the small print unmanageable. I have now Hesiod in hand, a noble edition, from the library, that seems to have been got up on purpose for the purblind.

On Sundays I read Chrysostom's Homilies on St. Matthew, a goodly Benedictine folio equally suited to me. Since you got me again among the Greeks, I have not been inclined to leave them, and I dare say you will find me two years hence still in the same company. Read I *must* while I can, though I may be obliged to shut my books when the sun sets; so that, if you think I can turn my reading to any account for you, you have only to set me my task. Would versions of choruses from Sophocles or Euripides be of any use? or would they, with all the able help you will receive from college tutors, be superfluous? Hesiod, I suppose, you will not read for some time. We may manage him together when you come. I am reading his "Works and Days" a little bit at a time; for when my vocabulary is at fault, the small print of my lexicons arrests me.

Thus the history of my Εργα και ἡμεραι is soon given. How I long, dear Bob, for an account of yours! Remember, my good boy, how great a comfort it will be to me to be enabled to trace all your steps. I shall be very anxious to know always all that you are doing, so that I may be enabled to fancy myself looking over your shoulder, or sitting opposite to you at your table, as we used to sit in our snug library at the Marina.

Tell me exactly how far you have advanced with Euclid and Algebra, and what books you are reading. Tell me always when you finish a book, and what you begin next; so that I may think sometimes of the things that are occupying your thoughts.

But remember, Bob, above all things, that, more than anything else, I wish to hear of your confirmed *health*. I am very far from urging you to work. It is as necessary for you to relax, for your "stomach's sake," as it is for me to relax for that of my eyes. You have hurt yourself by too close confinement and the anxieties of competition. Take

more exercise, then, and leave academic battles to be fought
by men of stronger *bodies ;* go quietly on, at no quicker pace
than your strength will easily afford, and you will still accomplish your purpose ; for you will gain scholarship and credit
enough ; but if, on the contrary, you overstrain your strength,
you will be compelled to shut your books altogether, and will
sow the seeds of disease that may last through your life.

*   *   *   *   *   *

Be sure that there is an absolute necessity for attending to
these rules. Take exercise for two or three hours every day,
and a large portion of it before dinner ; besides the exercise
in the open air, leave your books every now and then for five
minutes, and move about your room. Recline *sometimes* on a
sofa ; the more you vary your posture the better. By warm
clothing, exercise, and a good fire, you may keep yourself
warm. It is *necessary* that you should feel comfortably warm ;
for an abiding sensation of cold is sure to bring on some derangement of health. Wear flannel, then, and woollen cuffs
round your wrists, and warm gloves while you are reading. No academical honours are worth the sacrifice of
health ; read, then, no more than you can consistently with
your comfort, and don't set your heart upon the honours. *I*
shall not be disappointed if you don't reach a high mark, for
you will be unlike many who, at two-and-twenty, take a first-
class degree and then shut up their books. You will keep
yours still open, and will find many opportunities for bringing
your knowledge to account besides college or university examinations. Life does not end at Oxford. You will need
health and energy for further efforts ; and the reading of a
book or two more or less *there* is of little importance.

*   *   *   *   *   *

Don't imagine, Bob, that you are without talent for composition. When a man can translate well, he can *compose*
well. Many of your class, I dare say, knew the *sense* of the
Thucydides as well as you did, though your version was better

than theirs. You made your version better, because, besides
your accurate knowledge of the Greek, you had a just and a
refined taste for the composition of the English sentences into
which you converted it. Now, this is one of the two things
towards the composition of a good essay. The two things
necessary are *thoughts* and *style*. It is, at all events, something to be distinguished already for *one* of the two ; and as
for the thoughts, a man who has his eyes open as you have,
is not *likely* to fail in *heaping* up a store of ideas, to be
brought out when occasion needs. A few thoughts well
dressed up tell far more than *many* thoughts in a slovenly
garb.   *   *   *   *   *   *

As soon as I had read your letter, I took down Thucydides,
and read the three chapters you translated. They afford
plenty of exercise for ingenuity in furnishing a good version.

I read the piece of St. Luke, too, that ——— made you construe.   *   *   *   *   *   *

Nothing could be sweeter than that first news of yours
from Brasenose. The joy it gives me is not because your
triumph furnishes *me* with a proof of your scholarship, but
because I know it will gladden your own heart and relieve
the tension of your nerves, and operate beneficially on your
digestion. It was the sort of success, too, that I liked best,
—success in *composition.* The *style* of your *English* was
approved of. You *can* write English, you see ; and I know
that your *essays* will be as much distinguished as your *translations.* Good thoughts are easier found than skill in arranging
them and good taste in dressing them. You see that you
have language at your command, and have succeeded eminently, in spite of your want of practice. It is because you
have precisely the very thing you thought you had *not ;*
namely, in some sort, *genius,* or, in other words, a faculty,
and a rare one too, that *nature* has given you, enabling you
to *feel* what a good style *is.* It is analogous to an ear for
music. Nature, you know, gave Fan hers ; and you know,
too, that Nature has not given to certain worthy divines of

—— an ear for rhythmical sentences. You might stuff them chock full of Greek, and still they could never write you a decent version of Thucydides, any more than, stuffing them with Divinity, they could write you an eloquent sermon. As for " orator fit"—yes, true enough ; but only out of the *right stuff*. A silk purse, you know, is *feasible*, but not (as the vulgar rhetoricians say) out of *sows' ears*. This my illustration is, I find, as *ambiguous* as it is elegant and *new*. The ambiguity is in the parenthesis, the obliteration of which will make all clear.

But, Bob, no wonder *I* can't write, for I have neither read nor written for an age. I have done nothing but draw and play chess, and ride and pay visits, and talk to visitors. Never was my time so frittered away as it has been lately ; partly because I submitted to the interruption with more or less willingness, for the sake of my eyes, and partly because, whether I would or would not submit, the interruptions came, and are likely to come for some time. * * *

We never called on the Commissioners and Mrs. Commissioner, Mrs. Austin,[g] who is said to be a learned lady, and considers herself an equal member of the Commission. At length she sent me a message, to tell me that she desired the honour of my acquaintance. Captain Bouverie brought me the message, and took me to the lady, and I have had two long talks with her, and one with Mr. Lewis, one of the Commissioners, and shall have many more. * * *

* * * * * *

The new Governor,[h] too, has taken me up. Captain Bouverie, his cousin, is an old friend of mine. He introduced me to him, and the Governor asked me to dine with him when he was alone, and we had several hours' uninterrupted discussion of all the interests of his Government. He says he hopes to renew it, and has asked me to ride over the country with him. * * *

---

[g] The translator of Ranke's "Lives of the Popes," &c.
[h] Sir H. Bouverie.

His chief aide-de-camp, Captain Bridges, was the most intimate friend of my poor brother John.   *   *   *

But, Bob, I like a Greek book better than a chess-board, and shall be right glad to set to work again in earnest. I like doing something that may be of some use; and notes and versions *may* turn to some account. I want a good *Pindar*, and Hesiod, and *Apollonius* Rhodius. Will you get the best for me and send me them. You will want some Aristotle or Plato, or both. If you can foresee the treatises you are likely to choose of Aristotle, I suppose there are editions of them published separately, and you might send them to me.   *   *   *   *   *

To Madame Reboul he writes, the end of this year :—

Thank you ten thousand times for remembering me always with the same unvarying interest. The longer our absence from each other, the more firm will be our regard; because, if there were any caprice in it, it would not be proof against time and separation ; and when we do meet, as one of these days I *trust* we shall, we shall have that sort of confidence in each other that nothing but time can create. You always knew that I liked you very much and valued your friendship; but you might have imagined that a few years would obliterate the recollection of all your kindness to me; and *now* you will *never* have such misgivings, and I shall be equally sure, when I have the comfort of seeing you again, that you are, and always will be, all that you have been to me since the day that good Sir Harry received, at Malta, the orders to go and bombard Algiers. You and I became friends that day. It is almost thirteen years ago, and I remember, and see and hear you distinctly still, telling me to have no anxiety for Bob. It was just half-way up the great staircase at the Admiralty House.

Well, now, I will tell you something about him that I have just heard by the last packet. He entered at Brasenose College, Oxford, on the 11th of last month, and was, at his first outset, distinguished among all his companions. He was one of twenty-five young men, some of whom had been already two years at college, who were desired to write a translation of three chapters of Thucydides; and Bob's was pronounced the best of all, and read aloud, and proposed as a pattern for the imitation of the rest. The lecturer then invited him to breakfast the next day, and told him he had come to college so well prepared, that he could not fail of taking an honourable degree. Now, isn't this *very* good news of my good boy?

* * * * * *

CHAPTER II.

[1837.]

THIS was an eventful year in my Father's eventless and
monotonous life at Malta, for in it his second daughter's
marriage took place; a great stir was made by the Maltese
people to get him appointed to the Chief Secretaryship of
the island; and after nine years' residence at Malta, he spent
the summer in Switzerland with his family. However, he
shall describe these things himself in their order.

In January, 1837, he writes to his Boy :—

Never was my tranquil course of usual occupation more
broken in upon than during the last month. You know the
popularity I had among the Maltese; it has broken out in a
great blaze, and ended in *smoke*.

Here is a detailed history of what has happened. On the
18th of last month, Pirotti* told me that eight or ten members of the Maltese "Central Committee" (consisting of ninety-
six persons, elected by the whole population of the island, to
conduct their case before the Commissioners) had, in a private meeting, spoken of their wish to petition for my appointment to the office of Chief Secretary; that they had men-

---

* His clerk.

tioned it to their great leader, C——— S———, and obtained his cordial concurrence, and now desired to know whether the appointment would be acceptable to me, and what measures would, in my opinion, be most likely to obtain it. I received this message with some surprise; for although I had been accustomed for the last three or four years to hear frequent expression of such a wish among the Maltese, yet no recent mention of the matter had reached me.

My answer was, that I felt grateful to the Maltese people for such a proof of their goodwill, and desired, above all things, to be placed in a situation in which I might be useful to them; but that I could take no part in advising the measures to be pursued on this occasion, and must leave them entirely to their own discretion. On the 22nd December, Pirotti brought me a message, to inform me that it was proposed to frame a petition to the King in my favour, and to obtain the signature of the people at large; but that the Committee did not feel warranted in proceeding without my sanction. They requested, therefore, that I would allow two of their body to call upon me. I consented to their request; and accordingly received a visit from Drs. A——— and P———. The latter began by inveighing against H——— and the rest of the Government people. I desired them both to understand that I had no objection to their asking for me to succeed to the appointment on its becoming vacant, but that I would not allow the expression of a wish in my favour to be coupled with complaint against any one else. Nothing could be more distinct and peremptory than the terms in which I gave this reply; and the two gentlemen left me, to report it to the Committee.

26th December.

The son of C——— S——— came to me from his father and others, to show me the draft of a petition proposed to be brought forward. It was couched in the offensive terms against which I had already protested, and of course I refused to sanction it. S——— A——— afterwards came, and told me that he meant to move in the Committee for the adoption of a petition containing none of the offensive language to which I had objected, but simply praying for my appointment to the office on its becoming vacant.

27th December.

A—— came to me again, and signified that he and others had thought it best that the petition should not originate with the Committee, but should at once be laid before the people at large.

I read it for the first time, and was assured, not only by him, but by many other persons likely to know the sentiments of the community, that what it expressed was the general feeling throughout the country.

28th December.

The petition having been put into circulation, I waited upon the Governor and told him unreservedly everything that had passed. Short, I said, as his residence at Malta had been, I trusted that he knew already enough of me to be assured that I had not courted this expression of the favour of the Maltese.

Far from being connected with their agitators, or taking any part in political intrigues, I had no personal acquaintance with those called Radicals, nor with any of the members of the Central Committee, excepting one individual; and even to that individual I had not had occasion to speak for the last two years. There may, indeed, be others of my acquaintance among the Committee, but I do not know it; for, excepting the well-known names of Mitrovich and Camillo Sceberras, I have not even heard by popular report of what persons the Committee is composed. His Excellency might learn, I added, from those who know me, that I lived more than most people a life of privacy, occupying all my leisure among books.

He received me with remarkable kindness, and when I had done, put his hand to his heart, and begged me to be assured

that he knew how to appreciate the frankness with which I
had spoken to him, and was quite satisfied that I had used no
unworthy means to gain the popular favour, nor taken any
part in causing the petition to be put forth. Mamma and I
dined with him that day, and he picked me out of twenty-two
people to address nearly all his talk to me. I should have
said, that when I first told him of the petition, I gave him a
copy of it.

2nd January.

After repeated discussions in the Central Committee,
while nearly all concurred in the object of the petition,
some insisted on introducing complaints against H——.
Others objected on various grounds to its present form; and
others thought that, as the Committee was appointed for
specific purposes, and as the petitioning for a Secretary
was not one of these purposes, they ought not to adopt it;
and finally the majority decided against its adoption.
A—— called upon me to give me this information. The
petition had in the mean time been in general circulation,
and twelve or fourteen hundred signatures had been affixed
to it. The far greater number of people, however, of all
ranks, appear to be implicitly led by the Central Committee, and deferred signing till they knew the Committee's
decision.

The Committee having decided not to sign it, the people
will not. The H——s, the N——s, the G——s, and all
the underlings of office have, in the mean time, moved heaven
and earth to deter all *they* could control from signing it.
Every one connected with their offices, directly or indirectly—
all who fear them—all who hope anything from them, have
been deterred. The petition would not therefore be, what I
was led to expect it would be, the expression of the general
wish of the community; and therefore I desired that it might
be immediately withdrawn, and went to the Governor to tell
him so, and to explain my motive. I did not find him *this*
time in so friendly a mood. H——, and the rest, had suc-

ceeded in giving him the impression they desired. The whole tribe are in a ferment.

Besides the petition, a number of the chief people here wrote a letter to the Governor to be forwarded to the King with the petition, praising me up to the skies. It was signed by Sir Josias Rowley and Captain Bouverie, the Governor's cousin, and Lord Radnor's brother, when the Governor heard of it, and insisted on its *not* being sent to him. He told the Admiral and the rest, that it would be considered, at home, as an improper interference by persons who had no right to interfere on such a subject; and so the poor letter was dropped. *This* too must have been the effect of H——'s influence over the Governor. There was no attempt at any interference at all. It was merely a *testimonial*, quite natural for the heads of the *Naval service* especially to offer, on such an occasion. Besides those two, it would have been signed by Sir T. Briggs, Sir W. Elliott, General Wood, the Chief Justice, the Maltese Members of Council, the Dean and Chapter—and the *Bishop*, too, would gladly have signed it, if he had not been *afraid*. He is a *grand* friend of mine.

Besides all this, the two Maltese Councillors, P—— and De P——, volunteered to go to the Governor to testify that the wish expressed in the petition had been long and was universally felt among all classes; and Captain Bouverie offered me, unasked, all his interest with Lord Glenelg, which, through his brother, is great.

The Governor had taken me into high favour—I had dined with him twice, and his cousin told me he had conceived a very high opinion of me from the first, and all that he had since seen and heard of me, had confirmed the impression. But now all this is, of course, overturned. Nothing can be done without the Governor's support, upon which Captain Bouverie at first thought we might rely; and now, instead of his support, we should have his strenuous and, of course, effectual opposition. Why, Bob, you will hear of me next as the *O'Connell* of *our gem* of an island! But when H—— and his companions describe me as a *demagogue*, they will laugh themselves, and so shall I. A pretty demagogue! G——, N——, B——, and S——, are all candidates. If any one of the present set is appointed, despair will drive the people to resist, for they *execrate* all these names. You know how all the *civil servants* here, as they call themselves, are detested. My advantage will be, that I may ride through the country in security, and they must limit their rambles within the military works. Of course, this stir has made me more known than ever. Several leading people have sent messages to me, desiring to make personal acquaintance with me.

Every man in Vittoriosa signed the petition. So did those of Zabbar; and when it was proposed to them, they said they knew the good man, who had often ridden through the village with his Son.[b] Mr. Smith's Maltese clerk, to whom I have never spoken in my life, said the petition showed the feeling of the Maltese like a mirror.

Those at Burmola who did not sign, because they felt bound to obey the Committee, said they were ready to sign *with their blood.* Here is the petition :—you will see a word or two in it that you or I would correct. It was written in Maltese, translated by one hand, and retouched by another; but of course not at all by *me.*

"*To the King's Most Excellent Majesty.*

"The Humble Petition of ————, humbly showeth :—

"That the undersigned loyal and faithful subjects of your Majesty, having understood that your Majesty's Government has for some time past had it under consideration to allow the Chief Secretary to the Civil Government of these islands to retire at a fit opportunity from his present office, humbly pray permission to lay at the foot of your Majesty's throne

---

[b] In riding through the distant villages of Malta with my Father, I frequently heard the people exclaim to each other as he rode by : "Kemmuon ragel taiep,"—*Anglicè,* "What a good man that is!"

this their petition, relative to the filling up of that office, a matter of vital importance to the inhabitants at large, and to the substantial good of your Majesty's service.

"That in the executive branch of that high trust which is confided to his Excellency the Governor, your Majesty's immediate representative in these dominions, the Chief Secretary is the person to whom your Majesty's subjects look, as the official medium through which all that concerns them, individually and politically, must be conveyed.

"That for the due discharge of this important office, many and valuable virtues, talents, and other personal advantages are required :—perfect integrity, perspicacity of intellect, a cultivated mind, habits of business, firmness of character, joined to suavity of manners, entire impartiality, an abhorrence of all secret and sinister intrigues, a personal and intimate knowledge of the local interests of these islands, an acquaintance with their literary language,ᶜ a benevolent regard for all classes of the inhabitants, and a zealous desire to realize your Majesty's paternal wishes for the good government, happiness, and prosperity of this part of your dominions.

"That when all these qualifications do not co-exist in the person invested with the office of Chief Secretary, it is impossible that the inhabitants should not feel their interests to be more or less dependent on the character and conduct of subordinate persons, to whose assistance that high officer must resort, and by whose advice, though possibly given from the most interested motives, and without the slightest official responsibility, he must inevitably be guided.

"That an English gentleman, combining in himself the estimable attainments before specified, more especially if he were known to your Majesty's Government by a faithful discharge of other important trusts, would not only prove an invaluable auxiliary to the Governor in the various intricacies of the civil government, but would at the same time enjoy the unreserved confidence and respect of the people.

" That your petitioners with great humility beg to be permitted to present to your Most Gracious Majesty's notice a character such as they have described, in the person of Robert Clement Sconce, Esquire, an officer in one of your Majesty's civil naval establishments here, who, from the time of his first coming amongst your petitioners (about nine years ago), has, though perhaps imperceptibly to himself, so gradually and universally obtained the admiration and goodwill of all your Majesty's subjects in these islands (for all know him either directly or indirectly) as to have been long and generally regarded by them as at once the most efficient and most acceptable individual to fill an office of such public interest and concern.

" That should your Most Gracious Majesty be pleased, in your benignant desire for the well-being of your loyal, faithful, and attached subjects of Malta, indulgently to listen to the unanimous solicitations of your humble petitioners for the appointment of this gentleman to the office of Chief Secretary to the Civil Government, whenever it may become vacant, so distinguished a mark of your Majesty's royal favour would be received, as your petitioners are fully persuaded, by the population of these islands in general, with unalloyed feelings of gratitude and joy."

If this petition had not been withdrawn, by my desire, it would have been signed by some 3,000 or 4,000 people, notwithstanding the opposition of the Government people and the Committee. The letter which the Admirals and other leading people signed, or were to sign, was as follows :—

" It having come to our knowledge that a very general petition of the inhabitants of these islands to his Most Gracious Majesty is preparing, or has already been laid before your Excellency, couched in humble and respectful

language, and having for its exclusive object the appointment of Robert Clement Sconce, Esquire, to the office of
Chief Secretary to this Government, whenever it shall please
his Most Gracious Majesty to allow the gentleman at present
holding that high station to retire, we embrace with pleasure
the favourable opportunity of bearing our unanimous testimony to those rare endowments which qualify Mr. Sconce
faithfully to serve your Excellency's Government in that con-
fidential capacity.

" We further beg to assure your Excellency that we
are persuaded the petition in question does not originate
in the ebullition of a momentary impulse, but that the
opinion which has given birth to it has been for some years
past cherished by a large majority as well of the British as
native inhabitants, who concur in the estimate formed by us
of Mr. Sconce's fitness for so important a trust.

" Humbly hoping that your Excellency will take this
letter into your consideration, and will forward it, together
with the petition, and with your own powerful recommendation, to his Majesty's Government, we have the honour to
be," &c. &c.

   *   *   *   *   *   *

The Governor was buying a cow the other day of a Maltese
market-man, and by way of finding out, I suppose, what people
of his class thought, asked the man if he had signed the
petition.

" Yes," said the man ; " and it will be a blessing for us all
if Mr. Sconce is appointed."

This was repeated to me by a friend of the man to whom
he had related it.

B——, the Adjutant of Police, tells me the Committee
would have adopted the petition, if many of them had not
resolved to resist the saddling of the island with a *pension*
for ——. They say that a petition so worded would tacitly
convey their assent to his retiring peaceably in the usual way,
and they are determined to stigmatize him. The Adjutant

adds, that if the Committee had taken it up, there would have been 20,000 signatures. Even B—— told General Wood and Captain Bouverie that neither the petition nor the letter gave me a bit more praise than I deserved, and he has since professed to me his readiness to say as much to all the world.

The fuss has subsided; and as soon as the packet is gone I shall take up my usual pursuits, and forget all the agitations of the last month. They have been many and complicated.

Sir F. H—— in his ire offended General W——. They had a rough correspondence; and if H—— had not made the reparation required, there would have been a duel between them. You can fancy the feeling with which we looked on. It was exceedingly miserable; and of course I should not quietly have allowed the matter to reach such a termination.   *   *   *   *   *

What a sheet-full I have written for you on this matter! But it has occupied me for a whole month,—and not only me and us, but all Malta; and I know it is not a mere *précis* that will satisfy you when I am engaged in doings so deeply interesting to me. I have not told you enough of the warm friendship that Captain Bouverie has shown me. He is said to be cold and stiff and reserved in his manner. He is a man of few words; but to me he has been all warmth. I am quite sure that if ever he can serve me in any way, he will.

*   *   *   *   *   *

On the 9th of February my Father wrote the following note to Captain Bouverie :[d]—

My VALUED FRIEND,—Pray let me say a word about the paper I gave you. It contains a memorandum which I made from day to day (just as I related them from day to day to you while they were passing) of the various steps that led to

---

[d] Soon afterwards Admiral Bouverie.

the petition. My motive for giving it you was to recall to your memory the facts with which you were originally acquainted, in order that when you hear, as I dare say you will, the assertion that I myself got up the petition after two or three years of cogitation and machination, you may perceive at once the grossness of the calumny. But I wish you to make no *other* use of that paper. If it found its way into the hands of my adversaries, they would, at least, not deal candidly with it.

Above all, I should regret that your kindness to me should induce you to make any attempt to change the Governor's present impressions. My affairs have given you a great deal too much vexation already.

I should, of course, have been proud of his favour, and have valued it the more for owing it to your friendly offices; but in the consciousness of having not done, but suffered, wrong in this matter, I shall wait patiently until time may, perhaps, set it before him in its proper light, and show him that what I did was no more than he himself, or Sir F. Hankey, or you, or any other honourable man, would have done in the same case.   *   *   *   *   *

This was Admiral Bouverie's reply :—

"VANGUARD," *February 9th,* 1837.

"MY VALUED FRIEND,—For I cannot better express my feelings of esteem and regard for you than by addressing you in your own words, the full import of which I truly appreciate,—as for the paper you were good enough to give me, which I meant to appropriate to myself unless you desire me to return it, I will attend to your wishes about it. I had intended to have spoken to Sir Henry on the subject, and still may; for I meant only to have assured him he was entirely mistaken in supposing you had a hand in getting up the petition, and to express my hope that he may have a secretary who may serve him with the same zeal and ability, and with the advantages you possess on undertaking the office; but this I know is impossible.

'"The delay in the arrival of the *Confiance* makes me doubtful how or when I may get away; but be assured I shall be most happy to dine with you any day you may be disposed to name except next Tuesday.

" I beg my kind regards to all your family circle, and am most truly yours,

"J. PLEYDEL-BOUVERIE."

My Father's valued friend Signor M—— P——, a Maltese gentleman, lately writing to me, says, on this subject :—

" Your dear Father was deservedly esteemed by all my countrymen; so much so, that during the governorship of Sir H. Bouverie, on the retirement of Sir F. Hankey, they wished him to succeed Sir Frederick to the Secretaryship. A deputation waited on your Father, to ask whether he was willing they should apply for his appointment; and on their being assured that he would not have been averse to the appointment, but that he would not take any active part, a petition was set up here to memorialize the Government in England to select him as Chief Secretary for this place. That petition had already received many signatures, and would have been successful, if Sir H—— G—— had not been in the way with all his party in the Civil Government here.

" He had already used his influence with the Governor, who was his friend; and Sir H. Bouverie and the local Government clique threw cold water on the petition, and influenced many people against the prosecution of the signatures. Disunion was created amongst those concerned in the matter ; and as we were not then experienced in the way of petitioning, the memorial remained without its effect, to the grief of those most attached to your Father ; and more than one person had to suffer a kind of petty persecution for having signed the petition."

Three or four years after, M. Miège's[e] "History of Malta,"
in three volumes octavo, was published.   The following is an
extract from it :—

"Le Chevalier H——, Secrétaire en chef du Gouverne-
ment, auquel Sir H. Bouverie s'en remit dès son début,
comme son prédécesseur le Général Ponsonby, n'avait pas
compris que les habitants de Malte composaient une famille
qui devait être conduite par l'affection, et que l'Angleterre,
en agissant dans ce sens, pourrait se dispenser d'y tenir
garnison.   Fidèle au système de Maitland, et entouré
d'hommes intéressés à l'y maintenir, le Chevalier H—— en
était arrivé, par son langage peu mesuré, et à force de
mesures fiscales, oppressives, dont il était l'instrument, au
point de passer pour le principal auteur des souffrances du
peuple Maltais.   Attaqué de toutes parts, il n'eut pas la
force de résister à l'animadversion générale, et donna sa
démission.   La retraite du Chevalier H—— ouvrit la lice
à tous les ambitieux, et à Malte, comme ailleurs, le nombre
en est considérable.   Les Maltais n'eurent pas la prétension
de solliciter l'emploi de Secrétaire en chef pour l'un d'eux;
mais ils crurent pouvoir appeler l'attention du Roi sur celui
des Anglais residant à Malte qui possédait leur sympathie,
et dans une pétition adressée à sa Majesté, ils désignèrent
M. Sconce, Commissaire des vivres de la Marine.   L'emploi
de Secrétaire général est peutêtre plus important que celui
de Gouverneur; il exige non seulement un homme capable,
actif, rompu aux affaires, mais encore des qualités, des dispositions particulières; connaissance exacte du pays, bien-
veillance pour les habitans, circonspection la plus scrupuleuse
dans les actes et dans les paroles.   M. Sconce réunissait toutes
ces qualités; mais l'intrigue s'en mêla, et la pétition ne fut
point envoyée à Londres."

[e] Formerly French Consul at Malta.

In my Father's January letter to his Boy he says :—

Your last letter is not merry*f* enough to satisfy me; but yet we can't have everything *quite* as we wish, and we will comfort ourselves in thinking that you are well in health, and not dissatisfied with yourself in book affairs; and now that the new year has begun, we can say that *next year* we shall have you with us, please God, again.

* * * * * *

As for the *brackets*, you will find as good a place as you need desire. Don't fret yourself on that score. I am quite indifferent on such subjects, except only as they affect your own happiness; and if you are but *well*, I know you will satisfy *yourself*. The way to *keep* well is rather to be content with bracket number 3, than to read when you ought to be walking, or to make any *excessive* exertion for the sake of mounting to number 2. * * * *

About your money concerns I need not say much. *I* know you have not spent more than was necessary; and *you* know that to what you require for your comfort you are right welcome, my dear Bob. Our common purse, then, is at Stilwell's, and into that you have only to put your hand. I only wish it were deeper for all our sakes. The only use I should make of it more than I do make, would be an important one. I would live in England, Bob, for your sake now, and by-and-by for *Memmeck's* and *Bettoo's*;*g* ay, and now, for our precious S—— and F——'s sake, too; for Malta is not the best place in the world for them.

* * * * * *

In February he writes :—

You know quite well the joy with which we read your last letter, telling us of your *double-second*.*h* You have exceeded

---

f My brother at that time was subject to low spirits.

g Clement and Herbert.   *h* Double-second Bracket.

my hopes, and, what is better still, *your own ;* and the *cudos*
has had the good effect it ought to have upon your spirits,
and will have consequently upon your *health.*

*   *   *   *   *   *

In March :—

Here is most of " Antigone " for you.   Examine it well.
Mend it where you can.   Take your own sense, where you
don't agree with mine, unless you are thoroughly persuaded
that mine is best; but where you agree with me, try and
get so familiar with my phrases as to make them your own
and at your fingers' ends ; for I am pretty sure that, in
many places, they are strikingly happy.   There is no conceit
in my saying this to *you.*   I can estimate my own work quite
fairly.   Many people could do these choruses much better, *if*
they had as much time to spend upon them and were willing
so to spend it ; but *that if* is important.

I have twisted many and many a sentence about dozens
of different ways for the sake of a *syllable.*   The result is,
that the English reads fluently, and is in general even *closer*
to the *sense* of the Greek than a boy's word-for-word construing would be ; because the idea intended to be conveyed by a
Greek *sentence* may be conveyed sometimes more exactly by
making allowance for the difference of character between the
two languages than by a servile translation of separate *words.*
I have complied with your injunction not to work too hard.
This sort of work is not at all fatiguing ; for I have done
really the greater part of it on horseback.   I write a chorus
or a piece of one on a strip of paper, and always have one in
my pocket.   I know them nearly by heart, and, looking now
and then at my paper, as I canter along, it serves me for
amusement on the road to Sliema.   Then comes a game at
chess with the good old general, and then more chorus on the
way home.   At the rate in which I am going on, you will, at
all events, have your *four* plays in ample time for *Little-go.*

*   *   *   *   *   *

To Madame Reboul, at this time, he writes :—

* * * * Bob works always from the commentaries I have made for him, and still continue to make and send to him by every packet. He often ventures, on my authority, to differ from the hackneyed interpretations. The tutors laugh at his impudence, and told him once he was *wrong*. Little Bob proved that he was right; the tutor acknowledged it, and of course gave him great applause. This is great encouragement to me to go on, and so I spend all my time, as I have done for nearly three years, in writing for him. It is a very interesting occupation, and great amusement to me. I like the work for its own sake, and of course feel great additional excitement in the motive that engages me in it. Some of the things I am doing have never been done in any published books, and others have been done by people who had fifty times my scholarship; but then they went too rapidly over the ground. They had not the same object that I have, and did not give their *hearts* to the work as I give mine. Perhaps they did ten pages in the time I give to *one ;* and that makes a mighty difference, you know. * * * * *

The beginning of April my Father writes to his Son :—

Your last letter is the one giving an account of your contest for the university scholarship; and it is, you may be sure, deeply interesting to us. The utmost that could be done by your age you did. To succeed against men so much your seniors was impossible. No human industry or genius could collect at eighteen years of age the mass of knowledge that success would have required. * * * *

Your passage from Lucan was from the 8th book, v. 793. Its difficulty to you was the greater because the sense of the passage does not *begin* at—

" Hic situs est magnus."

If you had been allowed to read the lines preceding, you

would have seen that those words were quoted as the inscription upon Pompey's tomb; and then the poet goes on to
scold the inscriber for his petty notion that *that spot* was the
hero's tomb. " Take away these *saxa*, which imply a censure
upon the gods for their behaviour to poor Pompey. All the
empire is his monument—all Egypt is his grave. Erremus—
let us quit the shores of Nile, for all Egypt is his grave.
It has, therefore, become hallowed ground—αβατος, like the
temenus of the Eumenides." Why, it must have puzzled you
even to construe Magnus and Socer, for you could not have
known, without conjuring, that those are the terms by which
Lucan continually speaks of Pompey and Cæsar. However,
I can easily fancy that even a *small* difficulty must be mag-
nified into an insuperability, when one has to work against
time, and a clock is ringing the lapse of that time every
quarter of an hour into a poor wight's ears ; and your difficulties were anything but *small*.

One comfort to you is, that an examination of that sort
must be very improving. It sends you to the stores of your
memory, and calls up all your energies, and tells you your
deficiencies, and sends you to the right sources to supply
them for another occasion.

I don't know whence was taken your " Adfingens vicina
virtutibus vitia ; " but the sense of the words appears to be
similar to the following, in Cicero's " Partitiones Oratoriæ : "
—" Cernenda autem sunt diligenter, ne fallant ea nos vitia,
quæ virtutem videntur imitari. Nam et . . . magnitudinem
animi superbia, et liberalitatem effusio, et fortitudinem
audacia imitatur,—et religionem superstitio." Of course I
can't know, without seeing the context, what the author of
your sentence intended; but I should construe it, " God so
made the mind of man that his vices are near akin to virtues." I should illustrate the proposition by a reference to
animal and vegetable vitality. There is an uninterrupted
chain from man and monkey, through the zoophytes, to moss
and mushroom ; and the point where animal ends and vegetable begins can only be seen by scientific eyes. Just so it

is hard to pronounce upon the exact limits of liberality and extravagance, &c. &c.

Seneca, too, epistle 120, has something of the same sort:—"Sunt enim *virtutibus vitia confinia* . . . . . imitatur negligentia facilitatem, temeritas fortitudinem." Now surely this sentence of Seneca's contains the very same proposition as your Theme, and *explains* it too.

Take no more laughing gas. An eminent chemist has been here—a Mr. Roberts, a man of fortune, who has correspondence with all the scientific societies, has invented a mode of keeping rust from iron under water, such as the wheels of steam-vessels; and has received the thanks of some academy for a treatise on electricity. I told him of your achievement, and he said that it was exceedingly dangerous; that any impurity in the gas would be sure to give its inhaler consumption; and that there is no arguing on the opposite side from experience, because the injury may not show itself till long after the inhaling of the gas. However, it is as well to be on the safe side, and abstain from repeating the prank, especially as one's reason tells one that for great *excitement* one must in some shape *pay.*   *   *   *   *   *

In case you should be asked again what were the boundaries of Rehoboam's kingdom at his accession (for he soon lost ten-twelfths of it), look at the 4th chap. 1st book of Kings, vv. 21, 24, 25, which describe the extent of *Solomon's* dominions; and I believe it is not said that they were either enlarged or diminished afterwards until Rehoboam succeeded to them.   *   *   *   *   *   *

Now, Bob, for some *news.* If all goes as we hope, you will spend your next long vacation with us all,—not at Malta, but in Switzerland. Many and many a plan has been half-made and abandoned; and this is at last settled as far as human things can be. Aunt suffered so much from the heat of last summer, that she determined not to stay for *next* summer; and her determination was formed the more positively on your account, that she might go to England and take care of you in your vacations.   *   *   *

How can we manage it, then? Why, the only way is, for us all to go together,—not to England, but to the nearest place where a good climate is to be had; and that is just beyond the Alps.   *   *   *   *   *

In April of this year his beloved daughter Fanny was married to Doctor, afterwards Sir John Liddell; and in May my Father left Malta for Switzerland with his Wife and Sister, his eldest Daughter, and four of his little ones. Willie, the baby, was left in charge of the Liddells, who hoped to have followed us to Switzerland; but the cholera broke out at Malta, and Dr. Liddell, who took an active part in the measures for keeping it under, would not leave his post.

My brother Robert joined his Father at Bönigen, near Interlachen, on the 20th of June, 1837, and remained with him till the end of September; when he returned to England with his Aunt, to be at Oxford by Michaelmas.

We travelled in a great berline from Marseilles to Geneva; all the women and children inside, and my Father outside with the coachman, and frequently walking. He writes to Fanny from Gap :—

    *   *   *   *   I please myself with hunting the meadows and hedge-banks for Sally's old acquaintance among the wild flowers, and in finding new ones for her; and great has been our success in finding them. There are thousands of beauties. To-day we have passed many meadows whitened with narcissuses and purpled with orchises.
    *   *   *   *   After leaving Aix, the mountains begin; varied and very beautiful scenery, particularly some winding roads among the uplands. Cross the Durance over a new suspension-bridge, and keep close to the river all the way to Manosque. The country here is full of nightingales, who sang close to our windows all night at Manosque. This town has nothing remarkable in its appearance. Manosque to Sisteron; scenery more and more beautiful. Ascend a

high mountain; and gradually down again to the Durance
at Sisteron, the approach to which place makes a very
striking picture. Though Sisteron is by the river-side, it
is yet on high ground, for the Durance makes in its descent
a rapid descent. Sisteron is built on the side of an abrupt
rock, confined between which and an opposite rocky mountain rushes the Durance.   *   *   *   *   I got
up at four this morning (I do every morning) to sketch
Sisteron.   *   *   *   *   *   *

From Grenoble he writes :—

But, Fan, think of *this*. As we left Viselle to-day, and
drove along towards Grenoble by the side of the river
Romanche, or some such name,—a large torrent that con-
tributes to the Isère,—a mountain sloped down to the river's
brink. That mountain-side was covered with trees and shrubs,
all as wild as the Alps themselves. No human hand ever
planted one of them ; and among them were *Laburnums*, with
their long branches bending with their load of beautiful flowers
over the river, and gilding occasionally the mountain-side from
top to bottom. Wasn't *this* a sight worth coming all the way
to see, even if there had been nothing else ? But the approach
to Viselle from La Mure opens one of the most gorgeous scenes
eyes ever looked upon. You come suddenly to a mountain's
brow, and thence look down upon the town of Viselle, the
river on which it stands, and a most richly-wooded and varied
plain ; and such is the steepness of the descent, that it seemed
to me much such a view as one may suppose to present itself
from a *balloon*.   *   *   *   *   *

But, *above all things*, remember, if ever you pass this way,
to inquire at Gap and Grenoble, and before it and after it, for
Clairette. It is nectar. The cork flies out like a pistol-shot ;
and it costs from a dozen to a couple of dozen sous a bottle.
Then at Chaparcillan—and sooner, I dare say, if you inquire
sooner, ask for *Rosat :* it is a sort of red Frontignan, spark-
ling like champagne. They call frothy wines *moussu*, you
know ; so mind there's no mistake.   *   *   *

To Fanny, later :—

I told you when I wrote last that Mamma and I were
going to set out upon *our* tour. We went first to Vevay,
and arrived there from Yverdun in a day. At Vevay we
stayed five days, because we were at a very remarkably cheap
and comfortable inn, and surrounded with scenery for my
work. I did a good deal: the chief things being the Cathedral at Lausanne and the Castle of Chillon, inside and outside of Chillon. From Vevay we came, on Sunday evening,
to St. Maurice, by diligence, slept at St. Maurice, and came
on next morning to Martigny. Martigny is just twenty-four
miles from the top of Mont St. Bernard. Now, what do
you think, Fan? We did actually, Mamma and I, dine
yesterday, at the hospice, on the mountain-top, with the
monks! We stayed quietly here all Monday. Yesterday
morning, Tuesday, we set out, at six o'clock, in a little carriage drawn by one mule, which mule, besides drawing the
carriage, had on his back a saddle for ulterior use. In this
little carriage we drove twelve miles to a village, up the mountain, which village is called Lido. There we took the mule out
of the carriage, and let him rest and eat, and then I mounted
him, having first put Mamma into a chair borne by two men,
with two others walking by their side to relieve them, and
off we set for the hospice. Before we left the carriage,
though, I had made two sketches. There is nothing in the
way up the mountain very striking to us who have seen so
much of mountain scenery. There is not, I mean, by the
road by which *we* went, though I hear there is another road
more picturesque. However it was too long round, and we
were satisfied with achieving the great object of getting up.
It is a very remarkable scene — that hospice. The latter
part of the road to it is very steep and rugged, and nothing
is to be seen but rock and snow. The chief part of the day
had been extraordinarily hot—pretty much like Malta--and
we had been exposed in that great heat to a broiling sun.
Great was the change we felt as we reached the hospice, just
as the sun went down.

But I must tell you my story more in order. We saw, as we approached the hospice, numbers of people about—guides and travellers of various orders—though the gentlemen and lady travellers who had preceded us were all housed.

Lying at the door was one of the great dogs so famous in mountain story, and two or three others like him were near.

The prior came to the door to meet us, welcomed us cordially in two words, took himself our sack out of my hand, and showed us at once to a chamber, telling us that dinner would soon be ready. "Nous allons dîner," he said; by which we learned that we were to dine not by ourselves, but with him and his monks. As soon as we had washed our hands, we were shown not into the refectory of the convent, into which, it appears, ladies are not admitted, but into a large dining-room, in which a table was laid for twenty-two people, and about as many were assembled at it: ladies and gentlemen—some English, some French, some Russians—and the prior and one other monk were entertaining them; the prior occasionally blowing the *fire*, of which no one was gladder than I; for, after washing my hands in icy water, they were thoroughly numbed.

Then in came dinner at eight in the evening; only the prior and the one other monk sitting down with us, and none of the other monks making their appearance. They were all dining at the same time in the refectory, entertaining there seventeen *more* gentlemen travellers. They gave us the fare to which, we were told, they always limited their provision,—two dishes of meat, two of vegetables, and a dessert, with good ordinary wine,—ample in quantity, and all good. But what most surprised us, was the character of our entertainers. I expected to see gray-headed, queer codgers, very kind-hearted, but more like the monks of our acquaintance at Malta than like men of the world in their manners. But nothing could be more wrong than my guess. Our two entertainers were both young men, probably under thirty, very good-looking, dressed with perfect nicety, their shirt-collars well cut and starched, hair well-cut and combed, chins smoothly shorn, and displaying in their address the self-possession, tact, and urbanity of London men of fashion; good-natured, hospitable, obliging in the utmost degree, but not a bit *servile;* no cringing, but precisely the sort of easy hospitality that one receives from a gentleman who knows how to do in the best style the honours of his own house.

We soon made talking acquaintance with our neighbours at table, and enjoyed our evening, as presenting a scene for which there is no parallel.

But then the going to bed in such a climate! As soon as we got into our own room, after leaving the well-warmed dining-room, Mamma's teeth began to chatter, and she was *sick* with the cold. We covered ourselves with two duvets— *beds,* you know, filled with down, that serve for blanket and counterpane.

In the morning, at eight, we all breakfasted together, in the simple style in which we had dined. Before each of us was placed a white plate and a white *mug.* Coffee and milk were handed round, and poured into our respective mugs, and bread, cut in slices, was disposed along the table. In rambling about, we saw and spoke to a few others of the monks (their whole number is but twelve), and found them very inferior to the two who had entertained us. I suppose those two are picked out for the business of entertaining strangers, on account of the superiority of their address.

I will tell you more about them another time. They kill a bullock and three or four sheep every week; and at the close of autumn kill twenty-five bullocks and a quantity of sheep (I believe a hundred), and salt the meat for their winter's store; for in winter they give only salt meat to travellers. They can get no other; for their communication with the country is too difficult. I made two sketches of the convent. We returned to Martigny by eight this evening. It is now late, considering that we are to be up very early to-morrow, to begin our journey to the *Simplon.*

＊   ＊   ＊   ＊   ＊   ×

Many of the letters from Switzerland are missing. I find none from Vernex, where a part of the summer was spent. It was divided between Interlachen, the neighbourhood of Yverdun, and Vernex, near Chillon and Montreux; making expeditions from all these places. At Vernex, we lived at the same hotel with a most amiable Russian family,[i] who, though strongly prejudiced against the English, and not, at first, inclined to cultivate any intimacy with us, became so strongly attached to my Father, that they all gave him keepsakes of their own work, and embraced him with tears at parting.

His pencil revelled in the glorious Swiss scenery, after his long imprisonment at Malta; and he made an immense number of sketches, colouring a great many on the spot, and making exquisitely-finished drawings from them on his return to Malta. There was at Malta a little valley near Boschetto, containing about half a dozen fine trees,—a species of ash; and of these my Father had made some dozens of finished drawings, making portraits of them in every point of view. These were the only trees worthy of the name in the island; so his enjoyment of the various and beautiful trees of Switzerland, as well as of its mountains, lakes, and picturesque cottages, may be imagined.

My Father returned with his family to Malta the end of October, and writes to his Son at Oxford:[k]—

At midnight, came in sight of Stromboli, and found it firing: Mamma, Sally, and Clement got up to watch it. The show was not grand,—but two craters emitted occasional flames; but there was enough to interest people who had never before seen Vulcan's workings. He was not forging bolts for Jupiter, or even arms for Achilles; but it was something even to see him blow his forge. *   *   *

---

[i] Mesdames Fenger, sen. and jun., and Mdlle. Yachman.

[k] Describing the voyage from Marseilles, *viâ* Leghorn, Naples, &c., to Malta.

Speaking of the incivility we met with in the French steamer, he says :—

The French have discarded their old character for politeness, and affect the surly roughness of Americans. They talk of nothing but liberty and equality, and assume the liberty of being uncivil. Postilions and ostlers and cabinboys are all agreed to make no distinction in their address to gentlemen and to each other; nor do they allow anything more to the ladies. As for liberty, it must have in their conceptions a different sense from that in which we understand the term; for a French Count told me that they *had* it, and we only *talked* about it.   *   *   *   *

Speaking of Fanny :—

The poor little soul suffered a sad trial during the cholera, though she put a good face upon it. Her anxiety must have been intense; for Liddell exposed himself profusely to fatigue and sun, and *infection*.   *   *   *   *

Every one has spoken to me of Liddell's devotion to the general good.   *   *   *   *   *

As soon as we quitted the vessel, up I went, of course, to find my dear Mrs. Duckworth[1] and Annie, at Morrell's Hotel in Valetta. You can fancy the joy we had in meeting, after nearly ten years' separation. In their affection for me, I found them just the same as they always used to be.   *   *

Speaking of the reductions in the Civil Service at Malta, in consequence of the Report of the Commissioners,—

The *old* plan, the multitude of counsellors, seems to have been taken from Solomon; the new one, from the cook's oracle :—the broth *was* spoiled; *ergo*, there were too many cooks.   *   *   *   *   *   *

---

[1] She came to Malta with her sister, Lady Stopford, Sir Robert Stopford being appointed Commander-in-Chief.

In December, he writes to Bob:—

I am glad to find you agree with Paley in his opinions concerning the Christian Sabbath. This acknowledgment of mine will seem paradoxical to you; as you know that Paley's doctrines on that head are not those that I have myself adopted. The fact is, that though I believe more than Paley believes, I understood you to believe very much less.[m] I imagined your notion to be, that the ancient Sabbath was ordained exclusively for the Jews: that neither our Saviour nor his apostles enforced its observance: that, consequently, it was not binding upon Christians: that the fourth commandment was therefore abrogated; and that, as neither our Saviour nor his apostles had commanded the keeping of the first day of the week instead of the seventh, Christians were not bound by any *Divine* law to keep any Sabbath at all. Paley, however, has no doubt that the *assembling* upon the first day of the week for the purpose of public worship and religious instruction, is a law of Christianity of Divine appointment. He acknowledges that law in the practice of the Apostles. In agreeing, then, with Paley, you go much further than I imagined your prior conviction to lead you. But, in agreeing with Paley, you consider the *resting* on Sunday from our ordinary labours, except for the purposes of public worship, as an ordinance of *human institution;* whereas I have always followed the vulgar track, in considering myself as much bound by the fourth commandment as by any of the others. I say the vulgar track, because I believe that the great majority of Christians have thought and think as I do. I believe, too, that among the learned men who have recorded their opinions on the subject, and who think differently from Paley, there are some for whose authority you will feel as much deference as for his.

---

[m] At this early period of his life, my Brother's opinions on this subject were, I believe, very much those of the late Mr. Robertson. See his Sermon on "The Shadow and Substance of the Sabbath" (Col. ii. 16, 17).

What do you think of Horsley? "He is acknowledged by all parties to have been the ablest and most learned theologist of the times."[a] Read his sermon on the observance of the Sabbath. It is in the "Family Lectures." He says it is a gross mistake to consider the Sabbath as a mere festival of the Jewish Church, deriving its whole sanctity from the Levitical law. The contrary appears, he maintains, as well from the evidence of the fact which sacred history affords, as from the reason of the thing, which the same history declares. "The religious observation of the seventh day" (he continues) "hath a place in the Decalogue among the very first duties of natural religion. The reason assigned for the injunction is general, and hath no relation or regard to the particular circumstances of the Israelites, or to the particular relation in which they stood to God, as his chosen people. The creation of the world was an event equally interesting to the whole human race, and the acknowledgment of God as our Creator is a duty in all ages, and in all countries, equally incumbent upon every individual of mankind. The terms in which the reason of the ordinance is assigned, plainly describe it as an institution of an earlier age. 'Therefore the Lord blessed the seventh day, and *set it apart*' (that is the true import of the word 'hallowed it'). These words, you will observe, express a past time. It is not said, 'Therefore the Lord *now* blesses the seventh day, and sets it apart;' but therefore He *did* bless it and set it apart in time past; and He now requires that you, his chosen people, should be observant of that ancient institution."

He then alludes to the two days' gathering of manna. In Paley's opinion that transaction was the first actual institution of the Sabbath. Horsley, on the contrary, says that Moses on that occasion mentions the Sabbath as a Divine ordinance, with which he evidently supposes the people were well acquainted; for he alleges the well-known sanctity of that day to account for the extraordinary quantity of manna

---

[a] Preface to the "Considerations on the Lord's Supper," by Dr. Knox.

which was found upon the ground on the day preceding it.
" Indeed," continues Horsley, " the antiquity of the Sabbath
was a thing so well understood among the Jews themselves,
that some of their Rabbin had the vanity to pretend that an
exact adherence to the observation of this day, under the
severities of the Egyptian servitude, was the merit by which
their ancestors procured a miraculous deliverance. The
deliverance of the Israelites from the Egyptian bondage was
surely an act of God's free mercy, in which their own merit
had no share; nor is it likely that their Egyptian lords left them
much at liberty to sanctify the Sabbath, if they were inclined
to do it. The tradition, therefore, is vain and groundless:
but it clearly speaks the opinion of those among whom it
passed, of the antiquity of the institution in question."

And then, *the framers of the Liturgy.* They surely did not
consider the fourth commandment as rescinded, or they would
not have retained it in the Church service. They would not
have appended to it a prayer, repeated every Sunday by
millions, that God would incline our hearts to keep this law;
nor would those millions have concurred for ages in that
prayer, if the law had not in their opinions retained its force.

And which is the most *natural* way of understanding the
beginning of the second chapter of Genesis?

" Thus the heavens and the earth were finished and all the
host of them. And on the seventh day God ended his work
which He had made; and He rested on the seventh day from
all his work which He had made. And God blessed the
seventh day and sanctified it; because that in it He had
rested from all His work which God created and made."

I can only consider this (according to the note in Scott's
Bible) as *historical,* and not by *anticipation.*

"This," as Scott says, " is confirmed by the custom of
measuring time by weeks, which hath *generally* prevailed in
the world, and which is most reasonably accounted for by
supposing it to have arisen from an original tradition, handed
down from Adam and Noah to all their posterity."

He refers also to Genesis viii. 10, 12, and xxix. 27, to show that the patriarchs divided their time into weeks, and regarded the seventh day. In the former place, Noah sent forth his dove on three successive seventh days, and very probably *Sabbaths*. In the latter Laban speaks of fulfilling *her week* (the week of the marriage feast, as Scott explains it).

That the general practice, among Gentile nations, of measuring time by weeks, was handed down to them from their own forefathers, is more likely than that they imitated it from the Jews, with whom they had slight acquaintance, and whose institutions they would have had no wish to copy. As for the *antiquity* of this practice, I don't know whether *Homer* may be cited as a witness; but it is remarkable how often he speaks of the seventh day, and I see in one of the notes at ἑβδομάτη—ἱερὸν ημαρ (Fragment, v. 191), that the place is quoted by Eusebius and Clement of Alexandria. If I had time, I would refer to them to see for what purpose.

Hesiod, too, calls the seventh an ἱερὸν ημαρ, because *Apollo* was *born* on that day —τῃ, γαρ Απολλωνα χρυσαορα γεινατο Αητω. As for the argument that the mention of the Sabbath in the beginning of Genesis is by *anticipation*, and not historical, because the patriarchs are nowhere mentioned as keeping the Sabbath, it is quite as easy to believe that in this case the command was given and obeyed, although the practice is not recorded, as it is to believe that Abel and Noah offered animals in sacrifice, in obedience to God's revealed will, although no record of that revelation is anywhere found in the sacred history.

Paley himself, however, affords *two* reasons for hesitating to adopt his doctrine in this matter.

One is, where he says that it may be urged as an objection to his argument, "that the command which enjoins the observance of the Sabbath is *inserted in the Decalogue*, of which all the other precepts and prohibitions are of moral and universal obligation." Of course he answers his objections; but he does not even himself consider his answer as conclusive; for the terms he uses are, that this argument will have *less weight* when it is considered, &c. But, however

much the weight of the argument may be diminished by the
consideration he suggests, yet still it retains, in my mind,
very great weight. It appears to me that the mere fact that
this command was placed in the Decalogue, separates it so
absolutely from the mere ceremonial law, that the abrogation
of that law should not be considered as affecting this command.

Indeed, the fourth commandment appears to be, strictly,
like the others, of *moral* and universal obligation. For
though the light of nature did not prescribe to us that we
should devote one day in seven to God's service, and the
commandment, in separating for that purpose the seventh
day, is so far a positive law; yet, by natural and moral
right, *some* portion of our time is due to the service and
worship of God; and therefore the command to devote to
God's service *a* portion of our time is a moral command.

Burnet, therefore, calls this command *moral-positive.* See
his sermon, also in the "Family Lectures." In this sense,
too, Horsley considers it as a moral command; for he says
the Gentile convert (to Christianity) would spontaneously
adopt the observation of the Sabbath as a *natural* duty—a
branch, indeed, of that most general commandment, "Thou
shalt love the Lord thy God." And, in answer to the argument that our Saviour and his Apostles were silent concerning the observance of the Sabbath, Horsley insists that
idolatry and blasphemy may as well be justified by their
silence about the second or the third commandment.

The other argument that I derive from Paley on this side,
is where he says, that although the *resting* of the Sabbath is
an ordinance of human institution, it is nevertheless binding
upon the conscience of every individual of a country in which
a weekly Sabbath is established, for the sake of the beneficial
purposes which the public and regular observance of it pro-
motes, and *recommended, perhaps, in some degree to the Divine
approbation* by the resemblance it bears to what God was
pleased to make a solemn part of the law which He delivered
to the people of Israel.

Here, Bob, two reflections suggest themselves : first, that if it be only in a country where the Sabbath is established, that our conscience is concerned to observe it, there can be no reason why the peculiar circumstances of a country should not be considered as affecting the question; whether the law might not be with advantage *modified*, and whether by act of Parliament the shops should not be shut once a month instead of once a week ; whether Parliament should not sit on Sunday after church hours, and so forth.   But then, in the second place, if a question of this sort should be proposed, does not Paley furnish a suggestion to make a *doubt* whether we might not *perhaps* in *some degree* bring down upon us God's wrath, by following a course at *variance* with what He was pleased to make a solemn part of the law which He delivered to Moses: a law nine-tenths of which are confessedly binding to this day upon all mankind, and of which we cannot possibly *know* that the remaining tenth is not equally bind-ing ; though we do know, on the other hand, that it has not been distinctly repealed.

Finally, then, Horsley's belief may be wrong, but it is safe ; Paley's may be wrong, but it is unsafe.   On this account, Bob, I hope you will think that any pleasure you may have had in finding that your preconceived opinions tally with Paley's, and that your original thoughts were con-sequently *well* conceived, is not a pleasure worth the cherish-ing.   Predilections influence opinions.   But for this there would be more conversions.   Get rid of your *bias* then, and allow due weight to what you read on the other side, and I verily believe that, as Paley has done *something* for you, Horsley, and men like Horsley, will do something more.

*   *   *   *   *

In the next letter my Father writes :—

I have poked into the Critici Sacri for your profit, and find this : Genesis ii. 3.   Cartwright says : " Rabbi Salomon vult hoc per prolepsin, seu anticipationem, dictum esse."   Whereas

Grotius (to Exodus xx. 8) says: " Moses in Deuteronomio, ad verba φυλαξας την ἡμεραν των σαββατων ἁγιαζειν αυτην, addit ὁν τροπον ενετειλατο τοι ὁ Κυριος ὁ Θεος σου (sicut præcepit tibi Dominus Deus tuus), nimirum *jam olim, ab orbis initio.*"

Thus Grotius is agreed with Horsley, and opposed to Paley, in considering the Sabbath to be of *primæval* institution. But nevertheless Grotius thinks that the *rest* of the Sabbath was designed only for the Jews. You can easily find at Oxford a Grotius to refer to, and may as well read what he says; but it appears to me that if Paley had been persuaded (as Grotius was) that the words in Genesis were to be read historically, and not proleptically, his conclusion regarding *rest from labour* would have been different from that of Grotius.

Paley's opinion, that we are bound to abstain from working on Sunday, as inhabitants of a country in which Sunday is so kept, is taken from Grotius, whose words are, that we assemble for public worship, "non ex ultimo Dei apostolorumve præcepto, sed ex consensu voluntatis" (so far not at all like Paley). "Talem autem consensum, ubi in morem abiit, violare non est socialiter viventium. Sed in suos" (here again opposed to Paley) "otium non ultra indixit quam quatenus ad cœtus agendos erat necessarium."

Thomas Aquinas pronounces the fourth commandment "partim esse morale, partim ceremoniale: morale quatenus determinat aliquod tempus ad cultum divinum; ceremoniale quatenus diem Saturni ad hoc peculiariter destinat."

This I have already given you as adopted by Burnet.

As for Grotius, I can't understand how he comes to the conclusion that we are only bound by *fashion* to keep Sunday at all; for when he says that he understands the seventh day to have been set apart at the very beginning of the world, he adds, "Id fit læta grataque recordationi mundi a Deo conditi. Verissima enim sententia est Rabbini Judæ Barbesalhalis, et Rabbini Ephraini in Keli Jacar, aliud hoc aliud sequentibus verbis præcipi. Sanctus ille cultus causam habet mundum conditum; otium quod mox præcipitur, Ægyptianam servitutem. Illud *ad genus humanum* pertinet, hoc ad Hebræos solos."

Make what you can of it. It appears to me that the partim ceremoniale, partim morale, is the true character of the precept; that the Apostles made a change in the *ceremonial* part, by changing Saturday to Sunday; that all Christendom has received the practice of the Apostles for their law; that the *morale* of the original law is still binding upon us; that the engaging on Sunday in the turmoil of the world would unfit us for the special duties of that day, and that, *therefore,* the shutting of our shops would be necessary; but that, even otherwise, there is as much reason why *my* ox should rest one day in seven as Moses's ox. The *charity* of the law is universal.

With regard to the observance of the seventh day among the Gentile nations of old, Grotius says:—"Cognitionem aliquam venerationemque Sabbati ad alias etiam pervenisse gentes, et per secula aliquot mansisse, ostendit Clemens Alexandrinus, et in Præparatione Eusebius, Hesiodi verbis, in quibus ἰβδομον ἱερον ηιιαρ dicitur. Suntque Josephi, Philonis, Theophili, Antiochini ac Lucani eodem pertinentes loci."

As Divinity is one main business that you have on hand, I thought I should not mis-spend my paper in giving you these scraps. Let your opinion or mine be what it may, it is still desirable for you to know what eminent men have urged on one side or the other.   *   *   *   *

At present I am doing nothing but drawing. Lady Gore has asked me for one, and I have already done it: it is the Grindelwald, and it turns out well; very much better than the original sketch, and somewhat larger.

I am now doing the Giesbach for Annie Duckworth; and it will be, I think, far richer in colour, effect, and finish, than the sketch. By adopting the mode I learned of the Swiss artists, of keeping the paper sopping wet, not strained, but laid upon a board covered with saturated flannel, I am able to do, in a third of the time, three times better than I used

to do. All the vile mechanical difficulty of laying on colour
is at an end; and I could teach you to draw in a week as well
as I do, *if* you could call up, as I can, Nature's forms and
colours, with which my memory is stored, from long habit of
dwelling on what I see, for the purpose of imitating it. After·
the one in hand, I am going to copy the street of St. Ursola
from Mamma's album, for Mrs. Duckworth; and then I shall
go on working up the Swiss sketches.

You can fancy the rapidity with which I now colour a
drawing, from this: that instead of getting strong shade
and deep colour, as before, by repeated washes, I can lay on
any tint I please *at once*; I could not before, on the dry
paper, because there would have been on the surface the
opacity of undissolved colour; but the thoroughly wet
paper drinks it all in, and the effect is all the better; for
with any degree of force there is always transparency.

* * * * * *

CHAPTER III.

[1838.]

My Father writes to Madame Reboul in the beginning of this year :—

My DEAREST FRIEND,—In answering your kind letter immediately, I do not comply with your desire more than with my own cordial inclination ; for I am impatient to tell you how deeply I value such a proof of your warm-hearted recollection of your old friend, and how well I know how to share every feeling you express. Time is apt to make sad havoc with friendships when they are not refreshed by occasional intercourse. New attachments and habits usually obliterate the old. I have lived long enough to experience the truth of this, and have found it a very painful experience ; for my own nature is not changeable, and I have cherished deep regard for those whose hearts I have not found to retain an equally durable impression. Now in this your dear letter there is nothing for which I thank you more heartily than for the assurance it gives me of your entertaining no doubts of my continuing feeling towards you. For *two* reasons I delight in this your confidence in me. One is, that I like, of course, to have *justice* done to me,—and, *indeed*, this is no more than justice ; and the other is, that it is an additional proof to me

that you are preserving all your old regard for your friend.
Be assured, I earnestly beg you, to the very last hour of your
life, that I shall never part with one jot of my well-founded
regard for you. What it was, it will be always. Your kindness it was that used to take me out of my own miserable
thoughts, and that made for my little Bob such a home as
few children have found at such a distance from their own.
You cared for me because you thought I was worth caring
for; and if I can do nothing *else* to prove that your estimate
was not altogether erroneous, I will try, at least, to convince
you that I am at this moment, and always shall be, as
earnestly solicitous to retain your friendship as I ever was
to win it. I value it now, after eleven years of separation
from you, and now that I am surrounded by dear affections,
as much, ay, *quite* as much, as I did in the days that would
have been so dreary to me without it.   *   *   *

You know I have now *nine* children. Isn't it an awful
number? You are right in saying that my life has been
spent in the business of education; and great joy would it
be to me if I could make any skill that I have learned in the art
useful to *your* children. If I were happily near you, it would
be very interesting to me to give them all the help I could.
I always lamented that those fine boys were not placed at a
good first-rate boarding-school, where they might be subject
to classic discipline. It is not only a certain quantity of
knowledge that is requisite; but the most important part of
education is that discipline of the mind that fits it for
greater efforts when the days of school are past.   *   *

You know how *very* important *I* consider a thorough good
education. It is a common blunder to suppose that a certain
quantity of education is enough for a certain station, and that
more would be superfluous or useless. Now the truth is, that
in my official place little or no education—really none at all—
is requisite for that official business; and yet not a year has
ever passed over my head without bringing some occurrence
that has made me bless my stars for giving me a love of
books. I have either done, for myself or those dear to me,

some good, or averted some evil, by the possession of a power
that nothing but classic discipline in early youth ever can
confer,—the power of building an argument solidly, and
putting it upon paper in the most intelligible shape; the
power of thinking correctly and expressing thoughts forcibly.
Do you think I am perpetrating a vanity in pretending to
possess this power? Not you. I know who I am writing to,
and therefore, instead of minding my p's and q's, I put my
thoughts down carelessly as they arise. Everything, you know,
is measured by comparison. I am quite conscious that thousands and thousands of men have more of this skill than I
have; but I am equally conscious that I have more of it than
most of those with whom I have come in conflict: I ought
to have, because I have spent a thousand times more pains
upon it.   *   *   *   *   *   *

In January, 1838, my Father's fifth and last son, Charles,
was born. To his son, at Oxford, he writes, on the 24th:—

That is one of the great comforts I have in you, my
good boy, that you tell me distinctly just what you think;
and though there is warning, both in sacred and profane
writ, to mistrust our judgment of ourselves, yet the warning must have a qualified meaning. The γνῶθι σεαυτον is a
lesson in some parts difficult, but in others easy. You
may not yet have discovered its extreme difficulty in some
respects; but, I dare say, you have found out its easiness
in others. Most men know, in their own secret hearts, their
own strength or weakness in collision with others, however
shy they may be of confessing a disadvantage. But your
triumph in the Latin essays is right glorious. You would
not have been so distinguished if your compositions had
not been remarkable in *two* respects. First, they must have
been good specimens of *Latin*, in which you are conscious
of being pretty strong; and next, they must have contained
some thoughts remarkable either for originality of concep-
tion or ingenuity of application; and in *this* you have *not*

imagined your power to be as great as that of many of
your neighbours. Take courage, then, Bob. The *thoughts*
will come in proportion as your general reading and observation enlarges your store of materials. Read Byron, and
see if an immensity of reading was not necessary to the
furnishing of *his* thoughts.   *   *   *   I have
already set to work upon " Ajax," and written nearly a sheet-
full. It shall go by next packet.   *   *   *
I do most chorus while I am *fetching a walk;* and it is,
therefore, a salutary employment ; for I grudge the time of
walking when the walking stops my working; whereas a
chorus is a companion that allures me on, and I never do
one better than in the open air, either on foot or on horseback. I am rejoiced that you find them useful. They are
done with so much care that every word has been weighed.
To do them as I do, with scrupulous adherence to the Greek,
and yet to extract a good English, would be utterly impossible, without spending more time upon them than you
could spare from your other employments.

As for the *Sabbath*, you have written a capital defence of
your views upon it, and I dare say you will, at least for some
time, retain them. There are many varieties of opinion on
the subject, and all are supported by good arguments. One
alone is sufficient to me, and that is, the consideration of the
nature of the fourth commandment. When it tells me that
I must devote a portion of my time to the service of God, I
can't consider such a command as merely ceremonial. I
receive it as a *moral* law ; and, whether a code of moral
laws, of God's own framing, were given to Moses or me,
they seem to me, when once I have received them, as binding upon me as upon Moses.

But whether your opinions be considered right or wrong
by those with whom you have, perhaps, at Oxford, occasion to discuss them, it is desirable for you to know any
remarkable things that eminent men have written on either
side. I will give you, then, an extract or two from Hales'.
Chronology. But you may have the book, or, if not, you

ought to have it. Get it directly, Bob. It can certainly not
be superfluous in your library. He calls weeks the primæval
measure of time, instituted as a memorial of the work of
creation in six days, and of the ensuing Sabbath: that it was
universally observed by Noah's descendants during the pre-
valence of the patriarchal religion: that the days of the
week were dedicated by the Egyptians Chaldean Syrians,
after their decline to idolatry, to the sun, moon, and planets:
that so it was in Egypt during the residence there of the
Israelites. Dio Cassius, he says, tells us that the Egyptians
led the way in consecrating the days of the week to the seven
planets; and they were followed by the Greeks, Romans,
Hindoos, Goths, Germans, and Saxons.

A Pythian oracle is preserved by Eusebius, prescribing the
worship of these false gods on their respective days. That
the *week*, Hales says, was unquestionably derived from the
Divine institution at the creation, is evident from the word
Sabbat, or Sabbata, denoting a week among the Syrians,
Arabians, Christian Persians, and Ethiopians; as in an
ancient Syriac calendar (which he gives) expressed in the
Chaldee alphabet. The high antiquity of this calendar is
evinced by the use of the words one, two, three, instead of
the ordinal numbers first, second, third; following the Hebrew
idiom; as in the account of the creation, where we read in
the original "one day," which the Septuagint retains, calling
it ἡμερα μια. So in the Evangelists. It is remarkable, he
says, that from the earliest times sacrifices were offered by
sevens. "Seven bullocks and seven rams," by the Divine
command, in Job's days. The Chaldean diviner Balaam
built *seven* altars, and prepared *seven* bullocks and *seven* rams;
and the Cumæan Sibyl, who came from Chaldea or Baby-
lonia, gives the same directions to Æneas that Balaam did to
Balak:—"Septem mactare juvencos—totidem bidentes."

Then he quotes the ἑβδομη, ἱερον ημαρ of Hesiod, to
show the peculiar sanctity of the seventh day among the
older heathen writers, even after the institution of the Sabbath fell into disuse, or was lost among them: and Theo-

philus, Bishop of Antioch, who says of the seventh day, ἥν παντες ονομαζουσι,—" which all name," or distinguish ; " but most," he adds, " are ignorant of the reason why." " Instead of Saturday (concludes Hales), the last day of the week, and the patriarchal and Jewish *Sabbath,* the Christian world has adopted *Sunday,* the first day of the week, in memory of the *new creation,* or resurrection of our Lord Jesus Christ, which was also the day on which he made his successive manifestations of himself to his disciples ; and the day of the first-fruits of the Christian Church on Whitsunday ; thence consecrated to religious worship, and called the Lord's day in the Apostolic age. Consequently, the change must have been sanctioned and authorized by Him who was ' Lord even of the Sabbath.' " This, to show that a very great master of chronology is of opinion that the division of time into weeks was not derived by the Gentile nations from the Jews, but from the Patriarchs. 　*　　*　　*　　*　　*　　*

The 3rd of February he writes to Bob :—

Besides this letter to me,[a] there came to Sally the very sweetest letter I ever read ; indeed, not one, but two of them, for both are equally fit to make us love the writers. One is from Lady Bunbury, and the other from Mrs. Napier,[b] Bunbury's aunt. Lady Bunbury writes as if she desired earnestly to love Sally, and to win her love ; and uses the warmest expressions, put together in a dear woman's own sweetest way. 　*　　*　　*　　* I must in honesty confess that I could hardly help envying Sally the pleasure of answering such a letter ; and that if ever a heart overflowing with kindness, and a mind distinguished by delicacy and culture belonged to a human being, they belong to the author of that letter. 　*　　*　　*　　* We dined yesterday at the Governor's, and he did all he could to show his desire to make amends for his past incivility. 　*　　*　　*　　* He offered us

---

[a] From Sir H. Bunbury. 　　　　[b] Lady William Napier.

the use of his opera-box.   *   *   *   *   I have just
been trying a bit of chorus in blank verse. It is the bit
following where the enclosed sheet ends.

Ver. 362—ευφημια φωνει.

> Rash words repress ; nor, adding grief to grief,
> Thus aggravate the measure of your ills.

Ver. 361—όρατε τον θρασυν.

> *Ajac.* Behold ye me, the daring, the resolved,
> Th' intrepid in the shock of arms ; and now,
> Right valiant butcher of the flocks and herds
> Oh, deep derision ! oh, my insulted name !
>   *Tec.* Ajax, my lord, I prythee speak not thus.
>   *Aj.* Begone ! wilt thou not hence ? Alas, alas !
>   *Chorus.* O, by the gods, give way to better thoughts !
>   *Aj.* Ill-fated vengeance ! From my hands unharm'd
> I let the wretches part, and turn'd my rage
> Upon the bleating flocks, and hornèd droves,
> And bathed my falchion in their sable blood.

Is this close enough ? It seems the exact sense, and everywhere true either to the spirit or the letter. You know it is
possible to translate more closely by giving an equivalent
phrase than an equivalent *word :* that preserving the English
of each word separately, the *sentence* might not give the idea
intended. I am quite sure that some of my sentences, that
seem at first sight paraphrase, are in fact closer translation
than literal schoolboy English could make it. If you were to
try your hand occasionally at such work as this, I am pretty
sure you would find it profitable to your English. It calls
into play all the resources of one's vocabulary, and accustoms
the ear to judge accurately.   *   *   *   *   Then I
thought I should do well to dip again (after many years
since I was familiar with him) into Shakspeare, to mend my
blank verse; for I think I shall go on with all my future
choruses in blank verse; and for want of better occupation,
I may probably begin again, and re-do all my work in the
same way.   *   *   *   *   *   *   *   *

In a letter to his Sister, of the 22nd of March, announcing the birth of his first grandson, Johnny Liddell, he writes :—

I have written a letter to my poor Lady Gore, in answer to one from her telling me of the death of another daughter. This dear friend of mine has thus announced to me with her own hand, since I have been in Malta, the loss of her husband and three children ; and she bears it all with a courage and resignation that are admirable indeed !   *   *   *   *

To Bob, in April :—

We have had the great joy of reading your letter announcing the good news of the *passing*,[c] and the Fisher's exhibition. Of course I could have no doubt of your passing, and with honour too; nor could you have had any well-defined fears on such a subject; but you are a nervous rogue, and can't enjoy yourself when anything is hanging over you, however persuaded your reason is that its fall won't *hurt* you. The *smalls* now over, you are already beginning to fret about the *bigs*. But *why*, Bob ? If your success in life depended upon your taking a first class, or if the missing of the very highest aim were a disgrace, you might well be uneasy ; for the chances are necessarily against you. I don't expect you to win a first class. What right have I to presume that my son should be more gifted than the sons of ten thousands of my neighbours? But this I *know*, that you will leave college with a high character for industry, and acquirement, and good dispositions, and that you will not turn idler after you have taken your degree, as many first-class men have done. Henry Acland was here again the other day, and he remarked that most of the best tutors at Oxford were not first-class men. Don't fidget, then, on my account, my good boy. I feel *sure* that you will *not* get the first, because you yourself are so, and no one can judge of such a matter better than you can

---

yourself. But I know the many combined advantages that are necessary to such remarkable success, and I am not at all mortified by the acknowledgment that many young men have more *imagination* and *memory* than you have; perhaps —— has more of both. But you have good sense and discretion, a clear and correct judgment, quick penetration, and an accurate taste.

These qualities may not carry you to a particular point as quickly as others may reach it with other additional advantages; but they are quite enough to bear you through a long-sustained race; at the end of which you may reap more honour than all your present competitors. Remember, Bob, that all this game of life is not to be played at Oxford, and that, whether there or elsewhere, if you *do your best*, you are bound to leave the rest to a Providence which will surely dispose of it to a good end. But doing your best does not mean working to the prejudice of your *health*. Amuse yourself moderately, take exercise sufficiently, work bravely while you are working, and let the class turn out as it may.

*   *   *   *   *   *

No one ever did engage in the study of the Epistles without finding the difficulty that you find. Let a man's power be what it may, the difficulty must be sufficiently formidable, can never be wholly overcome, and is acknowledged still to exist by men who have spent a long life in struggling with it, like my old St. Julian's neighbour, Dr. Clarke, who does *nothing else.* But, Bob, the *few* who succeed, at last, in penetrating a certain way into these labyrinths, are those who, like *you*, find the pursuit *interesting.*

And, then, Bob, I am quite sure that in this sort of work more than most other sorts one gains strength as one goes. No mental discipline can be more salutary than such an exercise. It will invigorate your faculties analytical, synthetical, *mnemonical*; and, as you mean to use these faculties after you leave college, don't be discouraged by the fear you have of missing a " first class." Let that matter take its chance. The sum of a man's usefulness and happiness is not to be measured at the close of his *college* life.   Many a man has used his laurels for no better purpose than to *sleep* under them.   ⁂   *   *   *   *

You will want some knowledge of the affairs of the *Middle Ages*.   You would read Sismondi's "History of the Italian Republics in the Middle Ages" with equal pleasure and profit.   It is all as romantic as one of Scott's novels: it lured me on with quite as powerful a charm.   You would find it quite easy in the original French.   After a few hundred pages, you would scarcely have a word to look out.   Then, immediately after that, read Robertson's "Charles the Fifth," and "Philip de Commine's Memoirs."   Read that, by all means, in the original French.   Then get the "Life of Ezzelin da Romano," in Italian, and that will lead you to other similar books—amusing all these in the richest possible degree, and affording you a view of things all *new* to you.   You *must* have occasional light reading—and *I* never met with books that afforded at once so much relaxation and instruction.   They will give you subjects to think and write about—subjects that few people have much considered ; and the knowledge of history that you get in this way fixes itself much faster in the memory than anything you can get from general historians.   It gives you *points*, and from those points you make ramifications that help you to collateral matter, and to the overcoming of many of the difficulties regarding *dates*.   ⁂   *   *   *   ⁂

At this time my Father gave up his house at St. Julian's, and took one at Sliema for the summer months.   St. Julian's was considered unhealthy, on account of the mass of decayed seaweed that then lodged in the bay ; and the long rides in hot weather seemed to bring on the attacks of English cholera or diarrhœa, that now visited my Father more or less severely every summer.   Sliema was much less distant from his office ; and, after spending seven summers at St. Julian's, was agreeable as a variety.   However, my Father had but little enjoyment of it the first summer, for the new Admiral

Superintendent, being unwilling to sanction his sleeping out of his official residence at the Marina, he and his wife remained there, spending the evenings at Sliema with their children, and returning to the Marina, in a boat, at night.

In the summer of 1838, hearing of some changes likely to take place at the Admiralty, and my Father hoping that they might lead to his promotion and removal to England, wrote to his friends Sir H. Neale, Admiral Bouverie, Lady Gore, and Sir George Cockburn, to beg them to interest themselves in his behalf.

He says to Bob :—

All that I expect is that this step that I have taken *may ultimately* lead to my getting an appointment of *some* sort in England. It *may*, by reminding these friends of mine that I have been languishing for ten years in this banishment, and exercising the vile trade of a *baker*.   ❊   ❊   ❊
To get a good place in England would suit me just now gloriously; for so, I shall not have to look forward, as I must otherwise, to more and more *bereavements*. Sally will soon be leaving me. Liddell is looking for an appointment to one of the hospitals in England, and has such powerful friends that he will probably succeed.

You will be fixed in England. Clement must soon go, and then the little ones in their turn.   ❊   ❊   ❊

In July of this year, my Father and his wife suffered great anxiety about poor little Kitty, who was very dangerously ill with dysentery. He says :—

Yesterday was a terrible day ; but Liddell has, under God's blessing, done wonders. He was here all night. His assiduity is unwearied and his resources inexhaustible.

    ❊   ❊   ❊   ❊   ❊   ❊

About this time, as Kitty was recovering, my Father's house at Sliema was full of visitors. Mrs. M. Smith, a connection of his cousin Joseph Henderson's, was staying with us, on her way from India to England; and our cousin Georgiana Ewart[d] and her husband spent a month with us on their way to India.

In August, my Father writes to Bob:—

The two sheets I now send finish "Ajax;" and as soon as the packet is gone, I will begin "Philoctetes." I am not sure that the blank verse will answer your purpose as well as prose; but, at all events, you will find no difficulty in modifying it. The change of a word or a collocation here and there will be enough. I am hardly conscious of having relaxed the severity of literal version for the sake of the verse. Perhaps where, at first sight, you may think my construing too remote from the text, you may find it closer, upon nearer inspection; for you know that if these choruses were taken word for word, the English would be pretty nearly nonsense: there would certainly be little sense, little poetry, and no English idiom. I have tried, then, to construe the *words* as nearly as I could; but when they have been utterly untractable, then I have tried to express the *clause*, or the *sentence*, as Sophocles would have expressed it if he had been writing English. Whatever my success may have been, I am pretty sure you will find my version worth your studying; for though it might be much better than it is, yet I know you will find in it some words luckily translated, and here and there some curious felicity in the sentences.

Much of it, too, is more consecutively smooth,—makes a more naturally-connected sense than one easily gets in so close a translation of such queer Greek. However, in point of obscurity, "Ajax" has little or none, in comparison with some of his predecessors that we have dealt with; "Œdipus Col." for example.

I have copied out these sheets less neatly, if not less

---

[d] The eldest daughter of the Rev. Ed. Repton, Canon of Westminster.

legibly than usual; for I have been writing in bed. I am
pretty well again, and by keeping quite still, hope to be erect
by to-morrow; but I have had another (the second this summer—in Switzerland, you know, I had nothing of the sort)
of those internal commotions that would soon establish cholera,
if my glorious ally, laudanum, did not quell them. *   *
The primary disease is the only formidable one; and once
checked, that is formidable no longer. All it can do is to
make me change, for a day or two, my beef and beer for
macaroni and rice-water. The worst of its doings is, to-day,
in hindering me and my good Mamma from helping my
cousins and nieces eat Fan's dinner at Bighi. To-morrow
will break up our merry re-union. Mrs. Smith, that very
sweet little *niece* of ours (Joseph's wife's son's wife), will go
by the packet to England; and next day Georgiana, dear
affectionate girl, and her first-rate prize of a husband, will
begin their voyage to Alexandria. May they both retain life[r]
and health; and never did a couple come together with
happier prospects of connubial harmony. Both of them
have an unusual share of the first of all requisites, good
temper; neither, I am sure, is deficient in another requisite,
good principle; and both have quite enough of good *sense*.
As for Georgiana, no one can be *more* amiable; but her husband is quite *equal* to her. We all like him with an *unmixed*
liking. I have not seen in him one thing that I should have
wished for her sake not to have seen; and when *does* a man
spend a month in your sight without betraying some imperfection of temper, or at least of *taste?* All of us, great and
small, love him; and he will long remember us.

      *   *   *   *   *   *

For writing good Greek and good Latin you are making a
preparation that must be effectual. For grammar and idiom,
and choice of diction, you will soon cope with the strongest;
and if there be now some of your equals in age who excel you
in the *matter* of their essays, it is probable that you excel some

---

[r] Both, alas! died many years ago, leaving a daughter.

of them in scholarship. They may have spent more time than
you have in general reading, and you more than they have in
mere Latin and Greek reading. They may, therefore, be provided with more copious materials than you for their essays
on general subjects; for you must take into your account, in
estimating what you call a man's power of *original thinking*,
that he must depend for his thoughts upon his knowledge.

"Poeta nascitur." Yes; he was born to become a poet;
but always *provided* he took pains to lay in the necessary
stores to work upon. See what *quantities* of *things* Byron
and Milton *knew*; as well as Cicero, Brougham, Addison,
Knox, or any other eminent writer in verse or prose; and
especially, considering the early age[f] at which they were
written, see the wide range of varied reading displayed in
the Essays of your good Grandfather.[g] Well, then, when
you have had leisure to read more on general subjects, be
sure, Bob, that you will feel your thinking and inventing
powers grow to a *grand expansion*. You have, I know, the
groundwork of a *good taste* for composition. Walter Scott
himself could not have *imagined* all his imaginings if he had
not devoured books without end. General reading, in its
turn, and among it *light* reading (of a good sort), must be
desirable for you on many accounts; and your essay-writing
will gain by it beyond your expectation.   *   *   *

My Father now received kind and civil answers from all
the friends he had written to about his removal to England.
The particular appointment which he had had in view did
not become vacant, but they promised their good offices when
that or any other suitable one should be so; at the same time
Mr. —— added: "There are so many hungry expectants,
who have no pretensions upon the only ground that ought to
be attended to in selection of individuals for permanent offices
of great trust and responsibility, *i. e.*, peculiar fitness for the
duties required to be discharged, that I should not be sur-

---

[f] Sixteen or eighteen.   [g] Dr. Knox.

prised to see that important office,[b] where a thorough knowledge of the naval service, both ashore and afloat, is indis-
pensable, conferred upon some political hanger-on who never
served in the navy, and perhaps never even saw the sea.   At
any rate, you may, as I have already said, depend upon my
best offices, if I have the opportunity."

In September my Father writes to his Son :—   ·

When the last packet went, I was sick from the effects of
the fourth this summer of those internal attacks to which you
know I am subject in the hot weather of this miserable
Malta.   As usual, it soon passed off, and I have been since
as strong as ever.   *   *   *   *   I have said all
this,[i] because I thought it might by possibility enter *your*
head to try your fortune as a feeder of sheep in that new
world.   I hope better things for you.   I should like best of
all to see you in the Church, if you satisfy yourself, during
the time you have to think of it, that you are fit for the profession, and that it is likely to make you happy.   You might
also do well at the bar.   *   *   ·   *   *   However,
there is no hurry.   You have two years more of Brasenose.
In the mean time think; and if you finally decline the
Church, Bunbury may be able two years hence to tell you
the result of his survey, and you will judge which will best
suit you—to fleece clients in England or sheep in Australia.
If I were beginning my course, I should wish to make it in
the *Church*.   If I were free from the tie of my office, and
you went to Australia, I would try and go *with* you.
Wherever it be, I hope my latter days may be spent near
you.   *   *   *   *   *

I do not urge you to take orders, much as I wish to see
you in the Church; but I do entreat you, Bob, to pause
before you allow yourself to be deterred from thinking
further of the Church by such feelings as now possess

---

you. They are morbid. Your health has been probably impaired by too sedentary a life. Your temperament is naturally in some degree hypochondriacal. Your attention has unhappily fixed itself on *certain portions* of Scripture, which, isolated from the rest, may seem to convey a meaning that you would not attribute to them if you took the *only safe* course, of interpreting Scripture *by* Scripture. Abundance there is, amply enough for our purpose, about which there can be *no* doubt. Receiving and believing *that*, I am bound to *use* that in aiding me to understand those parts which are *not* equally clear. Where there are things hard to be understood, I will not attribute to them a sense contradictory to those declarations which have been made in plainer terms.

    *   *   *   *   I am not drawing, but have spent all my little leisure upon your plays. My leisure has been little, because I have had a good deal of sickness and semi-sickness this summer; and, besides, the hawk-and-buzzard life we lead, between the Marina and Sliema, has frittered away my time. *   *   *   *   *   *

Take care, Bob, not to hurt your health by pursuing too eagerly the trumpery honours,—for they *are* trumpery in comparison with the *cost*, if that cost is to be the sacrifice of health. But be wise in time, and don't hesitate to take my advice, and come and make a holiday with us at Malta, unless you are quite sure that you may with perfect safety stay at Oxford. At all events, put aside the *Divinity*. Many a poor man is a better *Christian* than the most successful of your divinity students. To take up and pursue such a study *merely* for the sake of gaining honours at Oxford, is to engage in it unworthily, and to incur the danger of punishment for presumption.   *   *   *   *   *   *

In the two remaining years you will become unfailingly an accurate scholar. Every step you take makes the next easier. It is like learning botany. It was hard to me at first to make familiar acquaintance with a genus, and puzzle out one or two of its species. But when I grew intimate with a dozen out of the twenty species the genus contained, I knew all the

remaining eight at first sight. In turning over the books for
the first twelve, my eye lighted so often upon descriptions of
those I was *not* looking for, that the moment my eye glanced
on them in the fields, I knew all about them. So it is with
particles, with Matthiæ's rules, with historical and geo-
graphical facts, topographical, chronological—in short, there
can be no doubt of your having found it so, and that you will
find it more and more strikingly so as you go on. Then
your love for the "sciences" ought to be very consolatory to
you. It is a sign that there is good stuff in your brain.

*   *   *   *   *   *

I have been exceedingly uneasy about you. I am persuaded that Aristotle and St. Paul together are injuring your
mind and body; just as food and physic, out of season or
proportion, may be converted into poison. Your digestion is,
perhaps, not naturally active, and you may have weakened
it still more by inattention to rules of health, which no man
ever yet broke without paying, sooner or later, the penalty.
Give your body plenty of exercise in the open air, and so
prepare for a good dinner; and remember that that dinner
will not digest if you think of Aristotle or St. Paul till at
least four hours have passed after you have eaten it. You
have now been at work twelve months since your holiday in
Switzerland, and you have had not only hard *thinking*,—in the
way of *study* I mean, but *care* on the subject of your future
profession, and *fear* of failure in your pursuit of honours.
All this has offended your *liver*, which is now avenging
itself by concocting bile of a bad hue. Your spirits are
injured by the effort you have made to reach a given mark
by a given time. You must pause and take breath *in time*.
If you go on in the same way, you will soon break down
and lose your health and your race together. As for your
taking orders, or preferring the bar, or any other profession, don't think about the matter *now*, but think only of
your *health*. Your case is not singular; many a reading man
has incurred more or less mischief by the same mistake. Let

us hope that in your case we are in time to cure it. Your
long vacation has been no holiday. Try and make a real
holiday, then, by coming as soon as you can to see us.

* * • * * * *

Go and see my dear Madame Reboul at Paris.

* * * * * *

In October he writes :—

My DEAREST BOB,—We are all confirmed, by the tone of
your letter to Sally that came the day before yesterday, in
the opinion we formed some time ago, that you are wearing
yourself out by an over-anxiety about your college work, and
that it is abolutely necessary for you to shut up your books
and make a holiday to come and see us. Come, then, at
once. Never care one straw whether your coming do or do
not diminish your chance of honours. Honours have a
certain value, and no more. By forcing yourself to undergo,
in the pursuit of them, such a degree of irksome labour as
must impair both mental and corporeal stamina, you are bidding too high for them, and the sooner you withdraw the
better. Don't be deterred for one instant by a notion that I
shall be mortified and disappointed. I shall have no such
feeling. I shall think only of your health and of your future
well-being, which are much more important considerations.
I have not the silly selfishness of desiring the reflected
honour of your Oxford triumphs. I wish you success of all
sorts for your own sake, and I am persuaded that your success in the more important business of after-life will be
best promoted by your attaching less importance to the object
of your present pursuit. Rude health, buoyant spirits, and
strong nerves, are necessary qualities in a candidate of high
honours at Oxford; and Nature has given you none of
these.

But yet you may do well enough for a bishop or a judge,
and you may lead a comfortable and useful life even without
the ermine or the lawn.

Come and talk nonsense, then, with Sally and Fanny and
Mamma, and help me make Swiss drawings and improve
our Sliema garden.　　＊　　　＊　　　＊　　　＊

In December he writes, in a letter, which crossed my
Brother on his way to Malta:—

I have not seen the Queen.[k]　All the world went to a levée
yesterday to be presented to her.　Of course I did not go.
The Maltese marquises and barons went in dresses of all
ages, from that of Louis XI. downwards; gala suits hoarded
up, and now exhibited, to the great amusement of Queen
Adelaide and her ladies.　　＊　　　＊　　　＊　　　＊

My Brother arrived at Malta on the 19th of December,
1838, my wedding-day, and remained with his Father till
the 15th of April following, when they parted, never to meet
again on earth.[l]

---

[k] Queen Adelaide, who visited Malta this winter.

[l] In a MS. volume of extracts from his Father's letters to him, beautifully
arranged by my dear Brother, with an index and a list of the subjects of each
letter, is written:—

"For nearly eight years afterwards he wrote to me every fortnight.　The
first letter after our parting dated May 15th, 1839; the last, before he fell
asleep, July 30th, 1846,—seven years and two months."

CHAPTER VI.

[1839.]

I SHOULD have said in the last chapter that Clement, then about nine years old, was sent home to school in charge of his brother Robert; and my Father wrote constantly to him too.

To Robert he writes, in May, 1839 :—

*   *   *   *   Do let me make haste to satisfy you that sincerely and heartily I agree with you on the *honours question.* I am glad you have relinquished the pursuit. You were not likely to win the first prize; and minor stakes were not worth playing for. But, according to my view of the case, I should not have heard of your decision with any regret, even if you had had a fair chance of a first class; because your health is not strong enough to bear either the hard work you would have encountered for such an object, or the anxiety you would have suffered during the doubt of your success. Neither you nor I, nor the Brasenose tutors, think the worse of your capacity for your declining to stand for honours which you would have been sure to win, if you had had from the beginning fair play, and, latterly, a better digestion. As it is, the first class would be clearly out of the question. The chance of a second *might* be open to you; but why should you sacrifice health and comfort for the chance of second-rate success, counterbalanced, as that chance is, by the risk of mortification?

It is quite certain that an attorney, some ten years hence, in doubt whether to give his brief to you or your next-door neighbour, would care little about your *second class*. Well, then, my dear good boy, you may be quite at rest regarding *my* wishes in the matter. On *any* subject concerning you, I can have no wish except for your happiness and your best interests; and on this particular subject I am satisfied that you have wisely consulted both.

It might be that I might be useful to you in such a case as this. For example: you might be pretty well convinced that the doing of a particular thing might prove of ultimate important advantage to you, and yet it might be, presently, disagreeable, and you might shirk it. In *that* case, I would urge you, by your filial allegiance, to swallow the pill; just as I would restrain you, if I could, from swallowing the pottage at the price of the birthright: but, in the present instance, my persuasion is (taking *health*, which is the main thing, into the account), that the course to which you are inclined is the one most favourable to your happiness in the general stock. By giving you present relief from the pressure of labour and care, it will improve your chance of health in after-life.

*   *   *   *   *   *

Mr. Roberts,[a] an A.R.A., came out of quarantine ten days ago; and he and his friend Mr. Cory have lived chiefly with us. He and I have had some sketching together, to my great advantage. He is a singularly clever fellow, and knows quantities of things that I could never have found out in my seclusion here, and that he has imparted to me. He is a frank, warm-hearted fellow too. Roberts is now going in the packet to England, and Cory to-morrow evening to Naples. We had all a rare treat in seeing Roberts's drawings of Jerusalem, Thebes, Balbeck, Petra, &c. &c., most beautifully-pencilled and beautifully-coloured drawings of the most magnificent ruins in the world. He gives *me* credit for drawing and

* He brought my Father a letter of introduction from Mrs. Scott (now Mrs. Ellis-Ellis.

colouring from Nature faithfully, and I made my sketches
with him as accurately and nearly as fast as his own; but
what he has in perfection, and I not at all, is a wonderful
knowledge of composition, and power of drawing things not
before his eyes. He can make a picture out of nothing, and
with the quickness of magic. He turned a bad drawing of
mine into a good one, by putting in some shadows, a cow,
two goats, a man, and some felled trees, dabbed down at
once over my colour without pencilling; and he gave me
reasons for what he did, to help me in my future work. He
afforded the Dean some such help in a drawing he is making
of St. Paul preaching to the Maltese.   *   *   *

This summer my Father passed chiefly at Sliema, sleeping
occasionally at the Marina, to see that all went right there.
Towards the end of June he writes to Bob:—

It is broiling hot; and though this is but the beginning
of summer, I have already been visited by the usual visceral
derangement. As usual, the laudanum happily prevented
immediate mischief; but it is now some time ago, and I am
even yet not cured. The care I take to shun the three things
that hurt me—sun, tough meat, and acid,—is as great as it
well can be; but yet I never have, for the last five summers,
succeeded in keeping free from this complaint, except in
Switzerland.   *   *   *   *   *

His children leaving Malta one after the other, and his
health suffering more and more from the heat of the climate,
made my Father desire more ardently than ever to be removed
to England; and giving up his long-deferred hope of *promotion*, he applied at this time for an appointment at Chatham
Dockyard. The following touching letter will show his
feeling.

My dearest Bob,—

      x   *   *   *   Before you receive this, you will
have heard through Aunt of the important step I took, and

well I know how anxious you will be for its leading us all to
England. Of course there are many reasons why I desire
very ardently that my application may succeed. In all the
time that I have had my present appointment, I never before
thought of exchanging it for one in an English dockyard. I
might have had a place in one when I came here; but I
always abhorred a dockyard; and the drudgery of its duties
is more unfit for me than ever, now that I am an old man;
and so is the subordination. No one in a public office could
be more independent, you know, than I am here; no one
could have his time more at his own command. In a dockyard all this will be very different; but having weighed the
pros and the cons in a fair balance, I am entirely convinced
that the preponderance of happiness for all of us is on the
side of the dockyard in *England*; and therefore I heartily
hope my present attempt will prove successful; and if it does
not, I will take the first opportunity to try again.

What I shall lose will be my independence and my leisure.
I shall be confined for most part of the day to my office,
casting accounts, over which I shall fall asleep. My business
will be to ascertain from day to day the total sum of a hundred
lines of figures, recording the issues of fathoms of rope and
pounds of nails. It is not, as here, when I complete a ship
with provisions, the issuing of a dozen articles in big lump
by my clerks, and the examination of the accounts by myself
once a quarter; but it is the *continual* issue of innumerable
small matters, which make long accounts, and cause great
trouble to the storekeeper as well as to his clerks. And then
the law is, in the dockyards in England, that no one can go
out of the yard without *asking leave* of the Captain or Admiral
Superintendent. At Chatham it is a Captain; possibly
some absolute ass, who will be my master, and whose accom-
plishments would hardly qualify him, if brains instead of
luck gave preferment, to execute himself even such trumpery
duties as I should perform and he control.

But my *gains*, on the other hand, will be so considerable,
that I am content to take with them all the disadvantages.

The latter I shall, I dare say, be able to make lighter than most people. My friend the Captain will probably like keeping good terms with me; and business of any sort I know how to dispose of and to shorten. I should make for myself more leisure than most of my brother storekeepers, and I should keep in my office other books besides ledgers. And when my day's work is done, we shall often be *all* assembled.

In Clement's holidays, and those the law allows *you*, you will both be with us. When Herbert's turn comes, and Willie's and Charley's, they too will be twice a year at home. Both Sally and Fanny will probably be in England too.

*   *   *   *   *   *

Malta would be more and more dismal to us, and England more and more inviting. It will be better for the health of all the little ones, and for mine, which is important, you know, considering what a tribe I have to take care of. I have only once this year been ill enough to resort to the landanum; not very ill then; but have been almost constantly out of order since the beginning of June. By living on rice, avoiding the sun, and in every other respect taking great care of myself, I may probably avoid danger; but I am losing stamina. And as I suffered in this way for two or three summers before I went to Switzerland, and have always so suffered in summer since, and did not in Switzerland, and never do here except in the hot weather, it is reasonable to hope that change of climate will cure the mischief.

After the long imprisonment I have had in this narrow cage, it will be refreshing, too, to see what is going on in the world. I should be able to get six weeks' leave of absence every year, and to move in any direction I chose, without the difficulty and heavy cost of getting away from this ugly *island*. Besides this, I might, not seldom, be absent for a day, and I hope there will be steam wings for me, so that I might see you sometimes in London.

But you would, I suppose, be able to spend all your long vacations with us. This would be an unspeakable advantage to us, dear Bob. It would, in some degree, spare your pocket, and diminish, therefore, perhaps, your difficulty in contriving to make your narrow income answer your purpose; but at all events you would have great comfort in a home that you might call your own, and where every face would speak a glad welcome to you. You and Mamma suit each other admirably; the young fry remember you as their best playfellow. Even little Charley remembers his use of the monosyllable " Bob;" and as for me, I consider you as my dear friend; and we have just such notions regarding each other as may best qualify us to give each other help and comfort. We can depend upon one another in all respects thoroughly. You can fancy, then, what it will be to me to see you habitually domiciled with us for some part of every year, and at other times, in my trips to London to alight at *your* door.   *   *   *   *   *   *

Living in London, in a large society, respected for integrity and ability, the chances of attaining something really good in the course of a certain number of years *must* be in your favour. You may follow *Brougham's* advice, and write a law-book. He says that through that sort of channel many a young lawyer has introduced himself to notice.

      *   *   *   *   *   *

I *dream* of the comfort of living within your reach. A railroad will run, of course, through Chatham, for the sake of Dover. One hour, then, will bring you to us. If this time we fail, I will try for the very next opening that offers.

      *   *   *   *   *   *

There is in your case more than common difficulty; for the labours of law studies would probably be too severe for your strength, and your spirits would be quite broken down by waiting year after year, as most young lawyers do wait, and wait in vain, for employment. If *I* had been a lawyer, I could have borne it all; and it would have been hard if, at fifty-two years of age, I had not been better off than I am with this petty appointment. It is true that Lord Eldon waited so long without a brief that he was just going to quit the profession; but it is also true, that, at last, the brief came and the Chancellorship. It is also certain that many of those who have had extensive practice have been men of very moderate talent. And does it appear that there are frequent cases of ultimate failure among men of competent ability, who pursue patiently the right path? *If* there *are* many such cases of absolute failure, they may well make you pause. How heartily glad on your account, dear Bob, I shall be if they let me live in England.   *   *   *   *

In September my Father writes to his Sister :—

You knew, as I supposed you would, before we did, the fate of my application to Lord Minto. I have had a dry letter from his secretary, simply to tell me that he had made the appointment before he received my letter.

Mr. Meek tells me that I stand so high in point of character at the Admiralty, and have so much of the esteem and good-will of every member of the Board, that I should be sure of getting some eligible appointment *if* political interest did not interfere. He says the Tories are pretty sure to come in before long, and that then my chance would be mended.   *   *   *   *   *   *

I believe I have learned to treat myself more successfully, and I really feel as if I was no longer subject to the evil that used to beset me. Diet has a good deal to do with it; but the chief good has been done by adopting the Maltese habit of going to bed in the daytime. Instead of working, as I used to do, more or less, in the afternoon,[b] I go to bed for two hours, and sleep sound, just as if it was night. By this practice, *regularly* observed, I have got the *habit* of sound sleeping at that time; and I suppose it has counteracted the internal irritation which the heat used to create. The differ-

[b] He rose between four and five in the morning.

ence between my present sensations and those I used to have
is so remarkable, that I now quite expect to continue free
from any return of the disorder.   *   *   *   *

In September he writes to his Son :—

Ever since your letter came, four-and-twenty hours ago, I
have been pondering on your speculations; and I only wish
it had been to a better purpose. You know how gladly I
would help you if I could. Why, Bob, if I were master of
my own motions, I should have energy enough to pack my
traps up, and go with you to Australia, to keep your spirits
up, and help set you a-going. But whether you would or
would not do the best thing in the world for the improvement
of your fortune by deciding upon emigration, I doubt with
precisely that measure of doubt that a man must feel upon a
subject on which he is utterly uninformed. Others have
made the experiment with success, and you might succeed;
but many have failed, and you might fail. Success in the
long run may perhaps be *insured* to men who possess certain
combined advantages; but must we not reckon among the
requisites for sure success, *a strong body, elastic spirits, knowledge* of rural affairs, and especially of the *treatment of sheep?*
Well, admitting this, you may not be unqualified; for an
out-of-door life might harden *your* body and drive out the
blue devils. The *knowledge* you might of course gain by
applying to the right means, and spending in the pursuit of it
the necessary *time*. But it cannot be mastered in a day.
Books will not give it. Judging by analogy, I should imagine
that it can only be collected among the sheep-walks and the
shepherds.   *   *   *   *   *   *
I *do* think that emigration would probably afford you
earlier means of marrying than any profession you could choose
in England; but I should not think that you could possibly
expose your happiness to greater peril than by marrying
before you are *tolerably* certain of being able to support your
wife and children. There is no suffering so bitter as that

created by pecuniary embarrassment, the pressure of poverty from day to day, affecting not oneself alone, but a wife and children. Don't run *that* risk, Bob. See your road at least a little way before you. *Then* marry.

But mind, all this is with the supposition that Australia is to be your object; but whether it is the object which in wisdom you ought to pursue, is another question. Is the bar the only alternative? I suppose it is. And in that case, is it not worth while, before you choose between it and Australia, to try and satisfy yourself whether there are not some means of entering and pursuing the profession of the law without any sacrifice of capital? You know there are eminent lawyers who began without *any* capital. How did they manage? When you talk to your friend —— again— he who told you that if he had your money he would jump at the bar,—see whether *he* knows, from any lawyer connections he may have, by what means a man with so limited a fortune may set to work.   *   *   *   *

Mamma wants you to go to the bar because she wishes you to gain a great *name* in the world, which she is sure you will if you turn lawyer.

But everybody is more positive than I am, Bob. I don't think any one can see the exact state of your mind as clearly as I can; and no one can be quite as anxious about your happiness. I have no *ambition* in my hopes for you. A man may be applauded, and yet not happy. I had rather know that you were enjoying health and content than hear you cried up as a prodigy of learning and eloquence. If I were in your place, I should certainly try the bar; I should make myself a sound lawyer, write law-books, work like a dragon, do patiently all a man could do to put himself in fortune's way; and I should in the mean time feel quite sure that it would come at last. Yet with this feeling, I hesitate to advise you to decide upon this course, simply because I have fears for your health. The confinement and hard reading, and waiting year after year for the desired vision of a brief, might be more than your constitution could bear. This is my one great difficulty. I had rather know that you had a robust frame and a light heart in Australia, than hear of your being a Lord Chancellor with an aching head and a sick stomach, and morbid spirits. The *only* decided advice I can give you is to dismiss from your mind peremptorily the notion of taking a wife, till you can secure the means of an adequate provision for her and the brats. On this subject you can't judge for yourself dispassionately enough. Just at first, the getting of the wife would be such prodigious delight, that in speculating upon it you would not allow due weight to the opposing argument. Be sure, Bob, that if you marry upon the mere chance of making money in Australia, the torture you would suffer till the die turned up would be terrible; and what if you threw a blank! Perhaps I am the only one among your friends that would not say *don't* go to Australia. *That* I *won't* say. In truth, I am by no means sure that between it and the bar, I should not, in your particular case, and with your constitution of mind and body, choose this branch of the alternative; but I would not choose without collecting, first, plenty of information. They say, all your dears here, and most people would say, " What a pity to throw away the fruits of Oxford upon Australia!" But *that*, too, weighs little with me. Wherever you are, or whatever your trade, the *learning* will not be thrown away. At all events, it will give you a better station in society, and larger means of varied and satisfactory amusement; but, besides that, there is no knowing what may turn up in the chances of life to bring all your learning to more profitable account : you are by so much the more in luck's way than you would be otherwise.

If you had decided ten years ago upon going to Australia, I should still have been glad that a thorough good education had been part of your preparation for it. Whatever you do, Bob, take your degree first. Never mind the small remaining time and cost. The degree is worth having, even if you take it to Australia.   *   *   *   *   *

In September of this year my Father's fifth daughter, Mary, was born. Soon after he writes to his Son:—

If I were my own master, I would seriously think about our going with you to Australia. But, Bob, I have been so remarkably well this summer that I could not possibly be invalided; and if I were to quit my post on any other terms, I should forfeit my pension. Would *that* be prudent? If I might go away at once, and take my half-pay with me, I verily believe that I should soon be in better circumstances in Australia than I ever shall be in Malta; and there is no country short of Cape Horn or Spitzbergen that would not probably afford me a more agreeable residence than this does. For the society of mere acquaintance you know I have small desire: I should be quite satisfied with my *dears* about me. But perhaps it is better that I should not have a choice in this matter; for if I had to weigh pros and cons, one chief *con* would be a very formidable one. The little people must be educated; and therefore they must be in England. On this subject there would be difficulties without end. However, if ultimately you do decide upon seeking your fortune in the antipodes, I *shall wish* that I *could* go with you; and if my health fails here, and I am allowed to retire, I will see whether I can't join you. My own personal inclination would certainly be that way. You and I might do wonders together.

*　　*　　*　　*　　*　　*

In November he writes:—

I am always anxious to know what you are doing and thinking about, and specially now that you are near the end of one important stage of life, and preparing to start upon another, where we know nothing of the road, and all sorts of chances may await you, and I shall not be at hand to put my shoulder to your wheel. O what a glorious thing *money* is, Bob! It is *power*. If I had it, I should be liberated from my prison, and I would be with you; and I should think nothing of a trip to Australia with you to explore the land,

and help you to decide upon the question of occupying it. But, Bob, what occurs to me is, that though, upon mature reflection, after you have collected the necessary knowledge to reflect upon, it may be well to try your fortune in that new country, yet it may be better to carry with you two strings to your bow. Most of the people who go there are qualified for nothing but graziers. Couldn't you make *some* advantage of the superiority you probably have over all the other colonists in point of education? Men of all professions will be wanted there. In no profession there can there be the formidable competition there is in England. Therefore will the chances of success in each be greater. And all the members of all professions may be land-owners and sheep-feeders.

If I went to a new colony, I would qualify myself to do *something* that might turn to account in case my grazing did not, or to add to my gains if it did. Whether law would be the best commodity *you* could take with you (for you have not a wide choice), is worth considering. Would it be worth while to enter at the Temple, and read, and make other preparation for being called to the bar, in case of trying Australia and finding it fail? Put all this together, and think in the train to which it may further lead.

But another subject for your thoughts may be *medicine*. I don't know whether you ever dreamt of being a *doctor*. But for *you* there could not, as I conjecture, be a better speculation. I verily believe that, with the preparation you have, you might in a marvellously short time gain sufficient skill to start with, and would improve it rapidly. Doctors are wanted everywhere, and you might be the only one there with a classical education. * * * * Why, Bob, with your Greek and your Oxford degree, and the *chemistry*, for which you have a taste, and which you might turn to large account, and with your grave character, and mellow voice, and quiet manner, and an understanding about equal to the combined store of one thousand such young gentlemen as I have named—your success would be *quite sure*.

You might look after your flocks as zealously as the mere graziers. But while sheep graze, shepherds whistle; and while your sheep graze, you may read and think.

* * * * * *

Later in November he writes :—

I can do little more than assure you how deeply interested I am in all your thinkings and doings, and how gladly I *would* help you if I could. But, my good Boy,[c] your stars have led you into a labyrinth, out of which I can see *no pleasant* path. That you will, sooner or later, marry Lizzy Repton, is, I know, if you both live, quite certain. The opposition of her parents may create delay ; * * * but it will not prevail with Lizzy to give you up ; and as for you, you always *were* (by your own confession, though *I* did not find it out) *"as obstinate as a mule ;"* and therefore they are not likely to argue you out of your love. *I* would not if I could ; for—yes, I *would if* I could ; for if anything *I* or any one else could say could make you change your mind, it would be charity to the poor girl to *show you up*. But I suppose all the Reptons know you well enough to be convinced that you will persevere ; and that Lizzy will be true to you as long as you are to her, they cannot long doubt. They may think it worth while to try for a time whether they *can* influence her ; but they will soon see the hopelessness of their experiment. When they *are* satisfied on this point, I take for granted they will not, out of mere anger, make their child more unhappy than they need. It would be very *unlike* them, for Edward Repton is of a tender nature, and I should not have loved his wife as I have loved her all my life, if her disposition had had any perverseness in it. Of course, Bob, you may take it for granted that it is *merely* their *love* for Lizzy that makes them wish you had

---

[c] He had at this time engaged himself to his fair cousin Elizabeth, third daughter of the Rev. E. Repton, Canon of Westminster.

been at Botany Bay a year ago. Could *any* one in their
circumstances feel *anything* *but* horror at their daughter's
engaging herself to a man without a competence, without a
profession, with the certainty of not being rich enough *for
years* to maintain a wife, without taking her to the world's
end, and *there* to toss up for the chance that may betide?

* * * * * *

But, my dear Bob, *be sure* that you are wrong to wish to
set out at once with a wife. Remember that the *children*
would soon come; that the expenses would increase *rapidly;*
and that the most grievous of all cares are those of poverty.
There is *nothing* that gnaws the heart worse than such a
plague. Its occasional visitation is bad enough ; but when it
becomes chronical, hectical, sticking fast all day and every
day, what is there so hard to bear? It will be much easier,
Bob, to bear for some time a separation from your dear Lizzy.
Work first by yourself. You are both very young. You will
be cheered while you are working, by the happy prospect
before you, and she will not be unhappy while she knows you
are working for her sake. * * * *

But, dear Bob, I have a sad sorrow hanging over me. My
own sweet Sally is just going to leave me,—and when *shall* I
see her again ! She is going with Bunbury and my beautiful
grandson to Marseilles, on her way to England, and will sail
four hours after the arrival of the mail from Alexandria,
which is expected to-morrow. * * * *

I parted from my beloved Father early in December, 1839,
for the *last* time !

CHAPTER V.

LIZZY—SOLITUDE AT MALTA—CHEMISTRY—VARIOUS ADVICE AND EXPRESSIONS
OF LOVE—NOTES—LETTER OF CONDOLENCE TO MADAME REBOUL—FANNY
LEAVES HIM—ROME—LETTER TO HANMER—COBBETT'S BOOKS—SKETCHING
—HIS GARDEN—H. KING—CONNUBIAL HARMONY—FUTURE READING—
SHOOTING.

In January my Father writes to Bob :—

The sheet containing *Lizzy's* letter and yours came a
fortnight ago; just too late to be answered by the return of
the packet. But I have written to her now, and, of course,
she will like my letter,[a] for nothing can be warmer than my
feeling towards her; and I dare say it expresses that feeling.
I had, certainly, very great pleasure in receiving *her* letter,—
the first offering of the love she means to give me for your
sake; and I need not say anything to convince you that she
will always be to me as my own dear child.   *   *

I have told my friends at the Admiralty to look out for me
for a vacancy at Greenwich, Woolwich, Deptford, or Chatham ;
but that I won't take a place in a remote dockyard. My object
is to be near London, to take care of the little boys at school ;
and still more, to be at hand to look out for *promotion.* *   *

What a solitude Malta will be to us ! Sally gone ; Fan and
Liddell going ;—then the only *friends* we had were the Abbate
and Smith,—and they gone too ! It is well for us that Mamma
and I are pretty constant in our companionship, and that we
suit each other as well as we do. We want our dear ones about
us for the sake of love; but we feel no want of society to
amuse us.   *   *   *   *   *   *

---

[a] This letter is missing.

Besides your welcome letter, the packet has brought me one from Edward Repton and his wife, written in the only spirit in which they *could* write,—full of kindness towards you and me.　　*　　*　　*　　*　　*

To see you and your wife before you go, would be a great comfort to me; but you and I are both too poor to do as we please. We must submit to the necessities that govern us, and look forward. Old as I am,[b] I have a good constitution, and may, not absurdly, indulge the hope of seeing you again in Australia or in England. Meanwhile, you will not be *lost* to me in your expatriation. We shall preserve a constant intercourse of such letters as will prove very valuable consolations to both of us. You would like me to *see* your works, and your prosperity, and your happy domicile; but I *shall* see it all in your vivid descriptions; and you will always know that every step you take is interesting to me. Each of us will know, while the other lives, that he has one friend in the world worth all others put together.　　*　　*　　*

It is very important that you should have some resource or other for amusing occupation besides books. A *little* application to *chemistry* for a short time, with such assistance as London or Oxford affords, might enable you to go on without help in your Australian solitudes; and I would, if I were you, go on till I overtook even Davy himself. It is a glorious thing to have some special work in hand,—some object on which to apply all one's leisure: it does more for a man's happiness than any variety of desultory work.　　*　　*　　*

Then the power of sketching would be a pleasant possession to you. If you could find time to take just twelve lessons of a good master in London, it would set you up: I had just that measure of teaching, and no more.　　*　　*　　*

While I remember,—before you go quite away, send me all the papers I wrote for you. You shall have them all again; but I mean to copy and polish them, to serve the young ones. They would not find elsewhere such help; and it would be a

---

pity they should not have it. It will be an amusement to me, too, for many a winter's evening.　　＊　　　＊　　　＊

In February he writes to Bob :—

The chief comfort I have in thinking of this is, that active employment will strengthen your constitution. I really believe you will be twice the man in Australia that you would have been in Westminster Hall. I said just now I was only sorry I could *do* nothing to make your way clearer for you. But yet, Bob, it will be something for you to know, when you are on the world's other side, that you have *one* sure friend; and though I have no money now, I *mean* to have some, for we are living so parsimoniously, that we shall save in future a great piece of our income. If ever, then, you are in want of money, I will give you all I can. If it should happen to you to be in such want, it will, I am quite sure, not be your fault, and we will *gladly* share with you our store.

　＊　　　＊　　　＊　　　＊　　　＊　　　＊

If I were you, I would in the next six months dive deep into the mysteries of digging, draining, dressing, fencing, watering, grazing, sheep and cow doctoring, knowledge of various sorts of soil, and all that a man ought to know who has to depend in a wilderness upon his own hands and brains. I would find leisure, too, for a little chemistry, and would take one dozen drawing lessons of a good master ; and after that I can *write* you lessons at leisure, and illustrate them by examples.　　＊　　　＊　　　＊　　　＊

To me, in March, he writes :—

I have not been able to draw *much* of late ; but I have sent one little dab to Mrs. Willes and one to Mr. Sleeman, by his son, who went home in the *Vanguard* ; and I have one of the palm-trees in the Marsa ready for Sir Thomas Acland, and a duplicate of it for Lizzy, and another in progress for Sir T. Acland, a repetition of the Acheron and the Shears. I have nearly finished, too, Captain Hunn's house and the Custom-house, which I have put in as a background to the Speronara that Bunbury copied. It is for Mrs. Duckworth, on her birthday, the 4th of this month.   *   *   *   *   From half-past six till eight I work every morning with Herbert, who is making *rapid* progress. He knows all the Latin nouns, adjectives, pronouns, and verbs perfectly, and has mastered one Greek verb. Then Kitty takes *her* Latin lesson too. Then I walk with Mamma, and often go to see Mrs. Duckworth; and, of course, I *read*. Bob is to send me my notes; and, when they come, I shall be employed in revising and copying them. He urges me to publish the Thucydides, and says that if he had stayed in England he would have published my Sophocles. Whether I shall ever venture to publish either, now that I shall be without Bob's help, I don't know; but I have motive enough for preserving them and putting them into a good shape; for are there not already Clement and Herbert, and Willy and Charlie, and Johnny and Henry, to whom they will be useful; and may there not be a dozen more Liddells and Bunburys, though of Sconces there are already enough, in conscience—no, no, the grandson Sconces will be forthcoming. In short, I may as well have a hundred copies privately printed for the use of my posterity.   *   *   *

On the death of Sir Harry Neale, in the beginning of March, my Father wrote thus to Madame Reboul:—

MY VERY DEAR FRIEND,—A letter from the Abbate[c] has told me the sad news by which you have been so deeply afflicted. That I should take part in your sorrow on *any* subject, you know full well; but you know, too, that the friend who has been taken from you was my friend too, and that I loved him dearly. No one either can understand the measure of your loss more perfectly than I do, enjoying, as

---

[c] He had gone to Paris with his brother Michele, who studied lithography there.

I once did, the privilege of living with you both, and sharing
your pursuits, and seeing that you were to each other all
that that good girl of mine, to whom you were lately so kind,
has been to me, and I to her. I see, at this moment, his most
benevolent face, and hear his joke and your merry laugh.
He made every one's heart about him expand. It was comfortable to me to be *near* the good man. It was delightful to
hear *everybody* agree in speaking of him as he deserved; and
a *multitude* laments his loss with you. I wish that could
be any comfort to your dear heart; but your love for him
was more than that of all the world put together. To
write to you on such an occasion as this is, of course, natural to me. You knew that I would write. But the
Abbate says: "Prendete la vostra penna e dite a questa
buona creatura, quel che sapete ben dire in simili circo-
stanze per ajutarla, per quanto si può, a portare la sua
afflizione."

This *is* the purpose for which I would fain write to you.
One *does* hope in such a case to do some little good. *I* feel
that hope at this moment, though I am conscious of knowing
no more than a child would know, what I ought to say to you.
I have no *wisdom* to help me. I can suggest no argument to
divert you from your grief or to lessen its pressure. If I were
with you, I would not attempt to do either; but then you
could not help seeing that my whole heart was occupied with
you, and that I *longed* to comfort you; and in your kindness
you would let my wishes count for something, and you would
answer them, if not with a smile, yet with *tears* perhaps, and
they would relieve you. But is there any case in which a
pen is so useless? My head has nothing to do with the
guidance of it; and as for my heart, the fuller it is—and you
know it *is* full of affection for you, deep and sincere, and
warm as it ever was and ever will be, even if my eyes never
look upon you again,—the more it hates such a miserable
expedient as this is. I have been *acquainted with grief*; and
I know that it hates words. I will not vex you with them,
but I will beg you only to think all that I feel for you.

*   *   *   *   *   *

In March his darling Fanny left him to go to England, *viâ* Italy and France, with her husband and child. He writes to her at Rome :—

The great things at Rome are the Coliseum, and St. Peter's, and the Pantheon. If I were at Rome again, I should go again and again to each of them a dozen times. The *walls* are interesting all round the ruined aqueducts; and the many churches full of ancient columns. But I would disregard all the modern artists except one painter, *Overbeck*, who is the best historical painter now alive; and one sculptor, Thorwaldsen, if he has returned to Rome. * * * *

Dwell as much as you can upon the sculptures in the Vatican and the Capitol; and some of the great pictures in the Vatican. You know the Transfiguration is the most renowned of all the pictures in the world. You will be sadly disappointed in it; for its general effect is far less striking and agreeable than you would expect from its great fame, as the best work of the greatest master; but the reason is, that the *colour* is not Raphael's. It has been restored and spoiled; but you are to look at the composition, and the drawing, and the separate heads, each of which is still Raphael's.

* * * * * *

To my husband he writes :—

MALTA, 16th *April*, 1840.

MY DEAR BUNBURY, or, better, my dear Hanmer,—for though by old use the former prevailed with me, yet the other seems so generally adopted among your new relations, that I don't know why I should make an exception; and if there be more of affection in it, it will on that account suit me better, as much as it suits them.

I am inclined, you know, to think of you and Sally as one; and I know you are inclined to adopt all her feeling towards me. No one can have a deeper conviction than I have of the great blessing of unbounded confidence and affection among all the members of a family; and do let us all do our best to

secure it. You will all of you be far away from me; but I
shall always think of you, and interest myself deeply in all
that concerns each and all of you. My nature, you know, is
ardent enough, and my memory quite good enough to preserve all the feeling I have for you now, in spite of all the
leagues and all the years that are going to divide us. Bob
gave me very great pleasure in telling me of the warmth with
which you had proposed his joining fortunes with you. You
are quite right in thinking that it would be absurd for you to
go one way and him another. Your united power will have
twice the effect that it could have divided. Two men may,
in succession, slay a dozen lions, though each lion might
separately be more than a match for one of them.

But the *wives!* What a blessing *they* will be to each other!

   *   *   *   *   *   *

You can fancy that I shall have an eager curiosity to make
acquaintance with every tree and every stone about you;
with every undulation of your ground, the species of your
grass, and all the very weeds; pools, wells, the colour of your
sky, the heat and cold, the sheep and the kangaroos, the
birds, the bipeds *unfledged*. While you are watching the
sheep, you will sometimes be able to sketch a little. Ever so
rude a sketch speaks a plainer language than words; and you
must describe your things to me with your pencils as well as
pens. Among the odds and ends I want to give you for
keepsakes, I begged my sister to get four things in the shape
of camp-stools or sketching-stools; and I told her she had
better get you to choose them.   *   *   *   *

If you find none that combine portability and comfort
in due degree, get them made on purpose. Umbrellas, too,
for fixing in the ground, would be very useful to you—
thorough good ones, well contrived. Will you order four
according to your own plan? and be sure and let my sister
pay for them.

There is nothing new here except the Neapolitan affair,
which seems a foolish one. The report is, that we are not to
make war upon the silly king, but only to seize his ships

where we can find them at sea, and take peaceable possession of them; not to use any steel or gunpowder. In the mean time the said king is calling himself a second Bonaparte; and his brother tells him it is very true, and that he really *is* equal to Bonaparte in all points except only *courage*. The *Belierophon* and *Hydra*, and a small sailing vessel, are gone to the neighbourhood of Naples, I suppose to pick up a straggling zebeck or so; and much will the honour and interest of England gain by their success. The French Ambassador at Naples is said to have gone to the King, to advise him to grant our demands, and to warn him that, if he persevered in braving the power of England, he would neither have the aid of France nor of any other power; and the blockhead refused to hear a word the Frenchman had to say, declaring that he knew his own business, and had made up his mind to all consequences.   *   *   *   *

Sir —— was actually going with his own three-decker, and his own flag at the main, with the *Bellerophon* and *Benbow*, on this fool's errand to Naples; and well it is he thought better of it; for *Neapolitans* to *laugh* at us would *really* be too bad.

I hear nothing about your state of health; and I think I may take for granted that you are going on gloriously. My hope is, that so thorough a change of air and scene will strengthen you *all*.   *   *   *   *   *

Ever most affectionately yours,

R. C. S.

To Bob, in April :—

I have ordered one or two books that promise to be useful to you.   *   *   *   Cobbett's " Cottage Economy " for my precious Sally, and Anne Cobbett's " English House-keeper," with my love to Lizzy; Cobbett's " English Spelling Book " for my Grandson, Henry Fox, with my love to the good little man ; Cobbett's edition of " Tull's Husbandry," for you and Hanmer to see if it is good for anything for your purposes, but it is to be his property ; and Cobbett's " French

Grammar" is to be *your* property. So, such as they may happen to be, there is one apiece for you all five; but you may form a *bookclub*, and so all five share together. Henry may help your orthography; Hanmer straighten your furrows; Sally set your house in order; and Lizzy sweeten the dumpling,—and so I well know you *will*, dear Lizzy.

To me, in May :—

Love is the best thing in this world; and very sweet is the comfort I find in hearing of kind hearts that love my dear child.[d] I will treasure up a faithful recollection of them all, that I may love them for your sake. Why, my chick, you will be so well off in this respect in your southern wilderness, that your days cannot fail to pass pleasurably with your husband and your baby, and Bob and Lizzy : there won't be one member of the colony as well off as you will be. I believe you will all go on together just as Mamma and I do. You know I have it all my own way, which is very agreeable; but then she is equally persuaded that she has it all *her* way : and both are right ; for the truth is, that my way is hers, and hers mine.   *   *   *   *   *

I heartily hope you will continue to like the good woman you have got to replace your nurse.   *   *   * But remember that if she is moderately young, and not intolerably ugly, she will be sure to leave you for a husband within six months of her appearance in Adelaide. You had better advertise for an *ugly woman*—though I am afraid there would not be one in the wide circuit of England who would see in her glass the required qualification. I suppose, in short, there *is* no such thing, as Dr. Johnson denied the existence of *bad wine.*   *   *   *   *   *

Bob and you do, to be sure, bewilder me, in sending me from Sydney to Port Phillip, and from Port Phillip to Adelaide. Adelaide of course it will be if Hanmer likes it

---

[d] In reply to letters from me telling him of the kindness of all my husband's relations.

best; for the *reasons* that make him prefer it will of course weigh equally with Bob, who can have had no leisure to collect materials for any opinion of his own. I shall have an intense interest in learning all I can about the country in which you are to live; and as for the letters you will write to me from thence, only think, my dear child, of *their* interest! I shall feel the most eager curiosity to know all the minutest circumstances that concern you, and everything about you. It is *then*, too, that your sketching skill will be valuable to me. *I* could make in an hour or two a *coloured* sketch of a house, or a hill, or a tree, or anything else that would enable you to fancy yourself looking at the very thing itself, and yet it would be a mere rough sketch. It is very *easy* to make sketches for such a purpose, when one is totally indifferent to their *effect* as *works of art*. A finished drawing takes time, and an artist-like sketch requires taste and knowledge of all sorts; but the operation is quite different when one's object is simply to convey a portrait of an object. You remember some of my boats:* Hanmer copied one or two. Well, they are roughly done, and none of them took me more than an hour or two; and yet they give as perfect an idea of the reality as one can desire. Well, then, you might quite easily do anything in that way. The body-colour gives you immense facility. Instead of leaving lights, or picking them out, you have only to paint them in, which is done in *no* time.   *   *   *   *   *

Speaking of the long drought:—

All the great wells in the Victualling-yard will be empty in two months. Everybody's wells will be empty in the towns, and all those in the country must be kept for drink instead of watering gardens, and cotton and melon fields. I believe I must pick out some few of the pretty things that I *can't* let die, and give up all the rest. I must spare

---

* The highly picturesque Maltese and Sicilian sailing-boats and vessels of various kinds.

a sprinkling of water now and then for the Hibiscuses,
the Pergularias, the great glorious double Oleanders, the
cut-leaved Bignonia, and for a few of the annuals, till
they ripen their seeds; such as those beautiful Escholzias,
of which Captain Wilson gave me a plant last year, from
which I have now a dozen pots, and *one* of them had
thirty full-blown flowers at once, as big as the flowers of
the single Hibiscus; and those equally beautiful pink Œno-
theras, the long spike, you know, that we had in the court-yard,
besides many in the garden. Sliema was full this spring of
magnificent ones, but I was forced to let them all die. The
Peruvian Nasturtiums I *must* save, and those dear English
sweet-pease. I have thousands of the pink ones they call
Painted Ladies. I have spared them a *little* water, and with
that little they have done wonders. I have quantities of all
sorts of coloured Rocket Larkspurs; and have immensely
multiplied my Ixias and Ranunculuses. The little Marina
garden has gained *renown* this year for its flowers. We have
had a hundred times more than ever we had. I have succeeded in getting immensely large and very double purple
groundsel. Our chimney-piece has been every day for the
last four months a striking exhibition. *   *   *

Our house is going to be thoroughly repaired; and so this
year I shall have no difficulty about living at Sliema.

   *   *   *   *   *   *

To Bob, in May, my Father writes:—

Your anxieties are now over, and so, I conclude, will be,
before you receive this, your residence at Oxford. You know
how impatient I shall be to hear that you have brought all
those labours to a happy close, and that you have entered
with a light heart and good courage upon the pursuits you
have next to take up. All is now, I trust, bright in your
prospect. If I were you, I should have no fears; but the
excitement of such an enterprise would be all pleasurable. I
can conceive no way of entering upon the active business of life

more interesting; for you are going with Lizzy to realize an
Arcadia.   Pastorals and poverty are combinations belonging
to our old overstocked western Europe; but you are going
to shear *golden* fleeces.   It must be impossible to feel
poverty in a country where you may buy wide lands for little
cost, where flocks find pasture, where gardens grow, and pigs
and poultry fatten; where the tax and tithe collector never
show their ugly faces, and where you will not want the
superfluous fineries of more artificial life. *I* have nothing
but cheerful hope; and I persuade myself that all four of you
are now equally in good spirits and good humour with the
lot before you.   *   *   *   *   *

Bettoo's lesson in Selectæ e Veteri describes to me the
sort of life you are going to lead.   You will bid Lizzy com-
misce similam (which must be construed semola), and she
will tell you After vitulum; and there will by the lac and
butyrum, and the panes sub cinere tosti.   By the bye, the
best *new cheese* you or I ever encountered was that made by
the poor people in the Riviere di Genova of *sheep's milk;*
though you will have no lack (and, therefore, lac enough) of
cows.   *   *   *   *   *   *

To me, in May, he writes :—

I have not been quite as robust of late as I am apt to be.
When Fan went away, I had a cold that affected my throat
and chest a good deal.   *   *   *   However it can't long hold out against the vigorous measures
I am now pursuing.   What *cold* can resist cayenne and
mustard?   One you know makes a plaster and the other
gargle; and I hope I shall want no other pharmacy than the
cruets, taking care to avoid the mischief of walking in the
sun, and then crossing the harbour in the comparatively cold
wind.   *This,* I suppose, has kept up the malady; for poor
little Annie[1] has been ill, and I have been to see her every

---

[1] Miss Duckworth.

day. It may be true enough that charity begins at home, but at any rate the maxim is not to my taste.

*   *   *   *   *   *

We have *visitors* with us. Henry King and his wife are here on their way to England from India.   *   *   * So we begged them to spend their few days at Malta with us. I was glad to show them what kindness I could, because you know his mother was my very dear friend, and I have more pleasure in paying a debt of love to a friend in heaven than I should have if she were here to acknowledge it. *   *   * Of all the people in whom I have been interested in their youth, I have not found any retain, after the lapse of long years, as much attachment as Henry King,[c] I am sure, feels towards me.   *   *   *

To me, in June :—

Hanmer will take as 'much care of you as I should, and I dare say he keeps you in much better order. Don't you remember how indignant little Fan was when Liddell said I must use my authority and make her ride? The fact is, I believe I cheated you both pretty much as I cheat Mamma. She fancies she has always her own way, and yet it is always my way. But " wisy wersy," as ——— says, I suppose you all think me cheated in the very same mode. I am pretty sure, too, that you and Hanmer are going on in the same track. One makes no sacrifice or self-denial for the other, simply because one always inclines just as the other does. When I hear that you both, and your mutual treasure, are all *well*, that will always be enough for me; for I am quite sure that in other respects all is *quite* right; and being right now, it is sure to be so till the end. The longer people live together in love, the more they love each other. You will nurse him all the more tenderly when he needs nursing, from remembering that his nursing you, when he was sick himself,

---

[c] A grandson of Admiral Sir J. Duckworth.

gave him a bad illness. So with daily and hourly deeds of
kindness, they are things to remember, and *are* remembered,
and make bickerings impossible. People do bicker who have
once loved each other; but not with the right sort of love,
and not people who have hearts or brains.

*   *   *   *   *   *

Please to give my love to your cousin Emily,[b] and tell her
that when she desired you to let her know how you found
" dear little Clement," she made for herself a passage right
into the middle of his Papa's heart. I rejoice, too, in
Pamela's recovery, and you may quite depend upon my com-
plying with your desire, by going to see them whenever *I
can.* You must always tell me of everybody that loves you
and that you love, that I may think of them as *my friends.*

*   *   *   *   *   *

Have you seen poor Mrs. Knox? Aunt tells us—what we
had before too accurately guessed—that she has a cancer!
Poor soul! I feel a most sincere grief for her, and for her
husband too. Mortality can know no anguish more appalling. I wish to write to him to tell him how I feel for her,
and for *his* trial too; but this is of all griefs the one that
mocks all sympathy. I do daily pray God to have mercy
upon her. Would that it were " the *effectual fervent* prayer
of a *righteous* man !" There is no better hope than that the
hideous death which is hanging over her may strike quickly.

*   *   *   *   *   *

To Bob and Lizzy in June :—

You will not shut up your Greek and Latin books, as most
people do, directly they leave college, and bid them a final
farewell. There is no knowing to what extent your scholarship may, by lucky accident, be turned by-and-by to profitable account; but there is perfect certainty that it will all
through life be more or less useful. Instead of letting my

stores perish from disuse, I would by degrees, and at convenient opportunities, *add* to them. I would now and then,
for my evening's amusement, even write Latin, and think of
Greek particles. You know I don't preach what I have not
practised, and with disadvantages, too, that would have
damped most men's courage; for after my Latin and Greek
books were first shut, I was engaged for years in so much
business, that I had little or no time at my own disposal, and,
shut up in a ship's cabin, I had no access to any books beyond
my own narrow shelves. My library, too, was unlike yours.
Duker alone had then handled Thucydides, and for one
difficulty smoothed, left a dozen unnoticed. *   *   *

However, you have had, for the present at least, enough of
Aristotle and Eton grammar, and I can fancy well the glee
with which you are both applying to other subjects. *Gunnery*
is certainly among the last to which I should have expected
you to turn. For *defence* you had better look into Robinson
Crusoe, and see how he built *his* castle; and as for kangaroos,
or furred or feathered game, you must tell me who bags the
first head, you or Bob; for my notion at present is that you'
will prove the better sportsman. I was a dead shot *once*.
Ranging the blue mountains of Jamaica with a practised
shooter, he aimed at a vulture high in the air, right over our
heads, and fired in vain, for the bird was apparently out of
reach. However, I fired too, and down came the big bird at our
feet. I could not very precisely aver that I ever stopped the
flight of another. But the Avunculus, as well as Pater, may
excite your emulation; for it was reported all through Ton-
bridge in my school days that Tom Knox had shot a duck—a
tame one. *   *   *   *   *   *

To Fanny in June:—

But you see, dear Fan, the Commissioners have done a
great deal for *me*. I shall be indebted to them for twelve

Lizzy.

shillings a day half-pay, in addition to my Agent Victualler's retiring pension; and my belief is, that the secretaries owe this to the correspondence I had with Sir George Cockburn. I only wish the law had existed at the time when I had completed the twelve years; for you see I gained no advantage whatever from the *ten* additional years' service. I was then only thirty years old, and just then I had a magnificent offer of help to induce me to try the *bar*, which, with my £216 a year half-pay, I certainly should have done; and it would have been hard if I had not done *something* then. Or even if at that time I had endeavoured to get such an appointment as I have now, and which in those days I would not have accepted, I should still have had a bigger pension in addition to the half-pay; in short, *anything* that I could have done would have been better than going on for ten additional years doing Secretary's work, which years were quite thrown away.   *   *   *   *   *

Mrs. Barnard and her two daughters are with us, and will stay with us till Captain Barnard arrives. I don't know whether his ship has yet left England, but Mrs. Barnard expects him by the end of next month.   *   *   *
She was so amiable a neighbour to Aunt and you at Tothill, that of course we must do all we can for her.[k]

          *   *   *   *   *   *

To me in June :—

As the time draws near for your going farther from me, my heart sinks at the thought of it; but I will keep a good courage, nevertheless, my darling, and so must you. I am quite persuaded that you are doing wisely, and that, as far as our short sight can go, you are making the best provision for permanent happiness by this present sacrifice. If God pleases, I may, without a miracle, live long enough to see you again; and in the mean time I am very far indeed from considering

---

[k] She was with him about three months.

my far-distant children as being lost to me. Though I don't
see your sweet face and hear your dear voice, I have you
always pictured in my heart; and shall always interest myself in your interests just as much as if I could follow you
with my eyes. The love that prompts your beautiful letters
and tells me the detail of all your doings, enables me to understand all the circumstances that concern you, and to trace
you everywhere so accurately, that you will never be hidden
from my mental sight; and in this there is IMMENSE comfort.
Let us make the most of it, my chicken. If God blesses you
with health and tranquillity and prosperity, you will enjoy it
all the more for knowing that it will give joy to your dear
Papa. You know how very, very much I love you; and so it will
always be a pleasure to you to occupy yourself in telling me
all that happens to you. We *can* then be to each other a
great deal, in spite of all the thousands of leagues between us.

     *   *   *   *   *   *

CHAPTER VI.

[1840.]

In June my Brother took his degree at Oxford, and was presented with an unsought-for "honour,"—a fourth class. In the beginning of August he was married at Strathfieldsaye; Mr. Repton having taken the Hon. and Rev. —— Wellesley's duties that summer. On the 9th my Father writes to him :—

Before you receive this letter of mine, your honeymoon will be approaching its second quarter. But no, Bob, it won't; for I foresee that it will be much such another as you know ours has been, shining for the last ten years without a cloud. Now, Lizzy, this is no flight of fancy, but a downright plain matter of fact, and a very encouraging one for you too, if you *wanted* any such encouragement after the experience of your own paternal home, and your sufficient experience, too, of your husband's disposition. Flitches of bacon are not so hard to win as the world fancies; or, in other words, there *would* be winners if the said flitches were but forthcoming. We should claim one *annually*; and rare prizes they would be, for all Barbar's are *rancid*. I do see strange goings on among married people, and have lately in very young and rather newly-married people too, and they married for *love;* but then they are deficient in *sense*, and that is enough to account for all sorts of miseries. Nine people out of ten, you know, have no brains; so out of twenty couples there is but one with a set apiece. Good tempers are about as scarce; and as for taste and sentiment, and sound principle, of course *they*, too, are *sometimes* wanting. Plenty of establishments, therefore, go on badly; but the comfort is, that not only one here and there begins well, but if it does, or only goes on right for a few moons, there will be no change till the end of the chapter. You know no exception to this maxim of mine; for though there have been, apparently, happy beginnings with bad endings, yet, if the truth were known, those beginnings were not *all right*. You are both of you wise enough not to expect to lead a life of undisturbed happiness; but you do expect, reasonably, to find in each other unfailing comfort in all your trials. And isn't this a blessed benefit? You have done wisely, then, my good children; and may God look upon you with His most gracious favour!   *   *

To me, in July :—

The packet has behaved well this time, for it brought me your dear letter last Monday, the 6th; so I had a treat for my *birthday*. I have now numbered fifty-three years, my darling; and though the Malta summers have not, of late, treated me well, I am pretty sure there are but few people of my standing who retain more of their energies than I do, or feel less in their limbs or spirits of the approach of old age.

      *   *   *   *   *   *

What a graphic account you gave me of your adventures that ended in landing you at Harwich! But whether you describe gardens of roses, or what you call the wretched little village of Walton, you make me think of the narrowness and ugliness of my narrow cage. Why even Walton must be a paradise in comparison with Malta; for there, I suppose, one might see a *hedge*, or a tree or two, and a *pond*, and a meadow,—and one wouldn't be hemmed in by a wide sea;—and probably a stage-coach passes near, or there may be a railroad

not far off. In short, it is not Malta, nor the dungeon of
Chillon. I was never in all my life discontented with my
domicile before, be it where it might; but, now *you are all
gone*, I am very, very sick of this dull scene. Can't you fancy
how continually I am reminded of you? The going to Bighi is
sad work. From the house where the Bowmans lived we hear
Miss Giungo's bravuras, and she sings many of your songs; but
they were very different when you sang them, dear; and when
will you sing to me again? Sing to Lady Bunbury two or
three of those well-remembered scraps, without any music,
and tell her it is for Papa's sake, because I loved them and
love you, and I will think I hear them, my precious.

＊　　　＊　　　＊　　　＊　　　＊　　　＊

Then I must look round my garden, or my exotics would
all perish from injudicious treatment or neglect. I have many
rare ones coming up; among them Jumbee beads and Job's
tears, and the Gloriosa Lily, and the giant Orchis, and strange
Cassias and Bignonias from Bombay and St. Helena.

＊　　　＊　　　＊　　　＊　　　＊　　　＊

To me, in August:—

MY BEST OF CHILDREN,—Best, I mean, in all the world,
except from Fan to Mary inclusive, but second to none since
children were invented by old Adam.　＊　　　＊　　　＊

I took Mrs. King and her baby to the church to-day for
her service and his. We and the nurse and clerk were
all the congregation. Loving, as I do, the memory of the
poor child's grandmother, it was very interesting to me to
join in praying for a blessing upon it. If she had lived, she
would have been Bob's Godmother.　＊　　　＊　　　＊

No, dear, I never read Aristodemo;[a] but I will for your
sake, though, of course, I hate the horrid man,—the old
Messenian, I suppose, that killed his daughter. Those Greek
and Roman killers of themselves or their sons and daughters

---

[a] By Monti.

are small heroes in my eyes; for patriotism had less to do with it than *temper*. They were angry with men and the Almighty.   *   *   *   *   *

I delight to hear of all the kind doings of your friends. Capital books they are that Edward Bunbury has given you. Happily you can take pleasure in books of the right sort; and they will richly interest and embellish your rustic life.

You are wise in reading Italian while you have it fresh. If you were to neglect it long, it would grow so rusty that you might be discouraged from refurbishing it. Mental stores are valuable enough to all their possessors; but you, who must depend so much upon your own resources, will have more especial need of them, not only for your own use, but little Henry's.   *   *   *   *

The time may come when some rapid steamer may take me to see you. If that time does come, there will be JOY in the farm; won't there, my chicken?

   *   *   *   *   Kiss my grandson for me, and ask Mrs. Austin to mount "the sweet child"[b] on a "sunbeam," and send him to see his Grandpapa. Aurora can take care of him, and I will open my shutter at five to-morrow morning to let him in.   *   *   *   *

To Bob, in August:—

We paid due honour to the 11th,[c] for all our household, with the good Abbate, the babies, the servants, and the boatmen, drank your health in champagne.

   *   *   *   *   *   *

In a former letter he had said :—

There will be grand doings here on that day; for, besides our domestic rejoicings, it will be the eve of St. Lawrence,

---

[b] "A Story without an End," translated from the German, by Mrs. Austin.
[c] Bob's wedding-day.

the great firework show at our town of Vittoriosa, and they
will give the saint more than his usual honours this time.

His Holiness the Pope has just sent over to our good
people some precious pieces of the Martyr's body. There is
a well-identified tooth, some roasted flesh, a small lump of
his unconsumed fat, and a link of the chain that bound him
to the fatal gridiron; and there is, moreover, a parchment,
under the Pope's own hand, leaving no doubt among the
faithful (i fedeli) that all this is genuine and true.

*   *   *   *   *   *

—— says an emigrant never prospers unless he can with
his own hands guide a plough and *load a dung-cart*. I say,
Bob, I *would prosper*, however. Make me an emigrant and
twenty-two years old, and see whether I won't apply my
labour to the most useful purpose, whether it be in handling
a pen or a pitchfork. The money I would make, however
unsavoury the means, be they only honest. The soil of Port
Phillip is, I hear, less ungrateful than that of Adelaide.
Where you are going, grass and corn and trees will grow. Pay
dear for good land rather than little for bad, that your labour
may be rewarded by the progressive increase of your crops
from year to year. No work can be more interesting than
the founding of an estate that promises to nourish your
children's children; the planting of oaks to furnish a broad
shade for them. Delighting as I do in a garden, what
intense pleasure it would be to me, in your circumstances,
to lay out my ground, and watch the first shoot of my
saplings!

The farm and its healthy business, the books to remind
you that you are something besides a farmer, and Lizzy and
a little nonsense for relaxation, you will lead a very happy
life, dear Bob; and I will share your happiness when you
paint it to me, and hope for the day when I may be my own
master, when steam has brought Australia nearer, and may
take me there to see you! What a day that will be for us
both, dear boy, if we live to see it!   *   *   *   *

To Madame Reboul, at this time :—

Never think of any private conveyances, but send me your
letter by the post. You know how little I am likely to mind
the paying of postage, and of *your* letters ! Why, you know
my daily *dinner* costs more, and you are equally sure that I
would give at least ten dinners for a letter from you. But,
happily, I can well afford both. *All* I desire to hear is of
yourself and your dear ones. When I hear nothing, I am
afraid that all may not be well. If you can tell me that you
are well and happy, and that you remember your friend, I
ask no more than that ; and to receive that assurance from
time to time would be very precious to me. *   *   *
If they⁴ do prosper, I shall contemplate the sending of all my
four young sons to join them. But if I live to accomplish
my wishes, they shall not go until each of them has had the
advantage of precisely the same sort of education as Bob's.
Each of them shall take a degree first at Oxford or Cambridge. For the sake of this important object it is that we
are staying at Malta ; for we *can't* accomplish it by any other
means than by living here economically, and saving some of
our money. Until this year we were never able to put by
anything ; but now that our numbers are so much reduced,
and dear Bob's expenses at Oxford are at an end, and we
have only the little ones at home, we can almost live upon
my pay, and put by our private income. The Malta summers
do me no good, but I must run some little risk for so important an advantage ; but if serious illness comes, then I won't
stay any longer, but get invalided, and retire upon my half-
pay. *   *   *   *   *   *
You see how I tell you of all my affairs. If I were near you,
shouldn't I talk to you of everything ? It is a friend's privilege, and very dear to me is the reflection that thirteen years
of separation have been far indeed from loosening our attachment. All my impressions of my dear friend's value gain,

---

⁴ Hammer and Bob, in Australia.

instead of losing, strength by the time that passes. Shall I
ever have the unspeakable happiness of seeing you again?
O yes, if we both live I *shall*; and if I grow in the mean
time a tottering old man, you will still find that your old
friend has a *heart*, and that it has undergone no change. Sages
have said that the hardest of all knowledge is the knowledge
of one's self. Of many things regarding this *self* of mine, I
dare say I have the usual ignorance; but I am quite sure
that in *steadiness of attachment* lies a characteristic that
honestly belongs to me. By the bye, Liddell, who has been
accustomed to speculate on the bumps on people's skulls, told
me I had a remarkable one just on the top of mine, and that
it meant firmness of purpose, or something of that sort,
though I forget the precise term; and no one ever had a
more decided *purpose* than I have,—that of cherishing your
friendship as long as I live, and of repeating your dear name
in my daily prayer to God to be reunited in heaven with all
those who have been dear to me on earth.   *   *   *
Accept, dear soul, the warmest wishes I can express for your
happiness. Nothing, you know, can be deeper, or more what
you would wish it to be, than the affection of your truest
friend,

R. C. SCONCE.

To Mr. Smith :—

We got your letter from Bonigen, and really interesting to
us it was. Of course it was particularly satisfactory to me to
find that you had been able to do all I chalked out for you,
and that you agreed with us in thinking that all you saw was
worth seeing, and well worth the trouble and the cost. I was
very glad, too, to hear again of my old friends, and the poor
washerwoman among the rest. If Queen Victoria would but
give us both our emancipation, I should like nothing better
than making another trip to the Oberland, and showing you
some of my pet recesses among the mountains beyond Chillon.
There is no spot I have ever known so full of sweet scenes
within a day's range.   *   *   *   *   *

Bob took his degree without asking for honours; but the examiners made him a present, unasked, of a fourth class. They never give a higher in such cases, and of course it is nothing to boast of; but yet it is quite enough for a shepherd, and more than one could have expected, considering the matrimonial and emigratorial speculations which have so long filled his brain. Be sure and manage better for Charles John and Percy. They are not likely to fall in love at Oxford; and in the vacation time I should recommend for them a couple of cages, all the better if fashioned like those of the *squirrels*, to give them air and wholesome exercise apart from the horrible danger of encountering pretty faces.

    *   *   *   *   *   *

To me, 3rd of September, he writes :—

Tell me that you are lords of a spacious pasture on the river side, and then I shall know that your sheep will in four years grow from hundreds into thousands.

The young Watsons are taking with them two Maltese asses. Tell me, Hanmer, by-and-by, if I shall send you some. Those of best blood and biggest bone are now sold for about thirty pounds apiece. You know the value of *mules* for steady work that requires power but not speed. I have four that have gone round in the mills every day except Sundays, eight hours a day for the last ten years. Horses couldn't do that. Four others were worn out in nine years, and the weakest four lasted eight years. The four that have completed ten years are still in high condition.   *   *

 *   * —— has a cadetship, and is going to India. How he is to get there I cannot tell, for Mehemet Ali won't let him pass. Said Mehemet defies us and our *holy* allies. The only answer he gives to their summons is, " The Lord gives and the Lord takes away, and blessed be the name of the Lord." They told him he should have ten days to think of the matter. " What," says he, " won't you take my answer now? You are like a merchant holding a bill at ten days'

sight, who refuses the money till the days are expired." He
said of the proceedings of the Powers, that it was solemn
trifling committed to vulgar hands. The old man won't yield
one inch, and the means of making him are not in our hands.
An *army* is wanted, and we can't furnish it. The Austrians
won't, nor probably the Prussians. The Russians would be
too happy ; but when we introduce the Cossack hordes into
Egypt, what a laugh there will be all over the world at our
cost.   *   *   *   *   *   *

At the same date he writes to congratulate Fanny on the
birth of her second son, and adds :—

I mean some day, like Mr. Cory of Norfolk, to give a grand
dinner to my *hundred* sons and daughters and grandchildren.
Mr. Cory, the young clergyman who came here last year
with Roberts the painter, told me that he was one of the
hundred at his grandfather's table. It was not an exact
hundred, but something *more* than that.

We must found a Sconcetown in Australia. By the time
Clement and his three juniors take up their abode there, it
will be already pretty well peopled, and they may as well
take out their four wives, for the sake of saving time. When
I am a robust old gentleman of sixty-five, Queen Victoria
will give me my dismissal from the biscuit-baking, and I can
go and assume the reins of government. While I go on as I
have done this summer, there can be no *invaliding*, for I have
been as well all July and August as ever I was in my life, all
sound and free from a single ache from head to foot. Some
of the usual threatenings came in the beginning of the summer, but they were easily got rid of, and I have learned by
long experience to manage myself so well, that I have now
little to fear from the old enemy.

I couldn't bear sleeping in my flannel belt ; but I found it
very much more necessary to wear it at night than by day ;
and by getting very fine flannel for the front only, with mere
cotton for the rest, the grievance was so much abated that I

bore it better, and now find it no grievance at all, but a most marvellous safeguard. And then, the suiting of due diet to the season and my idiosyncrasies, was a work that only time could bring to perfection.

It has taken me longer than the time usually allowed ; for one ought, if not a fool, to be a physician at forty ; but it has taken me thirteen years more.

To me :—

I have improved upon my plan of drawing upon glass. I use two glasses, one smaller than the other; so that the outer edge of the frame of one fits inside of the inner edge of the frame of the other. By wetting the paper and spreading it upon one glass, and *covering* it with the *other*, the very heart of the paper gets saturated, while the surface remains damp, for the air is excluded, and is defended from dust. When I leave off drawing, I cover up my work in the same way with the second glass, and whenever I return to it, I find it in the most beautiful possible state for taking colour.

The last thing I do before leaving off for the day, is to wet the paper at the back, and lay it down upon the glass, and then cover it with the other glass. Of course, the glass with which I cover it does not *touch* the drawing. It is like putting a smaller *slate* upon a larger, and just within its frame. I put on any quantity of colour so at once, and it dissolves and blends beautifully ; and I did a good sky all at *once*. By the bye, try some *trees* with three colours only,—indigo, lake, and gamboge. Put one wash with most of gamboge, and very little of the others, so as to be a bright rich yellowish green ; then, when that is dry, put on the dark parts with the *same colour*, but so *thickened* with lake and gamboge as to be almost a *paste*. I have seen some trees done so, and have tried it myself, and it answers admirably.

On the 4th, to Robert and Lizzy :—

My very dear Son and Daughter,—At last I have had
the happiness of seeing under your own hands that you
belong to each other, and I have one child more—an excellent child too; and you may be quite sure, my pretty Lizzy,
that, give me as much love as you please, none of it will be
lost; for it will be exceeding precious to me, and you will
share mine with Bob just as you will share all your other
properties.　Long may you both feel all the happiness your
letter expresses !　　　*　　　*　　　*　　　*　　　*

To them later in September :—

You will have time for *reading* on the voyage, so don't
forget to keep out a few books.　I say, Bob, all the young
ladies spend their time in working carpets.　I see nothing
but worsted-work going on.　——— *never* opens a book, but
always the *work-bag.*
Don't let Lizzy work.　You have an *understanding,* dear
Lizzy ; but most ladies live as if they had only *fingers.*　My
own dear wife works when work is necessary, as mothers of
families often find it to be ; but for her *amusement* she can
do something better.　Music, drawing, reading, are all a
pretty deal better.

To me about this time :—

　　　*　　*　　*　　*　　The war is begun in the East,
and the devil's game is likely to go on at a rare rate.　Beyrout has been battered down ; marines have been landed ;
Commodore Napier is Generalissimo in Syria.　The Sultan
has named a new Pasha to supersede Mehemet Ali in the
government of Egypt ; and so, of course, the old man will
fight to the last, rather than lose his fortune and his life, as
he would, in Turkish fashion, if he now surrendered.　I know
nothing but from reports, half of which are sure to be lies ;
but I believe it is quite true that the old Viceroy declared

his humble submission to the Sultan's will, adding, that he hoped his good master would in his generosity allow him, in consideration of all the services he had rendered to the Porte, to retain Syria for his life.   In answer to this submission, the Sultan and his advisers, the Ambassadors, with Lord P—— at their head, cry, Fire away!   Lord P—— hates Mehemet Ali with a passionate personal hatred.   They say the submission had a *condition* tacked to it, and was no submission at all, and was only a trick to gain time.   Most likely; but yet I should have reflected before I *fired*.

*   *   *   *   *   *

To " Bob and Lizzy," on the 30th of September, 1840, my Father writes :—

I hope this last word of mine that *may* reach you in England will not be too late, that so you may carry with you the latest expression of the love I shall always feel for you, and of our fervent wishes for a safe and quiet voyage for you, and a happy landing in your new country, and for all prosperity in all your doings there.   We shall wait with intense anxiety for some account of the progress of your voyage.   Some of you will now and then be able to write a line or two when the sea is smooth, to tell me how you fare upon the wide ocean.   If I were at liberty, I would go with you, even if it were only to help take care of my dear Sally and Lizzy and Henry on the voyage.   I shall *think* of you continually.

May the Almighty watch over you, and reunite us in Heaven, and bless my aged eyes, if it be His good pleasure, with a sight of you once more even upon earth.

*   *   *   *   *   *

In a joint letter to me, my husband, and our babe, he writes :—

You have made all your preparations, and bidden your dear ones farewell, and have now only to look forward with hope

and a good courage.   May a fair wind and smooth sea
carry you quickly away from the treacherous region of the
Channel, and bring my sweet Sally by degrees to an acquaintance with the life she is to lead for the next four
months.   It is a tedious time, my pretty child, for you,
whom the sea is apt to treat so unkindly; but if you are
blessed with quiet days at the outset, it is possible, I trust,
that you may grow accustomed to the ugly element, and
make good friends with it before you part.

  * * * * * *

I am heartily glad, dear Hanmer, that no *war* has yet
inclined the Admiralty to abridge your liberty of disposing
of yourself your own way; and I trust, that if war with
France does come, they will find people enough to command
the corvettes without disturbing you.   But the French are
obviously on the alert, and their hot spirits impatient for a
fray, and subject for a good quarrel not likely to be long
wanting.   There is a report here that the French Consul at
Beyrout has been rebuked by our officers for playing the *spy*.
Of course *that* would make his people sputter.   It is said, too,
that the French have made some bargain with the King of
Naples, by virtue of which they are to possess either Syracuse
or Messina. This would, of course, make *us* sputter. Several
French war-steamers have gone to their fleet in the Levant.
Three more are expected immediately; and the French
packets are all ordered to put themselves under the French
Admiral's orders, if he chooses to call for their services.   It
is wretched work, this Beyrout—beginning of a war which it
would puzzle Palmerston or Ponsonby to prove to be "just
and necessary."

When the high constituted authorities, whoever they be,
gave the word to fire, I wonder if it ever did occur to them
that it is an *awful word* to give, and that they will be
accountable for the *deaths* on both sides.   Passion, pique,
point of honour, or pelf, now and then perpetrates a homi-
cide; but if passion has anything to do with a *declaration of
war*, then the devil has done his work *thoroughly*.

My sweet little Grandson, take with you your Grandpapa's blessing. Be well and strong, and grow up to be a good and wise and brave man, just as you promise to be.

Heaven guard and guide and prosper you all.

*　　*　　*　　*　　*　　*

To me in October he writes :—

Thank you, my darling, for sending me the seeds; I shall love to watch their growth for my sweet daughter's sake. Mind, dear, I value a scrap of that sort for the sake of your sending it, much more than I should value the most gorgeous of flowers for their own—just as I value the little *lavender* bag you made for me. I always put it carefully among a heap of my pocket-handkerchiefs in my drawer, and think of you every morning when I take one out. It retains all its scent. *　*　*　* Of all the many experiments I have tried with little learners, my last has answered best. I gave them a little Latin book, with short easy sentences, and helped them to construe it. Then I extracted in one manuscript list all the substantives, in another all the adjectives, in another all the pronouns, in another all the verbs. In this way they got up the declensions, and so forth, synoptically, and very quickly; and when I put the book into their hands again, they will have it at their fingers' ends, and will be ready for something a step higher. They will run through a *hundred* substantives or adjectives at a lesson, and tell me their genitive cases all right. Put this into your memory-box for your little sweet. 　*　　*　　*

To Bob, same date :—

At the outset you must be content to risk little and gain little. *Slow* and *sure; no gambling.* I am *sure*, dearest Bob, that you are in danger of being tempted to speculate too deeply. Think of this for my sake. When you have added something to your store by the multiplication of your sheep, *then*, with your *gains*, buy horses and mills, and whatever else your experience of the place suggests.

Excessive caution may be the vice of my age; but head-over-heelsness is just as much that of yours; and besides, old as I am, I am conscious of having still a spirit of enterprise that would carry me a *fair* length. I am not sure that I should not myself rather err the other way. But you must hold up to yourself, in terrorem, the frightful picture of an utter failure; and then you will go to work so cautiously that you *can't* fail.

To Fanny at this time:—

But all is *not* quite well with you, my precious; for you have the pain of this SAD parting, and a bitter pain it is. Well for you, sweet Fan, that you have such dear interests at home. Your husband and your smiling boys are your little world, and you must be happy in it, as I am happy even here. We must seek content from our present stores; but we will shoot many a thought in the direction of our distant dears, and derive sweet comfort from their well-being, and from their love, however wide their separation from us. I believe in my conscience that if I were untied I should make a voyage every year between England and Australia, to see you all in turn.   *   *   *   *   *

To Fanny, in November:—

It is much pleasanter to talk about one's *children* than one's single child. Isn't it? One, you know, can hardly be called a *family*, and one likes to have a *family*. My wishes for you will be accomplished when the *daughter* comes to complete the group. Three children (three cows on a lawn, or three anythings) always do group much better than two. Mr. Gilpin, the artist and clergyman, actually bought a third cow for no other reason; and so you had better buy the other baby.   *   *   *   *   *

To Bob, in November : —

What an intense anxiety I shall feel till I know that you have made your first footing good ; and before I *can* know, one whole year must pass away ! Many a packet must come uncharged with its usual welcome freight for me ; but when once the series of Australian reports does begin, my hope is that it will not be materially interrupted. Utterly ignorant as I shall be, until you inform me, of all the circumstances of your new life, you must try if you can, by minute description, enable me to picture to myself every scene about you. I am glad to have made acquaintance with Grigsby, and King Charles, and the heavy Scotchman, and the carpenter^e (*vergeriensis*), and the pretty maiden from Ealing, who is, in process of time, I suppose, to be the said carpenter's wife.

* * * * * *

Have you left my *manuscripts* to be sent to me ? As you are gone, and I have heard nothing about them, you can fancy that I feel some little solicitude on the subject, seeing the many hours of thought I spent upon them (for many a day's work was sixteen hours long), and the natural hope I have of making them useful to the small people, who will soon be growing into Grecians. Suppose, my dear Bob, *you* take up some pursuit of this sort ; you would find it interesting as an amusement to fill up many an odd five minutes, and it might afterwards find its way to the press, or would, at all events, be a treasure for our own small fry.

Even at this distance we might interchange notices with pleasure and profit. Greek choruses, or any other things containing in small space subject for much thinking, furnish excellent employment for odd minutes. I had always in my pocket a Sophocles and a pencil and paper, and so did many a bit on horseback, in my boat, or waiting for people at the Lazaretto or elsewhere ; and if I were an *Australian shepherd*, such pursuits would naturally be suggested to me by the

---

^e Son of the verger at Mr. Repton's chapel.

leisure of a pastoral life. If I couldn't sing like Menalcas and Damœtas, I would meditate their muse.

By the bye, dear Bob, I have, among my odd readings of late, taken Tacitus's "Agricola," merely for the sake of recalling the time when we conned together its few difficulties. Wasn't there one at—" Nunc terminus Britanniæ patet, atque omne ignotum pro magnifico est. Sed nulla jam ultra gens "? The critics have made a puzzle of it. But from atque to est ought to be connected with *what follows*, and not, according to my Gronovius, with what goes before. " Our last recesses are now laid open to the view of the Romans. And though, while yet a large part of our island was unknown to them, their progress might have been checked by the fear of encountering a superior force,—the fear of the magnificum ignotum,—yet *now*, on they will surely come, for they see that *we* are the last—nulla jam ultra gens."

Small leisure will you have for many a day for such things as these; but you may look at your Tacitus a year hence, and tell me what you think of this.   *   *   *

To Fanny, in December :—

All will not be right *anywhere*. Everybody must have an annoyance. Mine, you know, is my *banishment*. My separation from so *many* of you. But you know, too, it has many alleviations; and it is encouraging to find that its purpose is likely to be answered in providing the means of educating the little ones. We shall take your advice, and give our friends no costly entertainments.[*] A leg of mutton now and then won't ruin us, and you know we *can't* turn *mere* misers.

    *   *   *   *   *   *

Precious daughter, it is *good* for me to write to you, and to read your dear letters. This intercourse with my distant dears is *all* I have to break the monotony of my days. Yet,

---

[*] He had always been in the habit of giving large champagne dinners (frequently of eighteen) to his friends and acquaintance.

thank God, there is very great happiness even in this monotony; for, if it is not varied by agreeable events, it is not
disturbed by *griefs* and *pains*. My health is good, my wife
good, and *all* my children good and healthy. BLESS you all!

To me, in the first letter addressed to Australia :—

Don't you know, my precious, what delight it would be to
me to do anything for you? And all I *can* do is to send you
a poor sheet of paper. I think of you continually, and I
feel as if you had just this moment parted from me. But,
besides all this, you know how impossible it is that I should
not feel more than common *anxiety*. I am as little apt as
most people to make misery.

We are in God's hands, and may well assure ourselves
that He will comfort us if we resign ourselves to His will
and trust in His mercy. But it is *not* His will that we
should always have light hearts, and mine cannot be light
until I am blessed with a certainty of your safety. In that
careful kindness of yours you meant me not to know you
were expecting another baby.

But we do know it, my precious child; and you must not
be sorry that we do. My earnest wish is always to know
every thing. I am sincerely *glad* that I have this knowledge.
At least, it enables us to pray to God with all our hearts to
help you in your hour of need.

*   *   *   *   A thousand kindest thanks, too,
for your precious present of the books—Sir Samuel Romilly's
Memoirs. You knew it would exactly suit my taste. It is
intensely interesting to me, and I have already found time to
read two of the volumes. But there is nothing in all the
book that interests me quite as much as the few letters you
wrote with a pencil inside the covers, "S. S. B. to R. C. S."
In pencil though it is, it will never be rubbed out, and the
book shall never be bound, that I may not lose them. My
special delight in your little epigraph consists, I believe, in
the fancy I have, that it expresses the *equal friendship* that
subsists between us.   *   *   *   *

To Bob :—

God grant that no evil has befallen you! My pretty Lizzy,
you have suffered sickness and terror. It has been an awful
outset of your voyage. And you, my dearest Sally, what
have *you* suffered? The newspapers from England are filled
with frightful descriptions of the tempests that prevailed
within a very few days after your sailing; and it is impossible you could have gone far enough to have been beyond
their reach, nor far enough from the land to have the good
sea-room that takes away from a storm its worst danger. A
good *ship*, I trust, you have, and a skilful captain, and that
Captain had Hanmer's active vigilance to aid him; but, above
all, we have God's merciful providence for our trust; and I *do*
trust that He will bring you in safety to the haven where you
would be.   *   *   *   You know well, dearest
children, how continually I am thinking of you, and wishing
that, whatever may be your troubles and dangers, I were with
you to share them.   *   *   *   *
That poor Miss Pendrill is gone, and a grievous loss she is
to those that loved her. She was one of the most sensible,
graceful, and engaging people I ever knew. A few days
before her death they had all moved out to Sliema, to the
house where formerly the Smiths lived, and after them the
Stoddarts. Two days before she died, when her two sisters
and mamma were by her bedside, she sent for me, to bid me
farewell, and spoke to me with entire composure. She said,
" I have had very great pleasure in knowing you, and I wish
our acquaintance had been earlier. You must follow my
remains to the grave, and, by God's mercy, we shall meet
again in Heaven. God bless and preserve you and all your
dear family. Pray for me, and pray that I may be spared the
pain of a severe struggle at the last." And she did die a
most peaceful death, without any struggle whatever. The
effort she made in speaking to me was the last of which her
bodily strength was capable.   *   *   *   *
The Greek notes are come safe, and I will set to work

soon. I am glad to see some emendations of yours, and only wish your pencillings had been more abundant. The chances are, that you are right in every instance, and that I shall take your sense rather than my own. Some of mine, I see, are mere blunders, natural enough when victuallers turn critics. " Ne sutor." Besides, you know the Thucydides never had a revision of mine. I wrote it as you had it at once, and not from a rough copy. By the bye, do you know the origin of Ne sutor ? Apelles exposed his pictures (per-gulâ—in the bazaı) for the criticism of the vulgar, " atque post ipsam tabulam latens, vilia quæ notarentur auscultabat, vulgum diligentiorem judicem quam se præferens. Feruntque a *sutore* reprehensum, quod in *crepidis* una intus pauciores fecisset ansas : eodem postero die, superbo emendatione pristinæ admonitionis, cavillante circa crus, indignatum pro-spexisse, denunciantem, ne supra crepidam judicaret, quod et ipsum in proverbium venit." This is in Pliny, Nat. Hist. book 35, where there is a great deal of interesting matter for us painters.   *   *   *   *   *

To Mr. Charles Smith, the end of this year, he writes :—

That you would decide upon retiring, I had small doubt, so I am not surprised ; but yet I had something like a hope the other way ; and little as it was, I cannot part with it without pain. Malta is bad enough under the best of circumstances, but what will it be to us now ? We had *one* friend with whom we could take counsel, or laugh, or grumble, without reserve, and now we have *not one*.

Our friend had the habit of coming in to us, and old and young always greeted him with an acclamation ; and now our solitude will be unvaried. But yet I am heartily glad, old fellow, for your sake, that you have escaped from slavery.

    *   *   *   *   *   *

I have been in bonds *all my whole life*, from the nursery to the school, and thence to the service of the King and his Admirals, and a hard service it is. Give this to Percy—

χαλεπον αρχεσθαι ὑπο χειρονος. I think it means, that "drudgery at best is bad enough; but the worst of all is fagging for one's *inferior*." This looks, sure enough, as if I fancied any Kings or Admirals could be my inferiors. Bless their hearts, they are mammoths and I a mouse; only, you know, it does sometimes happen that these big beasts (the mammoths) have no brains. I have seen one or two with their skulls as empty as my pocket. I wish I *could* turn gentleman too; but I must first fill the pocket aforesaid.

*   *   *   *   *   *

I have nothing to *tell* you. Our life is unvaried. I want my absent dears; I want a wood, and a field, and a river; I want the Water-colour Exhibition and the British Museum, and a railroad; but I *have* health and spirits and energy to amuse myself with the revisal of the work I did for Bob, and with my drawings when I have leisure; and I have a goodish wife and half a dozen rather sweet little brats about me. If agreeable novelties don't come, yet neither has pain nor grief come to disturb us; and with all my heart and soul I can thank God for allowing me what I am sure upon the whole an UNUSUAL measure of happiness.

I am using all diligence to grow rich, too; and if I live, there will be money enough to make scholars of all the boys, as well as graziers.   *   *   *   *   *

CHAPTER VII.

[1841.]

ATTACK IN A SCURRILOUS NEWSPAPER—ANXIETY ABOUT THE "ARGYLE"—
TEACHING LITTLE ONES LATIN—ACRE—HEARS OF THE "ARGYLE'S" SAFETY
—AND FANNY'S SAFETY—HER PRECARIOUS STATE—THE CHURCH AT PORT
PHILLIP—PLAUTUS—HIS PORTRAIT—THE GALLEY PRISON—ENGLISH CHURCH
AT MALTA—LETTERS TO LITTLE CLEMENT—NURSERY RHYMES AND LATIN
FOR LITTLE CHILDREN—LETTER TO MR. SMITH ABOUT THEM—LETTER TO
ROBERT.

My dear Father writes in low spirits the beginning of this
year, for he was suffering great anxiety about the *Argyle*,
which encountered, in the Bay of Biscay, one of the most
terrific gales that had been known for years, and in which
numerous vessels were wrecked. Of himself, however, he
says to Bob,—

I am as strong and sound, and almost as elastic as I was
ὅτε ἔιον Ἐρευθαλίωνα κατέκταν : Anglicè, when I shot the
vulture in the blue mountains of Jamaica; for that was, I
believe, my most signal feat of arms.   *   *   *

Speaking of an attack on himself and his department in a
scurrilous newspaper, relating to the purchase of wheat, he
says :—

At the Chamber of Commerce in Valetta the writer has
been abused for attempting to assail " Il più degno degli
impiegati."[a]   *   *   *   *

---

[a] The most worthy of the Government officers (*employés*).

To Fanny he says :—

My PRECIOUS, I am thinking of the *Argyle* night and day. I do hope and trust that all is right. But I have, somehow, a lump of lead upon my spirits that I can't shake off.   *   *   *   *   *

In another letter :—

My heart is sick for longing for news of Sally and Bob, and I fear there is but very little hope of our hearing from them by any crossing ship. What a time, then, we must wait! And how I shall jump for joy when a happy letter comes! Don't you think it will be the happiest day you and I have known for the last century, when we see their precious handwriting to tell us they are all safe and sound at Melbourne, and the little sea-born daughter all blooming and promising to her dear Mamma's content?   *   *   *

To me in February he writes :—

To see a letter with your handwriting on the outside of it once more will be such joy as comes but seldom in a long life. You know *men* are not like you poor whimping petticoated people, and my nerves are as well strung as most people's; but yet when that letter comes, and common sense would be in a hurry to read it, I am quite sure I shan't be able, for I shall *cry* a great big flood of tears, like a great *baby*. But before that letter comes, this, the last month of winter, must pass away, and we must go to Sliema and wear out the summer, and must return again to the Marina—and *then*, after that return, I shall watch from day to day. Think of the unspeakable interest with which every word you write will be filled!

All I can tell *you* is that your dear Papa is well, and that he loves you. But what histories you will have to give *me!* But the one word that tells me you are *well*, *that* will be enough. In *unum* vitam orarem. If I had not some *eighteen* several motives for desiring life, it would be enough to look forward to the reading once more of that word in your writing. Don't wonder at my writing *Latin :* I live among the Romans. Bettoo and Kitty and Mamma all talk Latin. The little things have a great fancy for this sort of work, and are getting on at a great rate ; and Mamma not only learns of course all she hears of it, but reads at a great rate too, for the sake of being able to help Mia and Willy when their turn comes.

I write quantities of baby-Latin, easier than the books make it, and affording varieties of exercise, sometimes for their puny understandings, sometimes for their rather stronger memories. They know the English of about *fifteen hundred* Latin words, and the Latin for as many English. I have written them all in a little book, and they go over and over them ; so that by constantly seeing them, they won't forget. I pick out such as are like *Italian*, and that is a great help. Of course, you know, Kitty soon learns that *luna* is Latin for the moon, *lingua* for the tongue, *mare* for the sea. In short, knowing as much Italian as she does, she has a great piece of her labour ready done. * * * *

As well as I can I picture you all in my fancy, and Argylina takes her place in the group. May all your hearts be as light, and your faces as bright as if (according to our Rev. friend of ——) they were painted by feathers plucked out of angels' wings. My dearest, I love you with my whole soul. Remember your Papa. He sends you his blessing from the depth of his heart.

The same date he writes :—

SWEETEST LIZZY,—Your married life has had a rude beginning. You have been very very sick in that horrid ship ; and, do tell the truth, haven't you often wished Bob among his books at Oxford, and yourself restored to your own green bowers at Drayton ? To tell *you* the truth, pretty Lizzy, *no ;* for you good women are no fair-weather friends.

You have borne the worse bravely, in looking forward to the better part of your bargain;

> And you and he have proved together

(except when you were *very* seasick)

> That love can make its own fair weather;

And his own

> Lizzy's laughing eyes
> Have been his clear blue summer skies,—

if your eyes *are* blue, my dear; but neither he nor you have told me that, and I don't remember.   *   *   *

The having of a number of good children is, upon the whole, an *advantage*, I dare say, and a *blessing*; but yet the wonder is that the havers of such blessings can ever sleep o' nights or digest their dinners. Ambiguous cares for the absent, and the impossibility of having all right among the many present, would fret one insupportably, if human nature were not itself a mere baby, and apt to be diverted every moment from grave interests by utter trifles. So then it is good for us in some things that we have this weakness. Yet we won't rejoice in it, for it is lamentable enough in the *main*.

*   *   *   *   *   *

To Hanmer :—

What I should do, if one could ride post upon a *wish*, would be to plant myself upon the Melbourne strand to meet you all upon your landing. *That* would be something like happiness, wouldn't it? But I would be in time to get some snug rooms ready first, and some *provy*, such as would tempt poor sea-worn travellers; bread and butter for the grand-children, oranges and mangoes, or whatever the Melbourne gardens or orchards afford. I am quite sure that if my power of moving had been like *Colonel Graham's*, I should have posted through India, and should actually have been in time. This is the way in which my speculations work. I think of you all, waking and sleeping.   *   *   *

But I ought to send you what news there is worth your having. You have heard of the rare luck of the navy people here—promotions and decorations without end. Your friend Napier seems to have carried off the great prize. All the Acre captains have been C.B.d, and all the commanders promoted; Bashaw Walker Commander of the Bathed; and Stopford, the good old admiral, has been left precisely as he was before. They have neither given him any honour, nor hinted the intention of giving him any. The Emperor of Russia has designed for him one of his grand orders; but when it comes, through our Secretary of State (which is the usual channel), the old admiral will *refuse it*. He thinks rightly, that any honour he may have earned should be given first by his *own* Government. You know the convention made by Napier with Mehemet Ali? It was not only made without any authority, but Napier sent it straight home to the Ministers in England, passing Stopford by, although he was within two days' distance of him.   *   *   *

By the bye, Stopford is Governor of Greenwich Hospital; but that is no *honour* with which to requite a *victory*, and still less so, as it was actually offered to some other admiral, and not to Stopford till after that other had refused it. I have not heard who that other was, but Stopford himself told me the fact. I interest myself in the old man for the sake of his kindness to Sally, in sending a line-of-battle ship to Naples for her accommodation; and to Fan, in getting a passage to Naples for her and Liddell in Lord F. Egerton's yacht. The truth is, he has always taken pleasure in doing good-natured things to all sorts of people.   *   *   *

Just as he had written these three little letters, my Father suffered the terror and misery of hearing of the alarming illness of his darling Fanny,—a spitting of blood which confined her to bed; and her husband thought of taking her directly to Malta. The very next day my Father heard together of her temporary safety and of us from St. Jago; and then he writes to Bob on the 14th February :—

MY DEAREST CHILDREN, all of you,—I have not yet felt all the joy I shall feel in knowing that you weathered the storm, and were so far safe and well. I was so much terrified by the imminent danger in which Fan was, that my nerves were shaken thoroughly; and though several hours have now passed since the happy news of *her* safety and your safety came, yet I feel a strange sort of bewilderment and shakiness, a sort of *lowspiritedness* still, and much more inclination to weep than to smile.

However, I am quite sensible of all the difference there is between my condition to-day and that of yesterday. The letters came just before we went to *church*, and glad I was to go *there*.   *   *   *   *   *   *

To Fanny he writes :—

You have frightened me out of my wits; but it's all over now, and all right, and I shall trust that you are not a bit the worse, and so *I* shall not be. If I didn't before know how *good for me* it is that you should be well, I know it *now*. Happily the *Liverpool* came quickly after the *Phœnix*. The first letter arrived the evening of the 12th, and I got the one by the *Liverpool* this morning at half-past nine. Don't you know, Fan, this is always the way people write, about what *they themselves* feel and suffer, just as if I was thinking only of *my* part of the suffering, and not a bit about yours. But are you soon going to be as well as ever again, my precious child? Won't you be *fat* and *strong* when warm weather returns, if there ever *is* any warm weather in England.

Thank you very heartily, my dear Liddell, for writing to me the *truth*. Whatever be the pain or the terror it gives, it is really right always to tell on such occasions the worst. Your letter expressed your own alarm too plainly not to awaken mine; but then, the account you have since given has its full effect the other way, because I can depend upon its sincerity.   *   *   *   *   *

Now, only think, Fan, what a deal I have written, and

have not said one word yet of that most precious, *precious* news you sent me of the *Argyle*. I thought, before you were sick, that I loved Sally and Bob quite twice as much as you; but then I found that I loved you quite as much as both of them put together. * * * *

I believe I have not had time yet to quiet down into the enjoyment of the *real happiness* that all this good news of to-day must give me. There never was a more precious packet than the *Liverpool* has been. I am sure I shall be quite glad *enough* of the good news from St. Jago, and I hope I shall be very grateful for it; but just yet I have been thinking even more about *you*. * * * * *

In a joint letter to me and Bob, a little later, he says :—

I am not apt to write bits of letters to you, but this must be only a mere bit, for the very truth is that I am a little *heartsick*. Well it may be sick, if Fan is sick; for you know she is tied and twisted and knotted about my very soul. Until I heard that you were *all well* at St. Jago, I loved *you* better a thousand times than all the rest, and now you know my affection is all centred in Fan. Only, my dears, *don't get sick;* for I shall contrive to love you even if you are well. * * * * * *

What *you* were to them all, good Hanmer, in the storm I well knew; and Sally's account of your doings was no more than a repetition of the picture I had already formed to myself. I can fancy you quietly cooking their arrowroot in a hurricane, while every other passenger was too sick or too frightened to help either himself or his neighbour. * * * * * *

To Fanny :—[b]

I know you have plenty of fortitude and patience, and that God has blessed you with a disposition to resign your-

---

[b] She had had a relapse, and the cough, which never again left her, was troublesome.

self to His good pleasure.   May He enable us to cast all
our cares upon Him, and our care for *you*, which is now
our *chief* care.   *   *   *   *   *

To me, in April :—

MY PRECIOUS SALLY,—There *is* cause for anxiety, for danger
is hanging over a head beyond all expression dear to us.   We
must all pray to God, fervently and faithfully, to avert it ; but
we must pray, too, to be enabled to submit with resignation
to His divine will, whatever it may be.   To us her removal
would be a fearful calamity ; but think what a gain to *her!*
But though there is ground for fear, there is, I am per-
suading myself, more ground for *hope*.   *   *   *

What provision has been made for the church at Port
Phillip?   At Melbourne, there is, of course, a chaplain ; but
in the country, wide apart as your settlements probably are,
how can you assemble at any church ?

There should be a *Bishop* of Melbourne, and he should
have under him clergymen to be sent by him round the
country, just as in the first times of Christianity in England,
and as, I believe, the practice now is in some parts of
America.

Mind and exert the influence you will soon possess in your
community to have this important subject cared for as it
ought to be.   *   *   *   *   *   *

To Bob :—

I have not had leisure for taking up books or drawings,
except in odd intervals ; but of those I am apt to make the
most.   For example, I always keep a book in my boat, and
the one I have had lately is Plautus.

In the twenty scraps of time I find in the course of a day, I
can read as many scenes; and right pleasant reading it is.   I
have read seven of the plays, and am going straight through the
whole. Most schoolboys have read "Aulularia" and " Rudens."
I don't know that you ever opened the book.   It will amuse
you exceedingly.   There is fifty times more spirit in the

dialogue than in Terence, and there is, to a Grecian, small
difficulty in the palæology. Barring his obsolete or coined
words, the Latin in general is simple enough for Herbert and
Kitty. I suppose you *have* a Plautus?—if not, I will send
you one. I don't know when I have enjoyed a book more
thoroughly. With the Variorum notes to help you here and
there, you will want little of a dictionary. I never take one
in my boat, and I suppose I get as much of the humour of
his jokes and allusions as a foreigner would be likely to get
of Sheridan's. Few Frenchmen would make as much of the
" School for Scandal " as you and I would of " Amphitryon."

    *   *   *   *   *   *

When you were three years old, Fan, and had a burning
fever, Dr. T—— told me he could do nothing more, and that
you would die. But I got a good man, called Dr. White,
who was surgeon of Chatham Dockyard, and he did a great
deal, and watched you all the night, and at last you looked
up, and said, " Kiss me, Papa." I dare say I cried like a big
baby ; and, to say the truth, I must wipe my eyes now while
I think of it.   *   *   *   *   *

Speaking of his portrait, which Mr. Alingham was painting, he says :—

He seems to be extra anxious to do it extra well ; and on
that very account is the more likely to fail. I suppose, too,
that my face is not very easy to copy ; for I believe I have no
remarkable features. All the *passport* writers to whom I
have sat, have described eyes, nose, and mouth as *ordinaires*,
which does not mean ugly, but only *much as usual* with regard
to length, breadth, &c.   *   *   *   *

In a later letter, when he had seen his picture, he writes :—

As far as I can judge, it will be like, when he has duly
furrowed the cheeks and forehead. At present it looks like
five-and-thirty ; but it is admirably painted. I don't know

when I have seen a head so separate itself from the canvas. It stands out just like a portrait by Raphael I used to admire at Naples; almost the only one I ever saw that did look like a real head, and not a painted one.   *   *   *

Captain Brandreth, the engineer sent out by the Admiralty, asked me as soon as he came where the galley prison was; for he said he had seen my report to the Admiralty in which it was mentioned, and that he was so much struck by the bit of history found so unexpectedly in a dry dispatch, that he took it directly to his "little friend Lord Dalmeny," who enjoyed it as much as he did, and said there was poetry as well as history in it.   In describing the site on which I proposed to build the new bakery, I said that a part of it contained "extensive caverns, where formerly the Knights kept their Turkish captives, and we now keep casks." This was all, and certainly it is but little; but I suppose there was something odd in it; for when I wrote it, I read it to Mamma, and it made her laugh. Of course I meant it for fun when I wrote it; and the caverns, captives, and casks were not accidentally alliterative.   *   *   *   *   *

To Fanny, in June :—

Our poor *church* is in a bad way.   Queen Adelaide was not lucky in her choice of an architect.   She was probably guided in her choice by the high constituted authorities here; but, however, by her, or by somebody, a *cabinet-maker*, a Mr. ——, was chosen to design and execute the work.   Well, some *cracks*, *splits*, and *crushings* began to appear in the columns of the portico before half the pediment was built upon it.   The Admiralty engineers were summoned to survey and pronounce; and what they pronounced was that the portico must all be immediately pulled down : and down it all is, accordingly.   The columns within the church, for the support of the gallery and roof, must come down too. *All* the work is *suspected ;* but it would be so great a pity to throw away the £6,000 already spent, that I believe they mean to try and coax the walls to bear a roof. Perhaps, after all, it may not tumble down; or, if it does, it may not be when all the people are in it. The Governor will just arrive in England to impart the pleasing news to the Queen. As soon as the accident was discovered, Captain Brandreth came to me, and said he hoped *I* had had nothing to do with the church! He and Mr. Scamp (who is a first-rate clever fellow) say they never saw in all their lives such an exhibition of ignorance. No, I had *not* anything to do with it; for the advice I gave was not followed.

Lady Louis wanted to ask the Queen to engage my assistance in her work; but I refused, because I *knew* it would be mismanaged; and I only begged Lady Louis to tell the Queen, which I believe she did, that *one* thing was absolutely necessary, and that was to get an architect from England, even at any price. What a disgrace it would have saved us! The Maltese are grinning at us, and have not the least doubt that Heaven's hand is as much in the work as it was when Julian tried, in spite of the Almighty, to rebuild the walls of Jerusalem. What made it more remarkable was, that just as the accident happened, a torrent of rain fell; enough to do great and universal good—and in *June!* No rain has fallen in June before, except once, in the memory of old people; and that was, I suppose, on some other great occasion of joy in heaven. They call our poor church the *Devil's Den*—"tochbah ta scitaun."   *   *   *

To little Clement, who was staying in June in the Isle of Wight, with the Liddells:—

Here is a funny present for you; for which, I suppose, you won't particularly thank me. You have had Latin enough at school; and so I dare say you would thank me much more for a packet of lollipops than for a Latin book. But yet, as we all must learn that vile Latin, I thought I might help you to put by a scrap or two in your knowledge-box without much trouble; and, you know, every little gained lessens the future labour; so I have copied for you some of the book out of which Kitty and Herbert are learning. They find it very easy, and certainly like my Latin better than Virgil's a great deal. I dare say one reason is, that my Latin is better than his; but besides *that*, I have had an advantage, that he had not, in drawing my subjects partly from that immortal genius Mother Goose. Though you are a much better scholar than Kitty and Herbert, yet this little book may not come quite as easy, in proportion, to *you*, because I took care to use almost exclusively the words with which they were already familiar. They have gone through it twice; and the second time it seemed so easy, that Kitty read and construed quite well *half* of what I send you, in one lesson. The Goosey part of my book naturally interests them very deeply; for what *other* book in all the world contains so much to make one laugh or cry, as one happens to be in the humour for a merry history or a pathetic one? and besides, there is a comfort in knowing that it's *all true*. Of course it must be; for I remember to have heard it all when I was a little boy; and my Grandmamma knew it all too. If you think it would be desirable to publish my work, tell me. You had better ask Queen Victoria to give me leave to dedicate it to the Princess Royal.

I suppose we should sell about a million copies for a penny apiece, and about half would be profit, and that would be two thousand pounds; and I can't do better than give it you to buy whips, sticks, and canes, if you have the same passion for them as you used to have.

EXCERPTA ET TRADUCTA

EX OPERIBUS

MATRIS ANSERIS, HORNERI,

ET VARIORUM AUCTORUM SIMILIUM.

CURA ROBERTI CLEMENTIS SCONCII.

TOMUS PRIMUS.

PRÆFATIO.[c]

Dicit parva Catharina, horridum opus est hæc lingua
Latina. "Selectæ e Veteri" me facit dormire: Phædrus dat
mihi dolorem capitis: Virgilius est certe pessimus inter
omnes hujus mundi homines. Virgilio soli debeo illam indi-
gestionem propter quam heri dedit mihi mater medicinam.
Non erat iter ad silvulam,[d] non fraga. In itinere ride-
bamus. Risus nemini facit malum. Cum fragis mixtum
erat saccharum. Quod est suave, quod est dulce, dat salu-
tem, non dat ægritudinem. Ergo Virgilius est qui meam
turbat bilem.

Pater mi, cur non potes nobis emere libellum parvulum
Latinum, facilem et jucundum, iis similem quibus ego, et
fratres parvuli et parvula soror, legimus illas pulchras his-
torias de Johanne et Gillia, qui dum portabant aquam de
monte, ceciderunt et capita fregerunt: aut si mavis alteram
illam de tribus pueris super glaciem æstivo die ludentibus:
aut illam de viro Thessaliensi qui ambos amissos oculos tam
lepide recuperavit; aut de crudeli facinore Johannis Viridis
felem in puteo submergentis: aut vitam Thomæ Pollicis, qui
tantos interfecit crudeles gigantes: aut mortem Galli Ro-

---

[c] All this is copied from the little MS. volume sent to little Clement.
[d] Boschetto.

bini, quem passer interfecit arcu suo et sagittâ; quem mori
vidit musca oculo suo parvulo, quem tantæ feræ tantæ
fleverunt aves. Ili sunt omnes optimi libri. Da mihi, pater,
unum ex his, et jace Virgilium, si vis, in ignem.

Bene igitur. Libri tales emi non possunt. Sed duos
dicunt esse modos per quos res obtineri possit; per amorem
aut per pecuniam. Pecuniâ non potest haberi Thomas Pollex,
non Johannes Viridis, non Homo Thessaliensis. Jam videa-
mus quod possit altero fieri modo, nempe per amorem. Non
sum ego validus bellator; sed omnia vincit amor, et vestri
amoris gratiâ, bone Herberte, bona Catharina, vincere possim
etiam illum terribilem homunculum Thomam Pollicem.

Siste, pater mi, inquit Herbertus, nimis esset illa pugna
periculosa.

Nonne melius foret primam facere pugnam contra Johan-
nem Viridem?

Prudens puer es, mi Herberte. Consilium tuum sequemur,
et ita incipit hic noster libellus.

DE CRUDELI FACINORE JOHANNIS VIRIDIS FELEM IN PUTEO SUBMERGENTIS.

Tintinnabulum, bim, bo!
Felis est in puteo.
Eam in puteum jecit quis?
Parvus Johannes Viridis.
Quis eam traxit e puteo?
Thomas Fortis, parvus homo.
Ut malus puer ille fuit
Qui felem aviæ submersit.

DE FACTO MIRIFICO VIRI THESSALIENSIS, OCULOS SAPIEN-TISSIME PERDENTIS, ET ITERUM REPERIENTIS.

Fuit Vir Thessaliæ,
Et sapiens erat mire,
Spinosam in sepem saltavit,
Et ambos oculos effodit.

Et quando oculos
Vidit effossos,
Cum sua omni
Potestate et vi,
In sepem alteram saltavit,
Et eos sic recuperavit.

DE FATO FLEBILI TRIUM PUERORUM, QUORUM OMNES PERIERUNT; SED RELIQUI FUGERUNT.

Æstivo die pueri tres
Per glaciem perlabentes
Omnes, ut accidit, inciderunt:
Reliqui fugerunt.
Nunc hi pueri
Si fuerant domi,
Sive per terram
Perlapsi siccam,
Millia dena minas pono
Pro uno denario,
Non omnes perdidissent hi tam
Misere sub aqua vitam.

DE PARVULO LANCES LAVANTE, PISCES EX OCULO TRAHENTE.

Parvus quando puer eram
Matris lances lavabam;
Digitum in oculo posui
Et pisces parvulos extraxi.

DE JOHANNE ET GILLIA DE FONTE PETENTIBUS AQUAM, CADENTIBUS, CAPITA FRAGENTIBUS.

Johannes et Gillia
Per difficilia
Montis cacumina
Petierunt flumina.

Vas impleverunt,
Sed non felices redierunt.
Concidit pronus ille.   A
Tergo dum sequitur Gillia
Post eum cadit.   Capita fregerunt,
Et aquam perdiderunt.

DE FELIS-FIDIBUS, INCITANTIBUS AD SALTUM, RISUM, CURSUM, VACCAM, CATELLUM, LANCEM.

Heididledidibus, felis cum fidibus !
Incipit vacca jocari !
Transilit lunam ;
Ridebis tu, nam
Catulus ridet
Dum talia videt,
Et lanx fugit cum cochleari.

DE SINGULARI FELICITATE JOHANNIS HORNERI, PRUNUM E PLACENTA EVELLENTIS, BONITATIS LAUDEM SIBI VINDICANTIS.

Parvus Johannes Hornerus sedebat,
Et festivam edebat
Placentam in angulo,
Pollicem inserit,
Et prunum extrahit,
Et clamat Quantus sum bonus ego !

De MERULIS in crustâ coctis,
Et non morientibus,
Sed canentibus ;
Jocum autem non amantibus,
In nasum serviæ vindicantibus.

De sex denariis carmen cano,
De secalis sacco pleno ;
De merulis bis denis
Et quatuor in crustâ coctis.
Apertam crustam quum viderunt,
Aves canere cœperunt ;
Ferculum nonne hoc egregium
Ad ponendum ante regem !
Rex in conclavi nummos numerabat,
     Dum Regina
     In culina
Mel et panem manducabat.
In horto lauta lintea
Suspendente servulâ,
Merula mordicus abrasum
Devolans aufert ei nasum.

LONGA HISTORIA, DE OMNIBUS REBUS, ET QUIBUSDAM ALIIS.

Urbs antiqua fuit, cujus nomen erat Troja. Fuit quoque regio cujus nomen erat Græcia. Inter populos harum duarum regionum fuit bellum famosissimum. Hujus belli Poeta, qui dicitur princeps omnium poetarum, scripsit historiam. Hujus magni poetæ nomen est Homerus. Nunc dicam vobis causam hujus belli. Trojani habuerunt regem senem Priamum. Priamus habuit quinquaginta filios, et inter eos Paridem. Is erat juvenis pulchræ faciei, sed mentem non æque pulchram habebat. Iis antiquis temporibus etiam regum filii fecerunt quod nunc ille noster bonus Robertus facit in Australia : pascebant oves. Sic quoque fecit Paris. Sedebat igitur inter arbores montis Idæ, qui mons prope Trojam est, dum grex suus pascebat circa eum.

Nescio quid faciebat Paris dum sedebat in umbra. Canebat forsan. Pastores antiqui temporis musicam amaverunt omnes.

Robertus in Australia non canit. Cur non canit Robertus ?

Quippe non est doctus in arte musica. Quid facit itaque? Legit libros, nam legere scit bene. Non solum scit legere, sed amat legere. Vide eum sedentem subter illam viridem arborem, cum libro in manu et oculis in librum fixis. Heus tu, mi frater, cave ne nimium sit fixus in librum oculus. Quid vis Herberte? Cur me suades ne faciam id quod mihi valde jucundum est? Mihi placent libri. Non mihi placet desidia. Non sum ego ignavus puer. I jam parve frater, lege librum tuum diligenter, sicut et ego diligenter lego. Valde bene, mi magne frater Roberte; sed legi fabulam de lupo rapaci, qui devoravit, aut si non devoravit, *laceravit*, innoxium agnum. Quis scit igitur si non veniat lupus, dum tu legis, et prædam faciat tuorum innoxiorum agnorum?

Ego scio valde bene, parve Herberte; et scio quod non veniet lupus. Et dabo tibi rationem manifestam cur non veniet lupus; quippe si non est lupus, lupus non potest venire; et lupi hic non habitant. Gaudeo, mi frater, et vale. Memento tamen, si non potest venire lupus, possunt errare greges, et tu potes perdere ovem dum quæris sapientiam. Me nunc abire oportet, et meum legere librum.

Robertum liquimus in pratis Australiensibus; ad Paridem redeamus in sylvis Idæ.

Sedebat igitur Paris, nescio quid meditans, et ecce ante oculos attoniti juvenis tres steterunt cœlestes Deæ, Juno, Venus, et Minerva.

Scis parva Catharina, scis parvule Herberte, Romanos, Græcos, et alias illius temporis gentes, coluisse deos multos, et deas multas. Hæ, quas nominavi, summæ dignitatis erant; sed jam videte si summæ erant sapientiæ. Rixam inter se habebant. Causam quæritis? Anne crustulum, inquit Herbertus, quod habet una alteræ cupiunt? Anne pomum?

Causa multo gravior fuit. In speculo se videt Venus. In speculo se videt Pallas. In speculo se videt Juno. Sum formosa, inquit Juno, inquit Pallas, inquit Venus. Ante omnes sum formosissima, inquit Pallas, inquit Venus, inquit Juno. Heu! Quantus in Olympo strepitus! Quis componebit talem litem? Dii nolunt judicare. Dixerunt id quod dixit Henricus: Unicuique est sua pulchritudo; Juno pulcherrima, pulcherrima Venus, pulcherrima quoque Minerva.

Formosus pastor Paris, ille judicabit, inquit Juno. Eamus ad eum, inquit Pallas, inquit Venus.

Ad Paridem veniunt. Pomum aureum Paridi tradunt. Jubent eum judicare, et pomum dare formosissimae. Ecce Herberte, de *pomo* erat lis dearum. Dixit Paridi Regina Juno, Da mihi pomum, et tibi dabo magnum regnum: dixit Pallas, Da pomum mihi, et tibi dabo sapientiam excellentem: dixit Venus, Da pomum mihi, et tibi dabo uxorem inter mulieres formosissimam.

Here ends the text of the only volume of this sort which I have been able to find, though many others are alluded to in the letters. In the little book from which I have copied it are lists of all the words occurring in the rhymes and prose, all carefully translated and analyzed for the little ones.

To Clement, a little later:—

My GOOD LITTLE MECCO,—I have not written much more of my Latin version of " Mother Goose" since I sent you my first volume, for I only go on just fast enough to have some always ready for Kitty and Herbert; and they don't get on very fast, because we go over and over again till we know every word, conjugating and declining thoroughly; and when they can do the Latin perfectly into English, I give them the English words to do back again into Latin. The only *poem* I have written since is about the blackbirds,— those, you know—four-and-twenty of them—that were made into a pie, and one of them afterwards punished the maid that made the pie, by nipping her nose off. I will send it you when I have a good lot to send with it. Last Sunday I wrote for them, in Latin, the account of Joshua crossing the Jordan; so that, you see, it is not *only* nonsense that I give

them. Next Sunday I mean to give them David's battle with
Goliath. It is, you know, in the Latin Bible; but I give them
the pith condensed, and in language they can better understand.   *   *   *   *   *   *

Speaking to Mr. Charles Smith, in a letter of June, 1841,
of the unhappy state of the church in Valetta, building by
Queen Adelaide, my Father says :—

Isn't this a dainty dish to set before the *Queen ?* *   *

By the bye, talking of dainty dish, &c., of course you are
aware that I quote from the immortal works of Mother
Goose, treasures to which adequate justice has not heretofore
been done; for I am not acquainted with a version of them
in any language. It is a deficiency which I am resolved
forthwith to supply ; and in order that they may be the property of the *learned* at least in all countries, I am engaged in
translating them into *Latin.*[e]

I dare say Percy remembers that I pointed out to him,
some eight or ten years ago, the beauties of one of her cele-
brated compositions ; namely that which treats of the amiable
child whose infant hands lightened so affectionately his
mother's labours.[f] Young as he was, he *washed her dishes,*
and well was his piety rewarded. *Other* infants have *put
their finger in their eye ;* but who but he has drawn from
thence what *he* drew ? *Pearls* have often been so produced ;
but I conclude that in this place the term *fishes* must imply
the OYSTERS and all ! Scholars of infinite taste in this depart-

---

[e] This idea was perfectly original with my Father, although I have lately
found that these nursery rhymes were very cleverly turned into Latin, and
published among a collection entitled " Arundines Cami," by Rev. H. Drury,
&c., in this very same year (1841). Mr. Drury's Latin is, however, far too
difficult for little children.

[f] Original—

> " When I was a little boy
>   I wash'd my mother's dishes ;
> I put my finger in my eye,
>   And pull'd out little fishes."

ment of literature, namely, Catharina Victoriensis and her no less distinguished relation Herbertus, have expressed in such gratifying terms their approbation of my plan, that I could not in conscience withhold from the European public this happy result of my labours. In the course of the next twenty years I hope to bring it to a happy conclusion. In the mean time the first volume, in 100mo, is ready for the press; and I beg you will immediately call at Buckingham Palace, and obtain for me the Queen's gracious permission to dedicate the work to the Princess Royal. Subjoined, I mean to give you a sample of my composition, that it may recommend itself to her Majesty. She will perceive that I differ in opinion with Horace and Virgil and other writers of that school, in preferring the use of Rhyme. But in this I am not only borne out by many sublime compositions of a later, and therefore, of course, a more refined age,—Drunken Burnaby among the rest,—but by the cordial approbation of the aforesaid Catharina and Herbertus, who disapprove entirely of Virgil, and are charmed with my much more readable verses.* * * * *

Now you know, Smith, how impossible it is for any one unassisted scholar to complete so mighty an undertaking; and my object in mentioning the subject to you (besides the dedication to the Princess) is to engage you to point out to Percy how much it will be for his advantage to shut his Juvenal and his Thucydides, and to join with me in this work, by which he will gain at once wealth and renown. He may begin with the "Dainty Dish," for I have not yet entered upon that. I should not think it would be more than he might manage with due diligence in a long vacation. The poems I have finished, besides those I send you, are —" Johnny Green," " The Three Sliders," " Jack and Gill," " Cat and Fiddle," " Jack Horner."

The notes will be philological, exegetical, philosophical, and historical; a lexicon goosianum, and copious indices.

---

* Here come some of the nursery rhymes before given.

Michele will be fully occupied for many years in furnishing spirited lithographic illustrations from drawings of my own ; and in order that they may be true to nature, I have agreed with Mackenzie to buy a cow between us. He is to have the milk, and I the profits of my sketch from the life when she makes the *jump* I am to teach her.   *   *   *

Kitty[b] has been reading the sheet I have just written, and says it is a rare pack of nonsense. At all events, Percy won't think so ; and of such subjects he must be a better judge. *This* I know, that I have just been giving Herbert his Latin lesson ; and my Latin nonsense has engaged his unbroken attention for an hour and a half. Would any *sensible* book do that? They are rapidly gaining a copious vocabulary, and every word of it well analyzed.   *   *   *

To Bob he writes, the following year :—

When *you* have small Latin learners, Bob, try my plan. All Latin elementary books are written to exemplify systematically grammar rules. The book is pretty easy in the very beginning, but soon gets out of a child's depth, like Delectus. No Roman writer is easy enough in point of style or subject for a child's capacity. But these small people can pick up Latin *words* if they are properly put in their way, just as they do Italian ; so I give them strings of the commoner words, and short easy sentences, culling them from all sources, and composing too. I am filling a third volume of this sort of Latin. They translate every day two pages of it into English, and write it back again into Latin ; and so gradually learn by mere habit, that it would be as absurd to say bonus puella as buono ragazza. Of course I give them all the easier rules by degrees, Propria quæ maribus, as well as syntax, and they learn the rules by heart here and there ; not going regularly through those formidable treatises, but gradually making acquaintance with them. I believe I meant to send you, but

----

did not send, some of our versions of nursery anthology. Blandi doctores, you know, dant *crustula*.[1] These have answered my purpose better than caramelle.[k]   *   *

In my last letter, dear Bob, were graver subjects. But I am obliged to keep many irons in my fire, and any work of mine interests you, as yours does me. My day is always deplorably short. I can't do half I have to do, and yet I often contrive to do two things at once. I can listen to the lessons and draw at the same time. My letters to you are generally written while they are going on. I wish I could afford to keep a reader, as Pliny did, to read to me while I am drawing. But I don't understand what he got by employing a notarius, a secretary, whenever he had a thought to put down : I could do it quicker myself. I should only want notarius to *copy*. That would save me a great deal of time ; when, for example, I have emended one of my speeches of Thucydides, till I have partly made it illegible.   *   *

My Father never had a study or private sanctum of any kind, but always sat in the library, which was a general sitting-room, and was never in the slightest degree disturbed in his work by the reading aloud, repeating of lessons, or the talking that might be going on around him ; nor by the pianoforte and harp-playing and singing in the drawing-room, from which he was only separated by folding-doors, and with which he was often in the same room. He had a wonderful power of abstracting and concentrating his ideas, —gained partly in early life, from having frequently important dispatches to write against time, and surrounded by noisy companions.

---

[1] Here, in the letter, are copied most of the Latin nursery rhymes which I have already given.

[k] Maltese sugar-kisses.

CHAPTER VIII.

[1841.]

THIS summer my Father lived very uncomfortably, having to
sleep at the Marina, and go backwards and forwards every
day between it and Sliema, where his family spent the
summer. He says:—

Portelli[a] has again and again offered to come and sleep at
the Marina, to enable me to be at home; but I can't allow
that, because he has *no* leisure. He is obliged to be every
day, and all day long, at the office; and to keep him away
from his family at night too would be a cruelty. I generally
get to Sliema between ten and eleven; then I spend all the
time till one in giving lessons to Kitty and Herbert, then
dinner, then an hour and a half's sleep, then a cooling ablu-
tion, and an hour or two of light reading is all that remains
of a usable summer's day; for in the evening you know
there are many visitors in the Sliema season * * *
Then I don't like keeping my boatmen up late, and on their
account I embark on my returning voyage at half-past eight.
To save time, I have a good lantern in my boat, by which
I read comfortably, and it is well worth while. I am altogether in my boat two hours every day, and they are glorious
reading hours; for you know there are no *callers*. But

---

[a] Acting as chief clerk.

altogether my reading is not much; for, except one or two
new books, I have read nothing but Plautus since I told you
I had taken him up, and I have not done with him yet; but
I have read sixteen plays out of the twenty. What an un-
accountable thing it is, that among all the modes of character
and business that human life affords, a man of Plautus's wit
should have been content to build all his plots on the same
form and with the same material. Adolescens loves Meretrix, lacks money; Servus assists him, robs Senex, cheats
Leno out of Meretrix, transfers her to Adolescens, and all
right. Miles brags, Parasita eats, each here and there, by
way of variety, and that's *all* the variety. But what a clever
fellow he was, Bob, out of such materials to make a most
amusing book. * * * * *

To Fanny, in July :—

I have had a good deal of work in my office, too; so that
I am not only away from Sliema all night, but much of the
day besides. One day I didn't get to Sliema till half-past
seven in the evening; and I always set out on my return at
half-past eight, for the sake of not keeping my boatmen out
of their beds.

Last night, however, neither they nor I were in bed till
one o'clock; for Mr. Mackenzie had a party, to which we
went. We met there a Captain Henderson, of the Rifles,
with whom we had before made some little acquaintance.
He gave a music party on the water, having the full brass
band of the Rifles in a boat out at Sliema, not within the
harbour, but under the rocks outside, in the open sea; and
numbers of people were there in boats to hear the music, and
Captain Henderson had a boat loaded with iced lemonade
and wine and cakes, which went about supplying all his
guests; and very beautiful music it was; but the one thing
that interested *me*, was a piece out of one of the operas that
my own dear Sally used to sing. Bless her precious heart!
But the reason of my mentioning this Captain Henderson is
this: he introduced himself to me as a neighbour and very

intimate friend of Robert Sconce's, at Stirling. He was
very near being a first cousin of Robert Sconce's; for his
father and my uncle married sisters (the sisters of Dr. Col-
quhoun); but his father's wife died early, and Captain
Henderson's mother was a second wife. Everybody speaks
of him in the highest possible terms. Some one told me he
had been upon his estate, and saw all his poor tenants enjoying every sort of comfort that he had provided for them.
He spends a quantity of money here; but he is the quietest-
mannered man you ever saw; he has not a grain of conceit
of any sort, and seems to be always busied in doing good-
natured things. He has shown a particular desire to be
intimate with us, and, of course, he will be, for he is just the
sort of person to suit us.   *   *   *   *

I have all the time been *remarkably* well. One of the very
hot days I was actually at work in my office the *whole* day,
and till half-past six in the evening, without suffering a bit,
and yet I had not only the heat to bear, but the plague of
multiplying and dividing, for which you know I have no
fancy. The Admiralty sent me out a new form for a bakery
account, and it was a puzzling job, and therefore fell to my
share. The common routine work, where there is *only* multiplying and dividing, P—— and all the rest do faster than I
can; but where there is complexity of calculations, they tell
me I beat them hollow; not because I learned in my youth
more of Dilworth or Cocker, but because the science even of
grammar helps me to investigate a truth with which figures
only seem to be concerned. Teach Johnny to *think*. Give
him a good *knowledge*-master, and he will *apply* his knowledge afterwards as he pleases.

We are going on so beautifully in our office, that it will be
grievous, indeed, if they rob me of Portelli. We are, of
course, in fearful anxiety about it.   *   *   *

Have you seen, Fan, Tytler's collection of letters in the
reigns of Edward VI. and Mary? It is one of our club
books that I have just been reading, and I think it would
just suit your taste, and amuse Liddell too. I can't bear

what they call a *general* history. Hume may tell me what sort of man Burleigh was; but I don't care what Hume thinks of Burleigh, and the less, because Lingard may give me quite a different account of him; but when I read letters written by, and to, and about Burleigh, I can form my *own* notion.

Oh, but dearest, if you could but transport me to *Ninham Farm* [b] I would shut up all the books! I should spend all my time in those beautiful *green lanes*. What a time it is since I saw such a scene! What would I give for a green lane here for our little ones to play in, with some of those venerable elm-trees, such as used to shade the lanes about Sydenham, lifting their heads as high as the topmast-heads of our stiff men-of-war, and throwing out branches that fall feathering over each other, as if on purpose to make lights and shadows for painters' studies.   *   *   *

To me, in August :—

My boat comes for me at night. It has always a good lantern in it, which I put upon the seat, and I sit upon a low stool in the boat, so as to have the seat for a table for my book, and I contrive to read comfortably during my voyage. After going clean through all the twenty plays of Plautus, I began Horace, and have read in my boat all the odes twice through, and shall read twice all the rest of his works. It is sixteen years since I read him last; but I find I remember much the larger part freshly; for at Tunbridge we were, in my time, great dabs in saying Horace by heart.

I have a mighty liking for these old books. Besides their intrinsic value, they interest me for their very antiquity, and for the sake of my early acquaintance with them. Be sure and make Harry and Argylina Latinists, and Harry, of course, a Grecian too.   *   *   *   *

I ought to give you all the news I can collect, for it must be interesting to you to hear, as often as you can, what is going

---

[b] Where she was staying in the Isle of Wight.

on on this side of the globe.　　*　　*　　*　　We have
London news to the 4th of this month, and *Galignanis* to the
6th. I read them last night; but there is nothing remarkable
in them, except the matter of McLeod and the Americans. The
law question, whether, as the English Government has taken
upon itself the responsibility of McLeod's act, he, as an
individual, is amenable to American jurisdiction, was referred
to the judges of the Supreme Court of New York, and they
have decided that what the English Government may have
done or do in the matter is indifferent; that Mr. McLeod,
in his own person, has perpetrated an illegal act, and must
in his own person take the consequences, and must consequently be tried before an American jury. These judges,
too, use language quite unlike the sober reasoning of
English lawyers, when arguing a point of law, or English
judges declaring their opinion and supporting it by argument. They talk like *angry politicians;* like men utterly
unfit for the business of important dispassionate reflection.
If, then, this is the character of the *judges,* what is to be
expected from the more vulgar-minded jury? The poor
man, then, is in great danger; and, if he is sacrificed, a war
will, of course, follow; and, for every hair of his head, some
scores of American and English heads will be laid low. I
am a thorough *antipolemist;* but, if I was Sir Robert Peel,
and obliged to go to war with America, I would levy an
income tax of twenty per cent., and send out, in two months,
forty sail-of-the-line and twice as many steamers, with five
hundred soldiers in each ship,—such a fleet as Nelson, and
such an army as Wellington had; and so make those bragging
people fear us as much as they now hate us, since it is plain
enough that they *do* hate us with all their souls. The more's
the pity; but *that's* one of the good things we owe to the
good old George the Third.　　*　　*　　*

While I am quoting Latin, I will just give you a word or
two from Plautus, that describe your *Papa's* condition with
remarkable precision. A brisk old gentleman says of himself, " Haud sum annos natus præter *quinquaginta et quattuor*

(you know, my chick, I was born on the 6th of July, 1787) : *Clare oculis video* (and mine are still as good as yours at a long focus; and, with my spectacles, as useful as they used to be without). *Pernix sum manibus; sum pedes nobilis.*" A very happy condition of body too; but, what do you think of Miss Hamilton, who, at seventy-four, walked last night, in the dark (and no moon), from Florian,[c] through the town and up to us at Sliema, to ask me about a *cow*. She might, of course, have have sent a note. But she had made the same expedition the night before; and finding, when she came to the door, that we had a *party*, she chose to retire unobserved. Her companion in these night excursions is a shrivelled Maltese woman, as old as herself, who carries a lantern before her; and Colomba[d] says they remind her of Diogenes hunting for truth.   *   *   *

Your first letter from Port Phillip is come ! *   *   *
Most humbly, and with all my soul, I thank God for all His great goodness to us.

To Bob, in August :—

Most dear Son,—The letter you wrote from *Forest-Hill Cottage* on the 4th of March is come ! Never brought letter with it better comfort on *all* scores. It tells me of the *safety*, the health, the high spirits, and bright prospects of my beloved children. And all you write, my good Bob, assures me that you are setting out with the best of all provisions,— a *right mind*.   *   *   *   *   *

The life of a woodman and a shepherd ought to suit you; and a light heart keeps the head cool. Whenever I have had any carking, I have felt my brow burn, and then away goes the appetite. You have had in your young life perpetual anxieties. All those examinations at school and college were hard pulls upon such nerves as yours; and then the difficulties of deciding for the Church, or the Bar, " metuens

---

[c] Some four miles.   [d] The housekeeper.

patruæ verbera linguæ." This is in *Horace*, lib. iii. Od. 12. But do, Bob, if you have a Horace at hand, read to Lizzy the second epode:—" Beatus ille qui procul negotiis." There is a line for Hanmer, the 6th,—" nec horret iterum mare;" and it will suit Sally too, for she will remember what a misery it was to see him embark. And a line for you—" *Forum vitat*," he wouldn't go to the bar. And a line for Liz and Sally—" Quod si pudica mulier *in partem juvat*," and " dulces liberos," and " lassi sub adventum viri. But *all* the ode is beautiful, and you ought, in your circumstances, to learn every word by heart, not this *afternoon*, but *now*, this very *moment*. * * * * *

To Fanny he gives extracts of our Australian letters, in case she should not have received hers; and says :—

They crossed the Yarra-Yarra by a ferry, paying two pence apiece for their passage. Ain't you glad to hear of that two-penny ferry, Fan? For you know they arrived at the very end of the summer; so that here is a clear proof that their river is a *real perennial* river. May its waters prove a Nile to them and their flocks, their meadows, and their cornfields!

* * * * * *

In this letter my Father says a good deal about his chances of promotion, through the interest of his friends Sir J. Pechell, Sir G. Cockburn, and others. He had been told, on good authority, that Sir John Barrow was about to retire from the Admiralty, and that *he* had been mentioned as likely to be his successor. However, he was far from being sanguine about it, and never spoke of it out of his own family.

About this time my Father wrote to little Clement at school :—

MY PRECIOUS BOY,—You will be at school again when this arrives. It is to tell you, what you know well enough without any telling, that Papa and Mamma love you dearly. But, dearest Meeho, you are growing a big boy now, and I have something more to say; and I think I may feel pretty sure that you will listen to it, and understand it. Well then, we hear with sorrow that you are low in your class, and that you don't like learning, and don't learn. Now I don't mean to scold you, or say anything to make you unhappy, but I do wish very much to say something to make you *think*. At your age, and with your sense (for you have plenty of understanding for your age), you can form some idea of the value of learning. You can distinguish between a man who has been educated and one who has not. You can understand that a man is in one main respect different from a dog; and that is, that a man has the power of reasoning, and a dog has not. Even *you* can reason already; not very wisely, but yet better than the horse you used to drive to water at the farm. The wild Indians who live in the woods of America can reason, but very imperfectly. You can imagine what difference there is between the mind of one of these poor Indians and the mind of an educated man.

Now, Mecho, if *education* makes this difference, can you have any doubt of the *value* of education? Now tell me, besides,—Don't you know that if a child were to grow up without exercising its body by walking, running, jumping, as other children do, it would have a poor miserable weak body? And can't you imagine that just so it is with the mind? You go to school to exercise your mind and make it strong; but if you don't *work* while you are at school, your mind has not its proper exercise, and does not grow strong. Some men have strong bodies, and some strong minds. Do you know what a strong body can do? Why not half as much as a *horse*. But don't you think a strong *mind* can do a great deal *more* than a horse can do? Think about this, Mecho, and then tell me. When the time comes for you to leave school and go to college, you may, if you please, have such a feeling as this:— How glad I am that I have worked hard at school, for now I may gain credit at college; but I am quite sure I shall get no disgrace. Or you may, on the other hand, have this very different feeling :—What am I to do at college? I have been an idle boy; I don't know half what other boys know; I shan't be able to pass any examination; I shall be brought to shame, and I shall make Papa and Mamma and Aunt very unhappy.

I say, my dear Mecho, you must *know* that you will be happier by-and-by if you work now; only it requires some *resolution* to set to work, and you don't try. But isn't it well worth while? You may take my word for it, that not only by-and-by, but *now*, you will be a *very great deal* the happier for working hard. Just try it a little while, and see. I did work very hard at school, and I got for my reward praise that I delighted in. I had never any anxiety about my lessons. Now you get *no* praise. You hear other boys praised, and you see other boys get prizes; and *you* will be *distinguished* by never getting praise or prize. Shall you like that? Isn't it worth while to take a little trouble to get out of the *stupid list*, and to see your name among the praised and the rewarded? Don't persuade yourself that, though you do no work now, you may fetch up your lost time by working hard when you grow older. Unless you begin at once, and work with great spirit, you will *not* recover your lost time.   ✱   ✱

Don't call this a dull lecture, my dearest little boy, but think of it seriously, for the sake of Mamma's and Papa's love.   ✱   ✱   ✱   ✱   ✱   ✱

To Hanmer, in September :—

Beware of the sun! It is apt to give no notice of the mischief it means to do; and when it does strike a blow, it is always a hard one. A hurricane may blow your house down; frost may nip one's nose off; but far-darting Apollo aims at the *brain*. Make a rest some day from your out-door labours, to write me a letter.   ✱   ✱   ✱   ✱

To me, at the end of a long letter :—

Do you see, my darling, how I have been writing? I have kept your precious letter before me, and have referred to it sentence by sentence. This is the only way to make the most of our poor intercourse. The notion people have of *answering* a letter is generally no more than the writing of one in return; but I like to dwell on all you say to me, and you may depend upon always receiving a direct answer to every inquiry your letters contain. This is a little like talking together, which is a thousand times better than each making in turn a long speech.   *   *   *   *   *   *

Thank you more than I can tell you, my pretty child, for describing the joy you had in first seeing on your table, at Forest Hill, my drawing of the Malta palm-trees; for you pictured your dear own self to *me* so vividly that I could fancy you before me. Don't I know exactly how it is that you "scream for joy"?—and can't I see you holding your hand up to look through it? Nobody ever did praise my pictures as highly as *you*, you know, my chick.   *   *   *

I shall fancy the *shimper* of your dear eyes when they light upon our views of Malta. It is a vile place to us; but it would be very precious to me if I were away and you here.

    *   *   *   *   *   *

To Bob, in September :—

Though we have the thickness of the solid globe between us, I never think of you as being lost to me; but, on the contrary, I am sensible of owing to you a great deal of happiness. In reading your letters, I see all that you *are*, as well as all that you are doing, and I assure myself that all my wishes for you are accomplished. Dear Lizzy, I gave him many a good lesson; but what should we have done, after all, without your help? If you had not taught him that love was better than law, he would at this moment have been straining his eyes over a disagreeable book in a dingy chamber at the Temple, with a pale face, a furred tongue, an anxious heart, and an empty purse. That he is at Melbourne now, is, you know, your doing; and he could not possibly, in any other circumstances, have led so healthy and happy a life. Whatever

had been his occupation in England, it must have been sedentary, and, in a great degree, solitary; and, in both respects
hurtful to his mind and body. You have made us rich, then,
good child, in all sorts of ways; for isn't it you that have
made his three per cent. twenty, and set him to work at
cutting, digging, nailing, ploughing, gardening?—and isn't
it a very sweet home that he returns to when his day's work
is done? Now do me justice, good daughter; for you know
everybody else thought Bob's love the ruin of his prospects,
and a wise father would have cudgelled it out of him. But
I was still wiser; for I was heartily glad of it from the very
first. This was lucky, too, you know; for he is, as his
honoured Mamma says, as obstinate as a mule, and so, of
course, the cudgel would only have hammered the love in
harder and tighter. As for the obstinacy, I suppose you
have found out, by this time, that its bump is not necessarily
a bad one. I hope not; for it is the biggest I have myself.
An obstinate fool or knave one had better avoid; but not a
good man obstinately bent on *loving* one, you know, Liz. So
I hope Bob's bump and mine are merely signs that what we
mean to do we persevere in doing; *tenaces propositi.* ＊ ＊

I have just heard that my friend Portelli is confirmed by
the Admiralty in his appointment of my chief clerk; and
great good news it is for us; for otherwise he would have
quitted us altogether, and he is my right hand. ＊ ＊

The long letter you wrote, chiefly on board the *Argyle*, and
finally on your arrival, has been about me ever since it came.
I take your letters and Sally's backwards and forwards from
Sliema to the Marina, and read them in my boat, and Mamma
asks me if I mean to wear them out in my pocket; but they
won't wear out, for they are carefully wrapped in a sheet
of paper that protects them, and I mean to keep them in their
proper sequence in a box specially allotted to them. ＊ ＊

You know, Bob, I read fewer novels than most people; but
I have now and then enjoyed a good one thoroughly. There
is a coincidence between us in Waverley's having sent you to
the history of Scotland; for I took up "Count Robert of

Paris" for an hour, some years ago, while I was waiting at Liddell's for him to come in and draw me out an aching tooth; and as soon as the operation was over, I went to the library and got a French translation of Anna Comnena, and ended with reading all the Byzantine historians through. I began Procopino, in Greek; but it was too slow work. I suppose even people who keep their Greek a-going more regularly than my little leisure allows, find their vocabulary often at fault in the wide range from Homer to Chrysostom, and still more to Comnena. Another coincidence, dear Bob: While you were analyzing Pusey's treatise on Baptism, I was fighting off a certain evangelical Dr. ——, a visitor here, who insisted upon my listening to his Calvinistic talk about it; and the weapons I used were naturally furnished me by some of the worthies cited in your tract (Catena Patrum). Of course my narrow shelves contain but few, but those few are giants (though they *do* find room on the narrow shelf); and having given him Luther, Hooker, Taylor, Wilson, Van Mildert, and Lawrence, it was as much as he could well expect from me, and quite enough to show him what ground I myself stood upon; though I was quite sure he would not have changed *his* for all the arguments and authorities that all the Church could lay before him. I hate all argument, but, most of all, theological; for all it does is harm,—good never; yet now and then one is so assailed that there is no escape.

  *   *   *   *   *   *

 The Calvinistic teaching about Baptism is this: Sedulo docemus, Deum *non promiscue* vim suam exercere in omnibus qui sacramenta recipiunt, sed *tantum in electis.* * * *

 Dr. P——'s view of Baptism is not, even by all the High Church party (how I hate *party!*), accepted as quite sound. The objection is, that he looks upon it as an act done in an instant, and accomplishing its purpose in an instant, and not rather as the sacrament of constant union with Christ, the assurance of a continual living presence; so that all the virtue and life of the creature should consist in its union with a Being above itself.

Two volumes of Mr. Newman's sermons were lent to us last year, and I read one of them every morning before breakfast, and lamented when I had no more of them to read. There was in *them* nothing controversial. For such reading I hope you will always find leisure, let your work be what it may.

Your albatross-shooting would have made me read again Southey's "Ancient Mariner," but I have not got his works. If you have, read it.   *   *   *   *

A great deal of chemistry may be got in a short time. Watson, the famous Bishop of Llandaff, was Chemical Professor at Oxford, or Cambridge, I forget which. When he first announced himself as a candidate for the office, a friend asked him if he knew anything about it, and his answer was, "Not one word;" and soon afterwards he began his lectures, and acquitted himself with great applause.

    *   *   *   *   *   *

I think I forgot to answer your question, dear Bob, about *Hesiod's Sunday.* Some years ago I mentioned it to you. About sixty lines from the end of "Works and Days" are these remarkable words: ἑβδόμη (ἡμερα), ἱερον ημαρ, τῃ γαρ Απολλωνα χρυσαορα γεινατο Λητω — The seventh day is holy, for on that day Latona brought into the world golden-sworded Apollo. Now just think, dear Sally, that Hesiod wrote those words *nine hundred years* before our Saviour's advent, and *only* seven hundred after the death of Moses. That he got them, second or *tenth* hand, from the Mosaic writings, is as clear as the sun itself. But compare the Biblical account of the creation of the sun and moon at *one time* with the mythological twin birth of Phœbus and his sister. That is remarkable too, isn't it? How could Gibbon gravely tell us that we owe our revelation of the *Trinity* to *Plato!* Did he himself think so? He must have been too keen an inquirer for that; and yet he could hardly have expected to cheat us. Plato, of course, got his notions from the same source as Hesiod. Pagan opinions were not inventions, but deformed versions of revealed truth.

    *   *   *   *   *   *

To Georgiana Ewart my Father writes, in September :—

Let your father's friends, the now triumphant Tories, make him* Bishop of Melbourne. We will have Liddell for our Physician-general; and if I live to a patriarchal age, I will go with my growing-up boys, and we will make among us a good name for the new colony. I can't conceive why people, who may there find room enough, and where an honest and industrious man must prosper, should go on struggling for his daily bread in overcrowded England. I consider Bob's circumstances as being already far better than my own, after all these years of toil; for he will soon have a better income, the life he leads is pleasanter, and more independent; the improvement in his circumstances must be progressive, while I have been for years standing still; I would not, therefore, accept for either of my young boys any Government place, civil or military. As for me, I suppose I must stay where I am, if I live so long, *eleven years* more; for the Government would not allow me to retire till I am sixty-five years old, and then I shall be entitled to a pension of £500 a year, and I may take it with me to Port Phillip.

* * * These are the castles we amuse ourselves with building; not unmindful that the tomb may claim its occupant before the castle.

In October of this year, 1841, he writes to Bob :—

What do you think of writing a *history* of your young settlement, with a description of its present state, and hints for its improvement? Its one most crying present evil is evidently the want of due provision for the duties of *religion*. The Romanists and the Seets are putting us to shame all over the world; and I am afraid we have special reason to blush for ourselves at Port Phillip. Fifty Maltese would not leave their land without taking with them a priest, and for that priest and his people a church would be built immediately;

whereas you at Port Phillip are thousands, and I hear of only *one* clergyman, and of your assembling in a *barn*. But I read of your *races* and of your *balls*, and four-guinea tickets. This is beginning at the wrong end, dear Bob. Stir yourself, then; invite the people to subscribe *largely*. Tell them that they must raise the money at the expense of some serious sacrifice. They must not be content to give only what they can give *conveniently*. They must be content to suffer some inconvenience and privations for the sake of accomplishing so necessary a work. They are bad calculators if they expect their sheep to bring forth thousands and ten thousands in their streets while they forget Him who gives the increase. Let us hope for a blessing upon ourselves and our substance when we have put away the accursed thing; namely, the worship of mammon. We may innocently gather gold, if we allow ourselves time for better things, and make a good *use* of it.

But yours is a case in which your *first fruits* are plainly called for. Shall I advise you, then, to spend the very first money you can command (for I suppose your purse to be now all but empty) in subscribing for the completion of your church? Subscribe for me too. Can I do better with the first £200 I send to Melbourne for my little boys, than give *half* of it for such a purpose? I *think*, if I were one of your community, I could write such a paper as would stir them up. At any rate I would try. By making a great effort, at all events, you would do something. Your newspapers would show what you were doing.

It would set a good example elsewhere, and would encourage Government at home, and the religious societies, to help you with a grant. You should have immediately a *Bishop of Melbourne*. Never rest till you get one.

Here is a fit field for your activity, dearest boy; and I shall love to see you engaged in it. I have read this to Mamma, and she agrees with me with all her heart in authorizing you to subscribe for us for your church. The mere putting down of the money would be doing nothing; but if

you can excite the people to join, then our example and
yours may do a great deal.

The way would be to call a public meeting, and then make
a *speech*, move your resolutions, put down your money; put
down a hundred pounds for me. Are any of you at Melbourne members of the Society for Promoting Christian
Knowledge? You ought, by all means, to be a member.
You ought to establish a district committee. In such a
community as yours it would do immense good, by getting
right books from the parent society at their very low prices,
and selling or giving them to the middling and poorer classes.
Then invite the parent society to aid you in the building of
your church, in getting more clergy sent out, in getting you
a Bishop.[f]   *   *   *   *   *

On the 13th of October his darling Fanny arrived with
her husband and children at Malta, to spend the winter with
him, she being too ill to risk a winter in England.

About this time my Father writes to Bob, speaking of the
Australian natives :—

The consequences of these murders and outrages must
necessarily be horrible. There was something of the same sort
formerly at Newfoundland. Some murders had exasperated
the settlers—ignorant men, of unrestrained passions; so that
if, by chance, one of our fishermen first caught sight of an
Indian, it was as much a matter of course to shoot him as it
would have been to shoot a hare. So, of course, with the
Indians; and so it will be in your country. Booty at first
tempts the starving natives, and then mutual deadly hatred
prolongs the mischief. You must do your part, dear sons, to
check such a devil's course. Our people must neither be
murdered nor robbed. As much severity as justice finds
necessary must be used to deter the natives from outrage,

---

[f] My Father did not live to hear of a Bishop being sent to Melbourne. The
Bishop of Melbourne arrived there the year my Father died.

but there must be no individual revenge. Hard enough it must be to deal with these poor people. To humanize their wandering tribes is not possible, and it is not easy to deter them, by fear, from aggression; for how are the individual aggressors to be known and apprehended? What police can spread its power over so wide a land? It would not be easy to identify even the aggressing *tribe*, and if you could, how could you get that tribe into your power, or how could you deal with it?   *   *   *   I am afraid no good whatever would be done even by apprehending and hanging the murderers; for the rest would simply consider it as an act of revenge. They would only be more cautious not to attack without a fair chance of impunity; but they would have two motives for mischief instead of one. It was at first hunger; but now it will be hunger and hatred.   *   *

To me :—

Mr. Scamp, the Admiralty architect, came out by the last packet, and immediately set to work, with his myrmidons, to demolish the *Galley Arches*, and prepare the site there for our new bakery. I wish they had put it anywhere else, for I can't bear the destruction of an old building. Do you remember old Donna Rosa? Her dwelling is only approachable by a great staircase contiguous to the galley arches, and in pulling down these, it is necessary also to pull down the staircase; so that her house will be in a few days blocked up. She could neither get in nor out, and so notice has been given her to quit by Sir ———. He thought (for he had been told so) that the poor old soul was living there upon charitable sufferance, and that he might turn her out unceremoniously. But I had understood, as clearly as the poor old woman could make me understand, that she had some sort of *right* to her house. So I set myself to work in her cause, and collected the evidence of *fifteen* old people, several of them between eighty and ninety, and one of ninety-two; and I have been able to prove indisputably that the ground on which her house, and Mr. S.'s and Mr. ——'s stand, belonged in ancient time to her family; that it was sold by them to the Knights; that in the contract for sale the corner of those buildings which she now occupies was secured to her family for their residence; that when the English took possession of the island, the first English Governors, Sir A. Ball and General Cameron, wanted to eject them, but were satisfied with the proof of their title which they brought forward, and confirmed them in their tenure; that Donna Rosa herself was born there; and that she has lived there until this day, her age being, as proved by the register of her baptism, eighty-seven last May. Sir John will forward all this to the Admiralty, and we shall get for the old soul a just compensation.[s] In the mean time I have taken a good house for her, with which she is quite content. Only she says there has been a *sentinel* under her window for eighty-seven years, and she is sadly afraid of being run away with when such protection is taken from her. *   *   *   *   *

My time is occupied continually with thousands of small works that prevent me from doing what I would if I could command it. What I can, of course I give dearest Fan. Latin Grammar takes up two or three of my morning hours for Kitty and Herbert. Queen Victoria has her claims; sick Mamma hers; introductions brought by every packet theirs. All I can do is to fill up odd scraps of time with some book that will bear interruption; and the book I have now is Ovid. According to my usual way, I shan't leave him till I have read him clean through, and probably twice: but it is surprising how much one *can* read by using up all the odd minutes. I have always the book in my pocket. If one likes a book, one is eager to open it; and so the way is always to have at hand a book one can really enjoy.

The great charm of Ovid, you know, is the wonderful facility of his language. His *verse* reads as if every word

---

[s] The stir he made in Donna Rosa's behalf was completely successful. She obtained what he asked for from the Admiralty, a pension of £20 a year.

naturally took its place where, with consummate art, he has placed it. Now you know what strict rules of art there are for writing Latin verse; and you know what queer contrivances English poets are reduced to for the furnishing of their measures and rhymes; and so you can easily understand that he must be a great poet who can make every word fit its place just as if art had nothing whatever to do with its collocation. I thought of the *Darabin*[h] while I read his *abuse* of a river that stopped him, by its unusual fulness, on his journey to his love. " Nec tibi sunt fontes, nec tibi certa domus. Quis gratâ dixit voce *perennis* eas ?" He calls it a mere mountain torrent, depending upon rain, with no springs for its source. But if a *wish* could make *our* stream *perennial*, plenty of us would alter it.   *   *   *   *

To Bob, in December :—

Let me give you first the subject always uppermost in my thoughts here, and always, I well know, in yours and my own dear Sally's. Fan is not worse. She is nearly the same as she was when Liddell went away, and as she was when I wrote to you a fortnight ago.   *   *   *

Some hope there still is; for there are many examples like those of Mrs. R——, whom you remember here. But we can only hope in *trembling*. We must *pray* too with all our hearts. All our poor little children pray God to look with compassion upon their dear sister, and enable her and all of us to put our whole trust in His mercy.   *   *   *

When she was a child she said it was *good for her* to be near me; and good it is for both of us to be near each other now.   *   *   *   We have, for a few days, a bishop here—Alexander, whose seat is to be at Jerusalem. He dines to-day at the Louis's, and they wished us to meet him; but I told Lady Louis I couldn't leave Fan, even for the Bishop of Jerusalem. They say *our* bishop is not to be appointed

---

[h] The little creek on our Australian farm.

till the church is built. Scamp hoped to complete it by the close of next year; but every step he takes discloses a new imperfection in the old work, and the poor man is puzzled everywhere. He has just found a part of the substructions based, not, as they ought to have been, upon the rock, but upon the remnant of an old and imperfect wall; so he is afraid to trust the foundations anywhere; and the underground work is so deep, that he would have to dig down, more or less in different parts, from ten to *fifty* feet, to examine them. Eight or ten inches of the base of a principal column was found projecting beyond the intended foundation of it, and resting upon nothing; and what has been used for *cement* has so little cementing or tenacious property, that it pulverizes under the touch, so that *snuff* would have been quite as useful a material. Not much like the old Roman mortar we saw resisting the waves of two thousand years at Baiæ, nor the old Norman castles in England, where the cement is as hard as the stone, and especially at Rochester Castle like *Travertine* stone, *shells* being mixed with it, and all in one inseparable mass.   *   *   *   *   *   *

Captain Basil Hall, who is still here, has interested himself mightily in my studies, and begs me to let him write to Moxon, his publisher, touching the publication of my Thucydides. He says Moxon would have the manuscript examined by his literary advisers, and if they reported favourably, he would pay me a sum of money for my leave to publish at his own expense, and for his own profit, a certain number of copies, leaving me the copyright. I have not yet set to work upon it, to revise and copy, for I have had no time; but I will begin as soon as I can.   *   *   *   *

CHAPTER IX.

At the beginning of this year the Rev. J. T. H. Le Mesurier [*] retired from the ministry of the Dockyard Chapel, and his congregation presented him with an address and a piece of plate in token of their respect. My Father was requested to prepare the address, which was as follows :—

" Impressed with deep and sincere respect for Mr. Le Mesurier, and with a grateful sense of our obligations to him, we are anxious to unite in offering to him our heart-felt thanks for all his zealous labours in our behalf.

" For twenty-two years he has been charged with duties beyond the measure of any mental or physical energies but his own. Five times every Sunday has he passed from the performance of one service to another, and never in all those years has the burning sun, the rain, the rough wind or sea, restrained him in his pious course. To visit us in our sickness, to carry consolation to the poor inmates of the hospital, to hold communion with the dying when epidemic distemper raged,—and his brave example was a useful

[*] Chaplain to the Forces at Malta.

lesson; to do good whenever it was in the power of his hand to do it, he has disregarded all considerations but those of duty to God and goodwill to man.

" We are persuaded that religion has not a more conscientious advocate, nor charity a more prompt or indefatigable minister of its varied duties, nor truth a more unflinching friend.

" With all our hearts we are grateful to him; with all our hearts we thank him; and, in the fullest sense of Christian benevolence, we bid him an affectionate farewell."

     *   *   *   *   *   *

To Bob he writes, in January, after speaking of the great improvement of his dear Fanny's health :—

Let us thank God with all our hearts for this His great goodness to her and us.   *   *   *   *

And at the close of the letter :—

We are all full of good hope. God's holy name be praised, for this and for all His mercies! I said these words just now in leaving our *dinner-table*, and with all my soul *thought of Fan*.

Speaking of his Thucydides :—

No one can judge infallibly of his own work. I do conscientiously *think* that my version is upon the whole the best English version there is. I may be a fool for my pains, but I am *not vain* in thinking so. I may make a great blunder, but I do really form my judgment without a grain of partiality; on the contrary, I am generally disposed to quarrel with what I do myself. I see more faults in my own drawings than other people see, and I could have no difficulty in *acknowledging* them to myself or to you. I know that Bloomfield and Arnold and all the rest of them are necessarily much better Grecians than I am. That is inevitable. They have Greek books in their hands every day of their lives, and I let *years* pass sometimes without opening one. I have a thousand other things to do. But, then, *common sense* has a great deal to do with such work ; and, above all, no one of them could have given his heart and soul to the work as I gave mine.   I am sure I have observed many places in the commentaries of great critics, where they have written nonsense and I should have written sense, simply because their experience of the affairs of the world had not taught them some particular matter bearing upon the sub-ject, and *my* experience *had* chanced to teach it me.   There was no superior wisdom that I could pretend to, but I happened to know some *fact* that they did not know ; and a very great light is often shed upon a cramp passage in an old book, by some scrap of knowledge that one has accidentally picked up.   Again, suppose such a passage as this were written in Greek.   It is from the First Part of King Henry IV., the last scene of act 1st :—

> " Dangerous . . . . .
> As to o'erwalk a current, roaring loud,
> On the unsteadfast footing of a spear.
> *Hotspur.*—If he fall in, good night : or sink or swim."

So in all the books, and Stevens's note says, " Sink or swim is a very ancient proverbial expression." By proverbial he means, of course, that in this place it is a *figurative* expression.   Not a bit.   It is used here in its literal sense, and there ought to be no stop at all at night. *Hotspur* means to say, yes, it is *so* dangerous to cross this wild torrent on the unsteadfast footing of a spear (whether laid across to serve for a bridge, as Warburton says, or used for a *leaping-pole*, which would have been the hardier way), that if a man tumbles in there is an end of him, *whether he can swim or not*, for the force of the water would dash him to pieces against the rocks.   This makes a clear and thoroughly satisfactory sense.   It is undeniable.   Mr. Pemberton[b] gave this pas-

---

[b] A gentleman who gave lectures on Shakspeare at Malta.

sage when he was here, and gave it according to the *books*, and when I told him my view of it he adopted it frankly. Well now, if this were in Greek, and Stevens and Pemberton had been far better Grecians than I, yet certainly I should have found the sense of the passage, and they would have missed it. Observe, that as the books give this passage, they make *Hotspur* say, " If he tumbles in, good bye to him ; but, as for me, I have taken my resolution, and I shall go on, whether my fate be to sink or swim;" and this is certainly *not* what Shakspeare meant him to say.   *   *   *

Pray, *pray*, dear Bob, don't follow Newman to the Pope's toe. He and his friends are now writing like downright Papists. I hear that something very much like celebration of the Mass is going on at Oxford. The *British Critic* is said to be under Mr. Newman's special superintendence; and one might certainly take it for an offspring of the Propaganda. In my conscience I am afraid that half England will return to the trammels it cost them so many sacrifices to shake off. The Maltese priests are chuckling at a rare rate, and glorying in their new allies. That ass Don —— told me Dr. Pusey would soon set us all right.

The February letters announce the birth of my Father's eleventh and last child, Sophia.

About this time my Father had the great satisfaction of hearing that his dear son Robert was to be ordained in Sydney by Bishop Broughton, who most kindly offered him the living of Penrith, in consequence of letters of recommendation from his friend Mr. Coleridge, of Eton; and on the 2nd of March, 1842, his Father thus writes to him on the occasion :—

No news could possibly be more welcome than what your letter brought me last night, telling me that you were at once to join, under the most advantageous circumstances, the profession for which you were always intended, and the only one for which you are, by nature and education, qualified.

Well done, my dear good Son! You are in a situation that
promises most admirably; and I trust you have as fair a prospect as you could desire of leading a truly happy life. My
hope is all the more sanguine, because I know you will do
your duty conscientiously. Your *business* will be to guide
your flock. If it takes up all your time, no matter. If it
allows you leisure for reading, that will be a most precious
relaxation, and will improve your power, perhaps, of being
useful.   *   *   *   *   *   *

I would not be in any *immediate* hurry to return to
England. Young as you are to have made such a beginning,
engaged as you are in a noble cause, with a magnificent field
before you, I would not quit it hastily for everyday work,—
for the ordinary work in England that ordinary men can do.
You will have a numerous family to provide for; and by staying some years where you are, you will *then* return to England
without those most harassing cares that want of money for
education can't help creating. I shall be most anxious to
hear that your parsonage is in a *healthy* country, that you
have a comfortable and pretty dwelling, and some decent
neighbours. I remember knowing Sir —— in London, and
a great goose he was: I met him at dinner at Jervis's, the
barrister's. Your Grandfather and Uncle Vi were there.
Sir —— talked about the Antip *"odes"* (odes, like odes of
Horace); and Jervis called out, at a long table-full of guests,
in his sharp lawyer's voice, "Sir J——, an*ti*po-des, Sir
J——;" correcting the poor man as unceremoniously as
he would a schoolboy.   *   *   *   *

Try, dear Bob, not to feel anything like vanity about your
reading and preaching; but remember that you are a poor
feeble servant of God's, engaged in doing His work, and that
you *can* do it at the best but imperfectly. I am quite sure
you will preach good sermons; better if, when you have a
good many prepared and are not so much pressed for numbers,—better if you spend six days upon one than six hours.
South said one of his cost him a *fortnight*.   *   * As for
manner, your sermon should be so learned by heart, and so

spoken, as to sound like *talking* to your congregation; otherwise, there is a want of *reality*. If I were speaking to you, and wished very earnestly to persuade you of something, I should naturally use tones quite different from those that anybody uses in reading a paper. I could not write a sermon well without working myself up to think that I had the people actually before me, and was speaking to them.

If I wrote a sermon under those feelings, I should certainly call them up when I was preaching it, and so I would make the people listen as if they had to do with a man who really had something to say to them. I would make them at least curious to know what it was I had to say. This can only be done by feeling one's self. That I should so feel I am sure; for many a time when I have been writing a sentence intending to affect others, I have felt tears come into my own eyes —a sort of *nervous* feeling that I have, but one that I am quite sure would make me eloquent.

If a man reads a sermon like reading out of a book, all the advantage is totally lost. I might as well read the sermon myself. But if I listen to a man who says the right thing as an earnest man does say it, I feel now and then an accent strike upon one of my nerves, and go deep into my heart. *Love*, you know, is seated *there*, and not in the brains.

I have just received a note from Lady Louis, to whom I sent one to tell her of what had happened to you. She says, " I am in an ecstasy at the intelligence you give me of your Son ! It does seem to me the most beautiful illustration of the Divine declaration and promise contained in the fifty-fifth of Isaiah that could have been exhibited to those who have eyes to see and to admire the wonderful development of God's purposes in some of the most mysterious dispensations of his Providence." And what she says is quite true. You seemed to be going clean away from the road to the Church, and have been brought into it by circumstances that would have seemed the most unlikely to occur. * * *

Among others, I have had to write to the *widow* of my poor *Brother*. He died at Jamaica last November, and has,

I fear, left her and her two or *three* children no provision. He had for many years a large income; but from the little I have heard I have scarcely any hope of hearing that he put by any store.   *   *   *   I have, of course, told her that I will help her if she needs my help.   *   *   * It is clearly my duty not to let this widow ꞓ and these orphans want; and you know, Bob, I should be a mere *fool* to attempt to better the condition of my own children, and to provide for them the means of *prospering* in the world, while I neglected such a claim as this. I know and am sure that it is much *better* for my *own boys* that I should pay to this claim all that is due, even though it should leave them without one penny. Isn't this sound economy? Not " Fiat justitia *ruat cœlum*," but fiat justitia; that so we and all belonging to us may be *guarded* from *ruin*, " Sicut in terrâ sicut in cœlo."   *   *   *   *   *   *

To me the same date, on hearing of the death of my seaborn child :—

Your loss is great. Poor little Harry's is a sad loss. But the child you mourn for is, we know and are sure, transferred to heaven. It was not granted to you in vain. You have been the means of adding one cherub more to the mansions of the happy; and when the close of your own lives is drawing near, you will think of the sweet little countenance that you loved to look upon, and will expect to see it smiling upon you again. And so it surely *will*.   *   *   *

How I long, my sweet Sally, to see some of your dear sketches! Every word you write is a word of precious interest to me. The sketching of *flowers* is very interesting where there are such multitudes of new ones; and though it is sad waste of time to finish them up as young ladies do, it would be very pleasant to sketch them slightly. I could give

---

ꞓ I have inserted this to show my Father's feeling towards those whom he had never seen. His assistance was not needed in this instance.

you a perfect idea of a plant with an hour's work. Captain
Basil Hall was struck with the banana-tree in our court-yard,
for it happened to be in very picturesque condition of semi-
decay, and he sketched it admirably in pencil with his camera
lucida, but didn't know how to colour it. For the sake of
showing him, I sketched it afterwards myself, and coloured
it. The outline took me one hour, and the colouring two;
and it was exceedingly pretty. He found my outline by eye
tally with his by the instrument, as if one had been an impression of the other. All the colour was put on at the first
wash, with no repetition whatever, so it looked very trans-
parent. Just try things of that sort in that way. Don't
attempt high finish; and you have no idea what beautiful
things coloured *sketches* may be of flowers or anything else.

* * * * * *

I am grieved to hear, dear Hanmer, of your worries and
fatigues. I know that you are not robust, and that you are
beyond example energetic; and so there is but too much fear
of your mind's being too active for your body. I know how
dauntless you are too, and therefore I am afraid of the bush-
rangers. You would fight half a dozen of them, and beat
them, too, with your one active arm and stout heart; but
there would be danger in the conflict, and for that I have no
fancy, and still less for danger that confers no honour. For
Heaven's sake get your police improved. * * *

I have been busily engaged for some time in revising my
Thucydides, and I shall improve it very much; but the publication of it must be at least deferred, for I have had a letter
from Moxon, the publisher, to whom Captain Basil Hall wrote
about it, telling me that educational books are not in his line,
and that Longman is the only man who, from his wide connection with schools, can make them answer. I may, when I
have finished it, propose it to Longman; but, at all events, I
will go on with it till it is quite finished, and it will be useful
to my Sons and Grandsons all the *more* for *not* being published; so my labour will not be lost, for it will enable Harry

by-and-by to make himself master of a very hard book with small labour.   *   *   *   *   *

To Bob he says, in March, about revising the Thucydides :—

I have done the first four speeches, and am pretty sure you will like them. As for the sense, I have only altered it a little here and there, particularly where you have suggested alteration ; but the language I have been able to make more idiomatical, more compressed, and more like original English. The speech in general can't read like an original English composition ; for it is essentially that of a man whose notion of making a speech was very different from a modern Englishman's. Two or three hundred years ago English orators were much more like Thucydides than they are now. Yet I have contrived to make the *separate* sentences real English and yet strictly literal, and consider myself, therefore, as having overcome a great difficulty.   *   *   *   *   *   *

You must always have in hand something classical : you can't *always* read divinity and write sermons. I wish you would take up some Greek book, and set to work upon it and make a thorough good translation, and notes for the construction, and whatever else may be necessary for entering thoroughly into the spirit of the author, and knowing accurately all that belongs to his subject. There are plenty of Greek books that *need* such help. Little has been done for Plato and Demosthenes : but there is a wide range out of which for you to choose.   *   *   *   *

Later in the month he says to him :—

By this time you are familiar with your new duties ; and I well know you are doing them *well*, Bob. You are *thinking* of your work. When you read the prayers, you *pray*. Most clergymen evidently do not ; they read with such tones as they could not possibly use if they were really praying. There is a mighty difference between repeating prayers and praying.

No one can read the prayers well, so as to engage the congregation to join fervently in them, without feeling what he reads. If a man *thinks about* his reading, and is ambitious of being *thought* by his congregation a good reader, it is not worth one straw. Let a man with the finest of all voices learn to read of Macready, and let him read the prayers without real feeling; and let another with a gruff voice trust wholly to his natural feeling for emphasis and cadence, and which will do most good? Just so in preaching. Supposing the composition equal, one man may read it in the usual way of a *good reader*, and send his congregation away in raptures *with him ;* and another will so say the same things, that some, at least, among his hearers will go home and *pray.* Dearest Bob, applause is very sweet; but you know they who seek it and earn it *have their reward.*   *   *   *   *

I had a long argument the other evening, at Lady Louis's, with an evangelical clergyman, who took it into his head to speak of bishops as partly useless appendages to the Church ; and asserted that reference to the Fathers was of small use on any subject, but that, as far as *their* opinion went, it was, regarding the real Presence, all in favour of the Romanists, for that he had lately " *looked over* " them himself and found it so! Looked over the Fathers !   *   *   I found he knew less of Cyprian than I did, and less, too, of Chrysostom, though I have only read some of his sermons on St. Matthew; very interesting, too, *historically.* But I have read, besides, Polycarp and Clement, and Hermas and Barnabas; and before I am much older I will read them again.

   *   *   *   *   *   *

In April he writes to his cousin Mary Repton, junior :—

My sweet little Cousin,—You have done a glorious deed for my dear Bob, and I do love you dearly for it. Of course I always knew that you were a warm-hearted and a very clever girl; so that I am not surprised at your exerting yourself in such a cause ; nor at your success in getting Coleridges

and bishops to do your bidding; but there is something wonderful in the suddenness and completeness of the success.
Bob's one letter that told me of the first step in this important matter, told me also of its complete arrangement; and a
blessed change of life for him it is! Don't you think he will
make a real good clergyman, Mary?   *   *   *

To Bob, in April :—

No more letters from Australia yet, but good Mary Repton
has sent me your correspondence with the Bishop, and very
great pleasure I have had in reading it. It was worth your
going to the world's end to make the friendship of such a
man.[d] I certainly never saw such an interest created by any
letter of introduction as the Bishop proves he felt.

    *   *   *   *   *   *

By way of a hint for making yourself heard. Somebody
told a Bishop Hinchliffe that they heard him better than anybody else, though he was far from having a loud voice; and
the Bishop said, "It is because I take care of the *consonants*."

    *   *   *   *   *   *

Speaking of Major Ewart, a connection of his, killed in
Affghanistan :—

Fighting is a bad trade, dear Bob; bad enough in a just
and necessary war; but who can persuade us of the justice
of this?   *   *   *   *   *

Dearest Lizzy, I think of you with very lively interest in
your new character of a country parson's wife. You have
made acquaintance with the poor people round you, and have
busied yourself about their children's schooling; and have
begun to set your garden in order, and your dairy and poultry-
yard and piggery. You will find time for all this, even with

---

[d] The late Bishop Broughton, of Sydney.

all the business your pretty Madeline gives you. I want to
hear a great deal more of my only granddaughter.

  *   *   *   *   *   *

On the 27th of April my Father writes in low spirits to me
and Bob, having just parted with Fanny, who returned to
England *viâ* Marseilles, where her husband met her. He
says :—

You can imagine that yesterday was a miserable day for
us. * * * I need not tell you how we miss our
sweet Fanny. Poor little Kitty was crying all day yesterday,
and is in no better spirits to-day. Fan was very fond of her,
and she of Fan, who says there never was a sweeter little
soul. She is now sitting opposite to me at the library table,
with a little Latin book in her hand; but she can't think
about the book, and I love her all the better for her distrac-
tion. *   *   *   *   *

I am very, very shaky to-day, and want a good cry, like a
baby. *   *   *   *   *

To me :—

Whatever you sketch, colour it from nature when you can.
All the great authorities agree, and my own experience has
amply proved it, that an hour's work from nature is more
improving and more interesting than a month's from memory
or imagination. Another useful observation I have made in
the long run is this: that it is generally waste of time to take
up a subject that does not offer a pleasing balance of *light
and shade.* Form and colour, or one or the other, have often
tempted me to make a sketch out of which I could never
make a good drawing, for want of light and shade ; and it is
absolutely necessary to put in the effect of light and shade
on the spot. *   *   *   *

To me in May, on his receiving my letter telling him of
the death of my child ; for he had only heard of it inciden-
tally before :—

At last that sad sad letter is come that describes to me the bitter suffering with which you have been afflicted. Deep indeed was the painful interest with which I read every word. Mamma and I have shared your pain, my precious child, and keenly have I felt the grief of being separated from you in your affliction and in all your hard trials. You are so very precious to me, dearest daughter, that indeed there is nothing but inevitable necessity that could prevent my being with you. I should not for myself care in what corner of the world it was. Your Bush would be an Eden to me, if we were all together in it, and all content. I have read many descriptions of mournful scenes, but never one so touching as yours.   *   *   *   *   *

Still it was a bitter grief, and was *intended* to be so. Religion was never intended to make us insensible. It teaches us to make a right use of our tribulation; but you know, dear, the *purpose* of tribulation would not be answered if we did not feel it. May your trials give you more and more strength, and more and more comfort in the best of all hopes! You have suffered a *present* loss; but you know that your beautiful babe was not given to you in vain. By God's mercy you will see its bright countenance again. It is looking upon you and loving you now, and *praying for you.* You know and are most sure that God has taken it to himself; and now, if you could, you would not wish it back again. You would bear your own bereavement for the sake of your child's unspeakably profitable change. And now, too, dearest, you are bearing your loss in the same spirit in which you would make a voluntary gift to Heaven, and therefore you will never be left without consolation; for all your recollections of what your sweet infant *was,* will be mingled with the blessed consciousness of what it now is, and will be for ever and ever. To you, by God's blessing, it owes all this, and when you think of it, my darling, I know it will mingle *joy* with your grief.   *   *   *   How I shall long to see the precious picture of your sweet children that

you have done for me!   *   *   *   When
you do landscapes, be sure and follow my plan of laying your
paper wet upon a glass. The man in Switzerland who told
me not to mount my paper, gave me a lesson worth all the
rest I ever had put together.   *   *   *   The
best blue for a sky is cobalt tempered with a very little lake
and a very little indigo. Rub a quantity of cobalt, and dilute
it enough, and tilt the plate so as to let it form a pool, and
then stand a few minutes, and pour it off into another plate,
but leaving behind all the sediment. In this way you will
have it beautifully clear. If your paper is thoroughly wet
except the very surface, which must be thoroughly dried by
dabbing it with a handkerchief, you may put on your colour
so strong that one single wash will complete the sky. If,
however, you find the blue not deep enough, you may add a
second or as many more washes as you please; but before
you put another wash, let the preceding one become perfectly
dry, and then wash it lightly with a large brush, not rubbing
it, but passing lightly over it, so as only to remove what
little colour will come off readily. Then dab that up and
dry the surface with your handkerchief, and immediately
put on another wash. But mind, the back of the paper must
be thoroughly wet all the time. It was precisely in this way
that I did Lizzy's picture of the palm-trees,[*] and in that
picture every light was left. Now you know, my chick, it
would have been quite impossible to have left the lights of all
those sharp leaves out of a clear deep blue sky, in any other
way, nor could they by any hand have been scratched out so
as to give the same sharpness and lightness. It would have
been quite difficult enough to leave even the illuminated
stem of the tree. I could not have done it.   *   *   *

To Bob, same date :—

A young clergyman has enough to do; but with all your
doings you have *two languages* to learn, which, if I were a

---

[*] The most perfect representation of Maltese *sunshine* that I ever saw.

young man and a clergyman, I would not rest till I had
mastered. German is necessary for you as a scholar, and
Hebrew as a divine. In two years you may do much in both,
only I should fear that neither could be comfortably managed
without a master. To set one a-going in some small degree,
such sort of help is necessary, but it is but little that a
scholarlike man needs of a master's help. Mezzofanti says
he can learn any language in a *fortnight*. You know I learnt
Portuguese, at Lisbon, almost wholly from books. I had a
master to give me the pronunciation, but he was of little
other use. As for Hebrew, it is certainly a disgrace in these
days for a clergyman not to know it. I don't mean for the
mass of worthy parsons who exercise the clerical calling, but
of whom little is expected; but that it would be a shameful
deficiency in a man who is beginning his career in these
stirring times, and has a fund of other scholarship, and a
student's habits. You know well, dear Bob, that a clergyman, who has brains in his head, may well store them if he
means to take an energetic part in the work that is going
on. You will be called upon continually to "give a reason"
when no little learning will enable you to give it satisfactorily to your own mind or the minds of your inquirers. I
should like to ask *Mr. Newman* why he is not a *Romanist*.
He may assert, this year, some small difference between his
opinions and the Pope's; but if he goes on at the rate he
has hitherto travelled, he may well intrench himself next
year at farthest within the walls of the Propaganda.

* * * * * *

The *only* peculiar doctrine of the Church of Rome that I
have not yet heard of Pusey's school's maintaining, is that of
the Pope's supremacy; but if they agree in all the rest, what
a trumpery motive for separation *that* would be.

* * * * * *

I do every day a bit of the revision of Thucydides, but it
is slow work, for the language, I find, will bear a good deal of
condensing; and then, after I have satisfied myself that I can
do no better, I compare it with Bloomfield's and the other

translations and commentaries. The result is, as far as I have gone, that though there are few passages in which my version differs from his, yet there are some in which, I am pretty sure, you will think me right and him wrong. I don't know how this happens; for he is a thorough scholar, and has evidently spared no pains, and shows in his notes that he has a large command of language. I am really surprised that such a man should not have made a more readable book of his translation; but as it is, however useful it may be to students, no general reader could get through it. I should have expected it to read as currently as Beloe's Herodotus, and still keep pretty close to the text. But I say, Bob, what reason could I give in a preface for publishing mine after Bloomfield's? He says of his performance that it was much wanted, because Hobbes was antiquated and incorrect, and that no other English translation existed but Smith's, which was too free and loose and faithless for students to use; but I could not with any decency tell the public that I meant to cut out Bloomfield.

I forgot to add, about the *German*, that I find reason every day to regret my want of it, and that, if I were younger, I would immediately set about learning it. They are, out-and-out, the best scholars. Their editions of Greek books make the Bloomfields and Arnolds look like pigmies. Their historians are the *Niebuhrs* and *Müllers*; and their poets Göthes, and others almost as great, of whom we can know little more than their names. Their histories we may read when Mrs. Austin chooses to translate them for us; but Müller is said to be the most eloquent of all historians, and when his German is made English, one may fancy that the loss is little less than Thucydides suffers when lowered down to Bloomfield.   *   *   *   *   *

To Bob, later in May:—

Live comfortably, but always economically. Begin at once to save *something*. You are likely to have no end of brats;

and there is terrible anxiety when there is no provision for one's wife and young ones in case of one's being suddenly taken away from them. There is no comfort in spending money like the comfort of reflecting that one is making a provision for one's dears.

Live frugally, that you may both accomplish this and give away largely too. My notion is, dear Bob, that people are too apt to be niggardly in their givings to the poor, and to justify the smallness of their doings in this way by pleading their large families. They forget that if money is necessary for their children, God's blessing is better still; so you and I will save what little we can by denying *ourselves* and not the poor.   *   *   *   *   *   *

Your tortoise is alive, and still growing, and may now, at the age of about eighteen years, have reached a full fourth of the size to which he means to grow. He has been heretofore remarkable for his love of solitude, but has lately taken to company, and strange company too; for the *cat* took a fancy to his snuggery between the trellis and the wall, sheltered by the thick old geranium in the corner of the garden on the right hand as you go up the steps, and there the old tortoise welcomed her and her four kittens, and they have gone on living together in queer harmony. The young cats jump upon him and nestle round him; and he and the old cat lie close together, with his head and neck poked out under her body, as if he liked the warmth of her fur. This is about as strange a fellowship as White's " Natural History of Selbourne " describes between a horse and a hen.

          *   *   *   *   *   *

To me, the same date :—

Your drawing, in a picturesque Alpine country such as I imagine Mount William to be, would be a glorious resource, and you would make yourself a real artist. Make studies of trees, such as I did at Blonay; only don't follow the plan I did of using only gray or sepia, but take colour at once, for it is really easier, and a million times more satisfactory. Don't choose any tree, or any other subject, for a study, without seeing in it a good effect of light and shade. Now, I must tell you another observation I have lately made. Shranz and I compared a drawing he had just made of the harbour, with my drawing of pretty nearly the same subject; and he agreed with me cordially that I had bestowed the chief pains on the right place, and he on the wrong. His buildings and shipping, forming the middle distance, were really well done, but did not keep their place; they came too forward; and the reason was, that he had comparatively neglected his *foreground*. He had made it up out of his own fancy, and there was no truth in it, and, consequently, no real *force*. This was the reason why it did not throw back the other parts of the picture. On the contrary, I had very carefully drawn and coloured my near rocks and boats from studies on the spot, and, therefore, they catch the eye at once, and, in fact, create the effect of the picture. Just so, if you sketch a tree, and mean to make a drawing from it, you must be sure to study carefully all that comes in between the tree and you, as far as your picture takes in, so that the foreground may be more forcible than the tree. Studies of near objects, such as picturesque combinations of weeds, rocks, water, animals, rustic figures, will, of course, help you to fill up a foreground. Remember what Mr. Coindet told you,—to sketch carefully all the *branches* of your trees. I don't know whether he added,—observe the beautiful variety of light and shade in the stem and branches.

* * * * * *

To Bob, June 18th :—

You are *setting out* in your profession with impressions which we may humbly hope are all right; and performing its important duties as they ought to be performed. Many clergymen, who have been for years asleep, have at length been awakened, and are doing *at last* what you have happily been impressed with the necessity of doing *at first*. Of course

I know that you owe the blessing of such a sense of your duties, under God's guidance, to Mr. Newman and his pious associates. In *your* case at least they have done good. So they have unquestionably in thousands of others. Only stop short when they would carry you too far.

That there *is* danger of being *fatally* misled, must be obvious to all who are not influenced by party spirit, a spirit which I heartily abhor. It is quite certain that Dr. Pusey, and I take for granted Mr. Newman also, deems it a heinous sin to address prayers to the Virgin. Dr. Pusey has said in terms that the prayers in the Roman ritual are all spoilt by this wretched perversion. But yet, if the reading of the Tracts[1] has created in some minds a temper to take all that Dr. Pusey and Mr. Newman would give them, and then just to take from the Pope what little he has to give that *they* have not already given; to *those* minds a million times more of harm than of good has been done; inasmuch as it is a far greater sin to pay to the creature the honour due to the Creator than it is to baptize at the end of the Church Service instead of the middle of it.

That there has been and is such a tendency in very many minds is quite obvious. And it is quite natural. The Tracts undoubtedly give us an impulse that *tends* towards Rome. To *that* I have not the least objection, because the width of our separation would not have been what it is except for human passions and infirmities. We *ought* in many things to be more like them than we are. But you know, Bob, the author of an impulse is not always able to control its consequences. The best billiard-player can't make a ball stop just where he pleases. That there is in the Tracts *danger* against which we have to guard, I should be blind if I did not see; and wise and pious as their authors are, I am shielded from the charge of presumption in entertaining this opinion, because I am bidden to entertain it by many of the *bishops*. I don't mean that the Tracts deserve all that has been said

---

[1] The "Tracts for the Times," published by Oxford divines at this time.

against them by the bishops. Some opinions have been imputed to them which they have distinctly disavowed.

But the good that these men may do is inestimable. Long before a "Tract" was written, I felt the great difference between the Roman Church and ours, in their making and our not making religion the daily business of men's lives. The day we sailed from Marseilles, fourteen years ago, in the good Bombard, the *Alessandro*, I went on board very early in the morning to see whether the captain found the wind fair to start. But there was not a man in the vessel. The wind *was* fair, and they meant to sail ; and therefore every soul had gone to church to pray for a safe voyage. And don't you remember that while we were at sea the old captain assembled at sunset all his crew, and never missed performing their vesper service, and with great apparent devotion too? Who ever saw such a thing in an English vessel? But now we may hope to see it.

You will do your parishioners immense good by bringing them to *daily* prayers in the church. Of course you will suit your hour of assembling them to the circumstances of the majority, so as to collect the greatest possible number ; and I know well you will make them feel that their meeting there is no matter of *form*. I wish with all my heart *we* could have daily prayers here. We have now on Saints' days, and Kitson is nothing backward in doing his part; but he could not assemble a daily congregation; for you know we are very few of us our own masters, and the sailors and soldiers and dockyardmen would not be *allowed* to go to church every day. They would not as things are *now* managed. But for this too we may hope to see a cure. The time may come when colonels and captains and Dockyard Commissioners will see it necessary to give their men time to meet every morning in the church. There would be no difficulty in the matter. There would still be time enough in the day to work for the Queen, even if half an hour were spared to the service of God. It will occur to the rulers of our affairs and the builders of our fleets to be just possible that

ten hours' work with God's blessing may have a better issue
than eleven hours' work without it. It never occurred to the
controllers of workmen that the *breakfast* hour was a loss of
time. But it has occurred to you, and so by this time your
farmers have learned, that the success of their labours
depends upon their own industry and the happy succession of
sunshine and showers; and that they can no more insure
their own strength to do any work at all, than they can the
falling of the rain. It depends upon my own industry, does
it? Then I will go to my field. This is what your farmer
used to say. It depends upon my own industry, does it?
Then I will go to *church*. This is what he will say.

My dear Bob, you must improve to the utmost perfection
you can the good *voice* nature has given you; and gain all
the skill too you can in using it. Your business is with the
hearts of your hearers, and sweet and appropriate tones tell
wonderfully. Just as the very reverse of melody and propriety was exhibited to us last Sunday by a good man, who
preached a good sermon and contrived to make it useless.
He had four notes in his voice, and bad ones too, and went
up and down every fourth word, demolishing of course all
meaning. When a man reads the prayers so, there can be
no reality in it. The most stupid of all jog-trot parsons
could not possibly use his habitual absurd tones if he were
really urging a petition in which his life or death depended.
It is very difficult for me to join with a man in a petition
when he shows me he is not in earnest; but he helps me very
effectually to join with him when by the earnest reality of his
prayer he makes me *feel* that we are praying for life to an
actually *present* God. Mouthing won't do it. Macready
can't teach it. Not one individual in one thousand has ever
learned it at all.

As for sermons, I am sure you have remarked that they
are generally much more calculated to tell us what our duties
are than to engage us to perform them. If I tell the preacher
I knew all he told me before, he will naturally answer, "O
yes, but we all need to be *reminded* of our duties." Quite

true; but we need very much more to be persuaded to act upon what we all know. In half-an-hour's sermon twenty-five minutes are commonly spent in telling us how we ought to live, and just the odd five minutes in an exhortation to live so. If I were a preacher, I would *reverse* the proportion. Very great skill is necessary to do anything of this sort with good effect; but no measure of skill can accomplish it if the *heart* is not the chief prompter.

You know, dear Bob, people have often given me things to write for them. Poor Sir Samuel Roberts wrote lately a memorial to the Admiralty, claiming what is called a "good-service pension." He dictated himself a chief part of it, and his wife put it together; but they were not satisfied with it, and I took it to do it for them. When I had done, I read it to their party, and after three or four sentences they all burst out a crying. Of course I meant it to touch not *their* nerves but *Lord Haddington's.* They said nobody in the world could have done it so well, and poor Lady Roberts hit the right nail on the head when she said it was because nobody else would so have *felt* for them,* and that without such regard as I had for my old friend, I couldn't have " thought of such words."

I dare say you are curious to know what I said, so I will write a bit of it; though, in truth, I see no great clever-ness in it. After an introductory sentence, I made him say, " He has many times addressed your Lordship's predecessors, but it was always for one single object; it was to beg for employment when danger was to be encountered, and honour gained, and he did not apply in vain. But those days are past, and very different must be his petition now. He has seen hard service, but he can see no more. All that remains of him is but a wreck, and he comes to your Lordship for the aid he needs." Then came a long list of his battles and imprisonments, and shipwreck, and it ended so: " If your memorialist attributes the ruin of his health to the labours

* There had been a friendship between them of thirty-three years.

and sufferings he has undergone in the public service, your
Lordship will not suspect that he can well be deceived.   It
is not age that has worn him out, for he has yet numbered
but fifty-four years.   The blow with which he has been
stricken came upon him suddenly; but he was laid open to
it by an habitual palpitation of the heart, which dates from
his shipwreck.   Of his many companions in that calamity
few are now alive.   His frame once seemed of iron; but one-
half of it is now no better than lifeless clay.   He gave his
strength to his country, and he now appeals through your
Lordship to his country to support the weak and shattered
remnant of him that yet survives."[h]   The pathos, of course,
consisted in bringing forward naturally, and in simple language, such as a seaman's vocabulary might supply, the
contrasted pictures of the warrior in his strength, and in
his palsy-stricken helplessness.   The idea might not have
occurred to me if I had been less able to put myself in the
poor man's place; and if it had, I might not have expressed
it so naturally.   I have filled a great piece of paper with a
small matter; but never mind.   All our little doings interest
each other.   We must always write to each other very frequently, and as we should talk.   Remember, dear Bob, that
I can't interest myself about your doings and your circumstances if I do not know them, and I can only know of
them what you tell me.   It is true that writing takes up
a certain quantity of time; but you need not grudge it to
me, for affection is not too abundant in this world and is
worth nourishing.   You can't do better than follow my plan
of writing at regular fortnight's intervals, you or dear Lizzy,
and let the letter be either long or short as your leisure may
serve.   *   *   *   What an odd coincidence it was that the cottage you first went to at Penrith
belonged to young Stilwell's brother-in-law.   The lady of

---

[h] Lady Roberts wrote to my Father afterwards that they said at the
Admiralty, "that so admirably worded and so clearly and yet concisely
drawn up a document never was presented before."

the cottage writes to her English relations thus (she little thought you or I would see what she was writing :—

"Our cottage is occupied by a new clergyman, just ordained, and appointed to Penrith and South Creek churches ; the parsonage, which is being built by subscription, not being ready for them to go into.   His name is Sconce, an Oxford man, whose attainments are spoken most highly of, and his views seem all based on an active anxiety for the performance of his duty.   He is young, and his wife I should think two or three years younger, with one piccaninny six months old.   Their advent to Penrith will be a source of much pleasure to us, when once they are comfortably settled in their parsonage."

But you are not to have all the praise to yourself, for our queer Governor has been giving *me* some.   I thought he had put me quite out of his good books, for he has taken no notice of us these two years, since the publication of Miège's book, that praised me at his expense and that of his myrmidons.   However he sat next Lady Louis at dinner the other day, and talked about me for a quarter of an hour, giving me credit for all sorts of high qualifications.   He says nobody ever comes to me for information without getting it, and a kind reception too.

The last *Galignani* says Mr. Tomlinson is appointed Bishop of Gibraltar.   Such, it seems, is to be his title, though Malta is to be his chief residence.   *   *   *   *
Mamma's dearest love as well as mine to you and Lizzy and Madgy.   May your present sweet prospect long remain unclouded.   God bless you, my dear good Boy.

To Lizzy, later in June, my Father writes :—

You will concern yourself with Bob's labours as my dear wife always does with mine, and help him, you know, when he wants a second hand.   You will both find the happiness that rewards successful labour.   It is a blessed thing, Liz, to be always thoroughly occupied.   Desultory reading for mere

amusement is not worth a straw.   One must have a pursuit
to which one is eager to give every available moment, and
such pursuits neither you nor your husband are likely to
want.   *   *   *   *   *

Can there be any situation in which a happy life is more
likely to be found than that of a real good country clergyman?   Especially, you know, Liz, if he happens to have taken
to himself a reasonable and pretty wife.   As for the beauty,
I should certainly bargain for that, just as Bob did; for you
are right in thinking that I enjoy pretty prospects of all sorts;
and painters, who have keen eyes, would naturally be expected
to pick out pretty partners.   Not all the painters do, however; for Bob's old acquaintance, ———, is going to marry an
olive-hued Maltese maiden that Mamma pronounces a downright *fright*.   The glimpse I had of her showed me chiefly a
span or so more of throat than the usual measure; but it was
convenient too, for the "piacere" of Maltese ladies is to
stretch their necks out of the street windows.

*   *   *   *   *   *   .

I have just been making a stir among the people here that
promises well, to engage them to subscribe in a body to the
fund for the endowment of our bishopric.   Many to whom I
spoke acknowledged that it was absolutely necessary to subscribe, and that there should be a public meeting for the
purpose.   But then the *Governor* should be consulted, for he
should preside at the meeting; and all the people most in
the habit of meeting him shrunk from the disagreeable business of suggesting to him to open his purse and interest himself
in getting others to open theirs.

But you know I don't mind cross faces; so I paid him a
visit, and after combating successfully an objection or two,
he agreed that it was all right, and that he would subscribe
and preside.   He asked me if I had any idea what people
meant to give—to regulate of course his own giving; and I
was glad to give him what information I could to enlarge his
ideas; so I told him Mr. Le Mesurier had already sent to the
fund in England £50, and meant now to add another £25,

and that I meant to give £30. If I had not told him this, he would probably have given £50, but now I think we may expect from him double that. The meeting is to be on the 1st July. I find the Governor is taking it up with spirit; for since I saw him he has suggggested that *ladies* should be invited to attend the meeting.

Wasn't it a saucy thing of me to go and ask him to give away his money at my suggestion, considering I have not been near him before these two years? However he was very civil. We mean to appoint a committee to collect what we can from the strangers who will come here in the autumn, and to write to all the communities of the Church of England on the shores of the Mediterranean, and consequently within the diocese, except Alexandria, which is in the diocese of Jerusalem.   *   *   *   *   *

To me, same date :—

I think of you continually, with anxious solicitude enough, and inexpressible tenderness. You know, my sweet, that I shall always think of you and love you—" dum memor ipse mei," as that sneak Æneas told poor Dido ; and the oftener you can tell me that you are well and happy—which includes the well-being of your dears, the more you will sweeten your dear Papa's down-hill life, and console him for such a dismal separation.   *   *   *   *   *

We are always going on precisely in the old way, only we have more schooling than ever, for Mia and Willy are now little Latinists ; and Willy is so surprisingly apt a learner that one must do all one can to help him. He has more power of application than I ever saw in a child, and more memory too. You know what a long job it is to teach a child the Catechism. He has actually learnt it by being sometimes in the room while the others are saying it. He [1] has gone

---

[1] About seven years old.

through quantities of Latin accidence, much in the way in which a man would. In short, he means to beat you all hollow.

To Fanny :—

I want you very much. I want to know every morning how you have slept, and whether you coughed much in the night. I want to hear Bobby call me Papa. I want you all to come and see me again this autumn. I did what I could to spoil you before, but I am sure now I didn't do half enough ; and if you will but come again, I will love you fifty times better. Only do try now. Wasn't the seton *dreadfully* painful ? Couldn't you give it me instead ? My poor Fan, I would wish it with all my heart, if wishing could but do any good, and I would pretty soon borrow your pain and bear it for you. There wouldn't be much magnanimity in it either ; for I am quite sure I should be better off when Mamma has pain if I had it myself, and so in your case equally.

To little Clement :—

You are a funny little sort of a monkey, not to tell us you were a *monitor* of your French class. Aunt has told us, and she says you would not, because it looked like *boasting*. Well, if you thought so that was a very good reason ; but you need not be prevented in future from telling us anything about yourself out of any such fear as *that* ; for I believe you have too much sense to be vain ; and there is no vanity in telling the truth to one's Papa and Mamma, *even* if it should happen to be in one's own favour. I always thought you would make a good Frenchman, because you made so famous a beginning that summer we spent in Switzerland.

*   *   *   *   *   *

CHAPTER X.

[1842.]

MEETING ABOUT THE BISHOP'S FUND—PALMER'S TREATISE ON "THE CHURCH"
—FASTING—NICKNAME "PUSEYITE"—THE CHURCH—ANTICHRIST—NEW-
MAN—SON TAKING PUPILS—WRITING LATIN FOR HIS CHILDREN—MALTESE
DOGS—LAY BAPTISM—WRITERS OF THE "TRACTS FOR THE TIMES"—
ROMANISTS AND PROTESTANTS—MICHAEL TOWEL—CONTROVERSY—BOSSUET
AND FENELON—LAY BAPTISM—PLAUTUS—FANNY—MUSHROOMS—CAUTION
ABOUT MONEY MATTERS—QUOTATION FROM MELANCTHON, ETC.—ZUINGLIUS'S
OPINION OF SENECA—SOCRATES—HOOKER—CATHOLIC ANTIQUITY—PRIVATE
JUDGMENT—WEARINESS OF MALTA—TRACT NINETY—DR. PUSEY, ETC.—
DAILY SERVICE—BISHOP OF GIBRALTAR.

BEFORE going on with the extracts from my dear Father's
letters, I must pause to speak of their beautiful regularity.
As I go on from year to year, and from month to month, I
find the four letters to his four absent children, generally all
written on the packet days about the 15th and 25th of each
month. This is the more remarkable, as two out of these
four letters were sent each fortnight to Australia; and, irregular as was the communication with Australia ten years ago,
I have not found one Australian letter missing.

He writes to Bob, the 15th of July, 1842 :—

The attempt I told you I was making to get up a subscription to our Bishop's fund, has succeeded well. The meeting
took place, and about £600 was subscribed.* £200 was con-
tributed by the Governor; £200 by Mr. Frere; and the other
£200 among the rest of us.   *   *   *   *

---

* In the manuscript book which I have before mentioned, of my brother's,
he here makes the following remark :—

" All my Father's doing, though, like a hundred other great and good acts
of his, it seems to have been quite hidden from the sight of men. God be
praised, he *hath* his reward."

Let the occasion, he writes, be what it may, people are apt to give no more than they can spare without making any *sacrifice*. Of course I could not give £30 without making a serious sacrifice, for it would pay for one of the boys at the Naval School for a twelvemonth; but then I ought to feel quite sure that if I give the money from a true sense of duty, it is quite impossible for my boys to be the poorer for it. No one can feel a more intense anxiety than I do to secure the means of educating my many young ones; therefore I will save all I can for that purpose conscientiously; but I must not weigh God's blessing against consols.   *   *   *

You know the seven sages and their sayings. *When* I am a sage, mine will be, "*Make your wants known.*" Many and many a want I have had supplied by making it known where its supply seemed hopeless. It is astonishing how often and strangely I have found help by using this maxim. Now all this, Bob, is apropos to almost nothing; for it was not at all surprising that Cleugh should have *Palmer on the Church.* Yet I asked him without the least in the world thinking it likely. However, he had it, and had just finished the first volume, and has lent it me; and it interested me so much that I read half the volume the first day, and would have finished it the second but for the packet. I have nearly finished it. Though I have read rapidly, it has not been the less profitably; for the thoughts are expressed so clearly, that the meaning of every sentence is visible at a glance. When this is the case, the faster one reads the better, for the easier it so is to preserve the chain of argument and obtain a general view of the whole subject. Of course one must afterwards examine it again in detail. A book once read is not read, for any useful purpose, at all. If I *could*, I would tell you what I think of the book; but the subject is full of such complicated difficulties, that I am bewildered in attempting to estimate its arguments. That it is calculated to do great good is quite certain. No honest member of our Church can read it without a certain degree of comfort in finding how much there is to justify our position. If I had been thinking of joining the congregation of the reverend and eloquent Mr. H——, of the Dissenting chapel at Valetta, I think this book would have deterred me: so it will furnish you with arguments to keep your own flock within your fold. I suppose it would have small effect in bringing back any who have already strayed, and especially any that have been educated in dissent, for early opinions on religious subjects stick fast; and the professors of all sorts of opinions are furnished with arguments on which they confidently rely. But, Bob, I am not quite sure that Mr. Palmer has furnished me with as good defensive arms against the Romanists as offensive arms against the Dissenters. Whether it is the fault of my understanding, or his argument, I can't yet tell; but I will see more into it, and of course I shall get more light as I read the rest of the book. At present I have an impression—or not so much as that, a *notion*, rather—that *in some of his opinions he is influenced by the notion that it is necessary to hold them for the justification of the British churches.* These are words of his own (applied, of course, to others), which you may see at the end of page 397.

I find, as yet, a difficulty in satisfying myself out of this book that the English Church forms a *part* of the one, holy, *visible*, Catholic Church, inasmuch as I do not find it in *communion* with ANY other part of that Church. As for the American Church, it is in fact one of the British Churches. The only *other* parts of *the* Church are the Roman and the Greek. The Roman Church did in fact excommunicate us. The Greek was severed from the Roman while we ourselves were Roman, and therefore was severed from us; and since our separation from the Romans we have not yet united with the Greeks.

It is true enough that the Reformers were not excommunicated by the *whole* Catholic Church (p. 389), for of course the Greeks had no part in *excommunicating* people who had long ceased to be *in* their communion; but I am afraid it is not candid to say that the excommunication was only received and acted upon by *some* of the Western Bishops,

who were " apparently " under the influence of the Pontiff
and Emperor.   The truth is, that *all* the Western Bishops
except the excommunicated were under the *influence* of the
Pontiff, just as every bishop in all Roman Catholic countries
is now.   The authority of the " Synod " of Trent will, I find,
be discussed more at large in the other volume.   But quite
certainly every Romanist would laugh at me if I told him
that the Council of Trent was not equal in authority to the
ancient œcumenical councils.   It appears to me that if the
absence of the Greek Bishops can be pleaded in bar of the
jurisdiction of the Western Church, we must deny both to
the Roman Church and to our own Church the possession of
any power at all of expelling heresy from the bosom of
either.

Again, how can Mr. Palmer, or any one else, deny and
attempt to prove, that whatever may be the measure of vice
in the Roman Church, the blind obedience professed by its
members and its well-marshalled authority are far better
preservatives against dissent and schism than our Church
possesses.   True enough they have their Jansenism and their
wide-spreading infidelity ; but the infidelity of Protestant
Germany is nearly equal to that of Romanist France ; and
Jansenism is *very* much less apparent in any Roman Catholic
country than dissent is in England.   Here in Malta our
1,500 English comprise a dozen various sects ; but the
120,000 Maltese are all true servants of the Pope.

The Romanists have a mighty hold over their people, and
are strong enough to rob us, as they are now robbing us by
thousands, of ours.   How is it possible not to confess to one's
own heart that their system has in this respect the advantage
of ours?   Hitherto we have not coped with them successfully in preventing schism ; but I believe it is not because
our religion is less good in itself, but because our clergy have
been asleep, and our Government more vigilant to injure the
Church than aid it.   Build more churches, ordain more
clergymen, and *you clergymen* fulfil all your duties faithfully
and zealously, and make your hearers feel they are worship-

ping in their money-bags a god without a heaven, and then they won't forsake you either for the Pope or Mr. Wesley.

That there must be immense difficulty in discussing the subject of " the Church," is shown by the total disagreement there is among our theologians in treating it. For example, Palmer says it would be vain to attempt to trace the visible Church in the Albigenses, Waldenses, &c.; whereas Faber writes a history of those people expressly to prove that in them the perpetuity of the sincere Church of Christ has, agreeably to the promises, been maintained. Does not this look as if men *took up* opinions merely because they seemed necessary for the conducting of their argument? I am quite persuaded that to talk of the Albigenses as the sole representatives, for a time, of the true Church, is absurd.

At page 253 I find something that shocks my candour; for it is an undeniable fact that Papists do not and cannot admit that there is salvation in our Church, and we do admit that there is in theirs. *Heber* said he had no higher wish than to spend his eternity with Fénélon, Pascal, and Borromeo. *He* does *not* doubt their salvation; whereas they were *bound* to doubt that of the holiest among us. To profess, because it seems expedient to the conducting of an argument, an opinion that one does not sincerely entertain, is not only unjust in itself, but as fatal to the argument as the inserting of a rotten link in a chain cable would be to the storm-beaten ship that depended upon it.   *   *   *

To me, in July :—

The best advantage I should derive from promotion would be that after a very few years I might retire with a better pension. However, I never have fidgeted about such things, and I now think less about them than ever.

     *   *   *   *   *   *

But oh, my dear dear Sally, I never made half enough of you, I am sure I didn't; and yet from first to last I don't think any Papa in this world ever doted upon his daughter as I did upon you. Let us remember past times, my chick, and look forward, and pray for each other, that we may love each other in Paradise.   *   *   *   *   *

I have had another letter from sweet Mrs. Napier,[b] desiring me to get Charles Edwards sent home.   *   *   *

To Bob, in August :—

In all your sentiments I agree entirely. I have not yet discovered that there is any difference at all between your theology and mine; and of course this is a very great satisfaction to me. Of the duty of fasting I have not the smallest doubt. In short, I had satisfied myself very many years ago that in all our practice, hatred of the Pope was too plainly mingled with the love of God.   *   *   *   I certainly shan't call you a Puseyite. Nobody has less taste for nick-names than I have, and I have a thorough respect for Dr. Pusey. He writes like an honest man and a gentleman. I am grievously afraid that he and his companions will, unintentionally, send crowds to Rome, but I am not afraid of his sending *you* there.

To Bob, later in August :—

I am afraid it will not be possible for me to find time to draw up anything like a complete exposition of my own opinions on the subject of your interesting argument—*the Church*. You have taken it from Palmer; and as I agreed with Palmer in his general view, so I agree with you in yours. Yet I find here and there a difficulty. There must, of course, be enormous difficulty in bringing one's mind to adopt unreservedly, and retain steadfastly, *any*body's opinions on this most important subject; because every book one reads has some course of reasoning or some conclusion different from those one has before been disposed to accept; and so we poor laymen have to decide between the Doctors.

---

[b] Lady William Napier, who died early in 1860.

In the *main* points I have little doubt. That the Church of England is a true Church, I feel thoroughly satisfied; and that I could not separate myself from her communion without committing grievous sin. I am equally satisfied that the Roman Church is a true Church, with all her corruptions; and I *always have* detested the Protestant fashion of calling her Antichrist. If Rome must be the Devil's throne, I can much more readily take Nero for the Devil than poor old Gregory, whom you and I saw blessing the tens of thousands that filled the wide area in front of St. Peter's. So must the Greek Church be considered clearly a *true* Church. And I can hardly conceive that there are any others. The Dissenters, who have voluntarily separated themselves from us, I can only conceive to be *out* of the Church altogether.

But, Bob, you and Mr. Palmer say a Church can only be a Church, *provided* it has neither separated itself from the universal Church by its own act, nor been cast off by excommunication. I have no wish to controvert your proposition; but yet I can't heartily acquiesce in it. Until I read Mr. Palmer's book I never saw this; and my notion was that we had *both* separated ourselves voluntarily from the universal Church, and *also* been excommunicated by it; and yet I felt quite sure that we were a true Church. I can't help still suspecting that we must in candour allow that we really did separate ourselves voluntarily from the universal Church; because, as members of the Western Church, we concurred in excommunicating the Greeks. *They* were already gone, therefore; and from *that* Church of which we subsequently remained part and parcel, we seem *voluntarily* to have separated ourselves, notwithstanding all the professions of the original reformers of their desire to remain in it: for the fact is, that their renunciation of the Roman errors made it *impossible* for them to continue in communion with Rome. We *voluntarily* adopted a pure religion instead of an impure one. By refusing any longer to address our prayers to the Virgin and images, we virtually refused to pray any longer with men whose prayers were so misdirected. We perpetrated what

must have been, in the Pope's eyes, a rebellion against his
just *authority*, and then had the impudence to offer him our
society on equal terms.

Again, we of the English Church can join in public worship
with French Protestants at Marseilles, or Swiss Protestants
at Montreux; but can we—do any of us anywhere—join in
public worship with Romanists?

Then for the other point of our excommunication; when it
is said that we were not excommunicated by the *universal*
Church, because the *Greeks* were not part of the Council, nor
we part of it, the objection to this argument seems to be,
that the Greeks could not be there, because they had been
excommunicated already; and as for ourselves, we were
already in open rebellion, and were *upon our trial;* so that
we could hardly have expected to be allowed to sit there as
judges. Again, while we were yet members of the Roman
communion, of course we considered the Roman Church (the
Church to which we ourselves belonged) *the* Church, *the Catholic
Church*, and we *did not* consider the Greek Church as any
part of the Catholic Church. We ourselves had acquiesced
in its excommunication. How, then, could we have said to
the Council of Trent,—You are not an œcumenical council,
because the Greeks are not among you? In communion
with the Greek Church we have not been since its excommunication by us and our then associates, the Romanists. With
the Greeks we had nothing to do. We were members of the
Roman Church, and by the Roman Church we were excommunicated. We had up to that time deemed ourselves, with
the Romanists, members of *the* Church; and by *the* Church,
therefore, we were excommunicated. I can't clearly see why
the Church to which we then belonged had not a right to excommunicate its rebellious members, just as we have now
to excommunicate *our* rebellious members.

I should be heartily glad to convince myself of the soundness of Mr. Palmer's argument, or, rather, of the correct
statement of his facts; because it would at once show, what
I believe to be truth, that the Church of England is part of

the true Church, and that Muggletonians are not. But the fact is that this, like many other arguments brought forward in a similar spirit, has too much the appearance of having been devised for *expediency*. It would be exceedingly convenient to us to prove the point; and *therefore*, perhaps, I am the more jealous in examining the proof. What I believe, I must believe *honestly*. I do satisfy myself that we belong to a true Church, whether we did or did not voluntarily forsake the Roman communion, or whether we were or were not excommunicated by competent authority. For my argument is, that fatal errors had arisen in the Church to which we belonged; that it was our imperative duty to renounce those errors; and that as the Romanists would not renounce them, the fault was not ours, but theirs; that they forsook *us*, in short, not we *them*. Then as for their excommunication of us; however their power of excommunicating, generally, may be denied or defended, I am quite sure that in exercising that power against us they acted *unjustly*. Nor is this at all surprising; for if they persisted in worshipping false gods, it was quite natural for them to curse those who worshipped the true. You see, then, that to make Mr. Palmer's proposition suit my convictions it would stand thus: that we of the Church of England *are separated* from the universal Church because we renounced errors which the universal Church would not renounce; and that if we have been excommunicated, it has been by an unjust sentence.

Of course I am aware that if I can say nothing better than this, I am on no vantage-ground with the Muggletonians; for *they* can say as much. It is true I should know they were talking great nonsense; but so it is equally true that the Pope thinks *we* are talking nonsense.

The plain fact, however, is, that the English Church is in absolute solitude. She is in communion with no other; and the cause apparently is that she alone has embraced *the truth*. Other Churches have found *new ways*, and persisted in them. We found we were going wrong, and returned to the *old way*. We profess that we desire to follow strictly the path in which our first Fathers in the Church walked; and we refer to the guide-books of antiquity to prove that we are following it. The Romanists, *even they*, can't do as much (though we have been accustomed to hear of their reverence for the Fathers, and our contempt of them), and in point of fact they do not attempt it. They are continually obliged to defend themselves by referring to the infallibility of their Church; for how otherwise can they justify the refusal of the cup to the laity, and the addressing of prayers to the Virgin?

Still less can the Muggletonians profess to be governed by reference to antiquity; and therefore I take for granted *they* shelter themselves under the infallibility of Mr. Muggleton; and so the Southcotians under that of Mrs. Southcote.

You see, Bob, I have not the least *wish* to disprove the claims of our Church; but, on the contrary, as zealous a desire to uphold them as you or Mr. Palmer; and if I point out anything that seems weak in your argument, it is not to direct you to a different conclusion, but to invite you to see whether you can make the argument stronger.

Again, I don't find that I can derive much satisfaction from the argument on which you and Mr. Palmer dwell—of the existence of Christianity in England before the arrival of Pope Gregory's missionaries; for though there probably were Christians in England before Gregory's days, and when his mission arrived; and though in Cornwall and Wales, perhaps, they may have been something like an organized Christian community, yet of that fact there can't well be any very decisive evidence; and whether there be or not, yet undoubtedly the Christianity that soon afterwards spread over the whole country was the Christianity not of Cornwall but of Rome. It can't in fairness be denied that England owed its Christianity *mainly* to the preaching of Augustine and his companions; and it must be granted that their influence is likely to have been felt all over the country. The learning they carried with them, and their civilization, must have given them an authority such as the poor British Christians of Cornwall could not have possessed. If, therefore, there were any differences between the Cornish *bishops*, if they had any, and Augustine, it must be taken for granted that Augustine soon settled them all his own way. If the fact were, and were sufficiently authenticated, that Augustine went to a country already *mainly* Christian ; if, for example, Canterbury had been already before his time a bishop's see, *that* would be of immense value to your argument. But the case is very different when we are forced to acknowledge that the *Saxons* at all events were pagans, and can't help doubting whether there was much Christianity even in the corner of the land that remained to its poor aboriginal inhabitants. I am afraid, therefore, we can't improve our case by proving that in some part of the island of Britain there were some Christians.

But, on the other hand, I should think our case a perfectly good one without any such argument. The truth is, that from the time of Augustine till that of Luther we were Roman. Was it or was it not our duty, when once our eyes were opened to the errors into which we and Rome had together fallen, to *renounce* those errors? Of course, we were bound to renounce them. They would not ; and therefore there was of necessity an end of our communion. Even Mr. Newman, who is no ultra Protestant, calls the Roman worship of the Virgin *idolatrous :* can any collateral arguments be necessary to prove that we were justified in ceasing to be *idolaters ?* He says, moreover, that the Church of Rome is " crafty, obstinate, wilful, malicious, cruel, unnatural as madmen are ; or rather she may be said to resemble a demoniac." Thinking this of Rome, how could we remain in communion with her?

But besides all this, and setting aside the historical question, whether we did or did not voluntarily separate from her, or whether we were or were not excommunicated by the Church, the true question for us at this day to decide seems to be whether we, the English Church of the present day, are *now* justified in *continuing* separate from the Church of Rome? If what our reforming predecessors did was wrong, we are bound to *repair* the wrong.

Now certainly, in considering this question, I should not care one straw whether there were or were not Christians in England before the days of Gregory and Augustine; nor should I stop to inquire whether the first Reformers quitted the Roman communion of their own accord, nor whether the Council that excommunicated them was or was not an œcumenical council! I should at once decide that I could not hold communion with an idolatrous church. Let the proceedings that created the separation be what they might, the separation itself was inevitable, and remain it must until they renounce, or we resume, the worship of the Virgin, of stocks and stones, and tobacco-stoppers. Perhaps you have forgotten the little image in the Cathedral at Lisbon, called Our Lady de la Pena (of the Rock), which was about the size of my little finger, and was shrewdly suspected to have been originally used for stopping a pipe. She had performed, in the eighteen months of her reign, when we saw her, just twenty thousand miracles. She was *invented* to serve a political purpose. The politicians devised the manœuvre, and the Cardinal, Patriarch, Archbishops, and Bishops connived at and acted in the farce. What sort of communion could there be between people who think as Mr. Newman does, or as you and I do, and the congregation of that church at Rome where you and I saw the Pope's certificate of the Virgin's *picture* in that church having *spoken* to his predecessor Gregory the Great? Of course, all the people who worship there are bound to believe that the picture can *hear* as well as speak; and without doubt, therefore, they *pray* to the *picture*.

You see, dear Bob, I have put down all this as it occurred to me, without much method; but you will make out my meaning, and will, I know, be interested in seeing how I occupy myself with the pursuits in which you are engaged.

Most of this was written while three of the young ones were round me, and seldom letting two minutes pass without a question about the genitive case of *ego*, or the perfect tense of *cano*, and other similar lore.

Have you got, or have you read, Newman's lectures on the

prophetical office of the Church, viewed relatively to Romanism
and popular Protestantism? I have read it through with deep
interest and unmixed satisfaction; and I shall quickly finish
it, and read it a second time. Clough has not yet given me
the second volume of Palmer. Putting down my letter to
read some of Newman before I go to bed, I find (p. 406)
this, which seems to justify my argument that it is quite
immaterial what sort of Council it was that excommunicated
us :—"*Who can* excommunicate those who have ever held to
that creed, and that succession, and those ordinances which
Apostles bequeathed them?"   *   *   *

Speaking to Bob about taking pupils, he says :—

If I were you, I would stick to the £150 a year, and not
abate anything, because the Sydney people will think your
Greek the better for being dear, and you will have boys of a
better class.

But, Bob, another important reason why it would be good
to take pupils is, that your work with them would greatly improve your own scholarship. You could not at college go back
to the grammar drudgery you were allowed to shirk at school,
neither could I sit down in solitude to re-learn Propria quæ
maribus for my own use; but scrap by scrap it gets into my
own head while I am hammering it into Bettoo's and Kitty's :
and so all the niceties of elementary scholarship would become familiar to you in beginning again a, b, c, with your
"young pickpockets." You had better *read* this sentence to
your class!

To me, in September :—

They[c] read only out of my manuscript books. I have
written about *five hundred pages* for them, and go on continually adding. Well I may, for Herbert reads ten pages
a day. I skim all sorts of books for the sake of picking out

---

[c] His little children.

odds and ends that suit them. All sorts of subjects, from all sorts of authors, come higgledy-piggledy : multitudes of short sentences with only a nominative case, verb, and accusative ; then rather a long story ; so that my books contain something of the histories of Socrates and Adonis, King Priam, Tom Thumb and Apelles, Narcissus, Maltese puppy-dogs, Diogenes, Julius Cæsar, and Jupiter. In short, I take down, as it happens, Plautus, Terence, Virgil, Horace, Lucan, Tibullus, Cicero, Justin, Sallust, Seneca, Suetonius, Livy, anything that comes ; and I am quite sure no Selectæ ever answered their purpose as well. The common Selectæ, and all other similar books, contain in the beginning half a dozen easy pages, and then they get full of dull difficulties. No purveyor for little children has ever thought of providing a *quantity* of *easy* Latin. Their object generally is to *exemplify rules*, and so pass on from one rule quickly to another. Then they talk about idiomatical niceties and peculiarities ; and all the while the poor boy has put into his memory no vocabulary. But in my way Bettoo has learned the English of, and got familiar with, hundreds and hundreds of Latin words ; and he has written such large quantities of Latin into English, and English into Latin, that he is getting familiar with grammatical construction by mere habit, just as, in talking Italian, he would naturally make adjectives and substantives agree. He would never say in Italian, buono donna ; and would be just as sure not to say in Latin, bonus puella.

*   *   *   *   *   *

Now, about the Maltese dogs. You know they were very famous of old. They are mentioned twice in Ælian's " History of the Nature of Animals," which I have never seen. But in Ælian's " Varieties of History," he tell us Epaminondas had one. Phædrus mentions them in *two* fables ; one about the man and the dolphin, and the other about the ass that wanted to sit as the little dog did in his master's lap. That little dog (though the English version does not tell us so) was a Maltese. Alciphron speaks of one accidentally killed by being caught in a trap set for a fox ; and now I have just seen in *Plutarch* this : " What a fool a man must be to fret because he can't combine the qualities of a lion ranging the forest, and a Maltese puppy dog nursed in a widow's lap." Isn't it very remarkable that such a trumpery little wretch should trace back his history 2,300 years in the writings of all those old Grecians?

To Bob, later in September :—

On the 27th of last month came three of your letters together.   *   *   *   I have read all these with very lively interest and unmixed pleasure; for, of course, I delight in seeing how thoroughly you are disposed to do your important duties, and, of course too, I find great comfort in seeing how perfectly all your opinions, as far as you have expressed them, coincide with my own. I am only sorry that I am so little able to help you by my own reading in the solution of your doubts. The question that chiefly engaged you, of the efficacy of lay baptism, and the propriety, or otherwise, of your rebaptizing children who had been baptized by Dissenters, and were brought to you to be received into the Church, seems to be quite as difficult as any one that could be proposed. You know, a clergyman in England, some short time ago, refused to bury a person who had not been baptized by a minister of the Church, and an action was brought against him, and a verdict given against him, in accordance with the judge's charge. A hard case this, Bob, that *lay judges* should have power to decide such questions, and that *the Church* should have *no power*. However, I find the case has been referred to by the Bishop of Exeter, in a late Charge of his; and the paper containing it having been sent to me, I am glad to forward it to you ; the more so as the Bishop of Exeter is considered, I believe, one of the ablest and most orthodox on the bench, and the Charge contains, besides, many remarks on the writings of your Oxford friends. You will see that it condemns the 90th Tract in the strongest language that can be used. I

have not seen the Tract; but from what I have heard of it,
I have no doubt that, greatly as I admire most of what I have
read of Mr. Newman's works (not all), I should dislike it as
much as the Bishop does. His book on Romanism and
Popular Protestantism is one of the most satisfactory I ever
read; but, here and there, there are expressions in it quite
unlike the gentle spirit one would suppose from most of
his writings to belong to him. I am much less acquainted
with the writings of Pusey; but from the little I have read
of his, I should feel pretty sure *he* would not use the rude
language I find, applied to the Romanists, in page 101 of his
book. It would have been perfectly easy for Mr. Newman to
give us quite as effectual a warning against their arts, without
calling them names. He can't *mean* what he says, in such
words as these :—

"Till God vouchsafe to restore her, we must *treat her* as if
she were that *Evil One* which governs her;" that is to say,
we must *hate* the Roman Church. Of course, we are bound
to hate *sin*, and therefore to hate its author the Devil; and if
we are to treat Rome as we do Pandemonium, what becomes
of Palmer's view of *the Church*, a *part* of which he recognizes
at *Rome?* A pretty portion of *the Church!* Why, we are,
according to Mr. Newman, to regard Rome as downright
Antichrist—as the visible church of Satan. How then can it
be any *part* of *God's* Church? and how can there be in it
"some things absolutely good," as Mr. Newman says in the
next page there are?

By the bye, one would not have thought that the author
of such a book should have been accused of *meaning* to make
us Papists. Of course he can have no such views; though it
is quite clear that some of his writings have actually sent
many to his *Pandemonium*. He did not mean it, but he has
done it.

Whether it was possible or not to take away from people
those errors which made their distance from Rome greater
than it ought to have been, and not to give them at the same
time a notion that they might go nearer and nearer still, till

at last they were hooked in by the Devil's claw,—this is a question there would be small profit in discussing. But it *is* profitable for me, and still more for you, who have to teach others, to reflect carefully upon the use we make of the light these good and able men have given us; and to think for *ourselves* while we are listening to them.

The good they have done is to the *wise*, the evil to the weak and indiscreet. But you know, Bob, there are nine men out of ten without brains; and then out of ten men *with* brains, at least nine are without an education to fit them for forming any judgment on such subjects; and even among the comparative few who have both brains and education, there are many who have flighty fancies, and go off like perverse rockets, any way but the right. It follows from such an argument as this, that the recipients of the evil are likely to be the more numerous. How that may be in fact I can't tell; but *your* business will be with *Penrith*, and I have sanguine hope that *there* the good may be unmixed.

But it is a *most* difficult task you have to perform; for *this* I know, that among the ignorant Papists *here* you could attempt no reform without a much greater probability of turning them into infidels than sober Christians. *Their* vice is *redundancy*; but strip them of their outer rags, and they will persuade themselves that their good doublet is equally useless. Our vice is nakedness; but once persuade us to put on the doublet, and we may easily take a fancy to the frippery also.

As for the Romanists, I hope, dear Bob, there may be none of them at all in your parish. If there are, of course you will be obliged to keep your people on their guard against them, for they are *always* at work. They are a thousand times more anxious to convert us than we them. This is natural. It is no concern for our souls that prompts them: they hate us with all their souls, because we quitted them, and remain apart from them as their *accusers*. They had rather convert one Protestant than ten Turks, because over us they gain a *triumph*. When we go back to them, we

humble ourselves before them, and their pride is soothed by
our confession of our folly;—we have maintained a controversy in which at last we confess ourselves beaten. This
sentiment is continually expressing itself in my hearing.
Our half-witted old drunkard of a warder, Michael Towel,
died a year ago. He had been, ever since I had known him,
a Methodist. The preacher at his chapel for some time was
a negro fifer of one of the regiments, and he and Michael
were a pretty equal pair of theologians. But poor Michael
was seldom sober enough latterly to go to church; so some
worthy Capuchins and Dominicans found their way to him a
day or two before he died, and made of him a right good
Catholic. It served their purpose beautifully; for they got up
by subscription a grand funeral procession for him, and
chanted their triumph all round the town.

"You see we are right and you are wrong," the triumph
says; "for here is your own Michael to witness against you;
and of all the English in Malta, poor though he was, there
was no one wiser or soberer than Michael Towel."

They tell us just in this way, and about as truly, that
among the English divines none have been more distinguished than Spencer and Sibthorpe. They *bray* and *crow*
about these men. But the truth is, the Spencers are all
worthy men, but all remarkable for the want of any superior
talent; and as for Sibthorpe, he was appointed preacher at
St. John's, Bedford Row, some years ago, and his congregation found him so dull that they contrived to get rid of him.
They are now crying up Froude as the "forte teologo" of
his day, since Dr. Wiseman has convinced them that, if he had
lived another year, he would have renounced his few remaining errors. Newman was perpetually in their mouths, and
they acknowledged him to be a writer whose works we might
profitably study; but now they hear, through their active
prompter Dr. Wiseman, what Newman says of them, they
are satisfied that Newman has no talent whatever.

I can't help now and then engaging in argument with
them, for they attack me; and when they do, I make a point

of never standing on the defensive. It requires no great
dexterity, with such assailants as mine, to parry a thrust or
two; and then I get rid of their chuckling by referring to
their indulgences and idolatries. That there are idolatrous
practices going on under our own eyes here perpetually,
they cannot deny. They call them *abuses;* but they are
abuses that all their bishops and their popes tolerate and
encourage.

But I hope you are free from any necessity for engaging in
any such discussions, for they are wholly unprofitable and un-
desirable. No Romanist ever begins an argument with me for
any other purpose than for that of crowing over me. Of
course, I can't stand that. It would not be right for my
cause that I should. But the feeling between two arguers
in such a case is precisely that of a pair of mere *fencers.* No
good is ever got by it; and the merits of either cause have
nothing whatever to do with the issue of the battle. The
cleverest arguer always wins; and it has, unluckily for us,
always happened that our champion has been the weaker.
Bossuet had it all his own way; for what Protestant of his
day was a match for him? and poor Mr. Pope was signally
discomfited by Maguire. One can't read any discussions
of that sort without seeing at once that all depends upon
the reading and readiness of the disputants. The less of
controversy we are obliged to engage in the better. I have
a thorough distaste for it. Keep your own flock safe, Bob,
in their own fold; and, if there must be controversy, leave
it as much as you can to those who, by filling prominent
stations, are called upon to engage in it; and, when you
must take your share, never use one unkind word. By the
bye, how much more reverence and affection one has for
Fénélon than for Bossuet. Fénélon met with mortification
and defeat, and bore it like an angel. There can't well have
existed a more beautiful character of a Christian gentleman;
and, though the other was a thorough good man too, one is
vexed with him for having had the upper hand, in anything,
of a man so amiable as Fénélon.   *   *   *   *

Dear Bob,—*All* that your newspaper editor said about the state of religion in South Australia was *not* bad; for example: "*Here we see no bickerings, heart-burnings, jealousies.*"

But are there not often such doings and feelings between different sets of people, all of whom equally *think* themselves Christian? We must make no dishonest compromise; we must not let our Church at Penrith or anywhere else sink into a sect. But we must be no parties to any bickerings, and we will neither express nor feel any heartburnings nor jealousies towards our dissenting neighbours. You may be attacked by Dissenters; but if you are, I know you will answer with no acrimony.

How you are to *satisfy* yourself on the subject of *lay baptism* I don't know. *I* can't bring my mind to any comfortable conclusion either way. Have you, or has either of your clerical friends, Bingham's works? He would, probably, show you all that has been said with any authority on the subject. To hunt the Fathers is useless without a guide; for what is to be made of their hundred folios—Greek and Latin books without, or with very scanty, indexes? Cyprian, you know, decided, with his council of a hundred or more bishops, that persons baptized by heretics must be rebaptized.

The Church of Rome was of a contrary opinion, and ultimately it was carried against Cyprian. The Church of Rome *does not* baptize again children who are baptized by laymen. Children, with apparently little chance of living, are often baptized by *Stilon*,[d] and his baptism is deemed enough. But yet, if *you* were to turn papist, they would neither admit your orders *nor your baptism*. They would rebaptize you with a *conditional* baptism; so that, *suspecting* you were not duly baptized before, but, not being sure, they confer a rite which, if needful, is to have effect, and if not, to be null and void.

---

[d] A surgeon at Malta, and a Roman Catholic.

I really don't see why St. Augustine's opinion on this particular subject should not have as much weight with us as it has on many others. I never heard that the *corruptions* of Rome had extended in any way to the rite of baptism; nor, in fact, can I see why any opinions the Roman Church holds on that subject now should not have weight. Such a question *ought* to be decided by the bishops. You may think, perhaps, that even the bishops in convocation could not make an invalid baptism valid. But yet you have no doubts in being governed by the *Rubric*; and if the Rubric were revised by *competent authority*, it might give you specific directions and leave you no choice. Le Mesurier confines himself, when a child is brought to be received into the Church, to the asking of the simple question which the service requires him to ask: Hath this child been already baptized or not? And, if the answer be affirmative, he does not inquire by whom; and so it may have been by a Wesleyan or anybody else—a layman, for instance. Neither —— nor —— seem to have any decided opinion. These are very sad disadvantages with which our Church has to contend. The fact is, *no* individual's opinion on such a subject is worth a straw. I should think that, in any case of doubt, you could not possibly do wrong in being guided by your bishop. Think of the arguments pro and con, that this proposition of mine suggests. The bishop may decide wrong, but he is more likely to decide right than you are, or than a *deacon* is.

To Bob, later in September, speaking of his nursery anthology:—

One would not expect to find such direct classical authority for the phrase "*nipping a nose off*," as there is in *Plautus*. "Nam si amabas, jam oportebat nasum abreptum mordicus." It is quoted in Ainsworth's Dictionary; but I was not indebted to the dictionary for it, for you know I read Plautus through last year, and found this nut for myself in "Menæchmus." I see in Ainsworth another mordicus, equally familiar to us, from Suetonius, from whom I have borrowed many bits for my young scholars. This one is the story of Julius Cæsar's jumping into the sea at Alexandria, and swimming with his Commentaries held in his hand above the water, and his paludamentum between his teeth : "paludamentum mordicus trahens, ne spolio potiretur hostis."   *   *   *

You would like very much to hear little Kitty make out page after page of my Latin books, about the Balearians and their slings, Cimon and his hospitable suppers, Augustus and his toast-and-water, Lucullus and his cherries. She knows that quinces are called in Italian *cotogne*, because they are in Latin *mala Cotonea ;* the Italian *cerase* comes from the Latin *cerasa ;* apricots are *mala Epirotica ;* and thousands of these odds and ends of all sorts that no printed books provide. There are thousands of beautiful bits to be had from Seneca too.   *   *   *   *   *   *

To me, in October, speaking of the sad necessity for dear Fanny's being closely shut up in her room all the winter, my Father writes :—

It is a sore trial for my poor child. But let us humbly thank God, my darling, for enabling her to bear it as she does. She has learned at an early age the most important of all lessons—that this world is not our resting-place. She is cheerfully resigned to God's will, and He will not forsake her.
          *   *   *   *   *   *
While I think of it, let me tell you that you must not say, "Mr. Johnson *left* on Monday." The verb *to leave* is an active verb and not a neuter, and absolutely must have its case after it. You may say, Mr. Johnson left *Melbourne*, or left *us*, but to say he *left*, in the sense of he *departed*, is to adopt the most thoroughly ignorant and vulgar slang. The *Spectator* has just been abusing some eminent American writer for using the barbarous phrase ; but you may trust me that I have not borrowed my notion of it from the *Spectator*.

Mercantile people use it; just as they say, "I avail of," instead of "I avail myself of."

I suppose you will think I never mean to give up my province of schoolmaster; but yet you have probably found out, long ago, that though some young ladies think their *education finished* at eighteen, or somewhat sooner, they are in a sad mistake. I suppose I know a good deal more than the young ladies, and yet I am quite conscious of the deplorably unfinished state of *my* education. I do what I can from day to day to mend it; but the *real* truth is, that the longer one lives and the more one learns, the more open one's eyes are to the extent of one's ignorance.   *   *   *

I have not been so well this summer as several others, for I have had more of those disagreeable attacks of petty cholera.

    *   *   *   *   *   *

Your meadows are kind in giving you not only grass but *mushrooms;* and your natural genius for cookery has turned itself to good account in turning them into catsup. There is no way of concocting them in which they are not admirable; and I remember, forty years ago, the fashion among the Tunbridge boys, of stewing them with milk. We used to get them in the fields there in quantities.

Horace says, "Pratensibus optima fungis natura est : aliis male creditur." *You* know more about them, botanically, than Horace did, and you know that all *agarici* are not eatable, and that no *boletus* is fit to eat. So please either to see your mushrooms yourself, or give your cook a lesson that she may know them accurately. At Castelamare they used to give us all manner of things in the mushroom shape, and so now and then poison us. All but the eatable species, which is but one out of two hundred, go in England, you know, by the delicate name of toadstools—by which name you will please never to call them; for though it may mean the toad's ottoman, yet it *may* suggest a much uglier idea— that of having sprung from a toad's *deposit.* Yet I dare say many a pretty lady has innocently talked of toadstools, just as the pretty dears use many other phrases they would not use if they knew their origin. Do you remember what a boletus is? It is like a mushroom, except that instead of having gills underneath, it is full of little holes, as if pricked with a pin.   *   *   **   *

To Bob, in October :—

Aunt says —— has sent —— orders for books and other things, and has not sent any money to pay for them. Do, my dear Bob, let me charge *you* to make, once for all, a rule never to let any human being say or think that it is possible for you to do anything careless, or indiscreet, or wrong, in any respect or degree, where *money* is concerned. It is impossible to be *too nice*, too rigidly punctual, too prompt to pay, too cautious to prevent *anybody* paying for you. It is perfectly astonishing how many men—and what sort of men—are apt to be *otherwise* than *quite right* where money is concerned; and you must be QUITE RIGHT.   *   *   *

I have read your essay with very great pleasure, for I agree cordially with you in every word of it. Your *own* argument, proving, from St. Paul's expression, his enduring all things for the *salvation* of the *elect*, that the latter word cannot be taken in the Calvinistic sense, is one that I should use with very great confidence. It seems an admirably satisfactory one; nor can any one deny that the coincidence between κλητοι and εκκλησια is likely to have a *meaning*. Have you read Archbishop Lawrence's Bampton Lectures on this question with the Calvinists? If any of your brother clergymen have it, you should borrow it.

When I am writing to you, I care nothing about connecting subjects, but put down just whatever occurs while I happen to think of it. Did you remark, in your rapid reading of Terence, the very striking words, "Advorsum stimulum calces"? They are in "Phormio," act 1, sc. 2. Of course, it was a proverbial phrase; but it is interesting actually to see it in a book two hundred years older than St. Paul.

Melancthon, quoted by Lawrence, says :— " De effectu electionis teneamus hanc consolationem, Deum volentem non perire totum genus humanum, semper propter Filium per misericordiam vocare, trahere et colligere Ecclesiam, et recipere assentientes, atque ita velle semper aliquam esse Ecclesiam, quam adjuvat et salvat." The word vocare here is obviously suggested by the meaning of the word Ecclesia. Do you know how Calvin expresses *his consolatory* views? "Neque enim prævidere ruinam impiorum a Domino Paulus tradit, sed ejus *consilio et voluntate ordinari*, quemadmodum et Solomo docet, non modo *præcognitum* fuisse impiorum interritum, sed impios ipsos *fuisse destinato creatos, ut perirent*." . . .

"Ecce, quum rerum omnium dispositio in manu Dei sit, quum penes ipsum resideat salutis ac mortis arbitrium, consilio nutuque suo ita ordinat, ut inter homines ita nascantur, *ab utero certæ morti devoti*, qui *suo exitio* ipsius nomen glorificent."

To form these frightful opinions, a Calvinist must take certain expressions of St. Paul, and interpret them in a certain way; and he must not only disregard the maxim that no particular law is to be judged of without taking the whole law into consideration, but he must leave entirely out of his account every word that our Saviour uttered and the Evangelists recorded.

In a note of Lawrence's I find this from Zuinglius, which will interest you :—

"*Senecæ viri sanctissimi fidem* quis non admiretur? Cum ait 'Sic certe vivendum est, tanquam aliquis in pectus intimum prospicere possit, et potest.' Quid enim prodest ab homine aliquid esse secretum? Nihil Deo clausum est. Interest animis nostris, et cogitationibus mediis intervenit. Sic intervenit dico, non tanquam aliquando discedat. Quis quæso hanc *fidem* in cor hominis hujus scripsit? Neque quisquam putet ista *in evacuationem Christi tendere*, ut quidam nos insimulant; *amplificant enim illius gloriam*. Per Christum enim accedere oportet, quicunque ad Deum veniunt. Unde *socerum Mosis* ne suspicamur quidem alia via, quam qua dicit, 'Ego sum via, veritas, et vita,' *ad Deum pervenisse*, qua *et Moses et omnes veniunt*."

In such a heart as that the law of God was unquestionably written; and though never baptized, he was called by an inward call to be a member of *the Church*.

Among the extracts I have made from Seneca* are these :—

" Miraris hominem ad deos ire ?   Deus ad homines venit, imo in homines venit ?   Semina in corporibus humanis divina dispersa sunt ; quæ si bonus cultor excipit, similia origini prodeant, et paria his ex quibus orta sunt surgunt ; si malus, non aliter quam humus sterilis ac palustris necat."   Had he seen the writings of the Christians ?   " Quid est præcipium ? Non admittere in animum mala consilia ; puras ad cœlum manus tollere."   By the bye, I had before put into my book the bit quoted by Zuinglius, as well as the rest, and a great deal more.   *   *   *   *   *

Xenophon's "Memorabilia" and Plato's "Phædon" contain very wonderful proof that Socrates was guided by a far better and holier light than that of mere reason.   Both these good men, Socrates and Seneca, spent their whole lives in endeavouring to deserve God's favour, and in preparing so to die, that, after death, they might be transferred to Heaven ; and they both did lay down their lives as cheerfully as if they had unbounded confidence in God's mercy.

Speaking of Hooker, my Father says :—

I suppose him to be considered the *first* authority in our Church.   For orthodox views, sound learning, and *judicious* treatment of all the subjects he discusses, I suppose the general voice of our Church would place him at the very head of English theologians.   *   *   *   *

Where can you find, Bob, a more competent examiner of the Fathers, or a more faithful reporter of their sense, than Hooker ? and, you see, he tells you that the general and full consent of the godly and learned in all ages allows the validity of lay baptism, and disallows its iteration.   You will surely tread on dangerous ground if you disagree with Hooker.

       *   *   *   *   *   *

_____ ___

* For the little one

Later in the month my Father writes :—

In the 138th number of the *Quarterly Review*, for March, 1842, I find some observations that I am inclined to extract for you, as containing a warning very much needed by numbers of ardent young men, who may quite unconsciously be led astray while they think they are following *Catholic antiquity*. *   *   *   *   *   *   *

And now, dear Bob, do let me tell you that when you spoke of your difficulty on the subject of lay baptism, and of your desire to ascertain the sense of the Fathers upon that question, I had serious doubts whether you were not pursuing a wrong course. I felt nearly sure that your true duty was frankly to lay the matter before your bishop, and to be governed in it by his directions. A bishop must be presumed to know better than a deacon what the practice of the ancient Church was, and what the rule of our Church is; and to interpret the Fathers much more justly, from his long acquaintance with them, than the poor deacon who has read none of their works, but only turned over their pages to hunt for scraps here and there bearing on one particular topic. At all events, your bishop is the head of your Church, and his authority is sufficient for you. The spirit in which you would submit to it would be a dutiful and humble spirit: the spirit that would dispose you to prefer your own private judgment in determining what the sense of the Fathers really is upon the point, after weighing in your own scales the authority of one Father against that of another, may *not* be sufficiently humble, and may not be consistent with a deacon's due deference for his bishop.

Take these thoughts of mine, dear Son, as you know I offer them. Nobody's theological skill can be much less than mine; but I hope I am on the safe side in feeling habitually a very deep reverence for my own Church and for its bishops, and a very strong sense of the danger of depending upon my own, or any one's, private judgment. And I am naturally anxious lest you should, in your veneration for Catholic antiquity, seek it for yourself, or without the guidance of our own Church.

Heretofore we have wofully neglected duties which the Church, our own Church, enjoins. Let us henceforth earnestly endeavour to fulfil them; but let us add nothing that our Church does not recognize, and persuade ourselves that we know better than she knows what Catholic antiquity is. Let us take for granted that Jewell and Hooker, and Andrews and Laud, Barrow and Bull, collected the true sense of the Fathers as well as we can; and I am pretty sure that there is no subject on which you may not more safely take that sense from them, or men like them, than from your own original reading for many years to come. Of course, it is your bounden duty to study the Fathers for yourself; but the fruit of such study is of slow growth, and you must beware of using it till it is *ripe*.   *   *   *

To Lizzy, in November :—

It *is* dull enough even for *us* to feel our imprisonment in so vile a cage hopelessly dragging on for the *fifteenth* year; for we can't even *know* here what the wider world is. From books, reviews, and newspapers we pick up some sort of notion of improving arts and improving society; but it is like looking through a fog, and looking without enjoying. Can't you fancy that to love books, and have no public library (for ours is so neglected that not a book has been bought for it these fifty years); to love pictures, and never see a gallery or exhibition; to love passionately fields and woods, and *never* to look upon a meadow or a tree, must be some sort of trial for the spirits?

But yet, dear child, don't think we *pine*. Very much indeed the reverse. I don't think there are any two people in the world who could more dislike their locality, and yet reconcile themselves to its privations more cheerfully; for good wife and I are exactly alike in *diligence*. We work hard every moment of our time   *   *   *

Speaking of Fanny to me :—

The pretty dear gives me the very great pleasure of hearing that your box of curiosities is safely arrived.   *   *   *
Fan says she has not only been *looking*, but *stealing*. The temptation was too great to be resisted, and she *could not* keep her hands off, and pilfered a squirrel skin and a couple of pieces of the cone of the honeysuckle-tree. Bless her dear little heart, how very glad I am she had something to afford her so much interest ! The monkey didn't very much scruple, I dare say, about sharing my little treasures with me, for she knows I would give her one of my eyes. What an arrival that box will be for us ! A million million thanks, my darling child, for such precious keepsakes, things provided by your own dear hands, while you were thinking of your own dear Papa.   *   *   *   *   *

To Bob, later in November :—

We should, of course, think it a great melioration in our affairs if I were summoned to a higher office in England. We have plenty of reasons, you know, for wishing to be there ; but yet it would be to me individually a life of labour and anxiety ; and I don't at all know how my diminished strength would bear that, after so many years of perfect quiet. This place of mine is in truth almost a sinecure. It requires about as much brains as would half fill a nutshell, and exercises even that small measure but seldom ; and I am by no means sure that I could begin again to work hard as I did in former times.   *   *   *   *

I think I am more distinctly conscious, within the last year, of having grown old, than I ever was before. *   *
  *   * This is an argument to reconcile me to my imprisonment ; but yet such an imprisonment as this is, does grow, after fifteen years, into a hard trial of the spirits. Few people could bear it more cheerfully than we both do ; but yet it *affects* us both,—good wife probably more than it would me, except that I suppose I feel any of her pains and

grievances as much as she does herself. You know, Bob, the
refreshment mind and body derive from a pleasant walk or
ride ; and that refreshment we never feel. We go out from
necessity, and drag our legs along over the same dull path,
gazing on the same stone walls, and return tired as much
after a mile's travel as I have been in Switzerland after a long
day's march over the mountains.

The days now passing are golden days, for my dear oldest
friend, Mrs. Duckworth, is with us, and will be till the 12th
of next month, when she will go on to Alexandria to meet her
daughter.   *   *   *   *   *

Since my last letter I have read No. 90 ;[‘] read it I have
with very great pain and disgust. Let Mr. N. beg the Pope's
pardon, and go to Rome if he pleases. Let him advocate the
Pope's cause if his conscience compels him : I should find no
fault with that. One only pities Mr. Sibthorpe; but one
can't help thinking Mr. N. *dishonest*. A bishop would not
speak as plainly as this in his Charge; and those who had
before learned to admire Mr. N. and love him, may probably
not allow themselves to think that he could do wrong; but
I don't see how *any* person, using his judgment freely and
fairly, could avoid applying to this composition the epithet of
dishonest. I did exceedingly dislike a previous tract of his,
No. 89; I think it was for *insinuating*, instead of plainly
stating his opinions; and this is written in the same spirit,
only that it has carried him greater lengths. Mr. N. has
done so much good and established so many claims to the
gratitude of our Church, that I don't like to allude to *him* in
speaking of the *tract*. I take the tract as a composition, without any reference to its author, and then I find it *detestable*.
No Jesuit ever wrote more jesuitically. When Mr. N. says
the Articles were never meant to condemn Popery as purified
by the Council of Trent, inasmuch as they were written
before the council was holden, and when it is answered that
the Articles were *revised and confirmed after* the Council of

---

Trent—originally written, I believe, while the council was
sitting, and nearly brought to a close,—how will he escape
from the inference?

I showed your last letter to Lady Louis, and she says the
simple, earnest, loving character of it is very delightful. We
dined yesterday with the Governor, and he talked about you,
and he said Lady Louis had been telling him of the beautiful description you had given of the Church in Australia,
and of your own happy condition.

       *   *   *   *   *   *

To Robert, in December :—

You say that though I dislike controversy, I need not be
afraid to read the Tracts, as their authors expressly disclaim
controversy. That is all very well: but, then, so may a man
knock me down and disclaim pugnacity. Could the author
of No. 90 expect that, when he told Englishmen that Invo-
cation of Saints was a doctrine of their Church, there was to
be *no controversy* about it? When I said, dear Bob, that,
with regard to some of the Tract doctrines, those especially
set forth in No. 90, *the Church* dissented from them, I suppose I meant what I certainly do mean when I repeat that
such is my conviction; that my Prayer Book does not teach
me those doctrines; that they are, therefore, not the doctrines
of *our* Church. That they *are* the doctrines of the Church of
Rome, Mr. N. tells us. It seems to me that the conclusion
to which any one would naturally come, in reading Tract 90,
supposing one had never heard of Mr. N. before, and had,
therefore, no partialities, would be this : This man thinks the
Church of England wrong and the Church of Rome right,
in at least nine points out of ten ; and, in his hearty desire to
escort the Church of England to Rome, he sets about giving
an interpretation to the Articles which he cannot *sincerely*
believe them to bear. I do not believe that, apart from
prejudices which disqualify him from judging truly, he can
attribute to the Articles the sense that Tract would persuade

us they *ought* to bear. I would have said the sense they
were *meant* to bear; but he does not even *pretend* that they
were *meant* to bear *his* sense.   However, as Mr. N.'s convictions have carried him nine-tenths of the way to Rome, and
he has, therefore, virtually professed that hitherto the Church
of England has been nine parts out of ten in the wrong, I
don't see how he can answer Dr. Wiseman when he asks
him, " Don't you think it *possible* that as you *have* discovered how very much of error you had, you may by-and-by
discover that some little remains?"

Now, dear Bob, it appears to me that Dr. Pusey can't
help being thoroughly right when he tells me that I can't
forsake the Church without committing a grievous sin.   I
am sure you would say just the same.   Then I am bound
to accept the doctrines of my *own* Church, and to reject all
others.   I must not listen to Mr. Newman if he tells me that
the doctrines of our Church are defective.   He may satisfy
himself that the primitive Church held other doctrines, which
we ought to adopt, and therefore he may, if he can, procure
the revision of the Prayer Book ; but until he does, that I am
not at liberty to follow him.   I do not clearly see why I
should not as safely believe the Pope when *he* tells me about
the primitive Church.

There is, in real truth, no one that acknowledges more
gratefully than I do the immense benefit conferred upon
us mainly by the labours of Dr. Pusey and his friends.   There
are now daily prayers in many churches in London, and
without doubt the time is at hand when *all* churches will be
open every day.

In the beginning of the last century there were (as I see in
a statement in the *Spectator*) 130 churches in London where
daily service was performed, and ten years ago *not one!*   So
in this very important particular it is not very far that we have
to be led back. Of course, I know that in the *cathedrals* there
was always service every day; but I also know that at *St. Paul's*
your Uncle Vade formed all the congregation ; and he, punctual in his attendance, was equally regular in his practice of

sleeping through the service. The time is coming when the churches will not only be opened, but filled. * * *

One word more about your theology. Of course, dear Bob, I think, as you do, that the unanimous voice of the immediate followers of the Apostles is the best interpreter of Scripture; but still I find difficulty enough remaining, for men differ as widely in telling me what the *voice says*, as they do in telling me what the Bible says. As for finding out for myself, I am quite unable to do that. I, or any one, may form my opinion of the matter; but whatever opinion he or I may adopt, we shall always be obliged to own that thousands of wiser men have judged of that voice differently. Of private judgment I know nothing. I have certainly no private judgment on such subjects. All the judgment I venture to exercise is in deciding upon the sense of the comparatively plain directions given me in the Prayer Book; as, for example, I decide for myself that what the service for Baptism *says* it really *means*, and, accordingly, I believe in baptismal regeneration; and so I believe that election regards the Church and not the individual; and so that I am forbidden to invoke the Saints. But I should not have the smallest faith in my own power, or in that of *any* individual, to decide upon any controverted point by a reference to the Fathers. All parties have quoted them triumphantly, just as all parties have justified all their peculiar opinions by referring to the Bible.

* * * * * *

I have just had a mighty treat in receiving a box from my dear good Sally, with Australian oddities of different sorts, but especially drawings of her own, which give me a most lively idea of her dwelling and the scenery round her. In one of the sketches there is a "vehicle," which, she says, is of *your* drawing. Very interesting to me is her dear little portrait of her son, and of the sweet little one that went to Heaven. * * * * * *

My Father had the pleasure, at this time, of making the acquaintance of the Bishop of Gibraltar. He went, with three or four gentlemen, to present an address of congratulation, from the members of the Society for Promoting Christian Knowledge at Malta, to the Bishop, on his arrival, and was received very cordially by him.

My Father says :—

He (the Bishop) was particularly struck with our library, in which we received him, and said he had not seen so English-looking a room since he left England.   *   *   *

I read every evening to Mrs. Duckworth and Mamma one of Mr. Newman's sermons.

CHAPTER XI.

[1843.]

To ROBERT, the 16th of January of this year, his Father writes:—

This has been a fortnight cut out of my usual employments, and given up wholly to my poor friend Mrs. Duckworth. She expected her daughter by a certain French packet from Alexandria, which ought to have arrived here on the 4th of this month, and until eleven o'clock last night neither the packet nor a word about it reached Malta; and in the mean time there had been a continuance of the worst weather an old sailor said he ever remembered in the Mediterranean.

Of course, Mrs. Duckworth has been filled with terror; and her nerves have been so much shaken by former great suffering, that she is less able than other people to endure such a trial. I have done literally nothing else the whole time than exert myself to calm and fortify and encourage her, and in a certain degree I have happily succeeded; for without some such help there would have been real danger of her going crazy. Happily she has a lively religious feeling, and could pray fervently; and I read very often suitable sentences to her, and she told me she felt them more forcibly than she had ever done when she had read them herself.

What a difference there must be, dear Bob, between one man's reading in such a case and another's. I believe there is only *one* way to read a prayer *rightly*, and that is earnestly to endeavour to feel every word, and to utter it just as one would if the awful presence of the Almighty were visible to one's bodily eyes. There could be no gabbling in such a case, no capricious or absurd habitual cadences, nor oratorical affectations.

Well, but at last we know that the missing packet put into a port of Laconia, and was quite safe; that Annie was not there at all, but on board of a packet which was not due at Malta till to-day; and that a son was most happily born to her a fortnight ago, on board the French packet *Leonidas*, while lying quietly in the Piræus.   *   *   *

Mrs. Duckworth says in a letter which seems to have been written a year or two after, and which I happened to find among my Father's papers:—

" Yes, dearest Sconcey, it is very true there is nobody's reading which ever did soothe and comfort me in sorrow, or interest me and beguile me, as yours and dear Mrs. Sconce's did; and even now, at a distance both of time and space, I look back upon the time, and am cheered by the bare recollection, knowing that the same words of promises and encouragements endure in all lands, ' yesterday, to-day, and for ever!' It is very pleasant to me to feel that the tones of your dear voices, and the tender kind spirit in which you read them, did indeed produce the solace I wanted. It is badly expressed, but I mean that it is very pleasant to me to feel that it is to *you* and your excellent dear wife that I owe my comfort."   *   *   *   *   *

And here I cannot help expressing my regret that I have none of my Father's letters to this dear friend; for in the letter from which I have been extracting, Mrs. Duckworth says :—

"I should find it *very, very* difficult, and indeed utterly impossible, to tell you how my heart thanks you for the most affectionate, the most precious, and the most beautiful of letters, which the post brought me three days ago. I do not think I ever in my life felt quite as I did when I read them! And I pray in all humility to Him who alone can change the heart, and give life to our endeavours, that the amazing privilege and great blessing of having possessed such friends may not be among the number of those mercies which the Almighty has granted me *in vain!*   *   *   *   *

"Oh, dearest Sconce, may He on whose mercy and loving kindness we can only rely, so wash *us all* clean in the blood of the Lamb, that you and I and all our dear ones may gain an eternal inheritance, where sorrow and sighing are not known, and where we *may* even be permitted to rejoice over those trials on earth and those friends who have led and guided and assisted us on the road."   *   *   *   *

To Robert, later in January, his Father says :—

I have given the larger part of my time by far to my young ones, according to their several wants, and that I am doing still. ·At present I am going over and over again the baby Latin that suits my four small learners; and Herbert's multiplication and division cost me best part of two hours a day. I can get no Englishman here to teach either Latin or ciphering, and therefore I am forced to do the drudgery myself. It *is* drudgery; for though one learns by teaching some things, yet you know I have learned such things as those well enough to need no more refreshing. However, I go on willingly, for their sake; and of course I am better satisfied so, than I should be to see them wasting *their* time. The main mortification is the waste of power; for, you know, my teach-

ing twice two, and hic, hæc, hoc, is like putting a dray-horse to
drag a wheelbarrow.   *   *   *   *

While Mrs. Duckworth was with us in her misery, I could
do nothing to improve my acquaintance with our good Bishop.
I have since asked him to dine with us; and he is coming to
meet a small party the day after to-morrow. We all like him
exceedingly. He is apparently just what he ought to be to
contend with all the difficulties of his position in such a society
as he will be immersed in, not only here, but in all parts of
his diocese, where his flocks are surrounded by enemies of all
persuasions. He preached last Sunday an admirable sermon
at our chapel. He neither *spouted* his sermon nor read it like
an essay; but addressed to us what he had to say in the tone
in which he would have spoken if the words had arisen from
the impulse of the moment. I listened to him willingly,
because I saw that he was himself interested in claiming my
attention. Of course, nobody can preach a sermon properly
who does not know it pretty well by heart, and who has not
sensibility enough to feel at the moment all that he is saying.

The day before yesterday he consecrated the Florian burial-
ground. It was the first important demonstration that our
Church has made in Malta; and I hope the Maltese will now
begin to think that we are not ashamed of our religion. We
have heretofore done all we could to give them a different impression. In their great delicacy of not interfering with the
religion of the country, our governors have always kept our
own religion in the background. *This*, at least, I hope we
shall do no more. Fancy our never having ventured to ring
a bell in Valetta to call our people to church! The Bishop
means to have at least six in the tower of the new church.
I had rather have eight, but I believe the tower would not
hold them.

Almost the whole of the English population was present
at the consecration. The Bishop perambulated the ground
preceded by a verger in purple, and followed by *ten* clergymen in their surplices and scarfs. So many clergymen were
certainly never assembled here before. It has happened

three times that we have been left for months together with *one* only to supply all the wants of the 5,000 English which there are generally here, including the troops.

The consecration service was read by the Bishop and his assistants on an eminent piece of ground, with all the large assembly round him, and all heard distinctly his clear voice.

* * * * * *

Nobody values more than I do the good your Oxford friends have done. But I can't so accept all the verba of any *magister*, as to adopt all the opinions in all the books he may write during a series of years, and to *change* my opinions just in proportion as he may happen to *change* his. I think Mr. N——— has changed his opinions between his writing of his earlier strictures on the Roman Church and his writing of the 90th tract; and I dislike that Tract most thoroughly. I can't help that; and I can't help thinking that it breaks down (for those who accept it) so much of the barrier between us and Rome, that we may at once jump over what remains, as Remus did over the first incipient bulwark of the same town. I see little left but the Pope's claim to the primacy; and as for that, nobody thought of contesting it till it became *expedient* to find arguments against it; and arguments of some sort are easily found on most subjects.

* * * * * *

At this time, from some expressions in my Brother's letters (or, as my Brother said, from the misunderstanding of some careless expressions), his Father was filled with terror lest he should desert his own Church for that of Rome; and the February letters to him are filled with the most earnest remonstrances. He says, in one:—

It is a misery, my part of which I am yet unable to measure; but its fearful extent appears even in this,—that so appalling a difference of sentiment seems to cut off all our intercourse. Not, my dear Bob, that it would, if it depended only on my disposition towards you, for I shall love you still, even if you become a Jesuit or a Capuchin; but you are yourself unable to write, even to me, on any other subject than this one that you have taken up with red-hot, unwholesome enthusiasm; and from this subject I must now wholly abstain.   *   *   *   *

The letter ends thus :—

With all the seriousness and affection I can express, let me entreat you not to seek your Jerusalem at Rome. You will find no peace *there*. Palmer, the elder and wiser, has told you that you cannot quit your Church without a crime, and your great master, Newman, has himself bade you beware of Rome, and called her a Demoniac. In the muddy waters of the Tiber you might find a haven, such as it is, from waves without, from the persecution you so much dread; but the fire of remorse would consume you nevertheless. Be SURE of this, dear son,—from the torture of most terrible misgivings you never could be free.

May God bless you, my dear son, and your precious wife and little one, and bless the birth and growth of your expected babe,—and give you a better mind!

     *   *   *   *   *   *

My dear Father's leisure at this time was occupied in doing for me ten coloured drawings of places in Malta that were most familiar and dear to me.

He says to me, in March :—

Do you remember a Miss ——, the daughter of a Maltese judge?   *   *   *   Well, said Miss is married to the son of ——, now also a judge, and the marriage was negotiated by a *broker*, who is also a *horse* broker : not a horse *breaker* mind, but *broker*, and the man's business is to furnish gentlemen with horses and ladies with husbands. My clerk, who is now married, used, before he was provided for, to have brokers constantly coming to him to offer him

young ladies; and Colombo's son, who now wears a long
beard like a Turk, has frequent overtures made to him
through a similar channel. By the bye, one of the Miss
——, Don V.'s niece, is married to a doctor at Casal Curmi.
Her brother came a day or two before to announce it, and
told us of the expensiveness of such affairs; for, said he,
according to the usage of the country, the young lady must
not only furnish herself with habiliments from top to toe, but
must provide *bed* too. We happened to land at the bakery
on the wedding-day, and sure enough there was a cart at the
parental door already laden with the bridal bed and its gear.
Isn't that a funny fashion?

To me, in March, after writing very strongly against the
spirit of the late Oxford writers, he says:—

But, on the other hand, my precious daughter, don't let
us reject the *good* we are offered through the instrumentality
of these writers. I heartily hope they have done *me* good.
They certainly have benefited numbers. They have taught
people to pray oftener and more earnestly—to think more of
the other world and less of this—to give more without grudg-
ing to God and His poor—to practise more self-denial.

Think of all this, my child, and do persuade yourself that
hitherto we *have* all been dreadfully wrong in dwelling so
much upon the trifles of this world, and disregarding so
much our own best interests.

We had an awful warning here the other day of the uncer-
tainty of human life. Poor Dr. Martin was visiting Sir John
Louis, and as he was passing from the house to the Admiral's
steps opposite, to get into his boat, the sentinel shot him
quite through the body, and in one hour he was a corpse!
There was no provocation. The soldier did not know him
by sight. Neither was the man mad or drunk, but simply
possessed by a devil to commit a murder!

*　　*　　*　　*　　*　　*

Later in March, to me :—

As soon as half-past nine strikes, I read every evening to
Mamma one of Newman's sermons (of which we have all the
six volumes), and we both find that they do us good.   They
make one think more seriously than any sermons I ever
read.   Don't let the mischief Mr. Newman has done deter
you from accepting all the good he is able to give you, which
is very great.   What a grievous pity it is he adopted strange
doctrines!   With them I have nothing to do; but I have a
very great deal to do with the question which he brings home
to me, whether I have not hitherto thought a great deal too
much of this world and too little of the next.   I have just
got from the Christian Knowledge Society a second series of
Bishop Blomfield's Prayers; very much better ones than
the first series that we formerly used, and Mamma and I
always say them together after our sermon.   I wish I had
put a copy into your box, but I had only just got it, and had
not made acquaintance with it.

As for *fasting*, the wonder is how it was ever possible for
us to have neglected a duty so plainly enjoined by Scripture
and our own Church.   However, *we* neglect it no longer.   I
believe my *duty* to be to avoid injuring my health,[a] and I am
not very strong, and could not go without a certain quantity
of food without suffering headaches and heartburns; but you
know one need not eat delicacies; so we omit the non-essen-
tials of food—eating our bread without butter, dining without
puddings and desserts, or wine, or beer, and eating what we
do eat sparingly, though not with so absolute a stint as to be
hurtful.   What we *can* do in this way we are undoubtedly
bound to do; and I know that you won't think that in this
or any other of my opinions I am betraying a predilection for
the *Pope*.   Our Church is all right, and its directions are

---

[a] My stepmother says that there is no doubt my dear Father's health *was*
injured by his fasting, not knowingly to himself at the time; but the fact is,
that *any* abstinence from food was injurious to him, as his feeble frame required
all possible support.

plainly set forth in the Prayer Book, but we have heretofore
been all wrong in disobeying its laws.

We and our teachers have been going on in a contented
jog-trot on the straight road to *ruin ;* for quite certainly all
the world has seemed to think this life all-important, and has
been over careful of its good things, and grievously, MOST
grievously, neglected heavenly things.

You and I will try, my dear Sally, to remember that our
time here must be short, and that the future life has no end,
and we will pray oftener than we used to do, and more
fervently, that we may be allowed to love each other *for
ever.* It is true I am old and you are young. There is a
difference between us of twenty-eight years. But what is that,
my child? Twenty-eight years to eternity! There is quite
as much reason, therefore, for you to think seriously as for
me ; and quite as much reason for you to wean yourself from
the trifles with which most people's hearts are filled.

*   *   *   *   *   *

To Bob, in April, after further remonstrance and argument on his dissatisfaction with his own Church, his Father
says :--

However, on these subjects I will write no more. You will
agree with me, dearest Bob, that it is better for us to lay
them aside ; for I am quite conscious on my part of the use-
lessness of laying before you the arguments of even the wisest
and best of men, with a view to the influencing of any of your
opinions ; and you would think it mere idleness to endeavour
to convince me that *I* ought to despise the bishops of my
Church, and to make my adherence to their communion
depend upon their sanctioning doctrines which they have
heretofore repudiated.

One thing I may mention as not being in the way of argument, but as a suggestion I wish to offer you with so much
love, that, for the sake of the love, I know you will attend to
it : be always on your guard, dear Bob, against theological

rancour. Don't hate people for not thinking as you think. Don't express yourself as if you scorned and despised all the world except the particular party to which you are attached.

You have been sensible of the influence of this sort of feeling, for you begin one of your letters by acknowledging that the preceding one was written " somewhat in anathematizing Palmer's spirit."   *   *   *   It seems *very* hard that religion should make men unamiable. It is doing this sort of mischief here at Malta now. A set of low-churchmen have got up a newspaper for the twofold purpose of proving the Pope Antichrist, and *our* bishop a liar ! One article is headed " Baptismal Regeneration no Doctrine of the Church of England." Think of such a publication in such a society as ours is at Malta !

One of the writers in this paper is a very amiable and clever man; but he is a thorough Calvinist, and the Bishop is not, and consequently he hates and despises the Bishop, and thinks he is serving God by assailing him. Hearts liable to be so disturbed must be filled much oftener with a bad feeling than a good one; just as Mr. P—— fancied himself the first of philanthropists, but he had not a moment's leisure to love the poor, for his heart was all day long occupied with hatred of the rich.

Fénélon and Bishop Heber were beautiful examples of the absence of this bitterness. Imitate them in this, dear Son. In urging your own arguments or controverting those of others, try and avoid crowing, and chuckling, and sneering. Persuade yourself that people who think differently may yet be honest and sane. How can you love your enemies while you are abusing them ?   *   *   *   *

For the gap there has now been I am very sorry. It has been caused by sickness in my *heart*. In other respects I have not been ill; but yet you would find in me a very great change. I have lost all the little flesh I had, and am little better than a skeleton. Of course, I have next to no strength. I had so many small attacks last summer of my usual summer malady, that they did me, I believe, permanent mischief.

Their effect—I suppose it was that, but it may be simply the effect, suddenly perceived, of increasing age—has been to change me from a young man into an old one. You know I had, when you were here, a great deal of strength and elasticity left; but I have now very little of either. I believe it would do me great good to spend a summer out of Malta; but without a clear necessity I won't do that, for it would do me no good to go alone, and Mamma and I could not leave the young ones; and if we went all together, it would consume full three years of our hoarding. * * *

The Bishop begged me to help him get up and support a periodical here, to counteract the detestable publication I mentioned to you. I should have been very glad to contribute; but he himself and his two capital chaplains will be absent from Malta half of every year, and I should have pretty nearly the whole labour to myself, for which I could not possibly find time. It would sadly disturb my peace, too, to be perpetually engaged in controversy with bitter adversaries,[b] whose productions prove them equally deficient in right judgment, education, and gentlemanly sentiment.

The person I before alluded to is going away, and the chief of the other contributors are —— and ——. * * The man has been in my house once, and made me a long oration, in the course of which he told me baptismal regeneration was a mere "figment," and that as for the Fathers and the old divines, it would be a great blessing for religion if they were all burnt. The other is the editor of a scurrilous newspaper, who sent his little daughter to Cleugh[c] to be prepared for confirmation. Cleugh talked to her as he naturally would, and gave her Mant's Catechism to read at home. The girl came no more till after a long time she brought back the book, and glibly told him, "We shan't come any more, for this is a bad book. See here, this is all popery, and so is this; so my brother won't come any more, no more shall I."

---

[b] Dissenters. [c] The minister of the Protestant church at Valetta

This was a pretty sample of the spirit in which the children had been brought up. Of course, if the father had a strong objection to the book, whether well or ill founded, there would have been no harm in *his* mentioning that objection to Clough; but he sent his little ignorant *girl* to lecture her spiritual pastor, and insult him. *These* are the conductors of a publication which they feel quite sure is calculated to promote the cause of true religion !

To me, same date :—

The last letters from dear Bob comforted me greatly. He gives me several reasons why he does *not* mean to become a Roman Catholic, and why he thinks it his duty to remain in his own Church. And most heartily do I pray that he may be governed in this most grave matter, and in all others, by God's gracious guidance. *   *   *   *   *
For the present he has quieted my apprehensions, but his impulses seem to be so strong and so sudden, that it must be very long before I can open his letters without fear of finding what I should consider the announcement of an hideous calamity.   *   *   *   *   *   *

At the end of this letter, he says :—

You will be surprised to hear that I have actually written by this packet for five months' leave of absence. Mamma and I suddenly made up our minds that it was necessary for me, and good for all of us, to get away for this summer. We shall go straight to Vernex.[d]

Later in April :—

Since I wrote last, no letters have come from Australia or England, and no event has occurred among us; but nevertheless we have been by no means in our usual condition, for

---

[d] In Switzerland.

we are all as much excited by the prospect of our summer's
holiday as prisoners may be supposed to be when they expect
to be let loose after a dozen years' immurement within the
walls of Chillon. Except the one holiday we made together,
I have been fifteen years in this miserable place. I have
made myself as contented in it as anybody well can; but you
know we have *no* resources except within ourselves. We
have *no* society. You have met in Australia with men whose
sentiments and pursuits are like your own; but there is *not
one* now in Malta with whom I have anything in common.

A walk or a ride in other countries does one good in various
ways, for it is often exhilarating; but here the most Mamma
and I can do is to vary our walk between the Capuchin
Convent and St. Clement's; and whichever way we go, half
of it is through our dirty town. We do this for the sake of
mere necessity. We should have more headaches and less
appetite even than we have, if we did not; but we come
home dragging our legs along and as much knocked up by
the two miles' effort as if we had been surmounting an Alp.
Give me books, and I believe there are few people who could
bear solitary confinement better than I could; but was there
ever mortal man, with sensibilities for enjoyment of any sort,
who would not feel his heart beat when his prison gate was
set open? Mine, then, is something like such a case.

       *   *   *   *   *   *

I have been hard at work in selecting the old unfinished
Swiss sketches, that I may take them back, and supply what
I left wanting; and I have made fresh outlines of some that
were not coloured on the spot, that I may colour them now.
I have cut one hundred sheets of drawing paper to fit my sketch-
ing-case, and I quite expect to fill them with one hundred
sketches. You know I made more than half that number last
time, when I had much more impediment than I shall have
now.   *   *   *   *   *   *

One lives and learns. Young ladies at seventeen say their
education is *complete:* mine is beginning. I have but just
learned how to cut a piece of India-rubber. Mr. Clifton told

me, and as you use things of that sort, I will tell you, that you
may turn the hint to account as successfully as I did just now.
I wanted to *split* a piece that was too thick, and it would have
been an impracticable matter if I had not set about it the
right way.   Dip your penknife in *water,* and it cuts the
India-rubber very much more easily than *scissors,* under
water, cut glass.

By the bye, among my preparations for Switzerland, I
have had a piece of glass framed of the size of my sketching-
case ; and I mean to sketch out of doors upon it constantly.
How the travelling artists will stare !   But I know by experience that I shall so be able to get a much faster and much
better effect.   Whenever I am not too much pressed for
time, I mean to make all coloured sketches.   And one of the
great pleasures I promise myself is that of sending you some
memorials of your old Swiss haunts, particularly of Bonigen
and Vernex.   *   *   *   *   *

The packet from England arriving at Malta on the 14th of
May, brought him his leave of absence, and also a letter from
his darling Fanny, telling him of her greatly increased illness,
and begging him to come to her : and on the 16th he set
off to go to her, with his wife and their four elder children.
On the 17th he wrote to her on board the *Scamandre,* and
said :—

You know already that I am on my way to you.   It is
good for me to be near you, and good for you to have me near ;
so you know we gave up our voyage to Switzerland, and are
doing as you desire. *   *   *   *   *

My Father stayed a week at Naples to show his wife and
children the Studii, and Pompeii, and Baiæ ; then went on in
a Tuscan steamer to Marseilles, spending a day at Civita
Vecchia, another at Leghorn and Pisa, and another at Genoa.
They stopped two days in Paris, where he says,—

You may well imagine how cordially we were received by
that dear Madame Reboul.

He had written her an affectionate letter from Marseilles, calling himself "her all unchanged friend (furrows excepted)."

He arrived at Haslar on the 13th of June, and found his dear child sadly changed, and even more reduced than he had expected. After spending a short time with her, he went to town to present himself at the Admiralty, and into Kent to see some relations. Of this he writes in June:—

All my official masters were very civil to me, and gave me generally to understand that I had established for myself a first-rate character. I think I made out too that in case of any vacancy that might be desirable for me, no one would be preferred before me, *except* a politician. If Sir John Barrow retires, Sir R. Peel will probably put in a political friend, without consulting the Admiralty at all. If Mr. Meek were to retire, that would not be a political place, and it would pretty surely be given to me. However, Mr. Meek is but half a dozen years older than I am, and has apparently not the least thought of giving up. If I had had any *luck*, I should have had, many years ago, the place he has; for I find that when he was appointed it was for some time doubtful between him and me, and that Lord Keith's interest did but just carry it in his favour.

I saw Sir John Pechell, one of the late Lords of the Admiralty, and a very warm friend of mine; and he told me that if any vacancy had happened in his time, the strongest possible fight would have been fought in my favour, not only by himself and Sir William Parker, who were my friends, but quite as zealously by Sir Charles Adam, who was as warmly disposed towards me as they were, though he had never seen me, but merely for the sake of my reputation in the service.

Lord Haddington expressed himself in general terms of great civility, and told me he should be happy to see me when I returned to town, and to receive any memorial I might like to present to him; and when I told him I should be glad to leave Malta, but could not accept a *dockyard* appointment in England, he said he thought I was quite right. His secretary, Captain Bailey Hamilton, told me there was no place lower than Mr. Meek's that was fit for me. He advised me to see Sir George Cockburn; but Sir George had been grievously ill, and saw nobody. Captain Hamilton said, " He will, however, see *you*, for we were talking of you only the other day." So Sir George did see me, and, like the rest, expressed himself in a very friendly way. In short, I am pretty sure that no one in the civil service of the navy would be preferred before me; but yet there seems not the least prospect of an opening for any preferment at all. ✻   ✻   ✻

He took Clement back with him to Haslar, where he was soon joined by his sister. He says to his friend Admiral Furneaux :—

You may fancy how Liddell's small house is filled when I tell you that he has made it hold (besides his own family) Mrs. Sconce and me, and five of our children, and my sister.

✻   ✻   ✻   ✻   ✻   ✻

On the 15th of July he wrote from London to his wife at Haslar :—

Then I went to Greenwich and saw Sir Robert Stopford, who said he was rejoiced to see me, and asked me to dine with him to-morrow, which of course I can't. He spoke as if he would gladly help me to get an appointment in England if he could, and told me it was likely there would be a vacancy at Greenwich. ✻   ✻   ✻   ✻   ✻

Sir R. Stopford said that it certainly was the intention of the late Admiralty to appoint me to Barrow's place if he had retired; and that a wish was expressed that he would retire, to make way for me.

On the 20th, he writes again to his Wife :—

This morning I breakfasted with Sir T. Acland, and there was Lady Acland and the youngest son and youngest daughter; but it was not a very comfortable visit, for during breakfast at least six different people came to him about as many different sorts of business; and directly after breakfast he had to go himself to M. Bünsen, the Prussian Ambassador, and he took me so far on my way to my own business. As he was going out of his own house, four people were waiting to speak to him. He was as cordial to me as he could be, and inquired after all of you, and sent special remembrance to Liddell ; but he was in a more rapid whirl than ever, drank half his tea standing, and left the other half undrunk.

Then I went to the bazaar, and bought the work-basket for my own sweet Fan, and the bustle for you; and the young lady at the bazaar of whom I bought it blushed most shockingly at the idea of selling a bustle to a gentleman ; so I did what I could to put her in countenance, telling her she needn't be ashamed of selling a bustle to an old gentleman, that my wife had told me to get it for her, and that really it was a very innocent transaction. Then she laughed, and thought me, of course, a very funny customer.

    *   *   *   *   *   *

In this letter he sent his Wife a copy of his memorial to Lord Haddington, and says :—

You won't think the memorial as *striking* a composition as some that you have seen of mine; but then you know I have not fought a lot of battles, nor been imprisoned, nor paralyzed ; so mine is but a tame history.

    *   *   *   *   *   *

On the 21st :—

The grass has not grown under my feet to-day. See what I have done, dear wife. After leaving Somerset House I called at the National Gallery. Oh, what beauties there are there! Many have been added since I saw it fifteen years ago. Correggio's Venus is worth most of the pictures you have seen in all your life put together; I must introduce you to her. Then called at Stratford Place, in hopes of a letter from Hooker; and sure enough there it was, to tell me he should be at home till noon to-morrow, but not after. But to-morrow I could not go to him, as I must go to the Admiralty; so I determined to go this evening. Started first for Paddington, dined by the way at a restaurateur's. Spent an hour with poor Elizabeth.[e] The poor thing is sadly forlorn; and I long to see more of her and cheer her. * * * *

Reached Kew Bridge at twenty minutes before nine, Hooker's house being more than a mile across the bridge in the country. At nine, saw Hooker in his beautiful *park*. He received me just as I knew he would: one of the finest, active, cheerful people you ever saw. * * *

I sat an hour with Lady Neale, who seems to love me better than anybody, barring Harry. * * *
She hopes you are coming to town, that she and you may be together while I am obliged to run about after my affairs.

 * * * * * *

My Father writes to Bob in July, speaking of his dear Fanny :—

She is sinking slowly. Her life may yet be spared for *some* months, but *not*, I feel assured, for *many*. She is visited frequently by the excellent clergyman of the parish, Archdeacon Wilberforce,[f] and he uses "the prayer for a sick person when there appeareth small hope of recovery." Our sweet SWEETEST Fanny joins in such prayers with placid resignation, and without evincing the smallest fear of death. I observed to the Archdeacon her remarkably tranquil state

---

[e] His brother Charles's widow.
[f] The Bishop of Oxford.

of mind, and he said he firmly believed it was on a good
ground.

After I had ended my little service with her the other day,
she said, " What a blessing it is to have you to read to me
and pray for me." It is an inexpressible comfort to me to
be with her; but what shall we both do when the time comes
that I must leave her ?   *   *   *   *

Very thin and pale as it is, her sweet face retains its
beautiful smiles.   *   *   *   *   *

My prayer is, that our Blessed Saviour will look upon her
in his mercy, and be ever present with her. He knows best
whether it is best for her that her days should be prolonged.
He will not willingly afflict her with protracted suffering.
We may, I trust, pray that she may not suffer protracted
pain. She has *great* fortitude, and hitherto she has never
shown for one moment impatience of her allotted trial.

      *   *   *   *   *   *

At this time my Father's brother-in-law, Dr. Knox, died
suddenly in the vestry of his church, at Tunbridge, and my
Father went there at once to try and help and comfort his
orphan children, and their afflicted Uncle Vicesimus. My
Father says, in a letter to Mr. Smith :—

I have been no less than three times to Tunbridge, desirous
of doing what little I could to divert his grief, and express
kindness to the children, and yet reluctant to *stay* away from
my dear interests here.   *   *   *   *

From Haslar, to his Wife in London, on the 14th September:—

She desired me to read the prayer for a sick person, which
of course I did, but not the one for a person apparently at the
point of death. I could not find in my heart to read that.
Neither of the prayers for the sick in the Prayer Book or
Liturgica Domestica are worded precisely as one might desire,
and so I had not been accustomed to read either to her; but

I told her we had never failed to pray specially for *her* when appropriate clauses occurred in almost every prayer, as in the brief sentence, " O Lord, make haste to help us! "

*   *   *   *   *   *

The *husband* God gave her is a mighty blessing to her. You would admire, as I do, Liddell's *most* tender and unwearied care of her.   *   *   *   His behaviour is not unlike her own, that of cheerful gravity and resignation.

*   *   *   *   *   *

Towards the end of September my Father wrote to me :—

For a long, long time I have had no courage to write to you, much as I have to say, and dearly as I love you. You know well, my darling, from my last letter, what our affliction is, and I feel *your* portion of it very deeply. Would that I could take it for you in addition to my own! But, dearest, if you saw what I see, you would be well assured that we OUGHT rather to rejoice than mourn ; for our precious Fanny is even now, in spite of her fearful illness, positively *happy*. She would not change her condition for that of health ; and happy as she is now, what a blessed change is awaiting her, and near at hand !

Wonderful it seems that her poor little remnant of strength should have supported her so long. Fearful expectoration, cough, fever, with alternate perspirations and diarrhœa, are all working the destruction of her now shadow-like frame. It is seldom that she is able to open her eyes and speak a word, or even listen, until towards evening; and then she generally feels awake, and free from any very painful or distressing sensations, and we talk with her, and she likes me very much to read to her and pray with her.

The good clergymen of the neighbourhood often visit her, to her great comfort, and especially the excellent Archdeacon Wilberforce. I wrote to him yesterday, by her desire, to ask him to come and administer the Sacrament to her, and all of us together ; and I dare say he will come this evening.

You know our sweet Fan's quiet fortitude. God's blessing has given it a good foundation, and it never fails her for one moment. Tears come into all our eyes sometimes, *except hers*. She speaks of death as if it had indeed for her no sting, no terrors, and as if she contemplated its approach without a wish that it should come one moment sooner or later than God in his mercy shall see fit. She has resigned herself entirely to his will, and is content. Her voice is very feeble and she can speak but little, and in whispers. She told me she wished she had strength to talk to me, for she had much to say. "I am so *perfectly* happy," she added. "I have not the least fear of death. I feel as confident as any poor human being ought to feel. I hope I am not presumptuous, and that all my reliance is upon my Saviour's mercy."

The last time the Archdeacon was here, after he had prayed with us, Fan expressed a wish to talk to him alone, and she did so, and told me afterwards that she had spoken to him just as she did to me, with unreserved freedom. The good man could only encourage her to feel more and more assurance that God would never leave her nor forsake her. Touching as these scenes are, *her* nerves are never shaken by them,—her *composure* is never disturbed; and when I am struggling to preserve the condition of my own countenance, I see hers wearing its wonted placid expression of cheerful content.

The Archdeacon asked her if she was able to think without pain of parting with her little children; and she assured him that she had been enabled to do even *that*. At first it *was* a very fearful thought; but her long illness, she says, has been a merciful preparation for her, and she now feels entirely willing to separate herself from all earthly ties. She knows that her treasures will be safe in God's merciful protection. She speaks very often of her dear Sally, and is having some little things prepared to send you. Among them is a pair of slippers of her last work. She told Liddell she would send some of her best clothes too, that she should never want any

more. She speaks of these things without any effort, or
emotion of any kind.

Her conviction is that her parting with all her dears is but
for a *moment*. She asked me if, in *eternity*, any number of
our measures of time called years might not be supposed to
pass like a mere moment; and so of course they will. It has
been, you can well imagine, a very great blessing to her and
to me, that we have been permitted to spend this awful season
together. I have got two months' farther leave of absence,
so that it will not be necessary for me to be at Malta before
the middle of December. It may be God's will that my dear
child's stay on earth should be prolonged beyond that time;
but, humanly speaking, her little remaining strength cannot
last *much* longer, and a sudden change for the worse may
come on at any moment.

We must not desire that her sufferings should be protracted. She is, I humbly trust, in God's great goodness,
ripe for heaven; and in her translation from a bed of sickness
and pain to a paradise of rest and joy, we must rejoice, and
not grieve. I shall lose, for the small space of my remaining
life, an admirable child, whose love has been precious to me
beyond all description; but I shall know with the most
certain knowledge that she is sharing the love of angels; that
God is rewarding her for all her goodness to me and to all
her dear ones; and that He will aid us all in striving to fit
ourselves for the blessed abode to which she is preceding us,
and where she will welcome us.

My heart bleeds for *you*, my darling Sally. Would that I
were with *you*, when my darling here no longer needs the
poor comfort I can give her, that I might comfort *you*.

    *   *   *   *   *   *

Poor Liddell bears as well as anybody could bear his awful
trial. Right nobly does he perform his part in nursing and
cherishing his poor sufferer. No creature ever bestowed
upon another more tender and unremitting care. He or I
are of course *always* with her; Mamma often; and in the
evening all three of us.   *   *   *   *

I have never told you, Hanmer, of my visit to Barton. I stayed but three days, for I could not bear to be away from Fan : but they were three *very* pleasing days to me. I hope your father liked me as much as I did him. He and Lady Bunbury and your brothers Charles and Edward, and that dear "Cissy"*—O what a *sweet* Cissy it is !—all seemed to open their hearts to receive me; and thoroughly amiable, estimable, and pleasant people I found them all. Nothing could exceed their cordiality, and I am sure nothing could be livelier than my sense of it, and my wish to make more acquaintance with them all. *   *   *   *

The letter to Robert of the same date was almost the same as the above. To me, on the 10th of October, his Father wrote :—

Mourn for your darling Sister, my poor dear, *dear* child, but in the midst of your mourning rejoice ; for God's mercy was marvellously displayed in supporting her through all her long trial, and in enabling her to retain to the last moment all her patience and cheerful hope, and Christian heroic fortitude ; and in transporting her from this scene of suffering to the abode of angels by a blessed death, which had no terrors and no sting. She breathed faintly, fainter and fainter, and then ceased ; and the moment in which the happy spirit fled— O my dear child, how can I describe to you, how tell what I would give, that *you* could have *seen* the appearance that *then* shone upon her *most lovely* countenance. It was nothing short of an angelic radiance, that told us of her transition to eternal peace and joy. I have no words to tell you how beautiful it was. It was not like the beauty of earthly things, but like the expression of a bright and happy angel's perfect peace.

And what a change is *that* for our sweet one ! Sadly as she had suffered, this world was a very painful abode for her, and we know and are sure that she is now in Paradise. It is *right* that we should, though with all humility, feel this

---

* Miss Cecilia Napier, now Mrs. Henry Bunbury.

perfect assurance; for it was in God's mercy that she put her whole trust, and the faith she felt was his gracious gift. She had had many most soothing visits from the excellent Archdeacon Wilberforce. At our darling's request he administered the Sacrament to us all on the 5th of this month. Happy was it that it was not delayed, for there was afterwards no such interval of repose as was granted to her that evening. "Oh, Mrs. Liddell," said the good man in taking leave of her, "what a blessing it is to have such a foretaste of heaven as you have; for you have a perfect assurance of going there!"   *   *   *   *   *

Four hours only before she expired she desired me to read a prayer to her. We could not help weeping bitterly while I read the solemn words, but she herself shed no tear; for God did, indeed, "give His strength to His servant, and help the *child* of his *handmaid*." She then told us that she felt no pain. Yet, what she had endured! and, what was she enduring still! And how should we, then, praise God that He has mercifully taken her to her rest. How she *needed* rest, poor child. How our hearts bled to see her quite worn out, and still forced to sit up, feeble and sore and sinking, and yet denied the dying comfort of a pillow! Yet she had *better* comfort; for ministering angels were supporting her, and the arms of Jesus were opened to receive her.   *   *   *   I had left her on Sunday night (the 8th), and went to bed, trusting, from her then comparatively tranquil state, that she might continue to sleep, and not apprehending any immediate change for the worse; but Liddell sent for me at one in the morning (of yesterday, the 9th), and I found her breathing so feebly, and with so much difficulty, that I feared I should never hear her beloved voice again. I helped, with Liddell, to support her in sitting up, and presently, to my unspeakable comfort, she said, "God bless you two, Papa." Liddell was crying bitterly, and she said to him, "Don't cry!" Again, almost within the last hour, seeing his tears, she laid her hand, with an expression of tender remonstrance, upon his arm, and made a distinct sign with her lips for him to kiss her. He had been holding her up for some time, while he was himself in a constrained position, and she said to me, "Perhaps you'll take his place, Papa; he must be very tired." For many hours we held her up by turns, her head bent forward, and her forehead resting upon one of our hands. While in this miserable condition of unrest, and struggling with the phlegm, which she had no strength to cough up, she said, "What a mercy it is to —— ;" the closing word or two I was not able to hear, but it was enough to show that she felt herself, at that moment of bitter trial, an object of God's mercy. We propped her up with pillows, which supported her back, and, while Liddell was adjusting them, she said, "It's very nice." She could not lie down at all, but was able, now and then, for a short time, to lean her head against the pile of pillows that supported her. At four in the morning she said, "What do you think it's o'clock?" I told her, and she presently added, "Then I'll take another morphine." At seven, "You'd better go and sleep, Papa." She then heard her pretty little ones getting up in the next room, and said to Liddell, "There's the children; don't let me see them or hear them any more." She wished not to be disturbed any more by any earthly interests. At half-past seven, putting her hand to her throat, "such an oppression in breathing,"— to Liddell (for it was his usual time), "An't you going to the hospital?" At nine, "Have you been to break-fast, Papa?" And, after that, "I'm in no pain." But, my dear child, she said this in answer to an expression of mine in admiration of the wonderful fortitude that God had given her, and what she meant seemed really to be this, "Why, Papa, I really have not anything very hard to bear." Mamma then came in, and said to her, "Heaven bless you, dear;" and Fan replied, "And bless you too;" and then added, "I can't pray." Mamma said, "We pray for you, and without doubt our prayers are heard." About eleven o'clock, she said to Liddell, "We shall meet in heaven." Her last words were, at half-past twelve, half an hour before she died, "*I was*

only dreaming." We thought we heard her speaking, and
on our asking her what she said, that was her answer.

She had been sleeping, precious child, and her dreams
were happy dreams. It is very likely that sleep came frequently over her towards the last, and she was probably
sleeping when her last gentle breath escaped. Did she not
die in the Lord, and do not we know that she is blessed, and
must we not rejoice at her blessedness? According to the
course of nature, she might have been expected to survive
her husband many years; and only think, if he had been
taken from her, how much worse her condition would have
been than his is now! Yet we must mourn for *him*, for
great is the claim he has upon our sympathy. He was to our
precious angel a most tender and most admirable husband;
nothing ever could exceed his incessant devotion to her, in
gratifying all her wishes, caring for all her comforts, antici-
pating all her wants, and exhausting all the resources of his
great skill to mitigate by all human means her protracted
suffering.   *   *   *   He asked us all to come
and pray this morning by the bedside where our darling lay.
I chose some of the beautiful prayers suited to such a solemn
season and read them, all of us weeping a flood of tears, and
all, I am sure, trying, as well as our poor infirm nature
would allow us, to lift up our hearts to God and implore His
merciful aid to fit us all for a blessed reunion with our departed
love, and with all our dear ones.

Be sure, my darling, that in all my poor prayers I think of
you—dear to me as my own soul,—and your husband and
little children, and my precious Bob and *his* little household.
        *   *   *   You will be equally sorry for the
love *I* have lost. Isn't it a *sad* loss, my darling? How she
doted upon her papa; and how intensely I loved her, too!
There was a tender, and fervent, and quite equal love between
us: she was to me even all that you are, my child,—more than
that is not possible. How grateful I am for God's goodness in
allowing me to be with her during her last trial, to exchange
words of love with her, to pray with her, to pray for her at

her bedside, to read to her, to help her when most she needed
help, to hear the last accents of her sweet lips, to receive the
last looks of her beautiful eyes, and the deep impression of
that *unutterable grace* that shed itself over her in the last
moment of her earthly life! She thought of you continually.

*　　*　　*　　*　　*　　*

Never yet did theologian compose a homily equal to the
lesson this poor, meek, single-minded, loving, confiding child
has afforded us in the example of her death. Words, words,
what are they? Our darling was no talker; but she gave
herself up to God, and He graciously endued her with real
wisdom. Let us think of her and imitate her. Young as
she was,[h] she had already fought a good fight. Few, and full
of pain, were the days of her years, but *not* of *sorrow;* for
God, in chastening, loved her, and made her to rejoice in that
pain as an assurance of His love. She told me what a blessing her long illness had been to her, in preserving her from
many sins she might otherwise have been tempted to commit.

See, my darling, how I go on dwelling on this subject of
deepest and tenderest interest. It does me good to dwell
upon it, though I shed many tears while I write. Tears
enough *you* will shed. I know you can hardly see through
them to read what I am writing; but they will do you good,
my darling, too.

The next day he added to my letter (those to me and
Robert are almost the same),—

We treasure all that is left to us of our loved one too much
to leave her to any stranger's keeping. The poor decaying
body now stretched upon her bed, and soon to be consigned
to the grave, will in its glorified form mount up to Heaven,
and there, by God's mercy, we shall see it again. We honour
it duly: Liddell never leaves the room, night or day, without
my taking his place in it.　　*　　*　　*　　*

---

[h] Twenty-six years old.

He himself composed that precious body in its winding-sheet, and he and I together will put it into its coffin. All the little LITTLE we can do to express our love, how sweet it is to do that little! We have chosen a place for her grave in the hospital burying-ground. It is immediately under a great elm tree; I will make a sketch of the place for you.

A little while before the poor dear was taken so very ill, and when she little thought her end was so very near, she told me to make a sketch of this house for her; and I did make as pretty a drawing of it as I could, and she dwelt upon it again and again with great pleasure. I will copy that drawing for you.   *   *   *   *

We shall *now* leave England, on our return to Malta, the end of this month.¹

A few days later he writes to us :—

She lies in the hospital burial-ground, a wide space surrounded with a wall, close to which, on the outside, are some elm-trees, immediately beneath the largest of which, an aged and majestic tree, is the vault. It will be covered with stone, and surmounted with a marble slab, inscribed,—

The Remains of
FANNY MARIA LIDDELL,
WHO DIED
OCTOBER THE NINTH, 1843,
AGED 26 YEARS.

We wished the stone to be laid before I went away, but it was not possible. It will be done in ten days more; and then some evergreen shrubs, which we have already selected, will be planted round it, and trained to embower it.

*   *   *   *   *   *

---

¹ The letter containing the account of my dear Sister's death is given almost entire, for the sake of her sons.

No being in this world better deserved love than she did. Few could know how excellent she was who did not see her in her last trial; but it is a very great consolation to me that I had *always* known her true value, and that *she knew* how I delighted in her and prized her love.   *   *   *

   *   *   *   *   *   *

You will be glad to know that a summer's absence from Malta has done me great good. I have not had a day's illness; whereas, if I had stayed there, I should scarcely have had a day's health; and my strength is consequently repaired in a degree that I was far from expecting.

My Father arrived at Malta with his wife and daughters on the 12th of November; having left Herbert and Willy at school in England. He says :—

We found our three young ones well. They had been admirably looked after in our absence by good Portelli and his nice young wife, and by Mr. and Mrs. Whitmarsh. What an immense treasure Portelli is to me! He did all my office business while I was away, as well as I could have done it myself; and the Commander-in-chief and the Admiral-super-intendent have both told me of the great pleasure they have had in their intercourse with him. He saves me "no end" of official trouble, and in all other things delights in giving me his friendly aid. Of course I do all I can to make his situation agreeable to him, and so we suit each other thoroughly. *   *   *   *   *   *

In another day or two we shall endeavour to settle down into our old business habits; but it needs *an effort*, my dear Bob; for one's ardour on most subjects cools as one grows older and becomes more and more sensible of the vanity of most of our pursuits. In one respect, and that a main one, my best hopes, I humbly thank God, have *not* been disappointed. My children are *all*, as far as I can yet judge, blessed with good dispositions; and whatever may be their failure or success at schools or colleges, it will not be a matter

of oppressive anxiety to me as it has been.   I will endeavour
to do my part well, and wait the result calmly.

   *   *   *   *   *   *

  You are a good boy for not being angry with me for what
I said about Mr. N—— and his Tract No. 90.   I think I
remember saying, in spite of my abhorrence of the tract, that
I still gave him credit for honest meaning.   If anybody else
had written it, I could hardly have made as much allowance.
But oh, how thoroughly sick I am of the profitless writing
and talking these disputes have prompted !   That you and I,
and all of us, may be guided in the right path is my humble
prayer; but I am quite sure that controversial writings do
me no good.   Wise and good men think as Mr. N——
thinks ; other wise and good men think otherwise ; but when
these wise and good men are writing against each other's
writings, they are animated by angry feelings, in which I
have no desire to share. * * * * *

  To me, same date, speaking of little Kitty :—

  She must now be *you* to me, and Fanny too !   My own
dear, dear Sally, and my own dear, dear Fanny, who is still
mine and yours, and happy, supremely happy, and yet looking
for an increase of happiness in our reunion with her.   May
God in his mercy prepare us for it !   This our bereavement
is a medicine to help us in that preparation.   How miserable
a condition this life is, and how *foolish* it is *not* to endeavour
to look forward to a better ! * * * * *

  I am going to make an effort to finish the drawing of St.
John's Church, which I began more than two years ago, and
after a fortnight's work upon it, have not touched it since.
  * * * * I think I got some little benefit by
a glance at the Water-Colour exhibitions in London, after
being so many years without seeing anything of the sort.
What I observed was an immense change in the system of
the artists in general.   They now produce much more forcible
effects with *very* much less finish.   When you look at a

drawing *close*, it is all unintelligible dabs : and yet those dabs tell at a distance most beautifully. The new painters seem to get a better result than the old ones, with a tenth part of the labour. You and I must try to do the same. I suppose one must look at the drawing in its progress, at a certain distance, and not care so much how it looks on close scrutiny. But then, mind, there must be a strong *effect* in it—plenty of colour, and powerful opposition of light and shade.

*　　*　　*　　*　　*　　*

To me, later in November :—

Sir Henry told me, though you have never mentioned it, that Hanmer had contemplated your coming to England, for change of climate. Most fervently do I hope it may not be necessary ; for I well know how unwilling you would be to make so formidable a voyage without your husband ; but if your health really requires the change, let that be the *first* consideration, important as it is to him and to your dear children, as well as to yourself and your own dear Papa too. You shall not come to England, my sweet child, without my seeing you. I would go most gladly to see you there, and think it more than abundantly worth while, even to spend one week with you. But perhaps it might not be amiss for you to spend the *winter* season at Malta, and then I would fetch you, and you well know what joy it would be to us to make much of you and my beloved grandchildren. To have you with me once more would be to me an inexpressible blessing.

Dearly as I have loved you ever since you were born, it now seems as if I had lost golden opportunities to express all the tenderness I feel for you, and as if the greatest comfort I could have in this world would be to make amends to you and myself by loving you more than ever. *Pray* always, my darling, that we may, by God's great mercy, be allowed to love each other in heaven, and to share the everlasting love of our dear ones who are gone before us.

Oh what cruel pain you have felt in the loss of *such* love as our angel Fanny's! There never was in this world a heart that could love more tenderly than hers: and who was ever more worthy to be loved! Who ever united more sweetness, and gentleness, and simplicity, with fortitude more absolutely heroic! You know the precious record I possess of her early affection for me and for you too. You know I have a little book in which she scribbled her baby memorandums after I left England in 1823. In one page is written: " Papa, who I love so much, is gone from me." And in another: "Sally is my only comfort now." *Dear* DEAR child!

*   *   *   *   *   *

To Bob, same date :—

While I was in England I wrote but seldom to you, dearest boy, and no oftener to my poor Sally. You can imagine the pain I felt in writing, for I knew what you would feel in reading the sad accounts I had to send; but now I will resume my old habit of writing once a fortnight, that is by every packet; and if my letters have no other interest, they will, at least, assure you that I am always thinking of you and loving you. I am afraid I am not as good as I have been as a correspondent, or a companion; for I find it hard to screw my spirits up for *anything*. I have done little or nothing yet, since I returned to Malta, except setting my young ones a-going with their lessons, after their long holiday, and making a beginning towards sorting my papers and tearing up rubbish. I mean, then, to make a catalogue of my books, which I never did before. I have not added very many to them since you helped me use them, but yet there are *some* additions.   *   *   *   *

You will be glad to hear that our poor church has got over its difficulties, and is to be ready for consecration without fail on St. Paul's Day, the 28th January. The good Queen Adelaide has promptly answered every fresh demand upon her for it, and has desired only that the work may be brought

to a satisfactory completion. There was a meeting of the
people here, in my absence, to subscribe money for an organ
and other church furniture, and for paying the organist's
salary. Though I was absent, they named me one of the
committee, and I am to attend a meeting of the committee
to-day. I suppose we shall collect £500 or £600; but the
people here are almost all poor. Most have but small incomes,
and you know they are great dinner-givers and champagne-
drinkers. I shall only subscribe £5, like most of the others.
By-and-by I shall be able to do more.

*　　　*　　　*　　　*　　　*　　　*

To Robert, in December :—

What a heavy, heavy loss is the loss of such love as my
Fanny's love! But I loved her too well to grieve for my
own loss while I think of what her condition was and what
I am sure it now is. The fearful trial she has passed we
have still to pass. Agonizing as it was to us to see her
bodily suffering, she herself seemed always raised above
it; and so entirely were pain and distress taken away from
the last close, that it seemed a miraculous transition without
death. *Never* did a human soul quit this earth more happily.
What can we who loved her desire more? I am content to
bear my own loss for the sake of my darling's gain; and
inexpressible is the comfort of having been allowed the
blessed intercourse with her of those last months. I think
of her waking and sleeping too. May you and I and all of
us see her angel countenance again, and share the same
blessed abode for ever.　　　*　　　*　　　*　　　*

To me, same date :—

I wish, my darling, I could sail away to go and see *you*.
If I had not many cables mooring me here, I should make
small hesitation. My own inclination would take me quickly
enough to William's-town, and there is no spot in this world
where I would rather be. There would be happiness enough

for me *near you*, and there is nothing in this life that I desire
in comparison with the joy of looking upon my dear child
again. We have not only *much* to make of each other, but
doubly much for the sake of our darling in heaven. We
have *not* lost her, but she is taken from our sight for a season only. While you and I live, we shall think of her, and
love her still, just as we did love her, only *more;* but the
place she has left we must in the mean time supply to each
other, and we must learn to pray more and more fervently for
God's merciful aid to purify our souls, and prepare us for the
blessed abode of which she is the happy occupant. *Don't
grieve* for her, my own sweet Sally, for hers is a most happy
lot. Her trial is all over, and she passed from earth to
heaven by a death so wonderfully blessed, that I have sometimes imagined it to be more like the transition of Enoch
than the painful passage through the valley of the shadow of
death, by which the other sons and daughters of Adam have
all passed. Doting upon her as we did and *do*, we must *really*
and *actually rejoice* in thinking of the happiness she now
enjoys.   *   *   *   *   *   *

To me, later in December :—

Most of my evenings have been spent lately in the severest
of all reading, that of St. Paul's Epistles, in Greek. They
are far more difficult than any profane Greek book, and you
may imagine it from the English version. There are plenty
of places there where you can't account even for the *grammar*.
Many there are where the sense might be made clearer by
other terms than those the translators have used ; but happily all that is *essential* in the sacred writings is as clear as
the sun. In one place (in the Epistle to the Colossians),
St. Augustine, quoted by Bloomfield, says: " Ego prorsus
quid dixerit, me fateor ignorare." I dare say you can construe *that*. But there is one little emendation I must give
you—not in the Epistles, but Acts, in the 17th chapter, v. 22,
where St. Paul makes his speech to the Athenians. In our

version he is made to begin by saying, "I perceive ye are
too superstitious." But the Greek word has a good sense
and a bad one—superstitious and religious,—and here he used
it in the good sense, "very religious;" that is, more attentive than others to religious matters. This is the sense
attributed to it, says Bloomfield, by most of the commentators for the last two hundred years; and how *very* much it
improves the speech! He had been walking about their
city, and saw evidences everywhere of their attention to
religion, such as their religion was; he saw their altar to
their *unknown god;* and he had so an excellent opportunity
to engage their favourable attention to what he had to say.
"I see," said he, "on all sides, proof that religion is an object
of deep interest with you. Hear me, therefore, for it is of
religion that I desire to speak to you." Don't you like that
alteration, my darling? * * * *

To Robert, same date :—

Sir —— asked me to dinner one day, prefacing his invitation by asking whether I dined out on *Sunday;* and I told
him I did *not.* * * * I don't mean that I
should think it necessary to make a rule not to dine out
under any circumstances on Sunday; but I liked much better
to spend my evening in reading my Greek Testament, and
then a sermon to Mamma, than in drinking wine with half a
dozen jolly captains, and listening to their talk. By the bye,
dear Bob, my Greek Testament reading lately has been in the
Epistles. I have often been daunted by the *first* that comes
in order—the one to the Romans,—and have stuck there; but
this time I thought I would try some of the shorter ones, and
have read Philemon, Colossians, Thessalonians, and Ephesians.
Dreadfully difficult they still are; but, happily, the difficulty
does not lie in essentials, and it is consolatory to see St.
Augustine declaring, "Ego prorsus quid dixerit, me fateor
ignorare." (See Bloomfield's note, 2 Thess. ii. 6.) No profane author could so damp my courage; for I should not feel

shackled as I do here. I should not pay the same deference
to commentators, and should fancy that I might here and there
succeed in discovering a sense which they had missed; but this
is out of the question in the sacred writings, for it would need
more than a life to read what has been written upon them by
wise and holy men, of whom I could never, in any one instance, persuade myself that they were wrong and I right.
But it is the mere *grammar* that makes the *first* difficulty.
The Greek seems nowhere so *dead* a language as in St. Paul.
A modern Greek will read Xenophon like a modern Greek
newspaper. Our *pilot* in the *Revenge*, a thoroughly un-
educated man, did read and construe our Xenophon; therefore, *Xenophon's* is *not* a dead language. But what would
Lambrinos (the pilot) make of St. Paul? Of course, it is easy
to conceive that in a *letter* much might be quite clear to its
receiver which would not be to any one unacquainted with
things of which the writer and receiver were mutually conscious. But an example in point is this:—In a letter Portelli
wrote to us from Malta, while we were in England, he said,
"The sticking-plaster has grown mouldy." Nothing went
before, or followed, that had anything to do with *sticking-
plaster*. A commentator some centuries hence would have
suggested an emendation; but to *us*, all was quite intelligible.
Something is to be supplied which *we* could supply, though
nobody else could. He meant to say, "The children have
met with no accident, such as *you* did, and Clement did, in
tumbling upon the boat's gunwale and breaking your heads,
so that there has been no necessity to *use* the piece of sticking-
plaster you desired Kieli to keep in the boat for fear of such
an accident." I don't know whether you remember; but it
happened once that, in getting out of the boat, Clement fell
and cut his forehead, close to the eye, so uglily, that Mamma
thought it right to take him at once to Liddell, at his house.
I did not go, because it was near dinner-time, and we had
eighteen people coming to dine with us, and they came before
Mamma returned; but as *she* was getting out of the boat,
down *she* fell, with her forehead on the point of the rowlock;

and a frightful wound it made. The recollection of this double disaster made her leave a charge that the boat should never be without a piece of *sticking-plaster*.

*   *   *   *   *   *

Take care of your *eyes*, too. Make short evenings, and get up early; the sun is better than lamps and candles.

CHAPTER XII.

[1844.]

At the beginning of this year my dear Father made a fresh, and I believe last effort, to be removed from Malta. As my Brother says in the manuscript volume I have mentioned before, "had he been recalled now, one of the most efficient servants the Queen ever had would have been secured to the Government, in all human probability, for many years. As it was, his universally admitted claim met with nothing but civil words. He endured another Maltese summer, and he died. The reward man refused, God has granted."

My Father says in a letter to Lizzy of the 17th January : —

By the last packet I had a letter from Bob's old friend Janie (Mrs. Bowles), to tell me that her uncle, Mr. Locker, was going to resign immediately his place as one of the Commissioners of Greenwich Hospital, in consequence of mental failure. She did this to give me an opportunity to apply for the appointment ; and I have accordingly written

to Lord Haddington, the first Lord of the Admiralty.   The
patronage may be with Sir Robert Peel, but I have begged
Lord Haddington in that case to forward my application to
Sir Robert.   I have written to my friend Captain Hamilton too
(Lord H.'s private secretary), to beg him to give me what help
he can, and to engage Sir George Cockburn's good offices.

I take for granted I shall only get a civil refusal, for the
place is so good a one that it will be scrambled for by politicians and people of parliamentary influence, who will be too
strong for such interest as mine to cope with; but then I
can't help that, and I shall escape the reproach of not
having done what I *could*.   I suppose Bob will like to see
what I said to Lord Haddington; so here is a copy of my
letter.   I have said all that was further desirable in the one
I sent to Captain Hamilton :—

" Your Lordship's kind reception of the memorial I had
the honour of presenting six months ago, assures me that I
may without impropriety beg your Lordship to think of me
in the filling up of an appointment which is now likely to
become vacant.   I have been informed, on no vague authority,
that Mr. Locker has tendered, or is about to tender, the
resignation of his office as one of the Commissioners of Greenwich Hospital.   If such be the case, may I hope that your
Lordship would consider me a fit candidate for the place?

" I served, as your Lordship knows, twenty full years
as an Admiral's Secretary; many of those years in active
warfare, at the battle of St. Domingo, at the forcing of
the Dardanelles, in large fleets, on the most important
stations, and commanded by admirals of great name, who
honoured me with their friendship, and have recorded it in
testimonials of no common emphasis.   To those twenty years
I have now added sixteen in my present situation at the head
of the Victualling Establishment at Malta; and of the effici-
ency of this department your Lordship has always received, I
trust, a favourable account.

" My health has suffered severely from too long a residence

in this climate. Of foreign service I have had a large share ; and deeply shall I be indebted to your Lordship, if you can, without injustice to the claims of others, make this an opportunity for recalling me to England."

This, you see, is a strong case. They can't say I have not a claim ; and I believe the general voice of the Admiralty would be that *no* one has a stronger. When I get my answer I will send it you. Meanwhile I shall probably not *think* of the matter further.

My Father, who had visited Mr. Locker when he was in England, knew then, from the state of health in which he found him, that he could not hold his appointment much longer ; and if he could have used this knowledge at that time, he might have had a better chance of success. But as there was then no idea of Mr. Locker's resigning, my Father felt that it would be wrong to take advantage of his knowledge, and never said one word about it to anybody.

On the 17th January he writes to Robert :—

Since I wrote last I have received as many as five of your dear letters. ＊　＊　＊　＊　Two excellent sermons too, "Thou art the man," and "Repentance." The latter is *super*excellent, and is almost the only sermon I ever read that looks to my own eyes as if I had written it myself. Of course, I have read a great many much *too* excellent in point of style, and in display of eloquence and theological learning, to look at all like anything I should have written ; for I have little enough of *Horne*, and far less of Taylor or Barrow. But this sermon of yours has precisely that quality that has now and then given great effect to a writing of mine ; it *comes from your heart*, and expresses itself in the forcible but simple language that a man (an educated man) naturally uses when he feels strongly, and means his hearers to march against Philip, not to cry, "What a fine speaker !" I never read a sermon better suited to its purpose. Too true it is, that upon most of your hearers it was probably wasted in a great

measure, though few, I hope, and possibly none, upon whom it
had not some good effect; for at least, if they listened at all,
it would be sure to raise their clergyman in their esteem.

Go on preaching so, and by degrees you will gain an influence that will tell more and more. A very *young* clergyman
has always uphill work to do. Youth is not often wise, and
grey-bearded men don't like young teachers. As you grow
older, you will gain, of course, more authority. In the mean
time, what has depended upon yourself you have done; for
you have made your people see that at five-and-twenty you
have the *gravity* of a presbyter.

I have received all the newspapers, and so made myself
acquainted with the political struggle in which you were
called upon to take a part; and it is quite clear that you took
the right one, and did no more than your obvious duty
required. There is a wide difference between using a legiti-
mate influence for a good purpose in the way you exerted
yours, and entering hotly into the broils of party politics, by
making speeches at electioneering dinners, with the accom-
paniment of bumper glasses and hip hip hurrahs. If the men
of Philippi had had to choose between a Christian or Pagan
magistrate, St. Paul would full surely have advised them to
take the good and reject the bad, though he would have
taken no part in the hip and hurrah.

Speaking of the new church at Malta:—

The font was given by Mr. Bowden, the writer of the Life
of Pope Gregory; so of course you will think it an orthodox
font; only it is too small. It is a marble copy of a good
Grecian vase. I should have liked it better if it had been
made from one of the old fonts, of which there are many very
beautiful. But then I don't attach all the importance you do
to the particular shapes and positions of church furniture. I
really do venerate *Christian* antiquity; but I can take what
the bad taste of others has provided for me without being
immoderately angry with them.　　*　　*　　*　　*

To me, same date : —

I saw the Governor (Sir Patrick Stuart) yesterday for the first time. Other people who did not know him have been presented at his levee, or by friends they got to introduce them ; but I go to no levees, and I had no ambition to be introduced at all. However, his brother, who was our fellow-passenger from Marseilles, and on whom I had never called, came the other day to see *me;* and upon my returning his visit yesterday, he said at once, " I am very glad to see you, for I want to introduce you to my brother." The Governor received me with such extra cordiality, that I am sure a good deal had been said to engage his prepossessions in my favour ; so perhaps he means to *patronize* me. I shall be glad if he does, simply that I may do something to put the poor Abbate[a] in his proper place. The fact is, that Bouverie's myrmidons have actually had him sent to Coventry by the Palace, for being my friend. The Maltese officials were always jealous of him for being mentally their immense superior ; and with —— to back them, they got Bouverie to slight him. You know the Abbate took my part strenuously at the time of the row about the Secretaryship ; and —— never, of course, could forget that : so ever since, when the dignitaries are invited to dine at the Palace, the ecclesiastical as well as the rest, the Dean has always been left out. At Ponsonby's table he was a frequent, familiar, and honoured guest, and often asked to meet remarkable strangers. At all events, I shall be able to talk to Mr. Stuart about him, and that may do him some good.   ∗   ∗   ∗   ∗   ∗

To me, later in the month :—

I have been thinking of you *more* than commonly of late, because I have been working for you. Don't you remember our many visits to Wittel Hassel,[b] and our sketching there? You know I began, and carried rather far, all on the spot, a

---

[a] Il Decano Bellanti.   [b] In St. Paul's Bay.

drawing of the chapel under the rock. It remained till the
other day in my portfolio just as I left it some eight years
ago, at least; but I took it into my head that I could make
something of it, and so I tried, and I find it will make really
not an ugly drawing, and a good deal of it is not badly done,
and it looks very natural, and is exactly like the place; and
so I thought I should like you to have it, for old recollections' sake. The old Abbate went with us more than once,
and he made a sketch there of our Angel Fanny as she sat
under the rock; and I will give you that sketch too, my
darling.   *   *   *   I have made a very pretty
little drawing of some more Boschetto trees : it was one that
I began many years ago, and put some colour upon it on the
spot one day that I went there with Mr. Allen, an officer of
Engineers, who was here for a short time, and drew well.
Some of his drawings have since been published; but he has
been dead some years. The trees are the first one comes to
in going out of the gate of the Boschetto garden down the
valley. I have put a parcel of goats into the foreground, and
altogether it has turned out well *for me;* only you know I
think almost every drawing I do *bad* as soon as I have
finished it. The palm-trees I did for Lizzy are an exception;
I don't think that bad, nor do I the view from our Sliema
gallery that I sent you, nor one or two in Mamma's album,
—one especially, looking from near the head of our creek
towards Burmola market.   *   *   *   *

We are not apt, you know, to stagnate in our stillness; but
it has been ruffled lately by unusualities; for Mamma and I
have actually been dining out two days running; first with
Sir Lucius Curtis, and then with the Governor.

          *   *   *   *   *   *

Speaking to Bob of the Governor and his family, whom he
liked much, he says :—

They have found out that I am learned in plants, and have
asked me for help. They brought me an Asphodel to name

for them; and the Governor asked me what the tree is that grows commonly here, and looks like Persian lilac.ᶜ I told him it was called Melia, and, therefore, ought to be Homer's μελιη χαλκοβαρεια. *   *   *   *   *

The lessons morning and evening interfere with my reading and writing, and I can do nothing while they are going on but draw; and a great comfort it is to do that; for while the little things are hammering at their small Latin, I can wait for them much more patiently while, at least, my own *fingers* are employed, than if I were doing absolutely nothing. I suppose you can fancy that it *is* rather a formidable effort for me to be still, at this time of day, dealing with *bonus* and *amo*.

I have refreshed myself, in the short leisure of the last three evenings, with reading through, once more, Tacitus's "Agricola," and the bits of the History and Annals relating to the Jews and Christians. Is there not in Tacitus an evidence that the Gospel of St. Luke circulated in his day? Just look (Hist. v. 5): "Nec quidquam prius imbuuntur (Judæi) quam contemnere deos (heathen gods), exuere patriam; parentes, liberos, fratres, vilia habere." Compare this with Luke xiv. 26; and *all* this, in its right sense, is strictly true. I turned to the place in consequence of a reference to it in Jeremy Taylor; but I can't put my hand upon the passage in which the reference is contained.

By the bye, dear Bob, have you read his chapter on Mortification in the Life of Christ? He does not advise us to *punish ourselves*. It is a difficult subject. If by inflicting upon ourselves voluntary vengeance, we could in any measure avert that of the Almighty, our Church would surely tell us so. But we are in His hands and not in our own. Do you remember the Capuchins at Gozo showing us the iron scourge with which they told us they flogged themselves? I am quite sure that, *if* they did, they were none the better for it. At all events, these are not subjects to be dealt with in the earlier stages of a Christian course, nor without the sanction

of deeper feeling than that of the poor Capuchins, men who, at
Lisbon, frequented the Lupinaria, and were met there in the
full dress of their order by the *Revenge's* midshipmen. As
for *our* Capuchins and other Frati and Padri, they are mostly
of the very lowest class of ignorant Maltese; but the Car-
melites are said to enjoy, more than any of them, the favours
of the fair. Do you remember ——, the Italian master?
He has a very handsome wife. Both are as good for nothing
as they well can be. They seem to have had a mutual understanding, and pursued their irregularities by mutual conniv-
ance, till they quarrelled, and she brought him into court
for an infidelity; and he defended himself by pleading *her*
intimacy with the Reverend the Rector of the University,
and the Reverend Superior of the Jesuits, Padre ——. The
Jesuits have for some time been trying to re-establish a
footing here, and they will succeed. They have volunteered
to take charge of the University, and to give the Maltese a
good education for *nothing*. They offer to bring a dozen or
more of professors,—of Italian from Italy, French from France,
Grecians, Latinists, mathematicians, medical, theological,
legal doctors. They would do it with all their hearts. They
are the Pope's zealous myrmidons, and here is a fine field for
them. Hitherto the Government has been able to fight
them off, for one of them (a singularly clever man) has been
preaching politics and something like sedition. That the
Romanist Governments have sanctioned the revival of their
order is not surprising; because, mischievous as they were in
other respects, they were without doubt the ablest of the Pope's
supporters; and, in the present state of the world, they are
naturally considered, upon the whole, desirable allies; but
their intriguing and dishonest spirit is precisely what it was
in their palmy days. That they should always be a formidable
body while they exist at all, is inevitable; for every man of
them is a picked man. They picked out a dozen of the
cleverest boys they could find here, and sent them to the
Jesuits' college at Rome. Out of those twelve there may be
one of a character that suits them, and then that one they will

make a Jesuit, and will train him with unceasing care. So it is at Fribourg, where they have a great college for general education,—they keep for themselves all the *very* best.

*   *   *   *   *   *

To me, in February :—

Mamma and I had a great treat last night. We heard a lecture by Dr. Keith, the author of the " Evidence of Prophecy." He was here for eight-and-forty hours only, on his way to Jerusalem. It is the second voyage to Jerusalem he has made in the last five years. I don't know whether you have read his book. It is a very beautiful one. His lecture last night (at the Presbyterian chapel in Valetta, for he is of the Scotch Church), was to show, by reference to the Prophets, that the " set time" for the restoration of the Jews is come. Just look at the places I am going to note: Psalm cii. 13, and several following; Isaiah vi. 7, to the end; Ezekiel xxxvii. 11, to the end; Daniel xii. 1 to 4. The psalm says, " Thou shalt arise and have mercy upon Zion, for the time to favour her, yea, the set time, is come; for thy servants take pleasure in her stones, and favour the dust thereof."

True it is that the minds of men *have* been turned of late to Jerusalem in a striking degree. The presence of a Christian bishop there is a remarkable proof of this. Isaiah says : " Until the cities be wasted, without inhabitant, and the houses without man, and the land be utterly desolate, and the Lord hath removed men far away, and there be a great forsaking in the midst of the land ; and yet in it shall be a tenth," &c. Now it is only of *late* years that there have been utterly uninhabited cities in Syria and Palestine, and there are now *many* cities literally without a man in them. The houses not, like those of Pompeii, mere walls, but with *roofs* and *doors*. Again, six years ago, Dr. Bowring was sent by Government to examine the state of the country, with a view to the affairs of trade, and he said in his report :

"The land does not now produce more than a *tenth* of what it is capable of producing;"—and when he wrote *that*, he knew nothing of Isaiah, and didn't care to know. The "substance" is in the land, for it produces brambles so thick that there is not room to plant a foot; and where a mountain-torrent has ploughed the surface, deep rich mould is disclosed.

But again, about the desolate cities. A traveller just returned from Jerusalem says he wanted to go and visit a city, the name of which I don't think Dr. Keith mentioned, and some Arabs he wished to employ as guides said, "No; we have just been driven out; there is *not* a man left there, and we cannot return." It seems as if the country, no longer protected and governed by Mehemet Ali's strong hand, was desolated by the quarrels of various Arab tribes, the stronger expelling the feebler, and yet the stronger too few in numbers to fill their places.

Daniel says: "Many shall run to and fro, and knowledge shall be increased." Did men ever run to and fro as they do now, in steamers and on railroads; and when did knowledge increase as it is increasing now? Ezekiel speaks of the "dry bones shaking." There is a great shaking among the Jews. They are stirred up everywhere. *All*, Dr. Keith says, have ceased to couple the Talmud with the Bible. All the Jews of one synagogue (I think he said at Frankfort) had agreed to let their children be brought up Christians. The missionaries of the Scotch Church have lately converted *thirty*, whereas so little impression has been made upon them till very lately, that when I was at Rome eighteen years ago, in the holy week, when the baptizing of the converted Jews is publicly performed, it was said they had of late been so unsuccessful, that, by way of going through the ceremony, one single Jew was baptized for the *third* time. Most likely the story was not true; but at all events it showed that Jewish converts were not common.

Voltaire (like Volney) bears his testimony to the truth of prophecy; for he calls Palestine a barren country, and says

the Israelites only fancied it a goodly land because they had
been forty years in a desert. So it *has* been deemed of late
years a barren country : it has been barren because there
has been a temporary curse upon it ; but its *substance* is still
there beneath the surface, and again it will yield corn and
wine and oil *ten*fold what it is yielding now.

Can't you fancy, my darling, from this poor little sketch,
how interesting such a subject would be, handled by a man
who has made it the study of his life, and who is full of talent
and energy and eloquence. One drawback there was, and
that was that he spoke such broad Scotch that one could
only understand him by dint of painful attention.

*   *   *   *   *   *

At the beginning of this letter my Father, speaking of his
application for the Greenwich appointment, which was backed
by several warm friends in England, says :—

I never feel the slightest anxiety about this or any other
such speculation. There is a good Providence that overrules
our affairs far better than we could govern them for ourselves.
As for myself personally, I am too old[d] to have any ardent
wishes about the whereabouts or condition of my few remaining days ; and whether it would be best for my little ones
that I should be in England I can't know. The cold
there might agree with me less than the heat here.

*   *   *   *   *   *

Before closing this letter he had received his answer, and
simply says at the end of it :—

A letter from Captain Hamilton is just come to tell me that
I shall *not* have the place at Greenwich. Sir R. Peel has
given it to somebody else.   *   *   *   *   *

---

[d] He was only fifty-six.

To Bob, later in the month :—

There is now only one place a vacancy in which would probably remove me to England, and that is Mr. Meek's; but there is now no talk of his leaving it (there was a year or two ago); and he may keep it, and most likely will, till I am no longer fit for work. The truth is, I feel as if there were not *much* work left in me. I am not as strong as I was in body, but the change of which I am most conscious is in the failure of my spirits. They are no longer elastic, and would not carry me through long labours as they used to do. Writing all day would make my head ache, and the responsibilities of an arduous office would shake my nerves. I had felt for some time these effects of old age creeping over me, and you can imagine, dearest Boy, how much they were aggravated by the bitter suffering of last autumn.

I do, I am sure, *rejoice* that my beloved Fanny, my unspeakably beloved child, is removed from a world of suffering. The way we have yet to tread she has most happily passed through. If her life had been prolonged to its full term, it would have been full of severe trials,[e] all of which she has been mercifully spared; and I bless God's holy name that she has departed this life in His faith and fear. But it is His gracious intention that bereavements should wean us from the world; and it is good for me that I should *not* take the interest I used to feel in the present scene. I trust His goodness will enable me to feel a livelier interest in heavenly things, and then I may hope to shake off some of the heaviness of heart which now oppresses me.

I have felt very much for you, my dear Boy, and for my poor Sally; for I know what your grief will be when you receive the sad letters I wrote from Haslar. *   *   *

To me, same date :—

How grievous our separation is when we most want each other! I want, more than I can express, the comfort you

---

[e] What a bitter trial to her would have been his own sufferings and death.

could give me, and I could do you good too in your grief. You and I have real sympathy with each other in such a bereavement. I know what you and our angel Fanny were to each other, and remember all that she was to me. Blessings, all blessings be upon her memory, for her sweetness was indeed inexpressible.

It is very melancholy and very mournful to think of the loss of so much love—lost to us in this world; and it makes the natural weight of increasing years more heavy to me. But yet I am content to bear the burden, for my darling is now exempt from all burdens, and cares, and pains; and angels love her, and she knows, perhaps, how we love her, and pray to be reunited with her; and if she is allowed to pray, how surely we know that she is praying for us to the merciful Saviour who heard her dying prayer, that He would receive her into the arms of His mercy! Oh that He may, in His great goodness, succour us in our last trial as He did her.   *   *   *   *   *   *

Every now and then I will contrive to do something in this way[1] for you, my precious; but I am tired of drawing, and tired of most of the pursuits in which I once took an eager interest. You know some variety of employment one must have, and I will resort to that occasionally. The main business of my short remaining life *ought* to be a preparation for its close; and I pray God it may be. My *relaxation* lately has been reading Tacitus's Annals,—about the hardest Latin there is; but as I am rather intimate with him, he amuses me for an hour or two in the evening, in spite of his crampness.

*   *   *   *   *   *

In April he writes to Robert :—

The packet that came on the 13th brought me no less than *five* very precious letters from you: No. 47, of the 6th of August, and 50, 51, 52, and 53, of the 4th, 13th, 16th, and

---

[1] Drawing.

27th of October. Here is an account that displays *primâ facie* your care for your old far-distant Father, such as he may well thank you for with all his heart; and trust me, dearest Bob, it is not lost upon me.

Nothing can be more to my mind than such letters as these. The one great consolation that we can afford each other is *love*; and as far as that goes, it is very certain that you and I will never be wanting to each other. Thank you, dearest Boy, for going back to my old letters to pick out affectionate bits. You need not ask me if you are not more worth loving now than you were when you rode upon my shoulders. It is quite true that I was wrapt up in you then; but it is equally true that if I had been asked then whether I should be content to have you grow up just what you are, I should have thought it the realizing of my best hopes. Be sure, dear Son, that I am *thoroughly* satisfied with you, and don't want you to be anything but what you are. I never did for a moment doubt that your heart was all right; and you may be sure I give you credit for as much goodness and cleverness as your good brother-clergymen in Australia can, while I love you a million times more than they possibly can.

Very, very sorry I am to have given you pain by writing as I did in my terror; but though you did make me think you were actually turning Papist, and so I naturally made a desperate effort to stop you, yet it was for *you* that I felt. I fancied you bringing upon yourself frightful misery; and it was better to wake you by pinching and pricking you, than to let you tumble into an abyss. This reminds me of one of our long-ago adventures,—when we slid over the head of our prostrate horse at the Scæan gate. The moment I reached the ground, I pitched you a yard or two forward, and you fell on your nose, and then fell a-scolding me: "The horse didn't hurt me, but *you did*; and you did it on *purpose*." I was afraid the horse might trample upon you in getting up, and so made haste to get you out of his way. Just so this last time: I thought you were in great danger, and I was myself in very great alarm for you; and what I wrote was under the

influence of that alarm. If I had loved you less, I should
have been less vehement; but the thorough *scolding* you say
I gave you, is no more sign of abated affection than that
pitch upon your nose was at the Scæan gate. And mind,
dear Bob, if the time were to come over again, I do verily
think nothing better could happen to you than *did* happen,
in your having fallen under Mr. Newman's guidance.

It is certain that he and his associates have done you
infinite good, have made you a devoted Christian, and all
that a good clergyman ought to be. You know I see many
young clergymen; but I see none, whether old or young,
who are in *earnest* as you are. You know I always *did* give
Mr. Newman credit (I use his name because he has been so
much more talked of than any of the good men who preceded or have wrought in concert with him, that his name
may well stand for all) for effecting a mighty reformation,
and I may well be grateful to him for what he has done for
you individually; but while I feel this, you must not think
me bound to follow him in his dreamy wanderings, nor think
me unkind for warning you if I see him leading you into
danger. I believe there is now something very like *craziness*
in his brain.

Of his pious intentions I am not at liberty to doubt. All
the world, all who can exercise any sort of candour in judging
of such things, agree that honest conviction has guided all his
writings; but yet, I am equally convinced that he has im-
bibed unconsciously the spirit of a thorough Jesuit. It speaks
in No. 90—it had spoken in a tract a little earlier, I think
89; but it has declared itself undeniably in his last sermons,
if the extracts I saw be faithful; and I can hardly fancy how
anything that preceded or followed such a sentence as I sent
you, speaking of the "present power and influence of the
Mother of God," can have so affected those words as to un-
Romanize them. When you promised me you would not go
to Rome, even if he did, you gave me very great comfort;
for *there* in heart and soul he *is*. The adopting of *all* his
opinions, *jurare in verba sua*, would now be hard for you, if

it be true (as I take for granted it is) that he has recanted what he wrote in " Romanism." It was natural that you should revere and follow almost blindfold, in your earlier steps, your able and pious teachers; but you will not respect yourself if you *continue*, at your age of *six-and-twenty*, to give up your mind like a piece of "pasta in mano sua," to be moulded at his or their will. This was the old Abbate's phrase, you know, applied to Mamma, who was, of course, in a great rage at the notion. He said she was buona, buona; pasta in mano vostra; and yet, poor thing, she thinks she has had her own way all her life long. So you think too, dear Lizzy, don't you? But Bob has equally cheated you; for, whether you know it or not, you have been *pasta*.

Do let me answer categorically a question you ask me— " Did you ever think I had a violent or sour temper?" No, no, dearest Boy. It has always been a great happiness to me to know, and every one that knows you has always observed, that you had *always* a most sweet temper; but once let a certain measure of fanaticism possess the most amiable man's mind, and see whether on that one subject of his madness he will not speak and write sourly and violently. Party spirit enters into *all* theologians, and no polemical bitterness equals theirs. Consciously or unconsciously they *hate* their opponents, and express their hate. Newman expressed hatred of the Pope *while he felt it*, and when he warned us to beware of him (of his Church) as *lying in wait to do us a mischief* if he could. The Abbate's observation when he read these passages, was, that Mr. Newman had brought shame upon himself by discarding the decencies of language, within which, by common consent, disputation was carried on in these more civilized days.

The style of your sermons is precisely right, for it is clear, forcible, and natural. Young gentlemen are apt to betray their youth by trying to write fine.　　*　　　*　　　*
You clergymen have immense advantage in being able to avail yourselves of scriptural language. What a glorious book our English version of the Bible is! The more familiar

with it you grow, the better, with your taste, you will write
your sermons.   I dare say you have observed, that a sermon
always tells better for being composed expressly for the day,
and treating of the day's service, and touching, if need be,
upon circumstances of the moment.   This gives a sure sign
of earnestness in the preacher, and bespeaks unfailingly the
attention of his hearers.   *   *   *   *

To Robert, later in April :—

I have very great hopes that several good men in the
Church, whom you have often spoken of as authorities,— I
mean Gresley, Palmer the wise, and Paget,—are taking a
lead which will be followed by a multitude of the very best
among the clergy and laity, and will tend to secure for us all
that is good in the Oxford " movement," and save us from its
frightful dangers.   You will, of course, soon see Gresley's
" Anglo-Catholicism."   I have just read a notice of it in the
" Church Intelligencer," the writer of which notice seems to
think on such subjects precisely as I do,—in short, as Mr.
Gresley does, and as I heartily hope *you* will; for it is not
possible for your eyes to remain shut to the plain fact that
the school of which Mr. Newman is the first and foremost, is
a " Romanizing school."   " Mr. Gresley (says the " Church
Intelligencer ") has spoken out very plainly what he thinks
of the conduct of those who seem determined to go as far
beyond the Church towards Popish dissent, as others have
gone below the Church towards Protestant dissent."   There
is, happily, " a numerous body of sound, Catholic, devoted,
and zealous men who are, in truth, the salt, and will ultimately prove to be, under the blessing of Heaven, the
stability and salvation of the Church of God in England ; "
and that you are one of that body I feel sure, from all your
warm expressions lately of attachment to this our Church.
   Speaking of that numerous body of worthy men, Mr.
Gresley says, " They have but one course to pursue; that
is, to declare their unabated attachment to their Mother

Church, to cling more closely to her than ever, and appeal to the good sense of those who seek after the truth, that the excesses of a few are not to be laid to the charge of those who never, in thought, word, or deed, have swerved from their allegiance." I am glad to see that Mr. Gresley thinks the perpetrators of these excesses are but few in number; for surely none of *them* could truly declare their unabated attachment to their Mother Church. Mr. Newman could not; for though he might (or might not), yet if he did, he would deceive himself. He may (or may not) have some feeling that will still keep him among us; he may think it necessary to remain where he is, but his *attachment* is not that of *affection*; and so of all who commit the excesses he has committed.

Some, of course, go beyond him. Mr. S. M——, for example, the member for Bucks, has given in his adherence to the Pope; a Christ-Church man, and, of course, a Tractarian disciple. But what a horrible calamity are these desertions! A county member marching over from our ranks to those of the Papists, carries with him a mighty influence for good to our adversaries and evil to us. His children, the heirs of his estates, will be Papists; their money will be spent in perverting the poor of their neighbourhood, and will be withdrawn from the schools they have heretofore helped to support, and from all the good channels in which it has flowed. This Mr. —— had a companion at Rome, who has also, it is said, turned Papist.

Mr. Gresley says, "He has never believed, and never *will* believe, that any of the writers of the ' Tracts for the Times ' will separate themselves from their Mother Church;" but his mere saying it implies a doubt. He *won't* believe it, though he doubts and fears. But is it not of Newman and Pusey, among others, that he speaks, when he alludes to the conduct of some of those who have been amongst the most prominent advocates of the "movement," and of whom he says, " It is a sad example of human infirmity that men, whose learning, ability, and piety seemed to mark them out as amongst the chief instruments of Divine Providence to restore their Church to its integrity, should have been carried away from their high object by the very eagerness of their zeal, until at length they have dared to *despise* the mother who has nurtured them. For a while charity forbade that we should believe the possibility of such a change.   *   *   * Their friends were unwilling to admit the possibility that those who had once appeared the Church's most devoted champions were really tainted with disloyalty. And now that the fact is too notorious to be questioned (so mind, dear Bob, and don't you question it), when the noblest minds have been beguiled and led on, step by step, until a shipwreck of faith seems impending, a sorrowful alarm is caused in the ranks of those who once marched together as allies. The mischief done to the cause of the Church by such excesses is incalculable." Most heartily do I hope, dear Son, that all this will appear to you as it does to me,—that these good men are bent upon restoring to us the *Church of the Prayer Book*, and that we can only do right by co-operating with them. If we want other doctrine than that which is *honestly* to be gathered from the Prayer Book, we *must* go to Rome for it; for few of us can long be blind enough not to see that no honest interpretation of the Prayer Book can give us the doctrines Mr. Newman professes to find there.

*   *   *   *   *   *

To me :—

Good Lady Gore wrote to Sir R. Peel and Lord Haddington and Sir G. Cockburn, to make interest for the Greenwich appointment for me, and she has sent me Sir G. Cockburn's answer. " You cannot be more anxious to serve Mr. Sconce than I am, nor can you have a higher opinion of his abilities; but I cannot hold out to you any favourable prospect of his obtaining the vacancy in Greenwich to which you allude."   *   *   *   *

Some letters of mine had miscarried, and my Father was anxious about me. He says:—

You said, when you were a little scrap, you would give a guinea for a letter from Papa, and how gladly would I so part now with one of *my* guineas. How I love to remember these little sugarplum-sayings! And now I may soon receive from you answers to my first letters from England—letters which wrung your poor heart in telling you of the grievous illness of our darling, and of the too sure termination of that illness. I think continually of the grief you are suffering, and feel it still more than my own. My course is nearer to its close. If, by God's great mercy, I may join my dear one in Heaven, and live with her for ever, it signifies very little what measure of suffering may fill the short intervening space. I have not the spring either of body or spirit that I had even until very lately; but it is much *better* so. It is sad, very sad, my chick, that you and I should be separated, when we so need each other's sympathy. You know how that blessed angel was twined about my heart, and well I know how precious she was to yours.

*   *   *   *   *   *

In the next letter :—

I have nothing whatever the matter with my health, and feel the approach of old age no otherwise than in its taking away my *elasticity* both of limbs and spirits. I can't interest myself in the pursuits in which I used to delight; but you know, my darling, it is better so, for it would be a sad thing if we were *never* to be *weaned* from this world till we were suddenly called out of it. Yet, I work with my children, and occupy myself a little with drawing, and find *some amusement* in books: for instance, I have just read *all* the works of Tacitus clean through, an hour or two at a time in the evenings. I like old books better than (most) new; and besides that, you know, I may help the young ones still with

their Latin and Greek; and to do that effectually, I must
keep my acquaintance fresh with the good old gentleman.

       *   *   *   *   *   *

To Robert, in May :—

I have just read a book called "Kings of the East," showing, that in the great battle before the world's end, *England*
is to be the Church's champion. There are certainly many
striking facts brought forward; but then, they are sadly
mixed up with trash. There is small profit in reading a book
of that sort, unless the author be content to go no more than
reasonable lengths, and the misfortune is, that *all* such books
attempt a great deal too much. From half a dozen words of
Scripture are spun out as many chapters of exposition, all
made, of course, to consist with some notion the writer has
taken up, and of which he is determined to make the most.

       *   *   *   *   *   *

To me, in May :—

I have an interesting word or two to tell you from my
friend Lord Nugent, who was our fellow passenger from
Marseilles. He has since been to Palestine and Egypt, and
came to see me, to give me an account of his adventures.
Here is something that will please you. He was passing
with his Arab guide through one of the gates of Hebron.
They were walking in the middle of the road, approaching
the gate, and the gate was like that opening upon the Street
of Tombs at Pompeii—in short, like that of Porta Reale or
Porta Marina, a big gate in the middle, and a little one for
foot-passengers on each side. Just as they were coming to
the *middle* gate, through which they were going to walk, a
drove of camels approached, meeting them; upon which the
guide called out in Arabic, "Let us go through the *Needle's
Eye !*" The gates of Eastern towns are commonly so made;
the big gate in the centre is for *camels*, for there are few
carriages of any sort in use there, and the side gates are

commonly called, and, no doubt, *were* called two thousand years ago, *needles' eyes!* Among the guesses at the origin of the scriptural expression, some interpreters say, you know, that there was *a gate at Jerusalem* called the Needle's Eye. But how much more satisfactory a solution we have now : it was not a particular gate so called, but the *general* name of the *side* gates, to distinguish them from the *camels'* gate. For a camel to pass through a needle's eye would be a clear impossibility ; but a rich man *may* enter into the kingdom of heaven, just as a camel might possibly, by *getting rid* of its *load*, squeeze through the lesser gate.

You have heard a great deal of the Cairo magicians, and have been bewildered by the wonders they enacted, as I have been. They claimed, of course, Lord Nugent's curiosity, and I am glad to find one can escape from the conclusion that they are workers of real devilry. Very keen observers, such as Captain Martin and Sir William Eden, Captain Ranier and Mr. Lane, have been all but dismayed by them. These conjurers certainly did, in many cases, describe absent people they had never seen with most minute accuracy. How did they do that? By mere collusion, Lord Nugent thinks, and Mr. Lane now thinks too, with persons who *had* seen them. Mr. Lane is at Cairo still, and has been there many years. He and Lord Nugent took their measures well for guarding against any collusion, and went with only one other English friend to see one of these Magi. They called for five or six remarkable people, and the man failed in every instance so totally that he never made one guess approaching the truth. Among others, he described Mr. Muntz with a chin like a lady, and this Mr. Muntz, a Member of Parliament, is remarkable for wearing a beard like a Capuchin's. They then asked for a man distinguished by enormous size, a prodigious mass of fat, and the conjurer described him as neither fat nor thin, and sitting with one ankle resting on the other knee, a position in which *I* could sit (when I have no lumbago) easily enough, but one as perfectly impossible for the fat gentleman in question as any of the queer postures of the

Chinese jugglers. When they told the man of his failures,
he said, " Ask me for somebody that has lost an eye or a leg,
and see if I don't tell you right." This was, of course,
affording himself a chance of a good guess, and they told
him so, but asked for Sir Henry Hardinge. The man
naturally imagined *he* might have lost a leg or an eye, but
which he could not venture to guess; so when they asked
him if he saw both his eyes, he said no, for his face was in
profile. Then, if he saw his feet. No, for they were partly
concealed by a cloak or dressing-gown that he had on. What
coloured gloves had he? White. Do you see both? Yes;
for he has his arms crossed. Well, it so happens, that Sir
H. Hardinge has lost a hand, and wears no sham hand, but
his coat-sleeve hangs down with *nothing* visible beyond it.

This magician was not Abdel Kader, the great man of all,
whose reputation is widest spread. So they went next to
Abdel Kader, and *he* failed quite as absolutely as the other;—
a total failure in every case. He said it was very remarkable;
but that since the death of *Othman Effendi* his power *had*
sometimes failed him,—he could not account for it. Upon
this, Lord Nugent observed Mr. Lane strike his forehead, as
if something remarkable had suddenly occurred to him; and,
on their going out, Mr. Lane explained what it was. The
conjurer had, undesignedly, given a clue to the detection of
the fraud. Othman Effendi was a renegade Scotchman,
who had risen to fortune and high place under Mehmet
Ali. He was an intelligent man, and useful to English travellers. He was generally of their party when they consulted
the conjurer, and Mr. Lane had not the least doubt that he
was in *league* with him. He contrived to get information
from the consulting parties, and to give it to the conjurer.
Whenever the conjurer did succeed, it was, they now feel
sure, by means of collusion with Othman Effendi or some
other. Mr. Lane remembers two remarkable cases of the
conjurer's success when Othman was present; one was in a
most exact description of *Burkhardt*, who was a *personal
friend* of *Othman's*, and the other of a man who was at the

time *ill in bed*, and whom the conjurer actually described as being so. Mr. Lane is not quite positive, but he thinks it most likely that he *told* Othman that the man was ill; and then, of course, Othman told the magician. Lord Nugent is writing a book, and Mr. Lane has authorized him to say that he agrees with him in the conviction that any success these people have had is only to be attributed to this sort of collusion.   *   *   *   *   *   *

Speaking again of his dear lost child :—

Are we not *sure* that she has passed from a state of long painful trial to a rest full of blessedness now, and of still more blessed hope? In this world we shall not look upon her sweet face again. Oh, how very sweet it was! But we will rejoice for her sake, and bear bravely our own loss, praying fervently to God that we may be reunited with her in heaven, and with her angel mother, whose image she was in mind and feature, in the soft speaking of her blue eyes, and the tenderness of her heart. My dearest, *we* must love each other more and more. You are many thousand miles away from me, but yet you are an unspeakably precious treasure to me. I cannot see you, but I can always think of you, and pray for you; and when I am writing to you, it is in some sort like being with you; and when your dear letters come, it is some sort like *your* coming.

*   *   *   *   *   *

To Robert, same date :—

I have that vile *lumbago* again. After nine years since I had the least touch of it, it laid its vile grasp upon me suddenly the day before yesterday, and how long it may keep its hold one can't guess. I have had it just three times: once for three years incessantly, then for a month, then for a year. It is not as sharp this time as before, so I hope it may be less tenacious. I went into the garden quite well. It was a beautiful morning, but there had been some rain the day before, and so there may have been some dampness in the air; and, in half an hour came the pain and tightening of the nerves about my back as suddenly as a gun-shot. But it is not any violent pain, and the mere inability to move quickly is less inconvenient to me than it would be to most people; so I shall try to bear it as lightly as it deserves.

*   *   *   *   *   *

To Lizzy :—

MALTA, 29th May, 1844.

MY VERY SWEET CHILD, — The packet has brought me many letters to answer and much work to do in little time, but the very first thing I have to do is to follow the impulse of my heart, and tell you how thoroughly I delight in your dear letter. How I love to see you taking your husband's part, like a brave, honest, affectionate wife as you are!

May you never have harder work to do for him than to convince me that you are right in your estimate of his worth! I love him all the better, Lizzy, for having made *you* love him so thoroughly, and of course I am more persuaded than ever that I formed a very wise judgment when I gave my hearty consent to his making love to you, when he ought, in most other people's opinions, to have been reproached with something like insanity.

Now, dearest Lizzy, I feel quite sure you have had wit enough to discover that there is no little of *self-love* in the desire men commonly feel for their sons' success at college and elsewhere; and you know I interested myself so much in Bob's school and college pursuits, that it would have been natural for me to feel more than commonly mortified at his not gaining the honours I expected him to gain; but yet, so cordially do I agree with you in being quite satisfied with him *as* he *is*, that I do not feel, and have not felt, the smallest particle of regret for what he has missed. He could not have been a better man or a happier. I am very sure he would not have been half as happy with a *double first* as he is *with you;* nor have done half as much good to himself and others as a college tutor as he is now doing as a parish priest.[g]

I had one selfish feeling in heartily working for him when he was at Tunbridge, and that was the desire to have him come and see me at Malta; which he could not have done between school and college if he had not won the exhibition of that year. Nothing could exceed the intensity of my desire for his success in that object, for the sake of the great happiness I knew it would give him as well as me; but for all the rest I have thought of nothing but his advantage, and have thought of it with the deep interest of very ardent affection. Ay, my dear Lizzy, for though we don't know much of ourselves, I think I can't be mistaken in thinking that I have a very ardent nature; and I know how to love as well as you do; and how I loved Bob *he knows,* and so you and he both know how I love him *now.*

Very, very sorry, then, I am for having given pain to you and him. I did think, it is very true, that he was growing crazy, and such a thought might well have frightened me out of the little wits I had, and so I may have expressed myself badly; but yet I well knew his heart was all right, and therefore it would have been both wicked and stupid to *love* him less.

Now, dearest Lizzy, I know you and he are thoroughly one, and so I will say to *you,* in answering this dear letter of yours, what otherwise I should have preferred saying to himself. It was not my misunderstanding of his expressions, not my want of skill in extracting their meaning, that gave me the painful impression under which I afterwards wrote. He did seem to me to be going, running, galloping into Popery —and at last in my dismay I talked to the bishop about it, and read him some of Bob's letters. He exclaimed with the same sort of amazement I had felt myself. I begged him to tell me if there was anything I could say that would be of

---

[g] My brother was at this time removed from Penrith by the bishop, to St. Andrew's, then the cathedral church of Sydney.

any use, and he suggested a word or two. I could not bear
to write anything to hurt my dear Boy. I showed the bishop
what I had written, and he would not let me expunge anything. He really did think, as I did, that this my dear Son
was likely, even by the next packet, to declare himself a
faithful subject of the Pope. I could not *help* entertaining
these horrible fears; and you see it was not my want of
theology that laid me open to them; for they were confirmed
by the cool judgment of a venerable person to whom I applied
for comfort and counsel in my deep distress.

Now then, Lizzy, kiss your husband, and tell him his late
letters have set my heart so perfectly at ease again, that I
shall certainly never *scold* him any more, and so you won't
have to scold *me* any more. And as for *love*, ask your own
dear heart how it feels for Madzy. You wouldn't *change*
her, would you, for the brightest little lady in either hemi-
sphere? Just so am I satisfied with my Bob; and thoroughly
content I am to have him just as he is. I may now and then
have opinions differing from those he has, or seems to have,
and then neither you nor he would like me not to say what
I think about them. I am sure he would much rather I
should treat him in this respect, as I always have done, with
unreserved frankness.

It happened only the other day I told him I did not like
his signing " A Poor Man " to a letter he published, considering the subject of the letter; but he knows I am as sure as
of my own existence that he is incapable of practising a
deception. It occurred to me that there was a sort of deception in it, and you and he will please to love me all the better
for saying what I thought about it.

*   *   *   *   *   *

I find I did my dear son an injustice in thinking (from
what he said about it) that he had argued unbecomingly with
the Bishop. Thoroughly satisfied I am that he did not, and
thoroughly sorry for having pained him by saying what I did
about it.

I wish, dearest Lizzy, I could spend more time with you

to-day ; but I have done what I could, and I am sure you will accept this little letter as an expression of my love for you, and of my earnest wish to set your good heart at rest, and to convince you that I love your husband almost as much, and think of him almost as highly even as you do. Think of *me*, dear, as Bob does. I am not a very cross old man. Bless you and your pretty babes.

To Robert, in June :—

*   *   *   *   I quite agree with Mamma, who exclaimed when I read to her your last sermon, " Upon my word, Bob is a capital writer of sermons ! " And she is a capital judge too, Bob. And I should like you to try and make some impression upon your strange legislative councillors. The newspapers you sent me have told me of their doings, and of the total absence of *Church* influence among them. If they are a fair sample of your people, the Church must be in a lamentable minority. There are, probably, many Irish and Scotch, Romanists and Presbyterians, among you, and among the English an unusual proportion of dissenters and *indifferents* ; arising from the cruel neglect of Church and State, in leaving such a population for the best part of a century without churches and clergymen.

Have you found any of these people open to conviction? Many, like poor Michael Towel,[h] left the Church because it was not religious enough for them. He preferred the black drummer to Mr. Le Mesurier, because his preaching was " more effectual like." But there *is* more life among us now, and there must be some among the hitherto dissatisfied, who begin to think you can teach them at least as well as the drummer can.

The majority of the dissenters are, I believe, more or less Calvinistic, and with them, of course, you can do nothing. The Calvinistic members of our own Church hate us bitterly

---

[h] An old warder of the Victualling Yard.

enough.   They have been assailing our bishop in the *Record*,
for not opening a crusade here against the Roman Catholics,
and on other scores.   There have been several letters of that
sort (I have seen none of them), and their author is a Dr.
——, who spent some time here two or three years ago; the
man, I dare say, I told you of, who came one day, in his great
regard for me, to show me the error of my belief in baptismal
regeneration.   He brought me a *book;* and in return I put
before him Van Mildert, Taylor, and several more, which I
told him I liked better than his.   Before that he was a
constant visitor at our house; but because I could not for his
pleasure give up my creed, he came again no more, but to bid
me a formal good-bye.   This is, of course, *mere* party spirit,
and a miserable spirit it is.   Are there *any* theologians free
from it?   ——'s five-year-old son is not, for he saw Charley
saying his prayers the other night, and told him he would
go to the Devil, for not crossing himself *as he did.*

*   *   *   *   *   *

No young writer of sermons ever wrote more like an old
one than you do.   You have always had good taste enough to
shun the use of *finery*.   There is no sentence of your writing
that has one particle of the foolish display that so often
offends us in the sermons we hear, never of Kitson's, but of
the chaplains who occasionally help him; one of them a very
clever young man too, who is rising into renown among us.
A writer of essays for his readers' amusement may deal in
prettinesses, for which he has leisure; but if I am earnestly
bent upon a point, I must go straight on; I take what I find
at hand to suit me, and nothing far-fetched; what helps me
and my hearers on, and nothing that would set my own
thoughts a-wandering and theirs too.   In short, nobody can
write well who is not in earnest; but a full heart is always
eloquent; and as you have good taste, and scholarship to boot,
you will do great things.

*   *   *   *   *   *

A large body of Cambridge young men expressed their

wish for the re-establishment of monasteries, a sentiment in
which I thoroughly disagree with them; but it shows that
religious feeling is at work at Cambridge too. Of course, I do
dislike opinions tending to work into our Church anything
that now belongs to Rome, and does not belong to us. Whatever is truly ours let us cherish, and let us repair where it has
fallen into decay; but let us borrow nothing from the Pope.
What monkery tends to is plain enough to people who have
lived, as I have, in Portugal, Italy, and Malta. Here and
there there is of course a good man among them; but generally they are the most ignorant and profligate of human
beings, the most venal procurers, and unblushing perpetrators
of impurity. At all events, monkery is no part of our Church
system, and therefore we must do without it as well as we
can.

By the bye, Government here having still set its face
against the introduction of a body of Jesuits from abroad, the
Pope and the Maltese have agreed upon a mode of carrying
their point at last; for a couple of dozen young Maltese have
been sent to Sicily, to be educated as Jesuits there; and when
they return, full-grown Jesuits, of course *they* must be received.
Some of the best of the Maltese families have sent their sons
upon this errand.

In the next letter, speaking of a young clergyman :—

He deals in metaphors, alliterations, and prettinesses of all
sorts, and talked of a good man becoming a jewel, which at
length, by the Almighty's *setting*, &c. I could not hear the
finish of the sentence, for that word *setting* stunned me.

*　　*　　*　　*　　*　　*

Do tell me where you found " church " said to be of Greek
origin (I suppose you mean Κυριου οικος), for Dr. Johnson
makes it Saxon, and Archbishop Whately says it is probably
no other than " circle," *i. e.* assembly, *ecclesia*. I should
hardly think it could be Greek, for, if it were, it would pro-

bably have come to us through the French (or Italian possibly), and there is no French word like it ; besides that, the formation of " church " from the words Κυριου οικος would not have been at all according to the process by which Greek words are commonly made into English; and besides that, our Saxon ancestors who first used the word church, didn't know a word of Greek, no not one of them. I have no time for hunting, nor books here that would help me; but the word church is, I have no doubt, older than Petrarch, who brought Greek into Italy, whence it slowly found its way to England.   *   *   *   *   *

To me, in June :—

I have always delighted in drawing for you, my chick, for the sake of the intense pleasure you take in what I can do for you, and the pretty praises you bestow on my doings, *da cuore* and *con amore*.

I have now something else I must do for you one of these days, if I live. I must copy for you a drawing I have made for Mamma, of our rooms : it has turned out very well, Mr. Allingham and Michele say; at all events, it is just like the reality, and when I look at it through my hand, so as to exclude the margin, it does not look like a picture, but like the very carpet and bookcases, and chairs and tables.

   *   *   *   *   *   *

Our summer[1] has *begun*, and, as usual, has begun to use me ill. I have been contending for the last four days with my old complaint, and have not yet subdued it. It is only in a mild form, but yet enough to weaken me ; for besides the disorder itself, I have a semi-starvation to suffer, living only on macaroni and rice-and-water.   *   *   *

I take immense care of myself, and no one can be more temperate or cautious about diet ; but it seems as if no care could ward off these vile disorders. I am not *ill* this time,

---

[1] He was obliged to spend the summer at the Marina.

as you may suppose from our having entertained a party at
dinner yesterday: there were Michele and his bride, the
Abbate and Luigi, the Portellis, and Mr. Allingham.

  *   *   *   *   *   *

 The first stone of the new dock itself is to be laid
to-morrow. It is to be an imposing ceremony. The
Governor is to be chief mason. Hanmer ought to be
here with his apron; and Sir L. Curtis has invited 280
people to be present, and to *breakfast* afterwards (at three
o'clock) under our colonnade, where a table is laid half
the length of the Marina, with canvass and flags spread to
keep out the sun,—but they *won't* keep it out ; and you remember what our Marina is, on the 28th of June, from three
to six in the afternoon ;—it is a furnace.

 We have just had a right royal visit. The King and
Queen of Naples chose to visit Malta ; and went away yesterday, after staying two days. His chief attendants were
our two Admirals, with whom he must have had a very
edifying intercourse, as he doesn't know a word of English,
nor either of them a word of Italian or French. * * *

 The King came alongside my wharf, and I received him at the
steps ; but finding the Admiral was at the dockyard, he shoved
off again, so I escaped the infliction of his society. What sort
of an infliction it was to those who endured it, you may fancy
from this,—that he went everywhere—through the streets,
over the dockyard, the new works, the forts—under the broiling mid-day sun, in a sciroc wind, with his hat in his hand,
and making all the twenty people who accompanied him do,
equally, all they could to court a *coup de soleil*. I have not
heard that any are dead yet ; but he must be surprised if all
survive it. His own head is double thick, and well covered
with hair ; but poor Colonel Tylden, the chief engineer,
walked by his side, with his poor old purely bald head
shining, and reflecting the sun in a blaze like a mirror. Sir
E. Owen invited him to a collation on board the flag-ship,
and he went to *restore* accordingly, after all his hot marches ;
but, unluckily, the Admiral had not given clear orders to his

servants, or his servants made a blunder; but so it did happen
that, hungry and thirsty as his Majesty might well be, there
was nothing, absolutely *nothing*, for him to eat or drink; and
at last tardily produced itself a bottle of wine, said, moreover,
to have proved sour.   Its ill-fated Majesty had reviewing and
cannonading to its heart's content; but its more vulgar appetites were doomed to disappointment, for they say he took the˜
Governor by surprise at St. Antonio, and found no better prog
there than sandwiches and tea, though this Neapolitan Majesty
looks as if he could bolt an ox and wash it down with a pipe
of wine.

To Robert, in July : —

If it were not that Mr. Newman has been heretofore your
guide, and that all his opinions have become yours, my great
dislike of the course he has taken would deter me from
reading a word he writes or others write about him; but, as
it is, it is impossible for me to see the progress of Puseyism
without thinking of you, and hoping that Uncle Vi has mis-
understood your letter, in supposing you a *"rank* Puseyite."
That he should think it " so much the worse" if you *were*,
you would not, perhaps, wonder yourself, if you knew the
lengths to which the heads of the party have now gone.

*   *   *   *   *   *

I told you some time ago of what Mr. Newman had said,
to engage us to offer our prayers to the Virgin Mary ; and I
have just read a notice of the lives of certain Saints, Mr.
Newman being the editor, which Saints are, of course, held
up to us that we may worship them too.   Saint Stephen
the Abbot, Saint Richard the Saxon, Saint Walburga the
Abbess, the lady who, rising from prayer, full of holy power,
bade the elements be still, and the winds and waters heard
and obeyed!   If this is part and parcel of Puseyism, do tell
Uncle Vi that you are *not* a rank Puseyite.   The most
forward advance of the party, or rather of its chiefs, had not
gone beyond the 90th tract when you last expressed your

concurrence with them; but I have a strong hope (not without anxiety) that you will agree with me in dissenting thoroughly from the views of the editor of these lives. He is not at all more a Jesuit in my eyes now than he was when he wrote No. 90; but I think, perhaps, he will be in yours. He wore a mask, and wears it no longer. My belief is, that he felt long ago a desire to lead us nearer to Rome than he then indicated. In the conscientious discharge of what he deemed a duty, he concealed the extent of his views, and advanced slowly, that he might not outstrip his followers. My hope is, that there are now not very many as far gone as he is, and that a great body of them, who had already gone too far, are turning back again. You won't wonder at my reading with anxiety on your account these strange writings of Mr. Newman's, after the very strong terms in which you have expressed your attachment to him, and your adherence to all his opinions. You believed that he had never gone from one thing to another, that he had been perfectly consistent all along, one writing being only the development of another; and just so, then, you may consider this panegyric of St. Walburga a development of No. 90, in which he told us the Church of England had no objection to our invoking her. I know *you* won't invoke her, for in one of your letters you disavowed that particular doctrine; but when you know that Mr. Newman does, it will be very hard for you to persuade yourself that he is wrong. By those of his friends who do not, or do not *yet*, invoke Saints, it will probably be said that these writings, like 90, are merely intended to deter over-zealous men from turning Papists, by showing them that they have saints enough for patrons and patronesses at home, without going to Rome for them; but if that were the primary motive of No. 90, yet obviously its tendency was to recommend to general adoption the Roman Catholic doctrines it treated of, and Mr. Newman did not at all object to its having that tendency, *or he would have said so.* You said, that if you were asked to point out the one man in all the world least likely to turn Papist, that man should be Mr.

Newman: you may still be of that opinion, thus far, that
he is not likely to quit our Church, individually, and join
the Roman; though really it is very wonderful that even in
that sense you should single him out; but do you think the
Pope can consider even Dr. Wiseman, or the whole body of
Jesuits, a more useful ally or better friend than Mr. Newman is? Does he not see that Mr. Newman is serving his
cause by remaining where he is a million times better than
by simply passing over? He has no wish to leave our
Church, but to hand over to the Pope *Church and all.*

Feeling all this, dearest Bob, it is natural for me to write
it to you. Of what use would be our intercourse, or what
comfort could there be in it, if I did not express all my
thoughts freely? But pray don't find in what I have said
anything to *hurt* you. One does not always know, or stop
to analyze one's motive for what one says. Mine, I suppose, has been mainly to justify my own long ago expressed
opinion of Mr. Newman as an unsafe guide, and my agree-
ment with uncle Vi in his "tant pis" of Puseyism in its
present development.   *   *   *   *

The day before yesterday, the 6th, was my birthday, dearest
Bob, and I have now completed fifty-seven years. I pray
God to make me deeply grateful for the mercy that has
spared me so long, and to teach me the true and full value of
every day that His great goodness may yet grant to me! I
am not strong, for I have no flesh upon my bones; but my
limbs are yet active and sound, my constitution still free from
any fixed disease, and my senses as fit for use as ever. Yet
I am reminded by the setting in of this summer, that
danger is always at hand.   *   *   *   *

I would not stay at Malta if I could help it; but, as long
as I can, without running *too* much risk, I *must*, for otherwise I could not educate my boys. For their sake I know I
must not persevere in bearing this climate too long; for my
life is of more value to them than many sterling pounds; but
I must not be in a *hurry* to resign my post. I should have
a much better chance of getting an appointment in England,

by retaining this in the mean time. I must fight with this summer as well as I can here, and think of getting leave of absence for some part of *next*.   *   *   *

To me, same date :—

The quiet of my official life will, I am afraid, be disturbed by the doings of the French and their fighting admiral, the Prince de Joinville. They have now a quarrel with the Emperor of Morocco, and have sent a fleet to his shores. We, of course, shall quickly have an equal fleet there too, for which I shall have to provide. That our fleet *will* go and watch the French is certain enough, for Sir R. Peel said so in the House of Commons; but does it mean that if the French attack the Emperor's town, we are to attack *them?* It would seem a hard case that a great European war should be created for the sake of these Moors; but on the other hand, I suppose we should not choose the French to possess forts close to the Straits of Gibraltar, which might become formidable to us. At all events, ships will come from England and give me, what I don't like, *more work*, and more anxiety, which I like still less. You understand that I deal in perishable materials, and that I am answerable for their preservation; and that when there are large quantities of such things to take care of, there is more danger of their spoiling than when the quantities are but small; and it is not as if any *credit* or *reward* were to be got by one's labour and one's cares, for mine are of too humble a nature for that, and so the best thing I can desire is *repose*.   *   *   *

I suppose you have heard something of Joinville's pamphlet? What a hellish spirit this young man must have! He goes to England with Victoria; the young Queen takes his arm, and shows him her comfortable house, and shares her loaf with him; and he returns to France, and writes and publishes an argument to show his countrymen how pleasant it would be to cross over, and burn down the said snug and hospitable dwelling. Some time after I came to Malta this amiable young gentleman came here, and was about as big

as Clement is now.   His heart must have made haste to grow
hard.   *   *   *   *   *   *

I must tell you of little Mia's[k] courage.   She is but a little
woman, you know, and I thought her in bravery not more
than a match for a mouse; but she had *three* teeth drawn
without uttering a sound.   Mr. Finney, the dentist, said he
had never had such a child under his hands.   You women
are in truth glorious endurers, and I am glad for poor little
Mia's own sake that she has so much in her of a most useful
virtue.   I gave her a dollar for her honorarium, and she
valued it far more for the credit's sake than that of the
62½ caramells for which she might if she pleased exchange
it.   The truth is, she will give it all away in sixpences to
certain old women who are among our visitors.

By the bye, do your Australian beggars ever say Thank
ye?   You know ours never do.   I gave an *old* boatman
double his fare the other day, and remarked to Chico, who
stood by, the man's cool thanklessness, and asked him if his
countrymen *ever did* say Thank ye; and he confessed I was
quite right, for they never did.   I think the last acknowledgment I had of that sort was at Gozo fourteen years ago,
and I was so struck with the poor man's unusual gratitude
that I added sixpence to the original penny.   Such appeals
are not likely to empty one's purse.   All these people, too,
who receive our pence and our shillings, feel quite sure we are
going to the Devil, and say so in terms of very cordial acqui-
escence.   Poor Mademoiselle Villes[l] has none of these
bigotries and hatreds, and talked about us to Rosaria, the
half-witted housemaid, and asked her if I must go to the
Devil.   "Ce Monsieur Sconce, qui est si bon?"   "Yes, yes,"
said the half-witted maid, "*Devil*, DEVIL!"

Later in July :—

I have been much better than I have ever been in summer
for the last eight or ten years, except out of Malta; and I

---

[k] Amelia.   [l] The French governess.

verily believe this is owing to the loss of our Sliema house.
Here is one proof more how little we know of what is good
for us. We fancied a summer at the Marina would be the
death of some of us, and we find that all are as well as if they
were at Sliema, and I all the better for not having a daily
journey in the sun.   *   *   *   *   There are *but
two things* that spoil the sweetness of the air; but the truth
is, that when we walk on the terrace in *front* of our house,
the odour of the drains contaminating the stagnant creek is
partly insufferable; and into our *back* windows comes not
unfrequently that abominable smell of fried oil in which the
Maltese deal so largely. From all such evils, however, we
escape for two or three hours every evening in our boat, and
I know little about them while I am busied as I am in the
daytime, or sound asleep at night.   *   *   *   *

Do you see Reviews, my darling? There is an article in
the June Quarterly, headed " Schism in the Papacy." The
article is not quite satisfactory, for it does not enable one to
judge of the extent to which the combination has spread;
but that there have been many of the Roman clergy concerned in it seems certain. I heard many months ago that
it had created a strong feeling at Rome; and the Pope was
certainly alarmed, for he ordered what is called a triduo—a
solemn service of three days — to avert the danger that
threatened the Church. It had an unexpected effect too;
for the people at Rome did not accurately distinguish between the interests of the Church and those of the State;
and, in the panic the triduo created, made a run upon the
bank, and well-nigh broke it.

But these German papists who want to marry, want three
other things : prayers in their vernacular tongue, communion
in both kinds, and no compulsory confession. To none of
this can the Pope consent; it follows that they cannot persevere without separation; and then away goes from their
creed the supremacy of the Pope, and his infallibility. All
this would be full of deepest interest if a large body were
agreed in the enterprise; but, as it is, I am afraid it cannot

be large enough to contend with the secular power that will be arbitrarily exerted to put it down. The Austrian Government, you know, forbids its subjects to change their religion, and so the inhabitants of Zillerthal migrated in a body to Prussia; but as *Austria* can't migrate to Prussia, it follows that before Austria can be reformed, the Austrian Government must be changed, which is not likely to happen in our time. The Jesuits meanwhile are adding more to the Pope's strength than the German malcontents are likely to take from it. The Jesuits, as the professed enemies of our religion, are naturally directing their chief energies to the countries within our rule. India seems to be their main point, and they are doing much more there than we have the means of counteracting. They have not only the advantage of absolute union in their own Church, a mighty power wielded by one unfettered will; but the theological enmity of the *Romans* well suits the national enmity of the *French*, and so *they* are co-operating most heartily with the Pope in trying to make the people of India more his Holiness's subjects than Queen Victoria's. To show how sensible the Pope is of the value of his Jesuit friends, he has actually made Padre Ryllo rector of the Propaganda. This is the man (a Polish Jesuit) who was sent out of this island by the Government for preaching unwholesome *politics*. A most active and unscrupulous partisan he is.   *   *   *

I paid the Bishop a visit yesterday, and he told me the Maltese newspapers had talked of his *audacity* in presuming to say grace at Sir Lucius Curtis's dinner, in the presence of Maltese. Sir Lucius had admitted to his table some six or eight Maltese; and *that* was a reason why the English bishop should not say grace for the two hundred and fifty English who were there assembled.   *   *   *   They really do behave, and we encourage them to behave, as if they were the dominant power, and might grant us just what little measure of toleration they might choose; as if we were bound to respect their religion and they at full liberty to insult ours.   *   *   *   *

To Robert, 15th August, in answer to a letter, after he had received his Father's, announcing Fanny's death :—

Habitual ill-health had for a long while deprived her of all enjoyment, and heart-breaking as it was to me to see her suffering, even *I* could rejoice more than grieve when it pleased her merciful Maker to take her away. I loved her much too tenderly to indulge any selfish feeling where she was concerned, and short as the remainder of my own life must be, it is time for me to learn how to part with earthly blessings; yet my Fanny was to me a blessing unspeakably precious. What is there as sweet as *love*, and what dear daughter ever loved more tenderly than my Fanny loved me; and not one grain of her precious affection was lost, for I doted upon her all her life long with my whole soul. Great, indeed, is the comfort I feel in having been permitted to be with her during her latter days. May God's great mercy bring us together in heaven, and she will tell me that her dear Papa's voice helped to soothe and support her in her last earthly trial. Dearest Bob, you asked me, in one of your late letters, why I never spoke to you of your angel Mother. You said we ought to commemorate our departed dear ones in all possible ways, and not content ourselves with shedding a few tears and dismissing them from our memories. Oh, my dear boy, you little know what sort of memory on that subject I had and have. My nature is, I believe, more apt than that of most people to keep what I feel to my own heart. The grief I felt would not have wrung me as it did for years if I could have talked about it, which I never could. But I forget nothing that has once impressed me. What I love, I love for ever. You, dearest boy, with the thick globe between us, may depend upon my never forgetting to love *you*. As for writing to you, the interest your affection engages you to take in my letters adds so much to the pleasure I feel in writing them that you need never fear any failure in my punctuality. To be able, even at this distance, to contribute something to your happiness is very sweet to me.   *   *   *

At this time my Father suffered from constant morning headaches, which became alarming from their long continuance, and which he attributed to a certain measure of malaria arising from his well-watered garden behind his house, and the impure creek.

To me, 29th August :—

You never told me whether the long-podded Jamaica bean, of which I sent you a quantity of seed, answered in your climate.   *   *   *   It is a first-rate vegetable. We have them growing beautifully in our Marina garden ; they run up twenty or thirty feet, and some of the beans are twenty-eight inches long. They are not fit to use when full-grown though, but must be cut before they begin to turn yellow. The Latin for it is *Dolichos sesquipedalis*. The more water you give it the better it grows.   *   *   *

All the drawing I have done lately is one I gave our good friend Mrs. Clifton, of a group of trees at the Boschetto, one that I had never sketched before. I was attracted to it by the effect of light and shade, which was very agreeable, five or six stems rising together, some brightly illuminated and others in deep shadow, backed by a dark mass of foliage overhung by branches catching the light, a couple of boys sitting under them, and some goats feeding. It cost me a great deal of work, and Mr. Allingham says it has turned out capitally, and so does Mamma. The truth is, some parts are beautiful, and some good for nothing ; so that if I were to do it again I could not for the life of me do the good parts as well, and should probably do some of the others much better. There is *always* a great deal of my work dependent upon luck. Don't be scandalized at my saying anything of my doing is *beautiful*, for I have no more vanity in the matter than if I was speaking of the doings of a Mr. Johnson or Thompson, and I have not in all my life made a dozen drawings for which I would give as many straws. *   *   *

*   *   *   *   *   *

To Robert in September :—

Do you remember my telling you, years ago, that in digging
out the earth that covered the old temple at Gozo, heaps of
the bones of *mice* were found there. I don't know whether
I referred then to the last chapter of Isaiah, ver. 17 : " Eating
swine's flesh, and the abomination, and the *mouse*." Those
mice were certainly not eaten as common food, but sacrificed
victims, and the eaters were *Canaanites*. Is not this, put
together, a curious piece of proof that Phœnicians (Canaanites) built these Gozo and Malta temples ? The Romans, you
know, had no objection to enlarge their host of divinities,
and so took Isis and Serapis from the Egyptians, and so most
likely from the Phœnicians borrowed their observance of
mice; for Pliny says: "Soricum occentu dirimi auspicia,
annales refertos habemus"—that auspices were continually
annulled by the squeaking of mice ; and Ausonius : " Qua-
drupes oscinibus quis jungitur auspiciis ? Mus." I got these
two quotations from Pitiscus ; and I gather from the two
together that so many cases of annulled auspices by the
squeaking of mice could not have been by mice that happened
to be dwelling or passing near at the moment of taking the
auspices ; but that mice must have been kept in the temples
on purpose to form a check upon the birds.

Phœnician lore is prospering. A German has taken pains
to collect all the existing inscriptions in that language, and
there are as many as fifty, mostly short ; but some with Greek
versions have furnished a key, and all are now intelligible.
The candelabrum in the old Valetta library that has two
or three Greek names upon it and some Phœnician words,
proves valuable in this way ; for one of the Greek names
is *Heliodorus*, and one of the Phœnician ab*shemsh*, and
shemsh is *Maltese* and Arabic for the *sun*. Another of the
names is equally translated. Our bishop has got the book,
and is studying the subject. Phœnician seems closely allied
to Hebrew. * * * * *

Have you read Law's " Serious Call ?" Mamma and I

are reading it now; and an admirable book it is. Thousands
of books point out one's duties; but few are equal to this
for the concise and striking form in which the arguments for
performing them are urged. Many a book that contains
good matter is dismally dull; but this has a lively spirit. I
can't read prosy writing. How far from wordy the inspired
writers are, from Moses to St. John. There is a wordy preface to our edition of Law, which I have taken the liberty to
glance at and skip.   *   *   *   *   *

Your old tortoise has gone on growing, and promises to
attain his ἡλικια by about the year 1870. By that time he
will be on familiar terms with the biped frequenters of the
garden; for he has already consented to some intercourse
with us, and came voluntarily the other day to eat a prickly
pear while I held it between my fingers. I value the poor
beast for having been your property, and supply him with
melons, grapes, and prickly pears to his heart's content.

In the next letter :—

I have been going on very steadily of late with my Thucydides, that I may have the copy ready for Clement by the
time he can use it, and that the original may go back to you.
The first material correction I have made is at the end of the
first speech. *   *   *   *   *   *

Then follow different versions and explanations of the
passage. Speaking of Bloomfield's and Arnold's Thucydides, he says :—

What a striking difference there is between Dr. Arnold's
character and Dr. Bloomfield's! Arnold's reputation as a
man of genius and a true scholar is far the higher; yet he
always speaks humbly of his own doings, and Bloomfield is
perpetually blowing his own trumpet, and calling other
people fools. *   *   *   *   *   *

To me, writing of his work, he adds :—

Then will come the Sophocles and Euripides; and it will be altogether two years' good work, or even more, for the lessons of the young ones occupy much of my mornings, and I am not strong enough for such work in the summer afternoons, and when the evening comes I like to read serious books,—Greek Testament, English Bible, good old Bishop Taylor, and others like him. It does one great good, my darling, to have such books much and often in our hands. If the one great object of living is to learn how to die, how much time we have all lost!   *   *   *   *   *

MALTA, 10th October, 1844.
From the Deanery-House at Citta Vecchia.

MY VERY DEAR BOB,—When I last wrote to you I was sick, without knowing what was the matter; but the malady soon unfolded itself in the shape of intermittent fever. I verily believe it had been affecting me the whole summer. The headache I had, more or less, every morning, was one of its symptoms; and the sciroc wind, that began with the beginning of September and has lasted ever since, gave it its full force. Physic, while I was breathing miasma all day and all night, had no effect, and the doctors found change of place absolutely necessary; so, not to go farther than I could help, I took possession, ten days ago, of the old Abbate's house here at Citta Vecchia, which stands high, and is ventilated very differently from our detestable creek, which is no better than a big cloaca, from the head of which they are scooping out, to make the new dock, thousands upon thousands of tons of the filth deposited there during the thousands of years in which a town has probably stood where Burmola now stands. The change of place has done me great good. For five days I continued free from the fever, and thought it would return no more; but return it then did, and stuck by me thirty hours, and pulled me a great way back. This is now the fourth day since the fit went off, and I am feeling tolerably

well, and making the most of my enemy's absence to lay
in munitions for the repelling of another attack. Good
Mr. Whitmarsh has been out here to see me; and has pre-
scribed, for the repair of my dwindled muscles, a sort of beef-
tea that you should, in case of need, know how to make. Get
an earthen jar big enough to hold two pounds of beef; get
two pounds of beef; remove all the fat; thump the lump of
beef with a rolling-pin, or some such instrument, and then
put the lump of beef into the earthen jar; get a bung that
fits the jar; cover the bung with a piece of muslin, for nice-
ness; bung the jar well up, and tie the bung down with a
stout twine; get a saucepan of cold water and put it upon
the fire, and put the jar into the saucepan, so that the jar
may be nearly, but not wholly, immersed, for no water must
get into the jar. Let the water boil, and keep slowly boiling
for a couple of hours; by that time all the juice that the beef
contained will be extracted from it, and will furnish enough
for two doses, to be taken with a little salt and a big slice of
toasted bread. Much nourishment is so to be had in small
volume; and it is a dish that you or I, who are not learned
in such arts, may make as well as a professor. Mamma is, of
course, here, to take care of me.

    *   *   *   *   *   *

You remember something of Citta Vecchia. It is like a
miniature Pisa; a place where there was once great bustle,
and now absolute stillness,—fine houses unoccupied, and
streets without a passenger.

It would be dull for most people; but in my poorly days I
move little from my sofa, and when my head is pretty clear I
open my books, and find in them all the company I want, as
long as I see Mamma's petticoat within a few inches of me.
When I say all I *want*, you know I speak of *accessibilities*;
for there are many coats and petticoats I should be glad
enough to see, if I *could*.

    *   *   *   *   *   *

When you questioned, dearest Son, whether all lowness
of spirits is not symptomatic of something wrong in our

spiritual state, you need not much have hesitated; for though undoubtedly it often is, yet quite surely it is not always so; for all the world knows that something wrong in the *bodily* state is often quite enough to account for it. For my own part, I am not subject to depression of spirits, though I have no longer the vivacious elasticity I used to have, and retained perhaps longer than most men are apt to retain it. That the approach of death should be welcome to an "earnest Christian," no Christian can deny; and I humbly hope God will bless my endeavours to become an earnest Christian, and support me under all my remaining trials. But, Bob, I do not think, because I am three years nearer to the grave than I was three years ago, that *that* is the reason why I have lost my buoyancy. I have grown pretty suddenly from a young man into an old one, but I do not lament the change; I have not the least wish to be young again. I am not, in that respect, like poor Mr. N——, who said, "Make me but eighteen years old, and put me down naked on Salisbury Plain!" You think a good man's old age ought to be the happiest time of his life: ay, dearest Bob, a *good* man's! But yet I hardly see why, except that he *must* soon have *done* with it. Old age is apt to be accompanied with many sufferings which must deprive even a good man of all *present* enjoyment; and as for that happiness which consists in looking forward to immortality, why should not a *good young* man feel it as intensely? A little more or less remaining pilgrimage ought to make but small difference.

*　　*　　*　　*　　*　　*

Little Mia brought me her book to construe a Latin line for her, "Platere, pluribus intentus minor est ad singula sensus." Platere, is O Thomas Platter—Thomas Platter, to whom this was said by his master while said Thomas was engaged at once in twisting rope and reading Plautus. I was so much struck with Mia's book, that I read it through. It is the autobiography of Thomas Platter, a Swiss, born in 1499, and contains some picturesque incidents which Walter Scott has woven into his "Anne of Geierstein." The good man was successively goatherd, beggar, student, ropemaker, painter, and professor of Latin, Greek, and Hebrew.

*   *   *   *   *   *

To me, same time :—

I must try, if I live so long, to keep my appointment three years longer, because, in December, 18 17, I shall have completed in it twenty years, and shall be entitled to a higher rate of pension ; but I will not spend those years in Malta. I have no doubt they will give me leave of absence for next summer and for that of '47. There will only then be '46 to contend with ; and my notion is, to spend the chief part of that summer here at Citta Vecchia, keeping up a communication with my office by means of a daily courier, and going in myself only occasionally. I am now satisfied that I must not try to stay any longer. While I went backwards and forwards all the summer between Sliema and my office, exposure to the sun gave me cholera ; and now that I have tried a summer at the Marina, it has given me ague.

*   *   *   *   *   *

Later in October :—

I am already pleasing myself with the prospect of quitting Malta *for good* after three years. Bob, perhaps, may live in England by-and-by, and so may *you*, my darling, and I may have the consolation of being near you in my last days. I should so be in England, too, when Clement would most want me, and when Charley must begin to go to school.

*   *   *   *   *   *

How strange it will be to me to be my *own master*, after having spent so many years in what is called *the service*,—that is, in a condition of slavery, however self-imposed, and light-yoked, and well paid,—to go where I please without asking such a man as —— *   *   *   * to mix with thinking people, to have all my boys with me in their holidays, and do them all the good I can.

Most people *who retire from business* are said to find the
repose they coveted less agreeable than they expected—their
time is apt to hang heavily on their hands; but such can't
well be my case, for I never yet had an hour that I could
not fill; and as for my *business*, I can't much miss that,
seeing it has not for the last thirty years employed me one
average hour in the day. The smallest of my left-hand
fingers would make an Agent Victualler, and its next neighbour an Admiral's Secretary in time of peace. In the busier
times before that, I had enough to do; but it was work that
interested me far less than such as my own tastes have since
provided for me.   *   *   *   *   *

In November, to me and Bob :—

Though I can't tell you that I am well, yet you need not
fidget, for I am firmly persuaded that my disease is of a mild
type, and will gradually give way as the winter advances. I
thought myself tolerably well towards the end of October, and
we moved from Citta Vecchia to our Marina home; but I
had not been there two days before headache began to return,
and then fever too; so we made another move, and are now
occupying the house over Zabbar Gate—I dare say you
remember it. It is one of the gates in the Cottonera lines,
close to St. Clement's, the open ground, which would sometimes in winter, when there is a sprinkling of grass upon it,
be called a field, and round which field you and I had a
gallop now and then sixteen or seventeen years ago, when
you first backed the matchless pony. This house of ours is
well suited to our purpose of breathing free air, for the
ground is comparatively high, and it is, besides, perched
on the top of the lofty building that forms the gateway.
From our drawing-room windows we look over the sea more
than half-way round the horizon, and over the lantern of
the St. Elmo Lighthouse.   *   *   *   *

I am still pretty strong for a sick man, for Mamma and I
took advantage of a cloudy sky yesterday morning, and

walked to Marsa Scala, a little harbour two miles beyond Zabbar. It took us an hour each way, and I came home not over-tired; yet I must add, that it was my *day's work*; for I could do nothing afterwards, not even read my new number of the Quarterly, though I did manage that after tea, which is generally my best time, and besides that, read a sermon of Wilberforce's to Mamma. In the afternoon I was not without fever.   *   *   *   *   *   *

Our particular object in returning from Citta Vecchia when we did, was to be present at the consecration of the new church on the 1st of this month; and a deeply-interesting solemnity it was. It is a very beautiful edifice, richly and properly fitted up. A thousand worshippers were present, and many hearts were undoubtedly full of the sense of the mighty blessing conferred upon our community by this glorious gift of the good old Queen. The Bishop *wept* when he began to speak of Queen Adelaide. Now, Bob, do remember, that in my *address* I spoke of *moistened eyes*, and the meeting said " Pooh, pooh ! " —— said *he* didn't cry, and the Governor said *he* didn't cry, and nobody did, so they scratched it out; but yet it was no unreasonable flourish of mine, for I was obliged to wipe my own eyes before I could write the words, and the Bishop has now proved that it was a subject on which tenderness might be felt, and might so express itself. The collection at the offertory that day was £112. Notice was given that there would be service every Sunday at eleven, and three, and at seven, and prayers every morning at eight. During the week we were at the Marina, Mamma and I, and Kitty and Mia, Charley and Mary, went every morning, and sorry I was that my sickness prevented us from continuing to go. There were always about forty present, and my hope is, that there will be more and more. There is no case in which more good may be done by example; for many who might not think it important to go, or think at all about it, will begin to think of it when they see their neighbours go. They will begin to think that people who begin the day by praying together, are

less likely to quarrel during the course of it,—that it *may* be
worth while to rise half an hour earlier, for the sake of giving
glory to God, and promoting peace and good-will upon earth.

  *   *   *   *   *   *

The next November letters give a somewhat improved
account of his health. In December he returned to the
Marina, by the Doctor's desire, the Zabbar house being too
cold for him; and the headache continuing and rather increasing, blisters were put on the forehead and kept open for
some days. On the 12th he writes :—

DEAREST BOB,—You bid me write you some sermons.
Just yet, you see, I am not fit for writing anything; but
even at my best I am afraid I could not write a sermon. I
can do nothing *unreal*. If I were a clergyman, I think I
could make my congregation listen to me, and make them
think and feel. I should have plenty to say to them, and
should say it very forcibly, because it would come from my
heart. But it is a very different thing when the mere *brain*
is to do the work. And such would be the case, even though
it would be *for you* that I were writing, because, "for you,"
in this sense, does not mean for your benefit, or for the purpose of doing good to you; but it means chiefly *instead* of
you, by supposing myself in *your* place. If you were in a
difficulty, out of which anything I could say would help you,
then I could write for you with the passionate earnestness
that would be abundantly *real*. But besides the difficulty of
fancying myself a clergyman, I should feel afraid of there
being something like presumption in my attempting to speak
in his language. You could not yourself have written such
sermons as you have written, if you had not felt while you
were writing them as if you were at the very moment actually
preaching them ; and I can't work myself up to feel as if I
were in a pulpit, even if it were right to try.

Of course, dear Bob, I have not the least doubt that if you
were to preach to your people a sermon of Barrow's, or perhaps

of Taylor's, you would put them to sleep; but that is no proof
that the good men were not eloquent. Their English is
obsolete, and their manner out of fashion; but they were
mighty masters in their day, and if they had lived in our
day they would have been equally mighty. Lord Chatham
must have been a pretty good judge of eloquence, and he
said he improved his own by studying Barrow. As for
Taylor, I can conceive nothing more awfully grand than
some passages of his sermons. He writes sometimes as
if he had the combined spirit of Shakspeare and Homer
and Demosthenes superadded to his theology. No one
makes me *feel* and *remember* more than he does. He does
me great good, and I am sure that it is in great measure
by means of his eloquence that he finds his way to my heart.
All you desire in a sermon is heartiness, plainness, unity
of subject, and reverence, quite enough too; but then that
HEARTINESS is the rarest thing of all. Where it is in due
measure, and in combination with a due share of brains, there
will be *no sleepers*. Your *heart* must write all your sermons,
and *your* heart will write them *well*.   *   *   *

Later in December :—

Since the last account I gave you of myself, I have mended
in one respect; for a couple of hollows, which had been
deepening in my cheeks, have begun to fill up again, and
everybody sees that I am making the improvement, Mamma
as well as the rest, and I am sensible of it myself. Yet the
headaches are not cured.   *   *   *   *

The Marina seems not to agree with me; though we can't
well account for the existence of unhealthy air in December,
even in our ugly creek. As soon as the coldest of the winter
is over, we shall get away from it and go again to Zabbar.
    *   *   *   On my further travels I am to
set out at the end of May, so as to be in England by the
beginning of the Midsummer holidays, and have my dear
Clement, and Herbert, and Willy to spend them with me.

I am speculating upon taking them somewhere to the seaside, where we have fine air for long walks, and undisturbed leisure for long lessons, to help Clement, particularly, forward in Greek and Latin, which have hitherto not much prospered with him.   *   *   *   *   *

I am still leading a sad idle life; but Mamma and the doctors are right, and I obedient. Of course, I can't leave my books *quite* alone. I took up my old Pausanias the other day. I had read parts of him on our way to Greece in days of yore. I looked to see what he said of a statue of Mercury, by Socrates, that stood in the Propylœa, and I found I had made a mark there in the margin, most likely thinking to myself, " Who knows whether that statue may not some day be found under this rubbish?" and sure enough, not the statue, but a fragment of the pedestal, has been found with Mercury's name on it. So has a piece of another pedestal been found hard by, with the name of *Thucydides*; and Pausanias says there stood there a statue, I don't clearly see whether he means of Thucydides himself or of Œnobius, the author of the vote for rescinding the banishment of Thucydides. In either case the name of Thucydides (and it is he of Olorus) would be found in the inscription. Isn't it interesting to see such proofs of the accuracy of a *guide*-book of seventeen hundred years old ? It was Giffard's " Tour in Greece" that told me of the finding of the fragments, and he mentions a third, bearing the name of another statue mentioned by Pausanias, and found precisely in the spot indicated.   *   *   *   *   *

I told you, in my last letter, we were going to lose the Whitmarshes. A sad loss it is; and now we have another,— Mr. *Kitson* is going to leave us. We could ill afford to spare such worthy members of our small community. The loss of such a man as Kitson is a grievous loss for us all : his talent is first-rate.

My Father, as well as other members of Mr. Kitson's congregation, felt that they could not allow him to leave them without a tribute of respect and regard; and my Father, who was always expected to take the lead in such cases, wrote as follows on this occasion :—

We have been so much accustomed to hear from each other expressions of esteem for Mr. Kitson, that nothing can be more undoubted than our sincere unanimity in wishing to pay to him a tribute of respect on this most unwelcome occasion. We do, with all our hearts, unite in acknowledging our serious obligation to him, in lamenting his removal from among us, and in praying that his future life may be cheered with the best of blessings. We shall always remember his impressive performance of the solemn service of our Church, his lucid exposition and faithful advocacy of sacred truth, his great talents, and matchless temper; and we trust he will do us the favour to accept a trifling gift, which we shall gratify ourselves in preparing for him, as a memorial of the impression which he leaves among his Malta friends.

Rear-Admiral Sir Lucius Curtis, who has kindly presided at our meeting, will be good enough to convey to Mr. Kitson the sentiments of the congregation.

CHAPTER XIII.

[1845.]

IN the beginning of January of this year is the first mention
of the *fatal* sore throat. My Father says to me :—

I always begin, I believe, by telling you what you most
want to hear, and that has been lately about my own health.
I have made good progress of late, my darling, and the best
proof is that in the last month I have gained two and a half
pounds weight, and weigh to-day 127 pounds.[a] I have got
the better of the headache, and should be stouter still if I
had not had a sore throat for a very long time, I believe
these two months, which prevents my going out as much as I
ought, for the least damp or evening air makes the throat
worse. I believe it is what is called a relaxed sore throat ;
but I have been very much subject to some such disorder for
some years past, and the least aggravation brings it to a bad
cough.   *   *   *   *   *   *

Speaking of this sore throat in the next letter :—

Whitmarsh thinks that *this*, and the fever I had, and the

---

[a] His height was about 5 feet 9 inches.

nine months' headache I am shaking off, are all referable to the visitations of *cholera* of the nine or ten preceding summers. If so, I shall be puzzled to spend *one* other summer here, which will be very convenient to me if I *can* manage it, for the sake of my increased pension.

Fancy what we should do with less than a thousand a year in England; with two boys at college together, and two at school, and four daughters to be provided with masters! We shall do it all if I live; but then the extra £50 a year will be valuable to buy us the egg-shells and nettletops on which we must be content to dine. But for this long malady of mine, I should be gaining strength and flesh rapidly, and I suppose it is not anything very serious: and if I do get rid of it, I may reasonably expect to enjoy as much vigour and activity as most men of fifty-seven.   *   *   *   *

In February, to Robert :—

You sent me in your last letter some notes on justification, with reference to a disagreement on that subject between Mr. Faber and Mr. Newman. What a lamentable thing it is, dear Bob, that there should be this never-ending strife among members of the same Church! It seems as if theologians could never be at a loss for some subject of quarrel. On they go, arguing questions which have been argued a thousand times, protesting that there is nothing new in their *matter*, and hoping for nothing more than to put it into some new form of words. To whom does such argument do good? It has been often remarked, that nine disputes out of ten would drop at once if each party understood the other's terms. Would not this be the case with arguments on justification more than almost any other subject? Is there any *real* difference, I mean *important* difference, even between Mr. Newman and Mr. Faber? I don't know what they have written, but may not their disagreement be more about "the *philosophy* of justification" than its essential theology? Would not both of them consent with such a view as this, of Bishop Van Mildert's?—" For Christ's sake, and in consideration of His merits and sufferings alone, our sins shall be remitted to us; but to render them effectual to that purpose, our own co-operation is indispensably requisite. On our compliance with the terms of the Christian covenant, our faith is reckoned or imputed to us for righteousness, notwithstanding the imperfection which still necessarily adheres to all human actions, and notwithstanding the innumerable transgressions for which we should otherwise be amenable to the tribunal of Divine justice." Then he adds: "With this simple statement of a doctrine in which we are all so vitally interested, let us content ourselves, without adventuring upon speculations leading to most dangerous errors."

Just such a warning there is in Bishop Taylor, who bids me "not fool myself by disputing about the philosophy of justification. These things," he says, "are knotty (hæc enim spinosiora) and too intricate to do any good." But when he tells me that "by the works of faith, by faith working by love, and producing fruits worthy of amendment of life, we are justified before God;" and that, "for our little imperfect services He freely and bountifully will give us eternal life," must we not *all* agree in *this*? Or can any of us disagree with Hooker, that "God doth justify the believing man, yet not for the worthiness of his belief, but for the worthiness of Him which is believed. God rewardeth abundantly every one which worketh, yet not for any meritorious dignity which is or can be in the work, but through His mere mercy, by whose commandment he worketh."

Further than this *I* must not attempt to go. I see in your notes some expressions that seem puzzling, but I have no wish to meddle with the *thorns*. Have you read Mr. Faber's book about the Vallenses and Albigenses? He depends upon *them* for the making out of a case *for our Church;* and I never read a more unsatisfactory argument.

    *   *   *   *   *   *

I don't know what we shall do without Whitmarsh. Dr. ―― prescribes for me *ex officio*, but not *ex animo*; and yet I am forced to apply to him, because if I go away on the plea

of ill-health, he will be called upon for his official opinion.   I
am glad to find that the whole of our small community
wishes to pay a special respect to Whitmarsh on his departure.
As soon as I found there was such a feeling, I set about cir-
culating a paper for subscription, to buy him a piece of plate,
and we put down our name for ten pounds.   *   *   *
Nobody has equal reason to feel obliged to him.   I have not
a copy of what I wrote for the subscription paper, but it was
this, or nearly :—

"Mr. Whitmarsh is going to leave us; and he must not
go without an assurance that he leaves grateful hearts behind
him.   Most of us have felt the benefit of his great medical
experience ; but all have known the willing exercise of his
great energies wherever suffering was to be alleviated, or a
friend was to be proved in time of need.   *He* will not thank
us for mentioning, but it is, nevertheless, a very sincere
gratification to us to know and remember his large-hearted,
unostentatious, silent, and sacred charities.   He has been the
friend of those who do not live to thank him.[b]

"We earnestly hope he will oblige us by accepting a trifling
gift, which we mean to offer to him.   May health and peace
cheer his remaining days, and those of his most excellent
wife : worthy as they are of each other, and united as they
will be in our grateful remembrance."

Later in February :—

My application to the Admiralty for leave of absence goes
to England by this packet, and with it a letter from Dr. Watt,
of the Naval Hospital, stating the absolute necessity of my
changing the climate ; and a letter from Sir L. Curtis, assuring
the Board that Portelli is very capable of doing the work in
my absence : so there will be no impediment.

*   *   *   *   *   *

---

[b] This alludes to the orphan child of Dr. Martin, who was killed by the
sentinel at Sir J. Louis's door.   Mr. and Mrs. Whitmarsh had taken care of
her for three years.

I never had any notion that my life was in the smallest danger; but I have lately discovered that —— gave me up in despair, and told poor Mamma I had organic disorder in the head, and might linger, but could not recover. Only think what *her* share of suffering has been; and all the worse for fighting against it, to conceal it from me.

*　　*　　*　　*　　*　　*

The only work I have done of late has been giving their Latin lessons to Kitty and Mia; and both of them are making a start.　　*　　*　　*　　*　　*　　*

You said you didn't know that you should teach your little girls Latin; but I think you would rather like the way I have managed with these small people.[c] They have been slowly picking up Latin, scrap by scrap, till they know a good deal; but while they have been doing that, the same labour has answered other good purposes, for what they have done has been little else than writing English translations of Latin bits of my providing, for I have made no less than five volumes of "Selectæ" for them. In this way they have learned *English*, *orthography*, *caligraphy*, without any trouble; and the Latin has been so much into the bargain; and very useful it is,—it makes them know their English, French, and especially Italian, better than they would know them otherwise.

*　　*　　*　　*　　*　　*

In March, to Robert :—

I find people expressing most unreasonable contempt for the preachers of borrowed sermons. I should not feel the least scruple in appropriating what I pleased; only I would take great care to steal like a Spartan.　　*　　*　　*

---

[c] He had said, in a former letter to me, "Do be persuaded, from my experience, that it is better not to trouble your children with book-learning while they are very young.　*　*　*　* The young learners are not the best. Let the little things run about and get strong, and don't exercise their brains till they have grown into some consistency."

I believe I am, upon the whole, better than I was when I
last wrote. I had some nights of such violent headache, that
I thought I had better not lose any time in getting away from
the Marina.   *   *   *   *   *

Mr. Christian offered me his house at Sliema, and we moved
to it at once, and are here now. It is the house in which the
Mackenzies used to live, a grand building, with a broad peri-
style round it on both stories. The Christians have had so
much trouble here, that they would not occupy the house
again, and their term expires the end of June. I sent him a
bag of money, to pay the four months' rent, but he won't
have it, insisting, that as he offered me the house for the sake
of my health, he can't in honesty make it a gain to his pocket.
This is gentlemanly dealing—isn't it? I do love an instance
of this spirit; and the spirit of Mr. Tagliaferro, who has
bought the house, is like it; for he has desired me to keep it
just as long as it suits my convenience, only hoping, he says,
that the air will be useful*to me; so we shall keep it to the
end of the year, and when I go away in May, I shall leave
Mamma with more comfort (to myself) than if she had been
stewing with all the poor little things at the Marina.

Later in March, after speaking of blistering his head,
which disturbed his sleep, and did him no good, he says :—

However, you need not fancy me suffering much either
from the maladies or medicaments; for I took advantage of
an interval of fine weather yesterday, and had a glorious walk
of *five miles*, exploring the hills beyond St. Julian's. I
stumbled upon a place we must have seen together years ago,
called the St. Julian's Machuba. Machuba is the name of a
remarkable *pit* on the other side of the island—a place where
the ground has subsided and made a great circular hollow of
a hundred feet deep and as many wide. This above St.
Julian's is much smaller. Near it are several of those
remarkable ruts, marking the wheel-tracks of ancient days,
with which Malta is intersected in so many places and so
many directions, that there can be no doubt of its having

been a place of great population and traffic. There is never an accountable terminus to any of these tracks, so that there must have been numbers of towns of which all traces have disappeared.

The Bishop, by the bye, is a great hunter of antiquities, and he and Sir Gardiner Wilkinson lately found and opened a tomb that had lain undisturbed for three thousand years. There were two skeletons in it and some pottery.

I can not only walk well, but dine well after my walk, and digest well: no wonder, then, the doctors are puzzled by the obstinacy of a headache that still returns every night, and an inflamed throat that has baffled their art for five months. I have now given up the hope I had of taking a sane body to England; and I suppose I must follow the advice everybody gives me, and go to Leamington and Dr. Jephson, who is famous for mending mucous membranes. Liddell, I am quite sure, knows as much of the matter as he does, only I can't stay any time in his neighbourhood.[d] My three dear boys would have small fun in spending their holidays within a stone's throw of New Cross.[e]   *   *   *

One of my grievances is, that I am seldom able to go to church. The damp of ours hurts me, and the last time I went I was obliged to come out. As warmer weather comes on, I shall, of course, get rid of this evil.

I don't choose to confess to myself how much I miss another old habit—that of snuff-taking. I can't touch it now; for some particles will always find their way to the throat, and in the condition of mine they are poison; yet like other things, so snuff—one *can* leave off even snuff.

     *   *   *   *   *   *

To me, in April :—

My condition is much the same as when I wrote a fort-night ago, pretty well (not very strong) in general health, but the throat quite as bad as ever.   *   *   *

---

[d] Greenwich.   [e] Where their school was.

I had a most kind letter from Mrs. Duckworth and Annie, asking me to go to them at Bordeaux, and travel to England with them, offering me *two* places in their carriage, one inside and the other out, that I might change as I pleased. I was sorry I could not have the great pleasure of being with them; but it will be desirable for me to lose no time. * * * * I mean to set out by the French packet of the 15th of May. * * * * But what sad work it is to go by one's self! I want Mamma to take care of me when I am well, much more when I am sick. I shall pass some wonderful scenery; but I have not the least pleasure in having anything to myself.

* * * * * *

To Robert :—

Thank you for telling me of Archdeacon Wilberforce's "Eucharistica," of the existence of which I was ignorant. I was lucky enough to find it at the Valetta bookseller's, and, of course, bought it. I don't think, dear Bob, there is any difference between Archdeacon Wilberforce's doctrine and your most excellent Grandfather's. * * *

That "church" is κυριακη οικια, of course, I must take upon the authorities you have given me. If Casaubon was satisfied, I may be; but it is hard to think how Saxons contrived to make the word. It is true Turner (Hist. of Anglo-Saxons) says, Theodore, Archbishop of Canterbury, and Adrian, who were sent into England by the Pope, about 668, were thoroughly acquainted with Greek. Whatever Adrian may have been, Theodore, of course, was, for he was a Greek by birth; and some scholars they had, too, down to Bede, but as Grecians, few enough, and of small power. Neither were the Saxon Bishops likely to bring home much Greek from the general councils; for Boccaccio says, no Italian scholar of his day knew as much as the Greek characters. From the time when Rome ceased to pay obedience to the Exarchs of Ravenna, the Greek language and literature, says Hallam,

had been almost entirely forgotten within the pale of the
Latin Church. The ecclesiastical language, he observes, was
full of Greek words Latinized; "but this process had taken
place before the fifth century, and most of them will be
found in the Latin dictionaries."

Talking of ecclesiastical Greek, you may not happen to
know that there are at this moment plenty of *Greek* bishops
who don't know one word or one letter of Greek. I mean
those of the Syrian Church. There is one here now, the
Archbishop of Tripoli in Syria. When he left his own
country, three years ago, he did not know one word of any
language but his vernacular Arabic. He can now read and
talk English, French, and Italian; and I have just given him
a Greek grammar, of which he means to make use. His
branch of the Greek Church, the head of which is the
patriarch of Aleppo, paid a sort of semi-obedience to the
Pope, but has been lately brought under his absolute control;
and the archbishop is a *reformer*, and would gladly join *us*.
So, he said, would many of his brother bishops and priests if
England would protect them.

Our bishop had a letter lately from twenty-five Maltese
and Italians, setting forth that they and others wished to
attend our church, but did not understand our language, and
begged to have a service performed *in Italian*, which there
will be. There will be no difficulty, for we have a Maltese
priest and a Sicilian who have come over to us.

Of ecclesiastical etymologies, I dare say I told you years
ago that "belfry" is not derived from bell. In old Italian
books one meets with "belfredo," for a tower raised by
besieging armies for assailing walls; and this *belfredo* had
more, therefore, to do with *bellum* than bell.

Of Casaubon, Scaliger, quoted by Hallam, says he was the
first of living scholars. Hallam supposes he meant to except
himself, but thinks that, as a Grecian, he had not a rival even
in Scaliger.   *   *   *   *   *

On the 13th of May :—

DEAREST BOB,—I am not surprised that you are growing a popular preacher. A sensible and earnest man can't well be otherwise. A good voice and good taste are of course additional advantages; and as I believe you have all this, you can't well fail. There *is*, of course, danger of being elated by your reputation; but against that danger you must fortify yourself as you can; for if you choose the other plan, of running away from the danger by preaching dull sermons, you will do no good either to your hearers or yourself. That *would* be burying your talent. You must turn it, then, to the very best account, and it will enable you to do immense good; and you will be grateful that your efforts are so blessed, and be enabled to bear with equanimity the praises of your congregation.

Popular preachers—ay, preachers widely popular among congregations not *all* fools—are sometimes most prodigious puppies and asses. I suppose you have heard of Dr. ——. Of all asses he was the chief, and turned out quite as much knave as fool; yet he was applauded sky high for his eloquence and sanctity. It is true, I suppose, that *all* men value praise; but it is certain that foolish men value it most. All our doings are, after all, but little doings. What is it one knows in comparison with what one does not know! Yet it is wonderful how the authors of the *very* little doings value their own performance! If a dozen people did each a work, all differing in degrees of skill, the self-satisfaction of the authors would probably be in exactly inverse ratio with their success.   *   *   *   *   *

The better you do, if you do it from your heart, the less and the less you will care for the praise. And oh, the ignorance of the praisers! What STUFF it is that pleases most of the ladies—and the gentlemen, too, dear Lizzy!

Well, dearest Bob, in three days more I am going—that is, by the French packet to Leghorn, and thence over Mount Cenis, where the snow is melted. I am just the same as when I wrote last ; not very sick, but yet my throat not a bit better. *Sad* for poor Mamma. I am sorry enough to go by myself, but more sorry still for her share of the suffering.

*　　*　　*　　*　　*　　*

To little Kitty, from Leghorn, 21st May :—

I know how sorry you were to see your dear Papa go away, and Papa loved you all the more for being sorry; and well I know I shall not see so sweet a little girl till I see my own dear Kitty again. *　　*　　*　　*　　*

When I was so very sick, I thought of what we read about Augustus Cæsar and his taste for the sea: navigabat *potius ;* he had a preference, a predilection for it. I wish I had had him in the *Dante.* But I suppose he made very little trips along the shore, and took care to land whenever bad weather was coming on. I heard a short dialogue on board between the two Englishmen, that would have made you laugh. " What's carter-vang?" asked the father. " Eighty-*four,*" said the son. So I suppose the elderly gentleman paid four francs more than he need. " I want to find my berth," said the senior; " what's *berth* in French?" This was far beyond the junior's vocabulary, and he made no answer. What a mess these people must make of their travels, not knowing the meaning of anything they hear, and not able to express a want.

When you see the Abbate, tell him the Commander gave us a bottle of *Orvieto* wine, that he got at Civita Vecchia; and that I thought of the *gusto* with which I remember him to have described it. It is just like very fine cider.

*　　*　　*　　*　　*　　*

On the 22nd of May, he writes to his wife :—

What a different place Genoa is from what it was this time two years, when you were close to me ; and what a dull room this is now ; and what a cheerful one it would be if I had but my own dear wife in it! There are a hundred thousand people in the streets, seated in chairs four deep on each side, all in their finest finery, to see the procession of Corpus Domini. Music of all sorts, and fooleries that we are used to, except that Capuchins and other such personages are in hundreds instead of dozens, and the municipality and functionaries of all sorts in their antique dresses. So I hear, but I have seen as little as I well could, though I have been out all day ; for the procession has been our great impediment, which we have done our best to avoid, though we could not help crossing it repeatedly. I say we, because my good friend Brown[1] was with me; and I don't know what I could have done without him.　＊　　　＊　　　＊　　　＊

I have been dining at the table d'hôte with thirty people, only two of us English.　＊　　＊　　＊　　During dinner two performers on the violin made music for us. They exhibited all sorts of dexterities, and (among the rest) performed a long, rapid, and intricate piece, both playing together on the same fiddle, standing opposite to each other, so that the big end of the fiddle rested on the shoulder of one, and the small end on the shoulder of the other, the two right hands working all the time with the fiddlesticks, and the two left hands fingering the strings. The German said it was new to him.

PAVIA, 24th May, 1845.
8 A.M.

MY MOST BELOVED WIFE,—Far as you are away from me, your influence reaches me, for I am in want of comfort, and find it by sitting down to write to you. You see I have dated my letter from Pavia. I wish it was quite true ; but the city gate is only a hundred yards off, in sight from the room I am writing in, yet into Pavia I can't go. In short, I am just in the case in which you and I were eight years

---

[1] H. B. M.'s Consul at Genoa.

ago at the Sardinian frontier, at Iselle and the foot of the Simplon.

At half-past two yesterday afternoon I left Genoa in the mail (a pretty mail!), expecting that my passport, which had been sent before to Milan for the signature of the Austrian authorities, would meet me here; and here it has *not* met me. The director of the post at Genoa assured me there was no doubt but that, at all events, I should suffer no inconvenience, as no objection would be made to my entering Pavia, where I might be perfectly well off till my passport came. Not a bit of it. The commissaire at the frontier says it is an "affare serio," takes me for the leader of a conspiracy against the Emperor, and won't let me budge. He sent a carbinier with me to an albergo close to the barrier, and won't even let me have my bag and baggage with me, but keeps it in his bureau for a guarantee. I made the good man understand that certain things I *must* have, and so I did in truth get all I wanted, such as razor and clean shirt, and these my writing tools. But such a place as this albergo is! much like the one into which you looked at Iselle, except that I *have* my room to *myself*.

Misfortunes don't come single. I should not care two straws for the discomfort if I were well, or as well as I usually am; but as ill luck would have it, I felt some *borborygmatous* commotions as I got out of the coach, and the usual indisposition has followed. I did not tell you that I had a slight visitation of it in the *Dante;* but it went off kindly, and so I dare say will this. I take all the care I can to avoid noxious food, and of course drink no wine, for all that comes in my way is poison; but there is no answering for any of the nasty cookery out of which one has to choose; and our supper at Tortona last night was filthy.

To little Kitty :—

PAVIA, 24*th May.*

MY DARLING CHILD,—Travellers by night sit by preference with their backs to the horses, to avoid the wind. The

coach in which I came had seats that held three. Of our
seat I had one corner, and a nice clean handsome German
gentleman the other.   Between us sat a mother and her
babe; and soon the pretty child began to cry, and cried (and
kicked its mother all the while) for four incessant hours!
The little dear was about two years old.   In all that time the
cleansing wave had not once bathed its cheek, nor its dear
mother's, nor the clothes of either.   The smell!—If I went
on describing it in this pathetic strain, I should harrow up
your soul as mine was harrowed.   But think of the complexity of ills!   An open window would have done wonders
for me; and I could not open it, for facing me sat a poor
man with a respirator, speechless with a *bad throat*, and a
breath of air must not blow upon him.   We were passing a
beautiful country, of which the bad, dirty glass shut out half
the view, while it kept in all the stink!   I am a little sick
this morning, and perhaps this may reasonably account for
it; but I bore it much more patiently than any of my companions did, and caught myself laughing at my queer circumstances as I looked into the glass just now while I was
shaving.   Levius fit patientiâ quicquid corrigere est nefas.

By the bye, little Miss B. and I had some Latin talk, and
I found she had not as good a master as you have.   If my
passport does come this afternoon, it will be all well enough;
but I should not at all fancy *sleeping* in this horrid place.
The bed in my room is what Mr. —— would call "sui
generis," meaning, I suppose, fit *for a pig*; sui being the
dative case of *sus*.

Bless you, my own sweet Kitty.   I have written a page to
Mamma, and now, after this parenthetical scrap to you, I
must go on with Mamma's letter.   I love you with all my
heart, my good little child.

11 o'clock.

I thought it worth while to go down and talk to my com-
missary again.   There are in my portmanteau all sorts of
credentials, which, as he fortunately reads English, showed

him quite satisfactorily who I am. Among the rest I showed
him the Admiralty certificate of my time served, and there
my salary of £600 a year is put down, and when he had
ciphered that into 15,000 francs, he necessarily set me down
for a high personage, it being, of course, more than any but
great officers get under his frugal government. All his fears
removed, he told me he would give me at once all the license
his authority allowed. He could not sanction my moving to
an hotel at Pavia, as he did not command in Pavia; but I
might walk about there, or where I chose, and dine, if I liked,
at an hotel there; and if the passport does not come by the
diligence, he will state my case to the proper authorities, that
I may move to an hotel fit for a gentleman. I then went
into the town and bought a few pennyworth of physic—five
drops of laudanum, and some peppermint and lavender—and
made a bargain for a gig to drive me to Milan, twenty miles,
in three hours, for eight francs, which is just the price of the
diligence—the mail, as they call it. If I am well enough, I
will set off the moment the passport comes, and so reach
Milan by half-past seven, or, more likely, past eight o'clock.
I should like, if I can, to be housed in a *good* hotel to-night,
and there are capital ones at Milan, though I saw nothing
that looked promising in Pavia.

A very little out of the road to Milan is the famous Certosa,
a magnificent old abbey, with walls of solid white marble,
lined within with costly stones and carvings most elaborate,
in marbles, gems, and metals; but if I go to-night, I can't
stop to look at it, as it would make me too late, and you
know, sweet, my first business is to *get well*.

Mind in your future travels to say no secrets in trust to your
neighbour's ignorance of English. All people seem to know
all languages. Two Germans in the coach last night talked
almost as well as I do; and when I spoke in Italian to the
dirty woman's dirty husband, who was outside, even *he*
answered me in English, and they belong to Nice, and in
degree he may be a tinker or a cobbler. *All* talked French
and Italian.

At daylight this morning we crossed the Po, in summer a smaller stream, but now as big as the Thames at London, and under the walls of Pavia flows the Ticino, little less. All the country round is watery meadow, with quantities of poplars and willows; though I have not seen one *Lombardy* poplar,—the straight trees so common in England : they are all *white* poplars, with more spreading branches. It is a nice country for malaria and fever; and the clerk at the barrier said his Government had sent him here to kill him.

*   *   *   *   *   *

The man who sold me the physic told me I did not look sick—"già si vede dal suo colorè; e fresco." You know I have had no fair play yet since I began my travels, with rough weather at sea, turmoil at Genoa, and *such* a night as last night—O such a night !   *   *   *

HOTEL REICHMANN, MILAN, 25th May.

*   *   *   *   The drive from Pavia to Milan is twenty miles, all along a dead flat, with a canal running on one side the road, and a river on the other, and often three or four rivers, in rows, on one side or both sides. All the land is wet meadow or inundated *rice*-grounds, frogs croaking all the way, and telling of malaria. My driver said the sickly season was not begun yet, but that everybody would be sick in summer, and some kept their fever five years. There was not a particle of beauty in the scenery, for there were still no other trees than young poplars (not one fine old one) and pollard willows. Nightingales abound, and I heard many singing. Fireflies sparkled in *millions*.

*   *   *   *   *   *

I have been out to see the Duomo, the marvellous Cathedral of Milan. What a gorgeous structure it is ! I wonder what possessed the architects to construct it of such minute blocks. Even the lower courses of granite, or some such hard stone (for all the rest is marble), are so small, that the sixth stone from the ground was not higher than my head, and half of the stones are not a foot long. Another thing that displeased me was, that the roof inside is painted to look like tracery, though it is, in fact, plain. There ought to be *no sham* among such immensities of grand reality. The marble was once white, but is now stained with rich tints of every modification of grey.   *   *   *   *

On the 25th of May he again writes to his wife, from Milan :—

My Italian was at fault in asking my way about the town ; for I heard constantly the word "Contrada," which means *street*. I observed afterwards written up at the corners, C^{da}, instead of S^{da}. The people all pronounce *a* exactly like French. *Paese* means a village. I knew that before ; for my first master in England, the maker of wax fruit, used it in that sense—so, I believe, does Manzoni. The clergy are *clean*, wearing breeches and silk stockings, and looking like English clergymen ; and the ladies have white and red in their faces, not dingy, like Southern Italians.

   *   *   *   *   *   *

26th May.

While I was at breakfast this morning, in came the poor man with the ailing throat, and he seemed rejoiced to meet me again, and begged me to go out with him to see the sights. It was raining, and I had not meant to go out at all ; but there are things worth seeing, and he had a carriage at the door, so I agreed to share the cost with him, and we set out, and saw several of the chief churches,—one remarkable for its great antiquity and for the tomb of *Stilicho*, as it is called, I don't know upon what authority. He was the General of the Roman Emperor Honorius, and is the hero of the poet Claudian. The Arch of Peace, a triumphal arch erected in celebration of the peace, is one of the most beautiful things that eyes can look upon. It is of grand proportions, of beautiful white marble, admirably sculptured with basso-relievos, and surmounted with a chariot drawn by six horses, besides a trumpeting lady on horseback at each of the four corners, all of bronze, and twice the size of life—most noble horses they are, full of nature and life-like motion. The ladies upon them are, of course, Fame and her deputies, proclaiming the peace, and good riders they all are. We went up to the top to see them in detail, and were well repaid for our trouble. Then the Amphitheatre—a gigantic one—of wider area than the Coliseum, begun by Buonaparte, and finished enough for use; and it actually is used for races of all sorts, foot, horse, and chariot, and it is occasionally filled with water six feet deep, for boat-races. It holds thirty thousand people. I suppose it is the only *modern* amphitheatre in the world, and the only one in which games are actually exhibited.

In the Brera Gallery, the great picture gallery of Milan, we saw some pictures of most of the old masters, but few of first-rate renown. The great sight of all was the remains of Leonardo da Vinci's great achievement, the "Last Supper" (not in the Brera Gallery, but in a large room adjoining the cavalry barracks). There is scarcely any one head that can now be well made out, though the general forms may; and some notion is to be gathered of the colouring and light and shade.* Of course we had everywhere to pay the showman; and I made my companion do that. You may judge I did wisely, for our sight of this wonderful work cost us only a quarter of a franc, my share, consequently, being five far-

---

* Speaking of this painting of Leonardo da Vinci, Mr. Harford says, in his " Life of Michael Angelo :"—

" Of his greatest work in painting, the ' Last Supper,' in the refectory of the church of S. Maria delle Grazie, at Milan, only a faint shadow now exists ; but in its perfection it must have been a perfect work of art. The skill with which he has surmounted the difficulty of relieving a long straight line of figures from stiffness and monotony, the fine disposition of the various groups, the speaking physiognomy of their expression, and the sublime tenderness with which he has invested the features and the figure of the Saviour, are such as to leave nothing to desire in this composition but that it had been executed with more permanent colours, and that barbarism had less rudely invaded its remains."

things. We kept our carriage three hours, and my share of carriage and sights together was four francs and a few sous; pray observe, too, that we not only saw the interior of the great theatre (this was my companion's taste, not mine; though it is, I believe, the grandest in the world), but had it *lighted up* for us with a dozen lamps.

I have made a good provision for the mountain, for I have bought a beautiful pair of very thick woollen stockings, and a pair of list thickly-lined boots to go over my shoes; and the stockings and boots together cost six francs. My friend and I may probably keep company as far as Strasburg. He is young and strong, and well, *except* his *throat*; and seems to have great reverence for me, and will willingly take all the trouble to his share. He is sensible enough, but has plenty to learn; and is curious, and finds my learning (such as it is) useful to him. He was as good as a laquais de place to me to-day, and better too, because he paid his share instead of being paid. * * * * *

I must tell you of the sage counsel my hackney-coachman gave me. It was raining, and I had no great taste for mounting to the top of the triumphal arch to see the bronze horses close. "*Go,*" said the man, "they are worth seeing, and 'giacche avete speso denaro per venire quì, spendetelo bene,' to a good purpose—get your money's worth." So, as I may never be at Milan again, and a journey through it costs some twenty or thirty pounds, I am glad I spent the five additional farthings to see the work of Leonardo. When once you are at a place, it is bad economy not to see all in it worth seeing.

Still at MILAN, 27*th May.*

Set out early with my young German and a young American who had been his fellow-traveller and had rejoined him, and went to the Duomo. Saw the tomb of S. Carlo Boromeo, enclosed in a crypt enriched with silver-gilt carving of marvellous workmanship and cost. Saw among the treasures of the church a bas-relief in gold and rubies, the work of Benvenuto Cellini, the prince of gold-workers. Went to the top of the dome, outside, upon the roof, and up to the lantern, and saw Mont Blanc and the Jung-Frau, and the whole chain of Swiss mountains. They told us we were 420 feet from the ground; and even up there every part of the building is of the finest white marble, and wrought with the same care and richness and delicacy as below. The pinnacles above the roof have innumerable niches filled with statues, the smallest not a foot high, and bearing close examination, as if they were meant for the chimney-piece of a lady's boudoir. The showman said twenty-five millions of pounds sterling had been spent upon the workmanship alone, exclusive of the material,—as much as the whole annual expenditure of the Government of England, not including the interest of the national debt. A great deal yet remains of the upper ornamental part undone; and the Milanese will continue to spend their money upon it for centuries to come.

We then set out to the Certosa, fifteen miles, and saw the richest church for internal ornament in the world. Marbles and carving can go no further. For many years it was untenanted, but has now a society of monks. Two were on their knees at the great altar; and as I could not go and scrutinize it while they were there, I asked some one when they would go away, and was told that night and day, for eight days after Corpus Domini, there were *always* two of them stationed to pray there.

The young American is very lively and good-natured, and talks German, French, and Italian. His English is nasal, and he says *my*, like his countrymen, with great emphasis; but the only bits of Americanism he gave me were, that he was *considerable* certain it would rain, and that it was very *aggravating*.

*　　*　　*　　*　　*　　*

BASLE, 31st May.

And always quite perfectly well, my precious wife, with the exception of the .throat, which is precisely the same. It has never been a bit worse, though I have been breathing

plenty of cold, damp air. It has rained every day for the
last eight days, and the sun has not shown itself for one
moment.

I have had no breathing-time, in the sense of leisure, and
it has been impossible for me to write since I left Milan, and
I have brought my letter on to Basle, as it must go through
France, and this is all in its way. And now, sweet, I will
give you an account of my journey.

On the 28th, at six in the morning, an omnibus took me,
in half an hour, to the railroad-station; and, by the railroad,
reached Monza in twenty minutes. There got into a diligence, and arrived at Como at eleven. Dined at Como, and
set out by the steamboat at two, and landed at Colico, at the
northern end of the lake, at six; hired a carriage, jointly
with my German companion, and reached Chiavenna by nine,
and there slept. The rain *poured* all day, 29th of May,—got
up at four, rain falling in torrents; the worst possible day
for the mountains. The diligence goes at six. What shall
we do? Wait for a fine day? We might wait for a week;
and what can we do in such a place as this? So my German
and I agreed that the least evil was to go on, and on we went,
with the inside of the diligence all to ourselves, for few
people would willingly face the Splugen in such weather,
none, it seems, but people with *sore throats*. Yes, there was
one other, in the imperial or sort of half-covered coupé, and
he was another young American, who *would* have stayed
behind if our example had not encouraged him. The first
word the man spoke told me his country, though his face was
downright English. He said he should *locate* himself in the
coupé. Well, dearest wife, but though I meant to brave the
snow and rain, I had not the least intention to get wet, or
feel a particle of cold; so I put on first, two shirts, two pair
of thick cotton drawers, and a flannel pair over them; my
thick woollen stockings, a flannel waistcoat, over them my
usual clothes, then my thick boots, and over them my list
ones, and then my thick great coat. The conductor furnished
me with a wrapper, and my German lent me one of his super-

numerary cloaks, for he had *four*, and one was a Greek
capote with a hood to it. Up the mountain and up the
mountain, clouds above us, clouds below, and rain never
ceasing, so that our view was close contracted, but yet all
the grander for the obscurity, and what glimpses there were,
were wonderfully rich in horrid beauty. At noon, after
having passed in the carriage between walls ten feet high of
snow, which had been cut away, we came to the end of the
cutting, and all was one wild wilderness of uninterrupted
snow. Lying upon it, without any covering, or any soul near
them, were some twenty sledges of various forms. Into two
of them we packed the luggage. Into another my German
and I transferred ourselves, and the American occupied
another. The horses were taken out of the diligence and
harnessed, one horse to each sledge, the postilions driving
two, and two men who soon made their appearance, the
other two.

With all my own quadruplicate clothing, and the borrowed
cloak which covered my head effectually, over my thick
Scotch bonnet, which I had tied on with a handkerchief over
my face, I had some of my blanket to spare; so we made
that an apron to cover our knees and feet, which were, besides,
protected by a wooden apron, with which the sledge was
furnished. It was a sort of rude gig, raised about a foot
above two parallel pieces of carved wood shod with iron, in the
shape of skates. Happily there was but little wind, and the
rain was less violent than any other part of the day—and
off we set !

The surface was at first level, and the good horse went
along merrily, only now and then putting his foot into a hole
where the snow was partially melted; but soon we began
to mount, and the partially beaten track was so irregular as
to require nice driving. The driver stood upon the sledge
behind us, and it was awkward managing the whip and reins
over our shoulders, and an inch or two the wrong way would
have overturned us into the snow; so, to my surprise, the
young German seized the reins; and a noble charioteer he

made! A very fine fellow is Von Trentorius (not *Sartorius*). He is a Prussian subject, but in the Russian service, and has driven *six* horses through the snow, four abreast, and two leaders.

In half an hour we came to the crest of the mountain, where there is a large building, the outpost of the Austrian dominion. Into this we drove, to have our passports registered; and the five minutes' shelter was useful to us for adjusting our coverings. The drivers munched some rye bread the while, and gave me a lump, which I found quite as good in that atmosphere as the best is apt to be below.

Off again, with a good courage, and not at all cold, only just knowing, if one put one's head out for a moment, that cold enough there *was*. Sometimes there was *nothing* to be seen but mere snow, and the track that preceding sledges had left. That track we followed, and presently came the descent; and then we soon found we were *not* following the course of the road, but making short cuts, and going down steeps far too precipitous for wheels. Well done, Von Trentorius! and well done you noble horse! Before us was a steep descent, but it seemed to end in a mere brink, over which one could only *tumble*. Not a bit; steeper it was than anything down which I had seen anything go except at the sport called the Russian mountain, which I once saw at Marseilles; and down we went much in the same way. The good horse crouched with his hind-legs under him doubled up, and his fore-legs stretched forward, and *slid* down; and two men, who seemed to have been in waiting, came and seized the sledge, one on each side, to keep it from oversetting; and Von Tren, with a steady hand, guiding the horse; and so men, and horse, and sledge, and all slid, scrambled, floundered, at a most rapid rate, and no accident happened; and in two hours from the time of leaving the diligence we got to the cleared road, and there we found another diligence, into which we and our things were packed, and our same horses harnessed to it. There, too, were dozens of sledges lying for the use of any travellers that might need them, and there we left ours.

By three o'clock we reached the village of Splugen, still very high up in the mountain, and there we dined, with appetites of *wolves*. At Coire, at the foot of the mountain, by nine at night, the scenery magnificent all the while, but the latter part the best. What they call the Via Mala has fifty times more of rugged grandeur than anything on the Simplon or St. Bernard.

Friday, 30th.

Left Coire at five in the morning in the diligence, and reached Wallenstadt by half-past nine. A steamer took us in an hour and a half to the end of the Lake of Wallenstadt; a row-boat, on the canal, in two hours and a half to the beginning of the Lake of Zurich—a great big boat with a cabin fitted up just like the cabin of a steam-packet. At the head of the Lake of Zurich we ought to have found the steamer, but it had been prevented by the rising of the water from passing a certain bridge; and we had to get into a carriage, and that brought us, by three o'clock, to the steamer, which landed us at Zurich at six. You see we had a variety of conveyances; but we took our places through, and the whole cost of the day's travelling was but fifteen francs.

The Hôtel du Lac at Zurich afforded us a comfortable dinner and lodging, and we had some grand people for our fellow-travellers, who dined in the *salle à manger* while we were dining. It was Prince Somebody—koff, a Russian; a remarkably fine, handsome young man, with two carriages filled with ladies and children, and one other gentleman; and one of the ladies was the far-famed *Taglioni*—all on their way to England together, where she is engaged.

Saturday, 31st.

Set off in a diligence at half-past eight in the morning, and got to Basle at six in the evening.   *   *   *   *

I made a point of getting to Basle last night, to stay over Sunday. I shall put this in the post as I go to church.

*   *   *   *   *   *

Basle, *Sunday, 1st June,* 1845.

*   *   *   * I have been to church both morning and evening. There was in the morning a large congregation in a good old church; but there was a great echo, and the clergyman spoke through his nose, without opening his mouth, and I heard imperfectly. In the afternoon there was a plainer speaker, and I got nearer and heard perfectly. The service was just the same as we used to hear at Montreux—first a hymn, then the Confession, then another hymn, then a long prayer, then a chapter from the New Testament, then the sermon, and then another hymn, and the *blessing*, and the good man prayed God to bless us and *our families*, and you may be sure I tried to join in his prayer with my whole heart. The Confession is word for word the same as in the other Swiss churches. It is read out of a book. The prayer is not read, but I remembered much that was the same as I have before heard, so that there was no difficulty in following it. After the afternoon service I went to look at the Cathedral. It is very ancient, and the outside is curious for its rude ornaments and unusual material, for it is built of *red* stone, and looks like brick, though it has a much finer effect when you see that they are large blocks of old stone.

By the bye, we passed, on the lower parts of the Splugen, on the Swiss side, quantities of beautiful *green* stone, like marble. The parapets on the road were made of it, and slabs were cut in some places, prepared for transportation. Do you remember two pieces of green stone on the corners of the balustrade at the Zabbar house? It is just the same sort, and would be much used if it were to be found where carriage is easier, for it is almost as handsome as the marble called Verd

Antique. At our *table d'hôte* dinner, at five, there were but five of us, one a German, and the others a young Englishman and his two sisters, very nice merry girls, and we talked a great deal. They, as well as I, are going to Strasburg to-morrow; but I meant to go by the six o'clock train, and they by the eight, and they agreed to get up a couple of hours earlier, that we might go together. In my walk through the town I found I knew more German than I thought, for I construed several of the inscriptions over the doors. One man kept a "Bier brauerey;" another said that "Tabac and spezerey waaren (were sold) bey Samuel Lotz;" another advertised that he was a "Gartner," another a "Schumacher;" then I passed through the Fischmarkt and the Münster Platz, which means the *Minster* (the Cathedral) Square.

Tuesday, 3rd June.

In the steamer going down the Rhine   *   *   * Yesterday morning I got up at half-past three, breakfasted, and set out at five in an omnibus to take us to the railroad. On our way we were stopped to have our baggage examined at the French frontier. At 5·50 started by the railroad, and reached Strasburg by half-past ten, the Englishman and his sisters and I having had the carriage all the way to ourselves. One of the poor girls, nineteen years old, is very pale and has been sick. She told me her two elder sisters had died of consumption, and her parents must tremble for *her*. Another elder sister was killed lately, by a stack of chimneys falling and breaking through the room in which she was. The brother told me she had had for six months a presentiment that she should not live. She had a bad temper, and in that six months entirely subdued it, and thought of nothing but preparing for her end, which came by so very unusual an accident.

We went to see the much-talked-of, but very ugly, monument of Marshal Saxe, and the very beautiful cathedral, the highest spire in the world, and saw the famous clock strike twelve, at which time *St. Peter's cock* flaps its wings and crows thrice, and certain other mechanical feats are performed. We dined at Strasburg, and set out again in an omnibus to go to the railroad station on the other (the right) bank of the Rhine at Kehl. After crossing the river, we were in the territory of the Grand Duke of Baden, and there again we had to descend from the omnibus for the inspection of our portmanteaus and bags. Left Kehl by the railroad at ten minutes after three, and in an hour and a half came to Baden-Baden station, where my companions left me, wishing heartily, they said, that we could have continued together, and giving me credit for liking them as well as they did me.

* * * * * *

At nine last evening we arrived at Manheim, where I slept. Up at five this morning, and set out at half-past six in the steamer for Cologne. We have now (eleven o'clock) just passed Mayence. There is no beauty in the Rhine yet— it is all a dead level, but there will be soon. The fine scenery begins at Johannisberg (the domain of which the Allied Sovereigns made a present to Prince Metternich), near Bingen, and continues as far as Bonn, after which there is nothing picturesque; so that it is but a little bit of the long river that gives it its reputation.

OSTEND, *5th June.*

And so, sweet Wife, my long journey has just reached its close. We reached Cologne on the 3rd, at eight in the evening, and slept there. Next morning I saw the cathedral, and Rubens's famous picture of the Crucifixion of St. Peter; set out by the railway at nine in the morning, and reached Brussels by eight in the evening. Set off again this morning at seven by railroad, and got to Ostend by noon.

The road from Cologne has been all flat and uninteresting, except that green fields, and trees, and flowering shrubs, and flowers abound, and are all beauties in my eyes. Yesterday and the day before I had pleasant companions: a very clever, frank young Englishman in the steamer, and a young English

newly-married couple yesterday in the carriage, which we
had to ourselves; both thoroughly nice people, very good-
looking, kindly-natured, and sensible—*but*—O what a but!—
the poor young man looked wofully emaciated; and when we
got out to walk, which we were obliged to do, to go over a
hill where the tunnel had broken in, he coughed a cough
that spoke of absolute consumption. The poor young lady is
not more than twenty, and seems to love her husband, but is
so merry that she can scarcely think him in any danger.

To-day my company was of a very different description.
There were five in the carriage with me. Four were fat,
middle-aged, ugly Dutchwomen, with green teeth and yard-
wide mouths, and gruff, grunting, croaking, braying, grating,
bawling voices, that never ceased going through and through
me, "located," as I unluckily was, in the middle of them.
Of course they killed me at last. Like the bold Trojans,
whom "non anni domuere decem, non mille carinæ," (Kitty
can construe that: domuere is third person plural, preterper-
fect tense of domo, to subdue; and carina is a keel, but
here, by synecdoche, a part for the whole—a *ship*). So I
survived

> A thousand leagues, sea storms, and Alpine snows,
> To fall a victim to four Dutchland frows.

The other was a vivacious young male of the same species,
who made his full share of the barbarous noise. I asked
them what hotel they were going to, and they said the "Imperial," and so gave me the means of escaping from them by
going to another.

Now, Mrs. Clifton,[b] can you wonder if I don't like women?
Haven't they been the death of me *twice* since I left you?

> I can forgive the charming creatures
> Any variety of features:
> But if they batter
> My ears with chatter;

---

[b] She was living in the house with Mrs. Sconce.

Or if, like George's fragrant bride,
Their shift, and petticoat, and hide
They will not wash,
My love they quash.

To-morrow morning at ten o'clock the steamer sets out for Dover, and promises to cross in five hours. If so, I shall be at Camberwell late to-morrow evening. I am a little tired with so much whirling along railroads, and have been a little put out in my digestion by irregular and generally late meals, and queer cookery; but I slept sound last night, and am pretty well to-day. As for the throat, it is only no worse. * * * * This is a poor, dull town, but it has an important fishery; and so the black gutters are garnished with garbage; here a pile of shrimp shells, there a rejected flounder, and so on. * * * * *

At Dr. Liddell's, GREENWICH, 7th June.

I have seen our two precious boys, and they are both of them pictures of health. * * * * *

Mr. Whitmarsh has seen my throat, and says it is a little more relaxed than when he saw it last; but by my own sensations it is no worse. He tells me Knox's house at Writtle is prepared to receive Harriet and me and our boys for the holidays, and that *there* I am to go. I don't know what may have been said about it, but I know *you* wish me to go to Leamington, and so, I take for granted, it will be decided.[1]

The first thing yesterday morning Liddell inspected my throat, and questioned me as doctors do who try in earnest to find out what is the matter, and what should be done. * * * He is persuaded that a fair trial of the effects of change of climate, and of improved general health, ought to be given to it, before resorting to *any* remedies, local or otherwise. * * * * *

---

[1] Dr. Liddell was not at home when this letter was sent off.

I looked in at the Water-Colour Exhibition, and missed poor old Hill's name among the contributors. I inquired for him, and heard that he died last summer. It made me melancholy. It seemed a great loss to me. I had known the good old man ever since I was a boy. * * *

I should like to spend half of every day in writing to you; for there is nothing that I do, or that happens to me, that I don't want to impart at once to precious wife. There is nothing I do that interests me half as *talking* in this way to my dearest *animæ dimidium*, and so doing what I can to mitigate for both of us this most distasteful separation.

* * * * * *

I have just been to pay a visit to Sir Robert and Lady Stopford, and have heard a sad account of poor Mrs. Duckworth. She was taken ill at Alençon, eighty miles from Paris. * * * My poor sick friend specially desired Lady Stopford to give her kindest love to me, and tell me she thought of me every day. Poor soul! I only wish I had known of her illness in time to go straight to her from Brussels. I would go *now* if it were not for my dear boys' holidays. * * * * *

At General Wood's in Norfolk Crescent, BATH,
14th June.

You need not be afraid of my forgetting you in my *vortex of pleasures*; for though it would be great pleasure, under other circumstances, to look upon the green fields and trees, and to see old friends who are thoroughly glad to see me, yet I have never spent an hour since I left you that has compensated for an hour's loss of *you*. It is quite true that, whether for a long time or a short one, you are worth everything else in the world to me; and I want no variety. I want *you*, and having you I care for little else. * *
Yesterday Liddell dined with my Admiralty friend Mr. Hay, whose acquaintance he made by my introduction; and Mr. Hay talked of me as if he was thoroughly desirous of doing all *he* could to help me. He says it is possible the

Secretaryship of Greenwich Hospital may be vacant, and asked if *that* would suit me; and Liddell said it would exceedingly well. It is £600 a year, with a house—and a sinecure.   *   *   *   *   *

How I wish you and I, my angel, had just such a house as this is, and here.[k] It looks over nothing but grass and trees, and distant hills, and you would not fancy yourself in a town.   *   *   *   My two drawings are in the drawing-room, and look well in their frames, but the one of the harbour is rather pale. It is very pretty, nevertheless, and Mrs. Wood looks at it with a magnifying-glass, and says nothing can exceed its finish. But the water-colour painters don't work in that way now. The drawings have a fine effect at a distance, but when you look into them you see *dabs* of all sorts put on in the rudest possible way, and many of them with body-colour. They totally (most of the artists) disregard finish.   *   *   *   *   *

You can easily imagine that these good friends do *all* they can to take care of me. Mrs. Wood looks after me much as you would. I have been drinking the Bath waters, and bathing in them. Liddell said I had better try them, and Mrs. Wood is of his opinion; but I don't expect them to do either good or harm, especially in one week. She shows me all the sights about the town, and this afternoon drove with me into the country. The General and I play chess in the evening.   *   *   *   *   *   *

18th June.

I have astonished Mrs. Wood to-day by walking up to Lansdown Crescent and all the heights of Bath, and coming back without being tired. But what an escape I have had! She made an engagement for me, not knowing, poor soul, my dread of the ladies, and *Miss* Macadam (of course, the lady that makes the roads—her Grandfather gave them the name)

---

[k] He *did* have a house in Norfolk Crescent, close to General Wood's, the following year, and moved into it a very few days before his death.

was to call for me in her carriage at five o'clock to-day, and
she and I to take a *tête-à-tête* drive.   Only think of it !   I
was ready to sink into the earth when I heard it.   I told
Mrs. Wood you would hear of it, and all Malta would be
scandalized, as well as Macadamized.   But there was no help
for it, and *tête-à-tête* I was doomed to be, when happily there
fell some raindrops, and a little wind rose, and it occurred
to Mrs. Wood, that as my throat was so bad I ought not to
go out; so she wrote an excuse for me, to my inexpressible
relief.   What in the world should I have done!   The dear
lady is *deaf*, too, and I have no voice.   We shall meet her
this evening, for we are all going to Mrs. Sankey's, where
she will be, and, of course, I shall tell her of my severe disappointment.   I can the more safely, as to-morrow is my last
day, and we are going to a great *flower*-show, and you know
I may very innocently fall in love with the flowers; and
besides, I shall neither have to listen to them nor talk to
them.   As for the party to-night, I shan't mind that, for the
General and I will play chess.   *   *   *   *

                                                                  Next day.

    I have just come in from seeing a flower-show in the Park
—*beautiful* things ; but some of our ixias and oleanders would
have made a good figure among them too.   The greatest
glories were the roses.   I suppose I have no very redundant
strength, for I was glad to come home and sit down as soon
as I had seen the flowers; whereas the rest of the people
promenade the lawns, to look at each other's clothes and
display their own.   The argument, you know, is, that the
Bath people in general are stronger than I am, though there
were plenty of elderly gentlewomen among them.   I mean to
get much stronger at Wateringbury, where I shall keep
earlier hours.   *   *   *   *   *

    He had engaged a cottage at Wateringbury, near Maid-
stone, for a few weeks, for the sake of being near his brother-
in-law, Rev. J. Henderson, who was then at Barming, and
there he went from Bath, picking up his son Willy from

Marlborough College, and his Aunt Van Sprang, by the way. At Wateringbury his sister and two elder sons, from the Naval School, New Cross, were ready to receive him. There, during the six weeks' holidays, my Father devoted himself to his boys. Teaching was for himself almost the worst possible employment in which he could have engaged in the state of his throat; but for his poor boys, this instruction from their precious Father, the last they were ever to receive, was invaluable.

In the first[1] of his almost daily long letters to his wife, from Wateringbury, he says:—

Clement has been construing and parsing Latin to me for two hours and a half, and knows a great deal more than I expected, and works with a most willing spirit, and has a good memory, and there is no reason why he should not do really well. He will gallop through my red books. Besides, some of the first volume, he has done this morning twenty-eight pages of the second, and in the evening will do more.

* * * * We had a very beautiful walk through meadows and bean-fields in flower, and among green lanes and plantations of various trees, and I thought I might as well make something of a *lesson* out of our ramble, and initiate my sons into the science of botany, and especially that part of it that may help their Latin reading. They have in Virgil, Propria quæ maribus, and *other authors*, abies, fraxinus, acer, quercus, and so on; and now they know the trees when they see them, as well as their English and Latin names. I showed them a few other plants, of which I thought they might remember the names, and *any* knowledge is so much gain when it may be had without painful pursuit. It is horrid *cockney* not to know the names of trees and of the commoner species of plants.

Again, next day:—

I have been occupied with my boys ever since I got out of

---

[1] The day after his leaving Bath.

bed at seven o'clock. Clement came in to me then, and construed, while I was dressing. After breakfast we all walked
into the woods, and said verbs as we went along, and Herbert
carried for me old Aunt's camp-stool, which she brought on
purpose for my use, and I sat down upon it in a beautiful
shady recess, and my boys deposited themselves round me,
and I believe we said, *short*, best part of a hundred verbs,
Clement doing each first, then Herbert, and then Willy.
Then we returned home, and Clement construed for an hour,
while Herbert wrote an exercise, and then Herbert construed
and Clement wrote.　　　＊　　　＊　　　＊　　　＊　　　＊

I slept last night but little. My throat hurt me, and kept
me awake. The evening was very damp in coming yesterday
from Maidstone, and I suppose it did some mischief. It has
generally been much as it was latterly at Malta, but now and
then a great deal worse, and then after a few days it gets
back to its usual state, but never any *better*　　＊　　　＊　　　＊
Just now my throat is excoriated, and smarts and burns; but
I have no doubt of its soon healing again, as it has done
several times before.

As far as I am individually concerned, my separation from
you is a great pain; but I bear it willingly, for the sake of
the very important good that I know I am doing to our dear
sons. Some important good I shall myself derive from the
change of climate; but Clement and Herbert will probably in
these six weeks make an advance in classics and mathematics[m]
equal to six months' school work.　　　＊　　　＊　　　＊

We try and make acquaintance with the birds, too, as they
sing for us. I used in my youth to know most of them by
their song or flight; but it is impossible to make much fami-
liarity with them and their doings if one does not go out
early in the morning, which is their active time. Two of
different sorts sang for a long while in a tree close to us. If

---

[m] They had a master for mathematic .

we hear them again we shall remember their notes, and if I
get a good sight of the birds, I shall probably know them.
The good boys enjoy their walks thoroughly.

*   *   *   *   *   *

Nothing can be more *regular* than the life I lead. Of
course it would be better for me if I had a *tutor* for my sons
who could and *would* do what I do, for I *talk* too much, and
have books before me too long; but it does me but little harm
in proportion to their great good; and when they are gone to
school I may be as idle as I please.

The letters to Robert and me at this time contain chiefly
repetitions of the foregoing.

To me, he says:—

I have not yet communicated with Barton; but if I can
possibly contrive to pay Sir Henry a little visit, I shall be
heartily glad. Vi Knox pressed me very much to go to him
at Writtle, and I should be sorry not to be with him a little
while. I may perhaps go from Writtle to Barton; but I shall
be hard pushed for time, and I must do, before all, what is
best for the errand on which I came,—that of repairing my
health, if I can.

In the course of a talk with a countryman, I told him I
knew this country when I was a boy. "Why, sir," said the
man, "that be a long bit agone, for I take you to be seventy."
I told Aunt Van, and she said sometimes I looked *a hundred*.
Yet I have not grown a bit *older* than I was at Malta, but a
trifle *younger*.   *   *   *   *   *

All the country people are civilly inclined and willing to
talk. I met a girl of a dozen years old, from whom I expected only a curtsey—the little *dip* they all give us; but
besides that, the little thing said, in passing, "It's been
a nice day, sir." I suppose I should soon make personal
acquaintance with all my cottage neighbours for miles round.

*   *   *   *   *   *

And here, you know, is my birthday, my darling wife; and I have lived fifty-eight years; and I hope I am grateful for the many blessings with which they have been filled, and that if it pleases God to allow me to number more years, I may make a better use of them.

We have been to church, and Harriet and I received the sacrament.

And now, this evening, I am going to *Dover*, and then to cross over to Boulogne. I received a letter by the post this morning from Colonel Douglas, telling me of their arrival at Boulogne, and of Mrs. Duckworth's having been again alarmingly ill there. She rallied from this attack, by dint of physicking and blistering; "but this fresh call upon her already alarmingly reduced powers is not unattended with considerable anxiety." I am longing to see the poor soul; and I am only *four hours* distant from her; so go I must.

I leave my boys plenty of work prepared, and, if they *please*, they may do it easily.

After two days' absence, having written in the mean time from Boulogne, he writes again from Wateringbury:—

We have done a good day's work, dearest. The weather has been fine, so that we have been able to do the out-door business as well as the in. We read hard most of the morning, but spared some time for walking and some for *jumping*. Willy and I are the best jumpers; Clem and Herbert may, by dint of practice, equal us; but they *can't* yet. I can clear, at a *standing* jump, seven of my own feet, and Willy can clear seven of his; but the other two can hardly do as much. Seven of my feet are equal to 6 ft. 2 inches, which is very well for a sick old man; though in my jumping days I could clear 9 ft., that is, ten of my own.

You see I am not very sick, either in body or spirit, though my throat is never one bit better: it does not oppress me, and I trust it will not. We may pray God to make us well, but still more to enable us to receive cheerfully and gratefully trials that may so be converted to our greatest benefit. I must not call this slight ailment any trial at all ; but slight as it is, what lasts a long while needs patience that one must seek from the right source, or it will fail.

Yet in the postscript of this letter he says :—

I am pretty well to-day, though I had no sleep last night. My throat kept me awake by the tickling of the phlegm, and partly by the pain of swallowing. There is a clock near my room, and I heard it strike every hour. I tell you always exactly how I am, whether better or worse, for I like to tell you the plain truth. I have certainly, habitually, more pain in swallowing than I had at Malta, and there is more phlegm created. * * * But I never had a headache.

It seems a long time since I wrote to you (though I have not missed a day), for it was early yesterday when I sent away my letter, and now it is night. My day has been all spent upon my boys and my walking, neither of which great businesses I put by, *even* to write to you.

* * * * * *

What Clement does is really important, for it will put him, in Latin, *quite* half a year in advance. You see, my darling, his six weeks' holidays bear an important proportion to the length of the ensuing half-year at school, which contains about *twenty* weeks. *Six*, you know, is little less than the *third* of twenty ; and as we do every day more than three times as much as he could do at school, the amount is easily calculated. * * * * *

What I tell him he retains admirably, and I expect him to gain special renown at his *naval* school by construing certain nautical phrases with a technical propriety worthy of his nautical sire ; for example : Æneas, ipse sedens clavumque regit, velisque ministrat, is, "He directs the steerage and *trims* the sails" (v. 218) ; and again (v. 229),—Vigila, et velis immitte rudentes, must of course be, "Keep a *sharp* look out, and *ease off the sheets*." Of course, if any of the *Council* hear him construe so, it will be worth a *gold medal* to him. They will think him specially inspired by the *genius loci*. So, of course, when Æneas speaks to his men, he must call them *my lads*, and my fine fellows, and *my hearties*, and so on.   *   *   *   *   *   *

Last night I did get some little sleep by sitting upright in bed. For some days I have felt a burning on my chest, which may be heartburn, showing that all is not quite right about the digestion, and *that* may account for the disorder in the throat.   *   *   *   *   *

Harriet and I just remarked that we should be glad to get a photograph of the old Aunt. I suppose her to be the handsomest old lady of eighty-four that was ever seen. She has no wrinkles, her cheeks are not fallen in, nor the form of her mouth spoiled by loss of teeth. Her eye is bright and the expression of her countenance lively and amiable. There is not a particle of the ugliness of age to be seen in her."

          *   *   *   *   *   *

I have *not yet* given myself up to the single pursuit of health; for, between Clem and Herbert, I have *talked*, at least, four hours a day, which is bad. Liddell says I have not given myself fair play, and that I ought to have nothing to do but to consult my own cure. Well, here is only one week more to work; for, after next Saturday, I don't mean my boys to open a book. They will be at home till the following Friday, but they must be whole holidays—those last four days. Good boys they are for having worked so much and so willingly, and I don't think my lectures have done me much harm, for they have been cheered by success, and I have spoken in a *low voice*.

          *   *   *   *   *   *

How thoroughly I should have enjoyed my ramble this morning if you had been with me, my darling Wife, and do tell

---

Mr. and Mrs. Clifton how glad I should be to have them of such a party; for they would have had a keen relish for the beauties of the scenery, and Mr. Clifton would have been as eager as I was to get a sight of the little bird that sang so loud and sweet and long a song in Sir John Shaw's hornbeam tree. I did see the little wretch, but could not make out his colour, and so can't find his name. I *had* once some knowledge of birds' music, but have forgotten almost all, and when I go out with the three sons, they chatter so fast that there .is small chance of getting close to a songster unobserved.

Harriet asked me just now if I had said all I had to say to my *sweetheart.* Everybody contrives to find out that I am over head and ears in love with my wife, and, of course, it must seem very absurd for an old gentleman like me to retain a propensity which people are so apt to outgrow. What I may come to there is no saying, but my *heart* is not old yet, and my notion is that, unless I grow crazy like poor ——, you will be my sweetheart till the end of the chapter. You know it never was my way to do anything by halves, and the *last* thing I should begin with would be *loving.*　　*　　　*　　　*　　　*　　　*　　　*

My brother Herbert says, in a letter to me from India :—

After 1845, I always kept a good place at school in mathematics, and I attribute it in a great measure to the pains my Father took in teaching me arithmetic, and especially practice. It encouraged me to take pains. He never uttered an angry word, although not a day passed without my giving him trouble with my Nepos. I was stupid and backward, but not obstinate. Our Father, you know, was always very active, and I recollect when we walked out he used to race with us, and how pleased he was to find that Willy could keep up with him.

To me, 28th July, my Father writes :—

If I had only myself to think of, I would not depend upon the doctors, for I feel sure they will do me no good, and may do harm. I think nature would work for me better than Dr. Jephson ; and my own inclination would be to set out at once for the old haunts about *Montreux*, and see whether I could not double my appetite and my strength, as I did once before, by tramping from morning till night among the mountains. But though I have a notion that such might be the better plan, I may be mistaken, and I am afraid to act upon my own mere guess in a matter that concerns wife and children. If I had a sanguine hope that the Swiss mountains would cure me, I might venture to turn my back upon the English doctors ; but I have not that. I only think it might possibly do some good, but when a disorder has lasted nine months (not a malattia allegra), one can't reasonably hope for a sudden cure. Lord Western, who died lately, about eighty years old, had a sore throat for the last thirty years, and tried all the physicians and surgeons in Europe without the smallest advantage. Yet the disease did not shorten his existence one hour, and he died of natural decay.

Here follow more little extracts from letters to his wife :—

All the rest of the day° I have been employed making a sketch for you of the view from our window. I began it yesterday before we set off to Yalding, so that I have spent just one whole day's work upon it, and it is done, and a very pretty and satisfactory sketch it is ; for Herbert, who delighted in watching its progress, and Aunt, have both paid it high compliments. It fills a page of my great sketch-book, and is highly coloured, and quite enough finished for what it pretends to be, no more than a sketch. It will serve to give

---

° From half-past eleven.

you an exact notion of our country, and will be an interesting memorial for Herbert.   *   *   *   *

31st July.

This is our last day at Wateringbury, and the boys' last day, poor fellows, at home.

Harriet has not only been preparing their boxes, but pies and other prog for them.   *   *   *   She devotes herself to these boys of ours in a way that you can have no idea of without seeing it as I have seen.

He then spent some days at his "dear old friend," Mr. C. Smith's, giving some hours each day to Mrs. Duckworth, who was very ill at Greenwich.

2nd August.

But now, sweet wife, I have an account to give you of my throat that you will be glad to hear. I took it this morning to Mr. Lawrence. I never saw a more prepossessing person than he is. His look speaks at once a clear-sighted and honest man. He looked at once into my throat, and told me, that as low down as could be *seen* there was really nothing whatever the matter with it.   *   *   *   *
Then I told him how it had come on, and how much worse it had sometimes been, and what my sensations were, and that it still felt sore, though much less than it has done, lower down. "Well," said he in a cheerful voice, "you may be perfectly satisfied that you have no serious disease, that the mucous membrane has been irritated by previous illness, and that having contracted that illness in a climate that disagreed with you, you will in all probability get rid of all the remaining mischief by leaving that climate for a better."
      *   *   *   *   *   *
He told me to sponge my throat night and morning with vinegar and water, to rub it with an oil for which he gave me a prescription, to create a little external irritation, and to get my skin into a healthy state by rubbing it all over with a

2 A 2

hair glove, to eat and drink just as I had been accustomed
to do, to keep as much as I could in the open air, and to
quit Malta finally as soon as I conveniently could. I told
him what my object was in trying to spin out the time till
the year after next, and he agreed that it was quite reasonable, but that I must be cautious to get away in time if I
was threatened with more sickness.

I told him that I myself was quite satisfied, from my own
experience of my own case, that his opinion was a sound one,
and that I had myself thought that I should do better by
going to walk about the Swiss mountains, than by putting
myself in the hands of the doctors.

   * * * . * * *

Now, sweet wife, in all this he agrees exactly with what
Liddell said to me, except that Liddell acquiesced in my wish
to go to Jephson; but I am sure he did so because he thought
it would be more satisfactory to *you*. * * *

Now, dearest, I desire, you well know how, to do just what
I think you would consider best for me; and I do feel
persuaded that you would heartily wish me not to go to
Jephson after what Mr. Lawrence has said.

At V. Knox's, at WHITTLE,
8th August.

Vi Knox is very warm in his expressions of interest, and
says, he rejoices with all his soul that I did not go to Jephson.
 * * * * He says he would give two
hundred pounds, or even five, to go to Switzerland with me;
but he has business which makes it impossible for him to
leave London. * * * * *

Last night, after Vi's dinner party of *twenty* had gone
away, and his nieces were gone to bed, and he and Tom
Knox and I were only left, he made a *pleasant* communication to us! The Superintendent of Police at Chelmsford had
been to him, and told him, that a gang of London house-
breakers had arrived at Chelmsford, and had resolved to
begin their operations by "cracking" *his* house and that

of his neighbour, Dr. Penrose, who is absent, and has left in his house only an old woman and a boy. The Superintendent informed Vi, moreover, that his *Butler* had been seen in the company of these robbers; yet Vi has great confidence in the man's honesty, and thinks he might have been accosted by them, and drawn into talk with them, without at all suspecting who they were. What was to be done? It was midnight, and no measures could be taken for getting help from without, and there were no beds in the house for either Tom Knox or me,[p] and, at any rate, I was not robust enough to volunteer to sit up all night, for the chance of *that* being the night fixed upon for the enterprise. But Vi would not let either of us do that, and he determined to go to bed quietly himself and take his chance, first making the Butler put the plate under his bed, and warning him and the Coachman (the only men in the house besides himself) that there were bad characters in the neighbourhood. He made them observe, too, that he had properly loaded his double-barrelled gun, and assured them, that *two*, at any rate, of the first-comers would infallibly be dismissed to Pluto. The night passed and the burglars didn't come.   *   *   *

SOUTHSEA, *12th August.*

(He came here partly to see friends, but chiefly to visit the Victualling Yard, and take a lesson at the Bakery there.)

Directly after breakfast I set off to *Haslar*. I need not tell you what I felt there. In going towards Dr. Richardson's I overtook him, and he took me to his house, and at once asked me to take up my lodging there.

  *   *   *   *   *   *

He said he knew I wished to visit the *burial-ground*, and had the key in his pocket, and would go with me. We went together. Close by the side of my darling's grave is that of his wife, precisely like it. It is similarly surrounded with

---

[p] He was sleeping at the inn close by, Mr. Knox's house being full.

shrubs, and overshadowed by the ancient elm. The trees planted two years ago are much grown; those newly added unite with them, and form one arbour. I looked up at the windows of the room where you and I last saw my Angel Child. God grant that you and I may see her again where there will be no more pain and no more partings!

*   *   *   *   *   *

I shall see poor Mrs. Duckworth for the last time (not, I hope, the *very* last time) to-morrow.

LONDON, 14th August.

At the often-repeated invitation of Sir Howard and Lady Douglas, I went to see them, and was received with all the cordiality they promised.   *   *   *   *

I found Mrs. Duckworth still improving, slowly; but after the Stopfords left her room to go and dress for dinner, she grew suddenly very nervous at the thoughts of taking leave of me, and said she could not bear looking forward to it; and I came away almost at once. She put into my hand a little ring, which she desired me to beg you to wear some-times for her sake, and the most beautiful pair of ear-rings that ever were seen, with her kindest love to little Kitty.

*   *   *   *   *   *

It was an inexpressible comfort to me to see our dear Sons thoroughly happy in their promotion. They were very anxious while the suspense lasted, and all the more so because they knew how anxious *I* was; and they were all the more happy in being able to tell me that all was right. The whole school was examined by Dr. Chambers, to enable him to class them anew; and of course the work we had done in the holidays told in the examination.   *   *   *   *

My dear Father stayed three days at Paris, chiefly with his dear, kind friend, Madame Reboul. He needed this rest before proceeding on his long journey to Vevey.

Speaking of Madame Reboul's daughter, he says:—

Mary is a glorious-hearted English girl,—frank and honest and affectionate,—and just, in these respects, like my dear Annie.

To Robert he writes, from Paris :—

I seldom say anything in reference to the favourite topic of your letters—the praises of Mr. Newman and Dr. Pusey, the doings of the party of which you are a stout champion. You know, dearest Bob, what my opinions have been on these subjects, and you can easily guess that nothing either they or you have written have induced me to change them. You and your friend Mr. W—— pity me for being old, and consequently unable to run as fast in a new direction as you do; but it is nothing new, dear Son, for young men to run too fast; and that multitudes have done so in this case will, I fear, be shown but too decisively.

Of course, you have heard—what no one, I believe, now denies—that Mr. Newman is about to declare himself a dutiful son of the Pope. Woful as such a consummation will be, it has, you well know, seemed to me inevitable. No one not in heart a Papist and a Jesuit could possibly have written that tract, the number of which happened to be the number of one of your late letters; and you made allusion, in numbering the letter, to what I had said of the tract, and that allusion meant, of course, that the tract was no more Jesuitical than the letter. Do you think so still? Can you think, if what we have heard be true, that the Church has not cause to rue the rise of Mr. Newman? Abundance of good and wise men will remain with us; but they will have to contend at once with passion, suspicion, and the Puritans, and those are fearful odds. You, dearest Bob, will, I am sure, be among the good and the *wise;* but *moderation* is an essential part of wisdom, and it will be more than ever necessary for you to *doubt* whether *all* the opinions, and customs and tastes of your party are just, and all opposing opinions, and so forth, untenable. Of course, you will protest against my use of the term party; but I can't help it. It has the characteristics of a party but too evidently.

I like to say to you just what I think; and one of my thinkings is, that the seal of a letter is not a fit place for the sacred symbol of the cross. There is no more reason why *you* should use it than all your neighbours—your greengrocer, for example, who professes to be a Christian as much as you. Would you put it upon your snuff-box, spoons, or coach-panel?

Vevey, *24th August.*

Ay, dearest love,[a] and not one jot the worse for such a journey, though I was fifty-nine hours on the road without a rest, except half an hour each day for breakfast and for dinner. I left Paris at noon on Thursday, the 21st, and got to Besançon on Saturday morning, at six. I had taken my place no further; but finding myself perfectly well, and not in the least tired, I came on straight, after just time enough to get some coffee, to Lausanne, where we arrived last night at eleven.

*   *   *   I was up this morning at six, got into the well-remembered *omnibus* at seven, and to the Vevey post-office at nine, and there realized the hope I had been cherishing all my journey of finding my sweet wife's letter.

*   *   *   *   *   *

Of course, I alighted at Vevey, at the old Faucon, poor old Mrs. Dreyer's.[b] To my great surprise, she knew me the moment she saw me, and before I opened my lips, and glad indeed she was to see me. She held my arm for five minutes, told me I looked as if I had been ill, asked most affectionately after you and the children, and thanked me with all her heart for remembering her and coming again to

---

[a] To his wife.
[b] He had lodged with his family at her house eight years before, for a few days, when she, like all the French and Swiss landladies, fell in love with him.

see her. She told me my coming was a remarkable *coincidence,* and asked a young woman, standing by, if they had
not been talking of me this very morning! By way of
amusing you, and my own fancy, in the diligence, I put
together a string of doggerel verses. They will show you,
at least, that I was not jaded in spirit.

From Paris to far Besançon
Without a rest is somewhat long;
And two nights' rattling upon a
French pavé wounds one's seat of honour.
As least of ills, though more I do pay,
I took a seat within the coupé,
'Tis roomier and far superior
To the rotonde or the interior:
Besides, one hopes there may not jump any
Fleas and so forth, from coupé company.
For grave and many are the offences,
Apt to assail poor travellers' senses;
And hard it is long nights to *associate,*
Boxed up, in contact close with *those ye hate.*
So 'tis a moment of suspense,
When seated first in diligence,
You wait to see what sort of faces
Will occupy the other places:
What sex, what bulk, what nation, may be
Some ell-wide monster or a baby.
Fatal extremes! No wonder *we* all *eyes*
Open to see what fate we *realize.*
Hard fate it is! a decent foreigner
Takes, for I've one, the vacant corner;
But in betwixt us jams a corpus,
A male one, bigger than a porpoise,
Squeezes my breath clean out and pinches
My small breadth into three small inches.
This brute appears an employé
Of Lafitte, rue St. Honoré,

> Lafitte Gaillard, the mighty *stager*, he
> Who fills all France with his *messagerie*,
> He's sent upon a special mission
> Of coach and horses' supervision,
> And curses the postilions, *for* it e-
> vinces his plenary au*thor*ity.

He would have cursed *me* too, and a most blackguard curser he was; but I kept him at arm's length, not *literally* —I could not do *that*.   *   *   *   *

I wanted you sadly as we merged from the mountains and first got sight of the plains of Vaud, the lake of Neufchatel on the left, and that of Geneva on the right, and the whole chain of the Alps in front, without a cloud. Mont Blanc illuminated and painted *rose* by the setting sun.

I counted upon going to church at Vevey, but the service began at nine, and I could not be in time; but, upon the whole, I don't know whether I was not more satisfied to read our own Church service, which I did before I began to write this, and you may be sure, dear wife, whenever the word *we* occurred I thought always of you.

    *   *   *   *   *   *

They came to tell me dinner was ready, and such a dinner never was provided for one appetite. The good old lady thought she could not do enough to tempt me to eat, and in she brought fish, flesh, and fowl—boiled beef, roast veal, mutton cutlets, stewed pigeon, roast chicken — vegetables various—stewed apricots, an apricot cake, a most beautiful-looking thing, currant jelly—preserved ginger, ripe peaches. Then she talked to me about her wines, and strongly recommended a small bottle of champagne; but, though I wouldn't have that, I thought I would venture upon some of the wine of this region, which I used to drink, and found it agree with me; so she produced a little bottle " of the vintage of '34," which she said was a renowned one.

    *   *   *   *   *   *

The good old lady's assiduities are unbounded and affectionate. She would give me her whole house, and be better pleased to take no money for it. * * *

He then passed some days in the beautiful valley of Simmenthal, between Vevey and Thun, stopping a day or two at different villages, and writing long letters to his wife from Weissenburgh, Erlenbach, Zweysimmen, &c., from which the following little extracts are taken.

The mountain air is cold, and the weather has been damp and dreary; but yet, if anything, my throat is rather better than when I left Vevey. It has not kept me awake, and does not hurt me much in swallowing; but there is a great deal of irritation going on, which creates an immense quantity of phlegm. * * * * I did expect when I left England, as I told you, that the evil was going finally away. I was all but absolutely free from it; but it has come back again, and I wish I could guess *why*.

* * * * * *

My want of German is a sad grievance. There is a church close to my hotel, but the service is, of course, in German, and it was useless my going to it. This is one of the comforts of home, to which I shall be most glad to return. The good people here[1] do all they can to take care of me, and nothing can exceed the liberality of their provisions.

* * * * * *

Oh, the difference between these mountains and the dockyard creek! This *valley* is more than 3,000 feet above the level of the sea. Tell little Mia I have found wild raspberries and gooseberries, and longed for her to have the fun of picking them. * * * * *

ZWEYSIMMEN, 3rd *September.*

I have been to Lenk, and spent a very pleasant day. I got up at half-past five, and began my journey at half-past

---

[1] Erlenbach.

seven, and got to Lenk at ten, driving at a good pace along a good road, with only little ascent. The valley ends there in a mountain something like those at Grindelwald, a brown rock towering some eight or ten thousand feet, the top all snow, and a glacier coming a good way down, but not *into* the valley, like the Grinderwald one. From this glacier the river Suime comes tumbling down, something like the Giesbach, more in quantity, but not picturesque. I spent three pleasant hours among these wild regions, made a memorandum or two to serve for sketches, and then repaired to the inn at the village of Lenk for some dinner. The man who keeps it is an Italian, and was glad to talk his own language with me.

The old man who drove my little char mounted his box without a whip. I never saw a coachman without one before ; but it would have been a needless affront to his good horse to carry one.   I never saw a quadruped so promptly docile. The man never *jerked* the reins, as the stupid Maltese do, and never made any of the queer noises that are supposed to be more intelligible to horses than plain English or plain German ; but when he wanted it to go faster, he said in a low, quiet voice, " Allez," and that instant the horse mended his pace—he never failed, and so he stopped when he was spoken to in the same quiet way. But when the rain came, and we were in haste to get home, and the man said " Allez " with a little increased emphasis, my patience, how the pretty mare did trot ! Strong, fat, sleek, handsome, fast, making nothing of her work, it was a pleasure to be drawn along by such a creature ; and I hope her lot will be like that of Eclipse, of whom it is recorded, that he was never touched by whip or spur.

The landlord at Lenk gave me beautiful trout from his stream, beef, mutton, and all sorts of sweet things, and took in return for them two francs, made my coachman a present of a drink of wine, and thanked me heartily, and shook hands with me. Civility is the general fashion of this country. I gave an old man sixpence for doing an errand for me, and he not only thanked me, but wished me health. He happened to know some French. As one approaches the Vaud confines, one meets occasionally with people who have crossed the border; but it is wonderful how strongly the line is marked of German on this side, and French on the other, of a mere conventional boundary. At Fribourg, the language of the upper town is French, and of the lower German; and there are hundreds of people there who don't know a word of the language that belongs to the next street.

Those *horrid* people at Zweysimmen did really put me into a horrid rage, by the cheating and cool impudence. I mentioned it to the man at Gassenay, where I slept, and, "Oh, sir," said he, "they are famous for it—look here!" and he showed me his book, where travellers write their names, and sometimes make remarks, you know,—and there was a warning to avoid the Crown Inn at Zweysimmen; and in a similar book at Château d'Oex, where I breakfasted, there were more than half a dozen notices of the bad character of the said Crown. I really do think I kept myself awake by brooding over my anger, and itching to make *my* entry in the book, which would, of course, have demolished the "Crown." However, I could not succeed in satisfying myself that my *motive* was quite right, and so I thought the safer way was to say nothing. It would have been good for future travellers to be effectually warned away from the "Crown," but would not have been at all a good thing *for me* to take revenge of the "Crown," and especially *behind its back.* Kitty and Mia, remember that somebody in the "Red-book" says, "I would punish you if I was not angry."

His remaining time in Switzerland he spent at Vernex, at the Hotel du Cygne, overlooking the lake, in which we had all lived together eight years before.

12th September.

It has not been quite so fine to-day; yet I was able to get a very pleasant walk and an hour or two's sketching, and so

brought home a glorious chestnut tree. In my walk yesterday
I met two young ladies, and they passed me to-day while I
was drawing, and so I took my hat off to them, and then they
stopped and asked to look at my work, and they told me there
was a finer tree a quarter of a mile off than the one I was
drawing, and they described to me the way to find it. "No,
no," said I; "I dare say you are not very busy, and I find it
too cold to sit still any longer, so, if you please, you shall come
at once and show me the tree." Of course, they liked nothing
better, so we took our walk together; and the great tree was
close, as it happened, to their house, so that I did not take
them out of their way. They are exceedingly pretty and
lady-like, so I shall go and sketch their tree and make love
to them. They have the grace of real gentlewomen, without
one particle of affectation or awkward shyness. I hear the
rain plashing at a great rate now into the lake, and I am
afraid there will be an end of my sketching and love-making.
It would be a great pity too, for though I can't bring away
the young ladies, I had designs upon at least half a dozen
chestnut trees of rare beauty.

  * * * * * *

I couldn't go and see my *ladies*, but one has been to *see me*.
I told you two very pretty ones made acquaintance with me
while I was sketching. It happens that one of the two—not
the Dutch one—is an acquaintance of the ladies who are
living at the Cygne with me. She is Russian; and there is
another young Russian lady living with her. This other one
came this afternoon to see the ladies here, and I saw her and
talked to her; and thinks I to myself, though Russia is a
wide realm, she may know the Fengers,[1] so I asked about
them.

"Yes, to be sure," said she; "I live in the same town,
Riga, and I know them most intimately; and the young

---

[1] The two Madame Fengers and Mademoiselle Yachman were the Russian
ladies spoken of at the beginning of this volume, with whom we formed so
close an intimacy at the Cygne, Vernex, eight years before.

Madame Fenger, who is now Madame Pescantini, is per-haps at this moment at Geneva. She was to come about this time. Mademoiselle Yachman has changed her name too, and has an English husband, Mr. Sharman, and they were lately living near Lausanne, and were to come for the grape season to Montreux."

Isn't this a strange coincidence? I have written poste restante to Geneva, to tell Madame Pescantini I am here and want to see her; and I have written to Mrs. Sharman for the like purpose. How glad they will both be if they really are here before I go. I am sure I shall be heartily rejoiced to see them.

The Russian girl who came here this afternoon and gave me this news is a frank, cordial little body," very much like the little Fenger herself, and tells me that, as my companions in this house are going away and I shall be alone, I must come very often and see her and her friend.

I have plenty of work at home for wet days, upon the slight sketches I have made; and to-day I have concocted a pretty little drawing out of an outline I made in five minutes while the diligence waited for me.

* * * * * *

As for my pretty Russians, nothing can be more constant than they are. They came to me while I was sketching to-day, and waited till I had done, and then took a long walk with me. These two girls soon got a notion, upon their coming to Vevey last year, that there was something wrong in their own church in praying, as the Romanists and Greeks

---

" Raikes says, in his journal :—

"The Russian women, generally speaking, have much frankness and sensi-bility in their character. A refined education forms their minds to the enjoy-ment of those scenes, both local and social, in which Italy abounds. This feeling is frozen up in their own barren country as soon as it is formed; but when they are allowed to visit foreign lands it bursts forth with redoubled warmth, and only renders them more wretched when fate or the Emperor ordains their return to Russia."

do equally, to the Virgin Mary and the Saints; and of their own accord they went to Mr. Malan, the most famous of the Geneva clergy, and begged him to instruct them; and they subsequently received the communion in his church. They now read nothing but religious books, because, say they, we must make the most of our time,—in Russia they won't let us have such books. I have made for one of them a little sketch of the cottage they live in, and the enormous walnut-tree close to it; and for the other I did the gate of the Castle of Blonay,—to their great delight.   *   *   *

I am impatient to tell you that my throat continues better. I have had no such days as yesterday and to-day since I left Paris: there has been less expectoration, and I swallow better. My Russian friend observed it to-day. How glad I am, precious wife, when I can tell you I am better! I really never do think about my throat without reference to *you*. When it is worse I am always picturing to myself my poor wife *fretting* about it.   *   *   *   *

I do all I can to improve my condition, and I suppose I am leading a healthy life. I get up very early, keep out of doors almost all day, sitting in dry sheltered places to sketch, and never sitting still if I feel the least wind blowing upon me, and always taking a good long walk, and not too long. These good Russian girls, too, help to make my day cheerful. They are warm-hearted, unaffected, and sensible, and thorough ladies. One of them, Catherine de S——, is of one of the highest families: her father is heir to the title of prince, and her sister's husband gives balls to the imperial family, at one of which the Grand Duke and heir apparent asked Catherine to dance with him, and she made an excuse, feeling shy.

        *   *   *   *   *   *

To me, he says:—

To my Geneva letter I have had no answer; for little Madame Pescantini won't be there, I am sorry to hear, till after I am gone away. I *am very* sorry, for I should have rejoiced to see her. But Miss Yachman I *have* seen. She answered my letter quickly, and I went to see her at a beautiful little villa she has close, to Lausanne. She has an English husband whose name is Sharman, and they have been married these half-dozen years.

She hugged me and kissed me much as you would, warm-hearted soul as she is ; and he received me quite like an old friend, for he said his wife had talked about us all a thousand times. She asked a great deal about you, and told me that the room I now occupied at the Cygne was the one "Sarah" occupied eight years ago. * * * *

To his wife :—

I have seen a salamander to-day for the first time in my life. It was lying dead in the path, but live ones abound here, though their time for going abroad is just my time for staying at home, namely, after dark, and especially in wet weather. It is a species of lizard, broad and flat, and in shape, but not colour or size, very like the wood-slave, the ash-coloured lizard that loves walls and old wood. The salamander is black, with a broad orange-coloured stripe on each side, from head to tail. The one I saw was eight inches long and one broad, but Miss Pfeil said she had seen them much bigger. How the fables about them were suggested I don't know; but it seems they love water much better than fire. * * * *

There has been more improvement still in my throat. It is improvement enough to be seriously grateful for, and you must join with me, sweet wife, in giving glory to God for it.

* * * * * *

My sketching goes on very badly. I can do next to nothing, for the grass is *always* wet, so that I can never go out of the road, and even then I can only sit in a sheltered place, and seldom long together. I have found a place that suits me well, but the patent dry days that I require are but few.[*] * * * *

[*] Yet the number of sketches he did make during these few weeks in

Speaking of a German artist who was at the the Cygne, he
says : —

He said I had all the talent of a professional painter, and
that my trees and mountains were *magnifiques*. They are
poor little dabs enough, and not at all what I like to carry
home to dearest wife; but, of course, I know that they are
better than amateurs are apt to do.　　＊　　＊　　＊

Now go, last of my letters! and tell my dear wife, if you
can, how thoroughly I love her.　　　＊　　　＊　　　＊

To me, from Malta, 28th October : —

I am again at my own dear home, after an absence of just
five months. I left Vernex the 3rd of this month. The
steamer took me to Geneva, the diligence next day to Cham-
bery, and next to Lyons, the steamer to Avignon, and next
day to Beaucaire, and then railroad to Nismes. I had never
been there, and was glad of the easy opportunity to see its
famous antiquities. I always pick up friends in a journey,
and this time I had been associated some days with two
Frenchmen, who joined me in hiring a carriage to the Pont du
Garde, the old Roman aqueduct, some half-dozen leagues from
Nismes. Next day to Arles, where there is a well-preserved
Roman amphitheatre and other remains, and next day to
Marseilles.　　＊　　　＊　　　＊　　　Most happy was I
to be again among *my own*. Few people are less fit than I
am now to wander about the world by myself, for you know
I want somebody to love, and to love me.

In November : —

But, dearest Bob, I am very sorry to hear that my sweet
daughter Lizzy was in poor health. Take great care of her,
Bob, for she is worth her weight in much better things than

Switzerland is amazing, and among them are many exquisite gems, surpassing
in artistic effect and beauty of colouring any of his earlier drawings.

gold. She is worth to you what my honest wife is worth to me.
These good women are *angels* about us. Millions of thanks,
my own good son, for your counsel and offer of all your good
service about the future education of my young sons. Well
I know, and well Mamma knows, and loves you for it, that
you would be to her and them a friend in need. Don't
think me such a goose, Bob, as to lament my ill fortune in
having *only* a thousand a year after my retirement. You
know I only meant that it would puzzle me to educate with
it eight children as I wish to educate them, and will, if I live,
at the cost of any sacrifice. My own wants are few. Wife
and I spend nothing upon ourselves. We will live in a wee
house, and be content if we can keep it *warm.* But, dearest
Bob, I have a dilemma to choose out of. For the last twenty-
two years I have only spent one winter in England. I never
could bear cold, and now it will pinch me more than ever. I
have great doubt whether I should not be nipped by the
frost. However, I must try. For my boys' sake I must
live in England, if I can. But for that, I would choose a
milder climate when I leave Malta. You are right, dear
son, in advising me not to stay here. I don't mean to stay;
but I will get through next summer here, or partly here, if
I can. If I find I am beginning to suffer I will go away at
once. Last year I had headaches for months before the
fever came; and if I had had the least suspicion what they
were leading to, I would, of course, have decamped. If any
such monitors come next summer, away I will go at once.

But I really have great hopes of doing well, managing, as
I mean to do, quite differently from past times. We have
that noble house at Sliema with the colonnade round it—cool
and far healthier than our Marina house, and there I mean
to live, and scarcely ever come to the office at all. There is
generally but little work doing in summer, and Portelli will
do it for me, only sending me routine papers to sign. In
this way I shall avoid my two great enemies, the sun and
the impure air of the dockyard creek. And please to observe,
my wish to hold my appointment as long as I can with safety,

arises not *merely* from the motive of the increasing pension,
but to retain as long as I can the chance of getting a place
in England. If a vacancy fit for me should happen while I
retain this place, I should now, while Sir George Cockburn
is at the Admiralty, have a good chance of getting it; but if
I were on half-pay, I should have *no* chance.

* * * * * *

To me, in November :—

I have been drawing in St. John's Church every day for the
last month and more. I began the drawing four years ago, and
got it about half done, and there it stuck—sometimes business, sometimes sickness, and twice going to England, having
interrupted it. I have now taken it up again, and mean to
persevere, if I have health and leisure enough, till I have
finished it, for it is worth finishing. I never sit more than
an hour and a half at a time in the church, so that my days'
works are short, and I suppose it will take me about forty
more sittings to finish it; and altogether I may have been
already sixty times. But it shows the whole church, and all
its detail of painting and carving; and there is not a bit as
big as your nail that is not carved and painted and gilt.
Mr. Hysler, the artist, sat by me the other day while I was
at work, and said it was the *very* church, exact in drawing
and colour and tone, and congratulated me on being the
first that ever succeeded in doing it.

There never *has* been a drawing made of St. John's, though
hundreds have done bits, and some have *attempted* the whole.
Several people have suggested that I should get the drawing
thoroughly well engraved by a London artist; and I dare say
some great printseller would be glad to undertake the publication, for it would be sure to sell, as it is *the* great ornament of

---

* When my husband saw this really wonderful drawing lately, he exclaimed,
"That isn't a *picture* of St. John's church, it is the church *itself*."—1856.

Malta, and the thousands of people who come here would most of them like to have a copy.

However, I must let Michele do it; for if he succeeds tolerably, it will be a gain to him, and the sale of his lithographies would not much interfere with the subsequent sale of the engravings, as there are people enough to buy both. He could make, of course, for himself, a very good drawing; but then he could not make one like mine without spending upon it as much time as I have spent, which would ruin him. * * * * * *

To Robert :—

I have received some of your "Southern Queens," and very interesting they are. Your own compositions in them of course interest me the most, and they are quite satisfactory; but besides those, there is the correspondence between our Bishop and the Roman, and there is the account of the New Zealand affairs. Oh, what a sad business our blockheads made of it! Stupid governors and incapable colonels are doing all they can to work ruin for our young colony there. Think of four or five hundred of our soldiers being marched up the country to attack a walled and a well-manned fortress, in which there were *cannon* too, without taking artillery with them, and a rocket brigade with just nine rockets for their whole ammunition, which nine rockets, too, were wasted. It must have a most marvellous effect in spiriting on the savages and intimidating our own people.

Lord Stanley, you know, has earned the credit of doing all he can to ruin the colonies; and, at all events, he has no wish to evince any particular affection for their interests.

Our Bishop has just returned from England. While there he wished to talk to Lord Stanley about the affairs of Malta, and had much to say that a good minister would have been willing to listen to; but Lord Stanley would not see him: he positively refused him an interview, thereby, of course, avowing his utter indifference, at least for the ecclesiastical interests of this part of his charge.

He seems to show special favour to the Roman Catholics, and especially to the Jesuits, as if he thought *that* was liberality,—his fair play being all on one side. He has sanctioned the establishment of a Jesuits' College here; and a tribe of Jesuits from Stonyhurst have come out to form it, and they have set themselves up at Citta Vecchia, and have already eighty Maltese boys in their training.

These Jesuits will busy themselves in undermining the lower classes of our people here, and in their active cleverness will have a certain measure of success; whereas if our bishop and clergy were to attempt the making of converts from the Maltese, Lord Stanley would rebuke them, and would remind them that when the English Government undertook the protection of Malta, it guaranteed to the Maltese protection for their religion, and so he would consider any *argument* with them as an infringement of the covenant.   *   *   *   *   *

In December :—

Do what you can to keep out of hot water with people who think differently from you. One is naturally tempted to hit hard in return for an attack; but when a man can afford to leave abuse unanswered, it is generally better for himself in most ways. The devil is sure to prompt us with *bitterness*, and then away we shoot poisoned arrows : *I* have, many a time; and very, *very* sorry I am for it.

The throat has been worse of late, and is pouring out phlegm in such quantities that all I eat can barely supply the waste; still I am not otherwise feeling like an invalid, and I have an excellent appetite, thanks mainly to good Mamma, who lately doubled it for me by making me buy a horse and ride him every day. I am still active on horseback, and gallop like a midshipman, and away I scamper just as I used to do years ago. It does me great good and improves my sleeping as well as my eating powers.

HOME HAPPINESS—HON. MRS. STUART—ROMANIZING CLERGYMEN—PHŒNICIAN
TOWER AND INSCRIPTION—HIS HORSE—INCREASED ILLNESS—PREPARES TO
LEAVE MALTA—LETTER TO MR. PORTELLI—JOURNEY TO ENGLAND—ILLNESS
—SUFFERINGS—LAST LETTER TO HIS SON ROBERT—HIS WIFE'S NARRATIVE
OF LAST DAYS AND DEATH—BURIAL—MY BROTHER'S LETTER TO ME ON
OUR FATHER'S DEATH—MR. KITSON'S LETTER.

To ROBERT, in January, his dear Father writes:—

I find in your letter a most comfortable picture of your
domestic condition. It is, I verily believe, much such a home
as ours is, where two people have one heart, the same principles and thoughts and tastes, helping and cheering each
other, never disappointing or vexing, except in the sense in
which poor Mamma complains that I give her more plague
than all her money, by being sick, by her neither being able
to cure me nor *part* cure me, by taking all or some of my
ailment to herself. * * * * *

The doctors have sent hither this season invalids of all
sorts, and among them an unusual number of *our* acquaintance,
among them that very sweet creature that was once called
Minny Gore—she is now the Honourable Mrs. Stuart, and
her husband, who is, of course, with her, is a Colonel in the
Guards. They dined with us the other day, and Mamma is
enchanted with my dear Minny,[*] who is not one bit spoiled
by the atmosphere of the Court, in which she has lived ever

---

[*] In a letter to me, Mrs. Stuart says, speaking of my Father:—

"It has always been a source of real pleasure to me to have renewed my
memory of him, as we did at Malta in 1846, and to have felt the *glow* of his
almost unique warmth of heart! as well as of his rare talents."

since she was grown up, and seems to love me as much as she did when she was a little girl. She asked a great deal about you and Sally, and remembers everything about Rochester as well as if it were yesterday.　　　＊　　　＊　　　＊

And lastly, the Prince and Princess of Capua, on whom I was obliged to call, from having seen a good deal of them formerly at the Woods'. They wanted our house at Sliema, and I was put to my wit's end to refuse it with a good grace. Happily I did contrive it.　　　＊　　　＊　　　＊　　　＊

By the bye—of Puseyism—Colonel Stuart saw two English clergymen kiss the vessel that contains Saint Januarius's blood, at Naples, the Saint that the Neapolitans curse when anything goes amiss, and the blood that the Roman Catholic Eustace believed to liquify by legerdemain, and not miracle. Another English clergyman knelt at the mass.

　＊　　　＊　　　＊　　　＊　　　＊　　　＊

Later in the month:—

Yesterday we all went to see the Torrejouhar, a fragment of a Phœnician tower, a mile beyond Goudia. We had two calesses for Mamma and the little ones and Mademoiselle Villes,[*] and the old Abbate went with us. I went on horseback. I had noticed often, years ago, a remarkable inscription on a stone forming the architrave of a house at Goudia, and yesterday I copied it. Here it is—a puzzle for you and any of your friends who have a taste for antiquarian lore:—

ΑΠΠΟ ΙΠϹΑΡΠΑϹΙΟΠΙS

Ϲ†Ι ⱮϹϹϹϹϹϹXXIII ᘓΙΘ XXIII ᘓΙ ⰂAΙⳐS

All I can make of it is, that the author of the composition knew a little Italian and very little Latin, and so helped out his Latin with the Italian. The C, instead of T, in incarnationis, must be an Italianism; and as he did not know the Latin for "of May," he wrote "di" for "of" in Italian, and added to it the *Latin* for May in the nominative case. The

R in incarnationis is in the Greek form, with a *very* little loop, ρ, so. The carving is elaborately and well done, the letters being left in high relief, and each letter three or four inches high. It seems odd that there should have been no Latinist at hand to submit it to—the parish priest, for example, who very probably knew that the genitive case of Maius should be Maii. I had a disagreeable ride, for my horse—which I only got a few days ago, in exchange, at a loss of course, for the one I first bought—*stumbled* so abominably, that I expected him every moment to come down upon his knees and nose.   *   *   *   *   *

The difficulty of getting a good horse is close upon a mere impossibility. The other shied so much, that a Maltese groom said to me one day, " Sir, that very pretty horse, but shy too much, and kill you some day, cause, you know, you *very* old man ; " and as I had no fancy for such a catastrophe, I got rid of him. I am still a good rider, except that I soon get tired ; and when I am tired it is a painful exertion to stick upon the back of a plunging beast : still, when I came home I was not knocked up, and contrived, without any disagreeable effort, to write most of the evening, scoring off a couple of chapters of my Thucydides.   *   *   *

In February, to me :—

Happily for *me*, dearest, I have no anxieties to trouble me ; for my difficulty is great enough as it is, in contending with my bodily infirmities. My throat has not been bad lately, rather better than otherwise ; but the headaches have come back, and have for the last ten days seldom been absent. I believe the *hot weather* has been unfavourable to me, for all this month of February has been so much absolute summer. There has been no wind, no rain, to stir the stagnation of the atmosphere, and the more pernicious stagnation of our detestable creek.   *   *   *

To-day I am pretty well ; but I can seldom do much more than give Kitty and Mia their lessons, read for amusement.

and take my daily ride. My horse is an admirable one. I have sold the second I bought, and gone back to the first; and having, in a great measure, cured him of his terror of *pigs*, he turns out in every other respect first rate; full of spirit and activity, most gentle temper, a mouth that doesn't pull against a little finger, very easy pleasant paces, and *never* trips. In short, I never had a better, and I am grateful to the good beast for the help he gives me. It amuses me to *skirmish* across the island, and revisit, after so many years, places formerly familiar to us.   *   *   *

March of this year is the first month in which there are no letters to his children!

In April he writes to me, and nearly the same to Robert :—

I am but little better; but yet in the last day or two I have gained something in point of strength. For two months I have been much more ill than before; yet the doctors are convinced that I have no incurable disease, and my own sensations tell me that change of climate, which has so often set me up, will again be of great use to me in removing many of my maladies and repairing my strength; though I am far from expecting that it will cure my *throat*, which has now been out of order seventeen months.

We are packing up for a final remove from Malta, and hope to get away before the end of next month. We can hardly yet quite decide which way to go. The least difficulty will, probably, be in the sea-voyage, but that would be quite formidable enough; and, if we can hire a carriage, and post through France for less money, that will perhaps be the best way.

Whether I shall be able to stay in England is very uncertain. An English winter would probably suit me as little as a Malta summer. Even for the summer I don't know whether I shall not be sent to the Eaux bonnes, in the Pyrenees, or to some of the German baths; both have been talked of. But, first of all, we must deposit the young ones with Aunt, who will take care of them if we are obliged to go away. We have spent the last winter in Malta, not thinking a winter here could be amiss; but I have had such a complication of maladies that it is hard to guess *what* climate we ought to choose. My head has been, for these two months, sadly out of order; no acute pain, but a stupifying weight upon it. The throat has been very much worse, and the medical people have now no doubt that the passages leading to the lungs are diseased. The increased irritation there brought on a cough that has now been long fixed, and another strange symptom in the shape of *hiccups*. For a whole fortnight this went on nearly all day, and much of the night. Then I had a most blessed respite, and now it is come again, and *occupies* me almost continually. I mean that it makes me *think* about it, and about little else; for while it is upon me it shakes me violently for hours together; and when I succeed in suppressing it, for an interval, with hot wine and water, which sometimes succeeds and sometimes not,—it would return again in a moment if I were not constantly on my guard to *struggle* with the rising air in my throat, which brings it on.

I am often obliged to sit motionless, holding my breath as hard as I can—never speaking. I write down what I have to say. My voice is all gone but a whisper, and even that I am not allowed to use. Perhaps when I gain a little more strength, as I may from the voyage, the bronchitis may be mitigated, and the hiccup which is caused by it may go away. By way of fighting the internal disease, the doctors have applied a seton to my throat, and Stilon has a good hope of its working a thorough cure; but in the mean time it is both an additional drain and a painful disturber of repose. The pain, however, is but a small matter; and, happily, none of my complaints are painful, and I have generally plenty of refreshing sleep. Upon the whole, I quite agree with the doctors in thinking that my condition is not worse than *precarious*; that I may regain a certain measure of strength, and may long go on like a creaking wheel. I have never felt the least despondency, and poor Mamma's trial is the heavier of the two. Yet we are both abidingly sensible of God's great goodness to us, and trust He will enable us, in all His dispensations, to praise His holy name.

I had a most welcome letter from Sir Henry Bunbury from Naples, giving me your latest news, a happier account than any I had before received, and especially of Hanmer's health. Sir Henry had just heard, too late, of my having returned to Malta, or he would have come to see me, or proposed our meeting at Messina. How glad I should have been of either plan if I had been in tolerable health.

I have not written to the Admiralty to resign my appointment, but simply to say that I can't stay at Malta this summer. Perhaps they will again give me leave; or, on the other hand, they may say, that as I had leave last year they can't give me more, and that I must resign. I don't at all care, for I have not the least notion of returning.

We came to Sliema the last day of February, and I have only been to my office twice since then.　　*　　*　　* Mamma is at the Marina, packing up the books; Mrs. Clifton and Mr. and Mrs. Portelli help her. We shall leave all our furniture to be sold by them after we are gone.

In May, he writes:—

I am so much better than I was when I wrote a fortnight ago, that I am impatient to write again, though I have little else to tell you. My voice is in a great measure returned, so is my sense of hearing.　　*　　*　　*　　*

Of my present condition you may judge something, from my having been able to pay eight farewell visits in Valetta yesterday, the first time I have been able to make any such exertion. Of course, I was carried about, with Mamma, in a calesse.*　　*　　*　　*　　*　　*　　*

* He had sold his carriage and horses a year or two before.

On the 18th May, in his last letter to his Son from Malta, he says :—

I received yesterday your letter No. 98, and you were quite right to make sure that its contents would be joyful to me. It gives me the *address of your parishioners ;* and though nothing they say in your praise can strengthen my own convictions, yet it is an immense satisfaction to find that the people to whom you are devoting yourself entertain, and take pleasure in professing, a right feeling towards you. This must be, of course, a mighty consolation and encouragement to you, and *therefore* it is that I rejoice in it. I am apt to *cry* about such things (neither for joy nor grief of my own), and that would have made it quite impossible for me to read a bit of your letter out loud ; but Mamma read that part to our friends the Cliftons, who shared our great pleasure in it.

Don't fret, dear Bob, because you can't get me to think as you do of Newmans, Wards, and Puseys, nor because I have small taste for scientific theology ; for it is enough that I think *of you* as you would wish me to think, and there are things enough in which we do thoroughly agree in thought, feeling, and taste. Mamma says of you that you are a chip of the old block ; and it is quite true, at all events, in the sense she mainly meant it,—and that is, in your great *energy.*

Of course, I dearly love to see it,—and to see it admirably directed, too. You know well the object of my intense care was your true happiness in this life and your preparation for a better ; and you can judge whether I am not more satisfied with you as you are than if you had been the humdrum occupant of the best living in England. You are doing your best, and doing it right well ; and you are loving your old Father even as he wants you to love him,—ay, Bob, and that's one thing in which we heartily agree, that in all this world *love* is the best thing of all. What should I have done in the last two years of sickness without kind hearts about me to give me love as well as needful help in my feebleness? What but love could even dress my seton for me, night and morning, as Mamma dresses it?

MALTA, 25th May, 1846.

MY DEAR PORTELLI,[d]—My last writing at Malta must be to you. I am going away in so precarious a state of health, that my return must be uncertain. However that may be, let me assure you that I shall never forget what you have been to me for the last eighteen years. I only wish you were likely to be my successor. Who could possibly fill the place better?—how many are there who could fill it as well? Exceedingly few. It is well known to the Admirals, to the Admiralty, and especially to our immediate master, Mr. Meek, how admirably you have managed the department in my repeated absences on account of ill health. If it were not for the entire confidence that is placed in you for ability and zeal, I should certainly not have been allowed the repeated leave of absence with which of late years I have been indulged. Mr. Meek has been told by me, over and over again, that you are worth your weight in gold; and Sir Lucius Curtis would adopt, with all his heart, the strongest terms that even I should choose in speaking of you; and well he knows that, intimate as the friendship between us is, it is impossible to attribute to private partiality one particle of the language in which I have a thousand times expressed my sense of your value.

God bless you, my dear Portelli;—thank you, with my whole heart, for the daily and hourly help, and for all the kindness for which, during so many years, I have been indebted to you. You know well the truth with which I am ever yours,

R. C. SCONCE.

---

[d] His chief clerk.

This is the last letter I ever received from my dearest
Father : —

MY OWN SWEETEST CHILD, — I had the happiness of
receiving yesterday your letter of the 12th of February,
giving a good account of the health of all your precious
house. And *now*, my darling, I may venture to tell you
that I, too, am pretty well. I could not have done so before,
for I have had a renewal of very grievous illness, and arrived
here, at Greenwich (on the 20th of this month), in a very
precarious condition, so that Liddell did not know whether
my lungs might not be incurably affected. Since then I
have slowly improved, but yet have contrived to make some
progress from day to day. * * * *

People with complaints of this particular nature are said to
be always unconscious of their own state; but I feel pretty
sure that I am really mending, and that the lungs are, for
the present, safe. * * * * *

We left Malta the 26th of May, and went in the French
packet to Leghorn. On board the packet I caught a cold
that fell heavily on my chest, and, I believe, created an
inflammation of the lungs. We paused one day there; and
then feeling able to go on, it seemed better for us to try and
get *home* than to run the risk of my being laid up in a strange
land.

We engaged a vetturino, with a big berline and three stout
horses, and on we went, by easy stages, to Genoa, Milan, Como,
Bellinzona, St. Gothard, and Fluelen; there we took the steamer
to Lucerne, and thence another vetturino took us in two days
to Basle; *steam*, by land, river, and sea, brought us all the
way from thence to Greenwich in six easy days. It was
often doubtful to us which might prove the lesser evil,—to
come on or to stop; but we always decided upon coming on,
and so we persevered from Leghorn to Greenwich, from the
30th of May to the 20th of June, without one day's halt. The
fatigue was, of course, very injurious to me; but the rest I

have since enjoyed is repairing the mischief, and I have a good
hope of being soon tolerably well. I am lower in condition
than I ever was—nothing but skin and bone,—but my appetite is like a wolf's, and my digestion admirable; so I flatter
myself that I must be imperceptibly picking up some little
solidity.

On our landing at Dover, good Uncle Joseph, with Clem
and Herbert, met us on the beach. Aunt would have come,
but was recruiting her strength at Barming, after a serious
attack of bilious fever. Next day, Mamma and I, and our
seven children, came to Greenwich, and Aunt joined us;
some at Liddell's and some at a neighbouring hotel.

On the 23rd they all went to Bath, leaving me to be taken
care of by Liddell,—and he *has* taken the utmost care of me.
We are to make Bath our permanent abode; and they have
taken furnished lodgings there till they can meet with a house
to suit us. They have had no luck yet. We don't mean to
live in the town, but in some country place near it.

If we can get such a place as Tothill,° only with a room or
two more for our larger numbers, it will suit us exactly.
Liddell wishes to keep me a little longer under his eye; but
as soon as I may safely go, I will make haste to join them. I
can't do much to help them hunt for a house, for half an
hour's walk at a time is as much as I can manage, and at
a snail's pace. However, my mobility will improve when the
beef I am consuming finds its way to my legs, which are
mere mopsticks.

Uncle Vi and his wife are coming to see me to-day. He
wants me to go with them to Writtle; but when I can go
anywhere, it must be to *Bath*. He says Bath must be too
hot for me in the dog-days: but these English people have
odd notions of *heat*, for I find this last day of June much
like a Malta December, and have been glad to add a flannel
waistcoat to my defences against the *cold*. The *lower* part of
Bath is, I believe, hot, and not very healthy; but we don't

° Near Plymouth, where we lived while he was with Sir H. Neale.

mean to settle *there*. Of course, my chick, it is quite settled that I am not to return to Malta. You see I could not escape illness there, even in the *winter*, this last year. I have come away on leave of absence, which I may probably spin out till October or November, and then send in my resignation.

I don't know what pension they will give me. The regulations on that subject are not just; for I believe, according to them, I can only claim £116 a year; that is to say, twelve shillings a day for half-pay as Secretary, and £250 a year for pension as Agent Victualler; and yet I should have been entitled to as much as that for twelve years' service as Secretary and fifteen as Agent Victualler; whereas, altogether, I have served, not twenty-seven years, but *forty*.

Good old Le Mesurier came here this morning and break-fasted with me, and inquired kindly after you, as he always does. Good old Smith paid me a visit the other day, and sent his love to you.

Liddell is gone this morning to the funeral of poor little Patrick Stewart, the youngest son of our friends Captain and Mrs. Houston Stewart. She is a most sweet creature, and we all love her dearly; she doted upon our angel Fanny. This poor little boy was but thirteen years old. Some unwise friend had trusted him with a gun—it went off while he was stooping to put on his shoe, and the charge went through his head and killed him instantaneously. The poor parents are composed and resigned. They are *good* people.

Heaven bless and guard you all, my dear child. I shall look forward to the joy of seeing you once more even in this world! Dearly do I love you, my admirable daughter. You are inexpressibly sweet to me.

The following are little extracts from his daily letters from Greenwich to his wife at Bath :—

How I do long to hear of you, and of dear Harriet and all the good little souls. I trust you have encountered no great perplexities. I am helpless just at the time when my help would be most useful to you, and I am deprived, too, of my sweetest wife just when I most want *her*. But you and I know that we have millions of mighty blessings to be thankful for, and a source of strength and consolation that will not fail us in any trial.   *   *   *   *   *

Liddell takes care of me just as you do.   *   *

I was at Church yesterday, dear wife, at the Hospital Chapel. Mr. Kitson read the prayers slowly and solemnly.

   *   *   *   *   *   *

I have been walking in the Park (as I always do for an hour after breakfast) and longing to sketch some trees; but there is too much wind. You may depend upon my doing no imprudences. My having an inclination to *sketch* is a sure sign of my being *better*.   *   *   *   *

I have as decided a preference, dear wife, as you have, for a house *out of the town*; for though you know I am as little dependent as most people upon external circumstances for my comfort, yet I can fancy nothing more detestable for a permanent abode than a street in Bath. London is bad enough; but there, there are museums, libraries, exhibitions; whereas, at Bath there is *nothing*. The poor little things could never go out without smart bonnets and smooth collars, and could have no independent out-of-doors play; and walking for exercise would be to you and me as disagreeable a *dovere* as a walk to the Capuchin convent. A walk at Wateringbury did one's *spirits* good; but in the Bath streets—my patience! why, the Capuchin convent would be out-and-out better; so do let's scour the whole circumference of Bath, till we light on something that will do.   *   *   *   *   *

I say, Willy, have you got your marbles with you? If not, I suppose we can get some at Bath. I can play at marbles with you, but I am afraid I can't *jump* as well as last year, because my legs have got no flesh upon 'em.

   *   *   *   *   *   *

Next Monday we are to go to Bath. Liddell and Johnny and Bobby to the Woods. * * * *

Here is your dear letter, and my good little Clement's. Thank the dear old fellow for it. I won't write to him now ; but I know how glad he will be to hear that I am to spend my *birthday at home*—only three intervening days.

* * * * * *

Whitmarsh came in just now, and I made him feel the calves of my legs, and he said, "Oh, there's muscle there !" In this matter there has been rapid improvement, and, of course, that is very encouraging. I could hardly be getting these mighty limbs if I had an internal consuming disease. So now, sweet wife, I have gladdened your heart.

* * * * * *

I am going on comfortably, and expect to be *pretty* stout again before very long. Very slow as the improvement is, it has made a wonderful difference in me within the last fortnight ; and though a certain quantity of local irritation still remains, yet there remains not a particle of that feeling of *illness* that it used to cause. Of course, that proves its diminution. * * * * *

Pray do tell good Clement how much I am pleased with his affectionate little letter—and a very satisfactory one it is too, in showing me that he can understand a piece of Latin without help. We must push him on now at railway pace, for his years at school will be few. We must get a *cheap house*, that we may afford him, for a year, a first-rate tutor.

* * * * * *

From Greenwich, writing to his Cousin Mrs. Repton, he says :—

I should have been glad to go and see you, my dears, but it is beyond my strength. *Talking*, too, is mischievous to me : a little too much of it two days ago pulled down all at once the building-up of a week.

2 c 2

And now I come to what my poor Brother calls "the last of his most fondly-loved Father's beautiful and affectionate letters :"—

BATH, 12th July, 1846.

MY DEAREST BOY,—Since I wrote to you twelve days ago, I have received two of your letters, 99 and 100, one just come, and I long to write to you directly. I took my paper out an hour ago, but sleep came over me, and I gave way to it willingly, for I was in pain.

My own dear Bob, you must not be disappointed if my letters are little more than short histories of my condition. They have been nothing else for a long time past. For more than two years I have been continually sick, and often severely ill, and at this moment I have a galling evil of a new sort. The seton that was put into my neck at Malta created an abscess, and a wide-spread erysipelas, and the sore is now a mighty big one, and growing every day wider and more angry.

I came to Bath a week ago, and Liddell came with me to pay a visit to the Woods, with whom he stays till to-morrow, when I must be transferred to a new doctor. Aunt is ill too. She has had an ague, off and on, these two months. For the last two days there has been no fit, and we are beginning to hope it will give way. Sad it is for poor Mamma to have us both ill together; but she has happily great help in nursing us, for all our good children are anxious to do their best, and it is very comforting to see the love with which they do it, Clement and Herbert claiming the chief share in supplying my wants. If you were here, you would think me still more your property; and I wish I *could* see your old face about me, and your pretty Lizzy, and the little daughters.

29th July.

The month has been wasting away, and glad, indeed, I am to be able, now before the packet goes, to add a little to my

letter, and to send you a better account of *both* invalids.
*   *   *   I have been struggling for the last
fortnight with greatly increased pain. The sore in the neck
allowed me no rest, day nor night, and the pain created
general illness, and the great discharge from the sore pulled
me down very low, and one of the remedies — a poultice as
big as your two open hands, kept night and day upon the neck
and over the collar-bones — gave me rheumatism in my head
and shoulders, and down to my fingers; so that, three days
ago, I could not possibly have held a pen.

But a blessed change took place in the aspect of the sore,
the discharge ceased, the pain abated, and allowed me a little
sleep; the poultice was removed, and the rheumatism went
away. The healing process is going on promisingly. It is
very slow and uncertain; but in the mean time, the *rest* I
enjoy is *exquisite happiness*. It is far from amounting to an
absence of pain; but yet, the mitigation is to me a greater
blessing than perfect health could be to people who had not
recently known what an ulcer in the neck of eight or ten
square inches *is*.

But now, dear Bob, you must remember that the *seton* was
designed to counteract internal disease, and that I had
grievous threatenings about the regions of my lungs.

The seton seemed to do no good; but the sore it made
was equal, in irritation and discharge, to twenty setons; and
it HAS done good, for I have now *no* morbid sensations
remaining in the chest, and so there is hope that the dangerous disease is suspended, or checked, or possibly even
cured. Yet *all* is not right within, for among the mischiefs
of the poultice (the great mass of damp so long enveloping
my neck), it brought back the disorder in my *throat*, that
seemed to have gone away after lasting twenty months. Still,
that is comparatively not a serious evil. It is far better, you
know, to have it in the upper region of the pharynx, or
larynx, or glottis, than down in the bronchial tubes or lungs.
I have not yet been able to get out of the house. The pain
allowed no locomotion; but for some days I have been able

to sit for three or four hours in the drawing-room; and when I *can* get out, I verily believe I shall be a sort of new man.

I received some days ago the "Divinity" you sent, through George Repton, and I hope to read it with great interest; but I must wait for more strength. I have no power yet to read more than short sentences in devotional books, a little now and a little then. For hours after the dressing of my neck I can think of nothing but its smarting. My scrap of dinner, and great draught of porter (for I have a mighty thirst, the effect, I suppose, of pain and enormous perspiration) wind me up; but then I grow sleepy, and am glad to put my head on my pillow again.   *   *   *

In answer to a letter of my Brother's about Mr. Newman's secession from the Church of England, he says :—

I gave you my opinion of Mr. Newman years ago, and there I let the matter drop. I believed that time would open your eyes; and I hope you know me too well to think that I have now any triumph in having made a right guess, while you made a wrong one.

One great difference between us—between youth and age—is, that you are *sure* of many things, and I have arrived at the conclusion that there is scarcely any *opinion* on which one can safely rely on any subject. I don't mean that you are over confident in *yourself*, but in those to whose guidance you have committed yourself.

30th July.

Here is the last day for the packet. I had hoped to be able to write to my darling Sally, but it is impossible. Send her the substance of this with my blessing. I have really a good hope of being able to send by the next packet a better account of my health. If the sore heals kindly, I shall quickly regain some strength. I am now exhausted with mere pain. God bless you, my good and very dear children, and enable us all to submit ourselves entirely to His good pleasure, and GLORIFY GOD IN THE DAY OF VISITATION.

These are my dear Father's last *written* words in my possession. The history of his few remaining days is given in the following narrative, written shortly after his death by his wife, and sent to his absent children in Australia.

On looking back at the mournful history of the last seven weeks, I now wonder that we were not better prepared for the impending blow,—that we did not see it was inevitable.

Blinded, I suppose, by the flattering nature of the disease, I had persuaded myself that it could not be consumption, and so, *at times*, hoped on to the last!

My precious Robert had for some time thought very badly of himself. He was apt to check my too sanguine view of his case, and only a day or two after he arrived at Bath (the 6th of July, the last birthday he was to spend upon earth) he observed that " it would be folly to reckon on such a life as his."

In spite of some favourable appearances—I mean the healing of the sore, and cessation of the cough—the weakness continually increased. For many days before we left Russell Street he was unable to dress without my help, and had scarcely power to wash and shave. Getting up and down stairs, and going out in the Bath-chair became more and more difficult. It seemed, indeed, as if both would soon be impossible, as it proved; for the very last time he attempted either of these painful efforts, was the day we came into this house.[1] We got him up to the drawing-room floor, and he never moved from it again. He got rapidly weaker, and my hope must have failed me entirely if it had not been for the cheerful manner of our young doctor, who at that time, as I have since learnt, knew little of the history of the case, and, deceived himself, always contrived to comfort me. I used to dread making my first inquiry of dearest Robert in the morning, as to how he felt, because every morning regularly he told me that he was " sensibly weaker." On the 19th of August, as we were wheeling him upon the couch from the

[1] In Norfolk Crescent.

bedroom into the drawing-room, he shocked me by saying,
in a solemn manner, as if to prepare us for the terrible truth,
"I think worse of myself to-day than I have ever yet done."
To some reply of dear Harriet's, he answered, "It would be
madness to shut our eyes to the truth; I have very little
more strength to lose, and if that little goes at the rate it is
going now, I can't last long." I determined to write for
Dr. Liddell immediately, and having taken the pen in my
hand, my beloved Robert said that *he* would dictate the
letter, and made me write down these dreadful words—"I
am grievously ill; my strength is fast going from me. I
want much to see you. Make haste and come to me."

The next day he rallied a little, and for the first time for
many days told us he did not think he had "lost any ground
in the last twenty-four hours." I was further cheered by his
asking me for the newspaper, and by seeing that he read it
with interest. On putting it down, he talked to me, as he
was always accustomed to do, of what he had been reading—
a debate upon the duty on sugar with reference to the slave
question. He told me how distinguished a part the Bishop
of Oxford had taken in it, and said, that "he had spoken in a
manner altogether worthy of a Wilberforce."

After this he took his dinner and dozed; about five o'clock
(he was still on the couch in the drawing-room) Dr. Liddell
arrived. This was the very earliest moment that he could
have come, and dearest Robert, who was rejoiced to see him,
received him with affectionate and most affecting warmth. I
remember his saying, "You are a good fellow, Liddell, for
making such haste to come to me. I wanted to see you, not
as a medical man, but as a friend; it does me good to look at
you." He had sat up longer than usual, and being tired,
Dr. Liddell soon assisted me in getting him into bed. Dr.
Liddell remained in the room, and when the tea was ready,
my precious husband begged him to take some at the bedside,
which he did. Thinking, I suppose, that the opportunity
must not be lost, dearest Robert talked to him about business
of various kinds, of his *Will* amongst the rest, and that even-

ing it was written fair and signed. He had almost lost the use of his dear hands, and felt so doubtful of being able to guide the pen, that he asked for a bit of paper, to try. He did just manage to sign his name for the last time. Having done it, he said, " Nobody would know that to be my writing; but you, Liddell, can certify that it was only the hand that failed me, and that I was of sound mind. My head is as clear as ever. At least, I am not conscious of any loss of intellect, and I think I could express myself on any subject the same as ever I did."

A delightful surprise now awaited him, a visit from his oldest and very dear friend, Mrs. Duckworth. In consequence of the bad account I had sent her the day before,[a] she and her daughter and her son-in-law hurried to Bath, and being just arrived, wrote to ask me when they might come to the house. In his weak state he was so little able to bear excitement, that I hesitated about reading the note to him.

He guessed the contents at once, and instantly exclaimed, with great eagerness, and crying for joy, " What—are they come, then! are they in the house—in the next room? Oh, bring them all in, it *must* do me good to see them." We told him they were waiting at the inn, and it was agreed that Dr. Liddell should go and fetch them directly.

The meeting between such very dear friends, under such circumstances, was what it would naturally be—each heart was full, and my beloved husband could not help shedding more tears. He said, " You mustn't think I am dejected. Oh, no! I am quite calm ; these are tears of joy." His other " dear friend," as he commonly called Lady Gore, had paid him a visit two days before, and being affected in the same way: he told *her*, too, that it was the great happiness he felt at seeing her that made him shed tears. He added, " I have always been more apt to cry for pleasure than pain." So many whom he loved dearly having come to see him, *did* give him intense pleasure, and I am glad, for their sakes, to

---

[a] To Torquay.

record it, quite sure that the knowing this will afford them
all lasting satisfaction.

The warmth and tenderness of his own most affectionate
nature made him peculiarly sensible of any kindness or
affection shown to him, and several times, in allusion to these
visits, he said, that he thought " few people were ever blessed
with so many real good friends as he had. They are glorious
friends, all of them. See how they have come from the
North, East, and South, to visit me, and there's Joseph[b]
coming too!" We were then expecting him ; but he wrote to
say, that he could not find any one to do his duty, and could
not possibly be here before the 26th. Early on Friday
morning, the 21st, my beloved husband complained of
increased weakness, and I myself thought I saw a general
change for the worse. He looked very ill, and his breath,
which had been short and feeble for some time past, seemed
to me shorter still. I felt alarmed, and fetched Dr. Liddell.
He soothed me in some degree, by not appearing to think
him any worse.

We were accustomed to pray together at this hour, and
Dr. Liddell joined us. Besides some other forms, we used
that morning a Litany for the sick, and my beloved husband
repeated every response earnestly and aloud. Dr. Liddell
then had breakfast by his bedside. They afterwards talked
upon business, chiefly about the retirement pension. I derived
a momentary comfort from hearing Dr. Liddell speak as if he
thought my beloved husband would live to enjoy it. At the
same time, he had told me the precarious condition of that
precious life. He compared it to a person standing on the
brink of a precipice, and added, " It is impossible to guess
which side he will fall over."

In speaking to Harriet, as she has since told me, he said,
that twenty-four hours might at any time make a fatal
change—a little more than twice that time showed how sadly
right he was. He left us about noon. My beloved Robert

took an affectionate leave of him; but there was nothing in his manner by which I could tell whether he did or did not expect to see Dr. Liddell again. He repeated, " You're a good fellow;" and I think his very last words at parting were, " God bless you, my dear Liddell ! "

Mrs. Duckworth came to us at one o'clock, and by that time I had just got him into the drawing-room. There was a solemnity in her manner which showed me that she feared he would not be spared to us much longer. Like a true friend, she was always trying to contribute to his comfort. A short time before she had sent him a cushion of her own knitting, and that day she brought him an eiderdown pillow. He thanked her for it in his own warm, affectionate way, and was pleased when I removed one of the other pillows, that he might have hers next to his head and face.

Finding that Joseph could not come at once, my beloved Robert was anxious to have the assistance of some other clergyman, and we talked to Mrs. Duckworth upon this important subject. All the clergy here being alike strangers to us, we agreed that we ought to send to the Rector of the parish, and Colonel Douglas kindly offered to find out who and where he was, for we did not know, and beg him to come. At the same time, he told us, that his Father, Sir H. Douglas, was intimate with the elder Mr. P—— (the former master of the Grammar-school, and a man of high reputation here), and after a little consultation, it was then determined that Colonel Douglas should call upon *him*, instead of the Rector, and request him to come to us in the evening. He then went away for that purpose. Mrs. Duckworth was sitting close beside my beloved Robert's couch. His behaviour, no less than his words, expressed the great comfort he felt in having her there. He often took both her hands in his, and many a time his dear countenance lighted up with pleasure as he looked upon her face. They spoke of their long friendship— how they had known and loved each other for forty years. He was glad to change his position whenever he could, and we moved him into the armchair, as usual, to eat his dinner.

Mrs. Duckworth took hers at the same table with him, and that was a pleasure to him. He wasn't able to sit up long, and returned to the couch—there he remained till about four o'clock, when he went to bed. Colonel and Mrs. Douglas, who had rejoined us, stayed with him for a little while, and then left the room.

I was alone with dearest Robert. He proposed our praying as a fit preparation for the Holy Sacrament, which we thought we were about to receive. The little table was prepared, and so I hoped were all our hearts. At six o'clock Mr. P—— arrived—not the elder, whom we expected, but a son of his. I never understood why the Father didn't come. The moment he entered the room he begged me to go away. We were all assembled in the next room, expecting shortly to be called to the solemn service we earnestly desired to join in; but an hour passed, and Mr. P —— still remained at the bedside by himself. At first we only thought he was injudicious for staying so long, and feared that my beloved Robert's little strength would be exhausted; and then we began to wonder at the strangely-prolonged visit. At last, Mr. P—— came in to us. He addressed himself to Harriet and me. He said a great deal, but what he *meant* I couldn't understand for some time. I was confused and agitated, and could only make out that he talked in a way I never heard a clergyman talk before. I supposed that he must have some peculiarity in his opinions. Harriet doubted his belonging to our own Church, and thought he must be a Sectarian minister of some sort. I understood him better as he went on. Having asked him if he did not mean to administer the Sacrament to us, he said, "No;" that he did not, generally speaking, approve of giving it to dying persons, because there was great misconception upon this point in the minds of most people. He spoke of it as a Popish practice, and seemed to suspect that we, like those he censured, considered it in the superstitious light of a passport to Heaven. I assured him that we had no such notion. I said, we had been taught to consider the Sacrament of the Lord's Supper as a powerful means of grace, on which account our Church enjoined the frequent receiving of it; that my dear husband had always been a regular communicant in the days of his health and strength, and that I could not possibly believe there were any just grounds for denying him now the consolation of this holy ordinance. To this he replied, that he must act conscientiously, and do what he thought best for my husband's soul. His own conviction was, that it was better for him *not* to take the Sacrament in the present state of his mind. "*Why?*" I asked most anxiously. He said, "Your Husband has told me he does not *feel peace in believing,* and therefore," he added, " he is not in a fit state to receive the Lord's Supper."

I was unspeakably shocked; but I summoned courage to say, "If by '*peace*' is to be understood a perfect assurance of salvation, I am not at all surprised at his words. I believe that this is granted to very few people, and many of the most eminent Christians are supposed to have died without it. I am fully satisfied that my beloved Husband has a humble hope, and that it is well founded, not on his observance of outward ordinances (Mr. —— had spoken of these as being a *snare* to many), not on any doings of his own, but upon the mercy and merits of our Redeemer."

He then said he did not wish to seem harsh or unkind, and that he would go home and think over the subject, in case we should still desire him to administer the Sacrament, or that he would get some other clergyman to do it. I told him this was not necessary, as we were expecting my brother in a few days. Alas! He asked me if he should come the next day. I didn't know what answer to make, doubtful whether his visit would be a comfort to my beloved Robert. Should he not wish to see Mr. —— any more, it would be easy, I thought, to put him off, and therefore I accepted his offer of calling next day at noon. This is the substance of what passed between us. He must have stayed with me for at least an hour.

Harriet left us, and went to our beloved Robert, with whom she had some conversation upon Mr. ——'s strange objection to administer the Sacrament. Happily, he was not at all disturbed by it, as I feared he would be. He saw that their opinions on the subject were quite different, and he calmly retained his own. He feared, though, for me, knowing my greater weakness in every way; and when Harriet remarked on the strange manner in which Mr. —— expressed himself, he said, "I hope he is not saying anything to distress dearest wife." On my return to his room, I was agreeably surprised at finding him quite calm and placid as usual. I merely asked him if Mr. P——'s visit had given him any comfort; he said, "A doubtful comfort, owing to the very great difference in our religious views."

That evening he rallied wonderfully; he was able really to enjoy the society of our kind friends. Once, taking hold of Mrs. Douglas's hand, he said, "I do love to see you all about me." She and her husband had tea in his room, and after tea all the rest of the family joined us. My beloved husband sat propped up in the bed with pillows, and smiled and talked to us all in turn.

He was quite himself: his manner was full of that quiet animation which always distinguished it, and made it so attractive to everybody. We remarked how strong and clear his voice was. At Harriet's request he repeated a few lines of Spanish poetry,[1] and at another time some droll verses of his own. He made us all as cheerful as he was himself. It seemed *impossible* that he could be so ill as we feared, and for a brief interval I forgot my fears.

Between nine and ten o'clock Mrs. Duckworth got up to go away. Good Colonel Douglas, who was always glad to put in a word of comfort, congratulated me on the seeming amendment, and said he thought there was good ground for hoping that my beloved husband might yet recover. Alas! He slept in the night at intervals, but was frequently disturbed by shortness of breath; and the next morning he told me he was weaker than ever. I soon perceived it. Every-

---

[1] From "Don Quixote," of a knight, Lancelot, so well served by ladies.

thing still went on as usual. He had his cup of milk,—the
first nourishment which he always took in the morning; then
we prayed together; then he was shaved; and then the doctor came to dress his poor dear neck. The sore never looked
better: it was healing as well as it possibly could, and the
pulse was good, but there was no improvement in the state
of the tongue, and I followed Mr. Stockwell out of the room
to talk to him about that. I asked him if it was indeed
thrush? He said, "It isn't exactly what we call thrush, but
it is just as bad." I mentioned the healthy condition of the
sore, which we had all along been told was a good sign. He
replied, "*If* the neck heals, there is no reason why the tongue
should not;" but he gave me no encouragement to hope that
it would.

My beloved husband determined on seeing Mr. P——, and
I shall ever be thankful that he did. Whatever are Mr. P——'s
opinions, he is a pious, good man, and his visit afforded us real
comfort. Before he arrived, we had read a passage from the
Bishop of Oxford's "Eucharistica" to dearest Robert. Part
of it was a quotation from Hooker, stating the importance of
the Lord's Supper as a means of grace. He said, "Show it
to Mr. P—— when he comes, and say that that is quite my
own view." I did so; and when he had read it, I told him
(being afraid he might try to argue with dearest Robert) that
my dear husband was never fond of religious controversy,
and could not possibly engage in it now; I ventured to add,
"He thinks he must be safe in holding opinions which have
the authority of Hooker and the Bishop of Oxford for their
support." He answered in a low voice, and I only caught
something about his differing entirely from the Bishop of
Oxford; "but," he said, "I don't come here to argue, but
to preach." He did better for us than either: he read some
scripture, and then prayed most fervently. I never heard a
man who seemed to pray more from his heart, and I felt a
humble confidence that he would prevail. My beloved husband
joined in the prayer with equal earnestness.

When Mr. P—— was gone, he made an effort that was

very painful to him, and got up. Hitherto he had always
been able to help himself a little in the putting on his
clothes, and I dressed him without further assistance; but
from the greatly increased weakness he could now do nothing,
and I was obliged to call the maid. Something told me that
we were putting on those clothes for the last time! He could
hardly stand for a moment; and by the time we had got him
on the couch, he was so much exhausted that he said himself
he must not attempt to get up any more. After wheeling
him into the drawing-room, I thought he looked quite like a
dying man. My feelings got the better of me, and I could
not help crying. He said, "Don't cry: when the trial comes,
the way is to screw one's courage up to bear it." He then
quoted Jeremy Taylor's direction to the dying man to send
away "the women and the weepers." I told him I always
thought the bishop hadn't a *wife* when he wrote that, and I
said, "You wouldn't like to send me away, though I do cry,
would you?" He replied, "Oh no, that I wouldn't;" and
caressed me tenderly, which of course made me cry all the
more.

Mrs. Duckworth came in soon after. Having left him
apparently so well overnight, she was not prepared for such
an unfavourable change, and was the more distressed by it.
He said something to her about Annie's "having her pillow
back again, when he had done with it." Poor Mrs. Duckworth tried to express a hope she could not feel, that he
would long want it for himself. *Once* more they were to
dine together. For the last time we helped him into the
arm-chair. He expressed a readiness for his dinner, and ate,
or rather *swallowed*, as much as he had done for some time
past. Ever since his poor mouth had become so sore, he
had become quite unable to masticate, and only took what
he could take with a spoon. For several days he had
found great difficulty even in drinking, owing to wind and
phlegm which rose in his throat whenever he attempted to
swallow. To-day there was more of it than ever, and I
was dreadfully shocked at the rattling sound it made,

such as I had heard before on the near approach of death, and only then.

Colonel and Mrs. Douglas came in soon after he had dined. He returned to the couch, and remained upon it for a little while, when he wished to go to bed. Colonel Douglas assisted in putting him there — never to leave it again! The exertion of getting to bed fatigued him sadly; but this soon went off, and he then told us that he felt pretty comfortable. Nothing particular occurred during the rest of that day. He revived towards evening, as he commonly did, and talked occasionally. We took tea in his room, as we had done the evening before. Wishing Mrs. Duckworth to taste a "Sally Lunn," a famous Bath tea-cake, he had desired one to be got. When he ordered it, he jokingly said, " It's one for her and two for myself." Poor dear soul, I reminded him of his words, and begged him to try and eat a bit. I put a scrap upon his tongue such as one might have given to an infant. Nothing in the shape of food could well be softer, but he said it felt hard and rough to him, and he was *unable* to swallow it. He got some sleep that night, but was restless, and often disturbed; and when he awoke up the next morning, which was earlier than usual, I observed that his breath was shorter than it had ever yet been. He was still weaker too, and less able than ever to move himself about in the bed. He said to me, " I haven't a bit of muscular strength left." When I was dressed, and ready for our prayers, he told me to read the 51st Psalm. Then I read some passages of Scripture from a book we were in the habit of using, " The Pious Christian's Daily Preparation for Death and Eternity."

After reading and praying with him, I felt inclined to talk to him more unreservedly than I had ever had courage to do before, and I said to him, " Since it does, indeed, appear to be God's will to take you from us, I want to know if you wish to die, or if you would rather recover." He paused a little, and then said, " I can't say that I *wish* to die."

" You think of *us* more than of yourself, I suppose, and

would like to live chiefly for our sakes." He replied, " It is great suffering, either of mind or body, which generally makes people desire to die, and I have not suffered enough to be weary of life. If it were to please God to give me strength from this moment, and restore me to tolerable health, I could still enjoy life. However, having been brought so very near the gates of the grave, it would be a pity to have to go through it all again. The best way is to put oneself entirely in God's hands, and desire only to do His will."

In answer to something I said about my own share of the trial which seemed coming upon us, he told me, " I am always praying to God to comfort you in your sorrow."

That morning the post brought him a letter from dearest Bob; No. 101, written on the 7th of April, 1846. I read it to him. Some time afterwards he said, " I want to write to dear Sally and Bob, but I am not able." Turning to Harriet,[k] he said, " Tell them both that I love and always have loved them with most inexpressible tenderness, and that I value them both most highly. Tell Bob I have received his letter. I am sorry to hear he has so many causes for vexation, but I have no doubt it will all come right at last. Call him Puseyite or *What-ite*, he is a glorious fellow, and though I have not agreed with him in all his opinions, yet I know him to be an excellent parish priest, and most devoted clergyman."

Harriet and I thought it sad that the poor boys, the two elder ones especially, should not see their dear Father again, and we expressed our wish of sending for them. At first he partly objected, but his love for them and for us prevailed over other considerations; and, after a minute or so, he said, " Very well, send for them; yes, do. They are thorough good boys, and have always behaved most affectionately to me. Clement and Herbert both loved to wait upon me."

Poor fellows, there was no longer time to send for them.

----

[k] In her letter to me she says, " And then, dear, he spoke with so much energy, his whole soul seemed in those words."

For several days we had observed that he made a point of
noticing the three little ones whenever they happened to
come into his room. He always caressed and spoke to each
of them separately.

To-day, Sunday, the 23rd, when he first saw Kitty and
Mia, he said to them, in a very serious manner, "The
great work you have to do now is to pray to God for your
dear Papa. I am not able to pray much myself. Beg
God to enable me to bear my sickness patiently, and if I
die, to take my soul to heaven." He then spoke to them
of God's goodness to him in sparing him from pain, and
expressed his great thankfulness for this mercy. Nothing
could exceed the *patience* that he showed throughout all his
long and trying illness. He had suffered a great deal in
various ways, but *never once* did the smallest murmurs escape
from him.

Mrs. Duckworth and Colonel Douglas came together after
the afternoon church. My beloved husband was unable to
talk much. More and more phlegm seemed to be collecting,
and he could scarcely spit up any, which distressed him
extremely. A gasping came on, and every now and then he
wanted to be raised up suddenly in order to breathe better.
The difficulty of breathing and swallowing had so much
increased that he could take very little nourishment. He
dozed occasionally. About four o'clock in the afternoon the
elder Mr. Stockwell called. He had not seen dearest Robert
for six weeks, so that all he knew of the case was from his
son's report. He asked some questions, and felt his pulse,
which he said was *good*. Dearest Robert told him how he
was oppressed by the phlegm and unable to cough it up.
Mr. Stockwell said, "You seem to have a cold." These
few words, spoken perhaps at random, produced a strange
effect upon me, which I now can only *wonder* at. The idea
that what had alarmed me so much before was merely a cold
got possession of my mind. Dearest Robert had been suffering a good deal lately from rheumatic pain, which he attributed chiefly to getting uncovered, and thereby chilled in

bed. I thought the air-passages, too, might have been affected in the same way, and felt satisfied. It was a blessed delusion for the short, the very short time it lasted.

My beloved Robert himself was not so deceived. He now *felt* that his departure drew very nigh. Several times that I spoke to him about his having caught a cold, he made no answer. The last time he said, "I suppose I have; it makes *no difference.*" As the evening advanced he slept more, and whilst he slept, he made a louder noise than usual in breathing. Still strangely blinded to his real condition, I was pleased at his sleeping so much, and thought it would refresh him. Mrs. Duckworth said she hoped it was good sleep; but the very remark showed she had misgivings about it. Harriet brought back some of my alarm, by saying, she thought he was "*very ill.*"

Between each sleep he awoke gasping, and was eager to be raised. About eight o'clock I brought him an egg beat up with milk, thinking that better than wine for the *cold* I even then thought might account for the accumulation of phlegm!

He took some, but was too much oppressed to take it all. Soon afterwards Mrs. Duckworth and Colonel Douglas left us, intending, as we supposed, to return to their home the next day. Throughout the evening their manner had tended to cheer me; but it seemed changed just as they were going away, and I was greatly saddened by the alarm I thought it expressed. My beloved Robert seemed to be asleep when they went, but he was not, and a few minutes afterwards he asked me if they were not gone. I said yes, and he replied, "Ah! they did wisely to avoid saying *Good-bye!*" He lay quiet for some time longer, and then started up and gasped frightfully. *All at once* the awful truth burst upon me. He must, indeed, be dying!

Harriet was alone with me. The poor children had all gone to bed. He wanted to move perpetually, and we called the maid to help us. We moved him about from one position to another, but he found no relief in any. His distress was very great. As he struggled for breath, he called out, "I can't breathe—I am suffocating;" and if we went close to the bed, he said, "Don't come near me; go away." At ten o'clock we sent for the doctor. I knew *then* that nothing could be done; but I thought it would be a comfort to see him. When he came, he tried to cheer me with a hope I could no longer feel. He said the pulse was perfectly good, and whilst that was the case, that there was a possibility that medicine might relieve him. He told me to give him a camphor draught that we had by us, to enable him to throw off the phlegm. Dearest Robert told him that he had already taken two that day without the slightest benefit. He said, "Then they are not strong enough, and I will send you some that *are.*" In the mean time he proposed giving brandy and water. My beloved Robert said he did not think he could swallow it, but that he would try. He got it down, but it had no effect.

Mr. Stockwell behaved in a very kind, feeling manner, and offered either to stay with us or to come again, whichever we preferred. We begged him to go home then, and return in a few hours. He soon sent us the medicine; but when I asked dearest Robert if he would take it, he said, with marked emphasis, "*Nonsense, nonsense!*" He continued in the same great distress, sometimes motioning to us to lift him up, and then directly afterwards wishing to be lowered. The struggle for breath was dreadful. Once, when it was at its worst, he said "Pray for me." I took up a book, thinking he meant me to pray out loud. He said, "It's of no use," meaning, of course, that he was too much engrossed by his bodily sufferings to join us. We knelt by his bedside and prayed silently. At another time he called out in a loud voice, "O God, save my soul." He spoke fast, as if afraid he should not have breath to finish even so short a prayer. Once I said to him, "I am afraid you are suffering sadly." His only answer was, "God's will be done." The cold perspiration was profuse from head to foot. It made him feel so cold about his arms and shoulders, which were outside the bedclothes, that he frequently asked for more covering.

Once, after telling me to cover his shoulder, he said, " It doesn't signify, I shall soon be cold all over." The cook came into the room—Harriet said to him, " Here is the kind-hearted cook come to see you." He said, " God bless her !" I said " And haven't you a blessing for Otway ?" (the house-maid, who had always waited upon him with singular kindness of feeling, and he was very partial to her in consequence.) " Oh, yes, that I have—God bless her too ! I have blessed her many a time." At two o'clock the doctor came ; some one got up to go to him, and there was a little stir in the room. Dearest Robert asked the cause of it ; and when I told him that the doctor was come, but that I had desired he might not be brought up stairs, he said in a very faint whisper, " I shan't want him any more." The perspiration about his head and face annoyed him, and from time to time he told me to wipe it away,—he would say, " forehead," " nose," " mouth ;" and whenever I wiped near his mouth, he generally said, " Quick, quick !" as if my hand kept the air from him. I frequently dipped my finger in wine and water and wetted his parched lips and tongue. Sometimes he would say " Enough," and this, I think, was the *very last* word that dear tongue ever uttered. Once, when he still seemed to be suffering a great deal, I could not help praying to God to *release* him. My beloved Robert heard me, and though he could not speak, he reproved me for it by a sign which could not be mistaken.

To the last he seemed to retain all his faculties. Within half an hour of his death, I said to Harriet, " What a blessing this is,—he is amongst us to the very last ; thank God for it." He directly said, " Amen." Long after he ceased to speak, he turned his eyes towards us and pressed our hands. The struggle gradually subsided, and the breath grew fainter and fainter till *half-past three*, when, as I humbly believe, my beloved husband entered into his *eternal rest*.

I have omitted one thing ; but it is important, and I must add it here. I asked him if he felt easy in his mind, and happy? He said, " I have a humble hope,—a very humble hope." This was some time after he had said, "Oh, God, save my soul!"

Until the arrival of his brother-in-law, the Rev. J. Henderson, everything was done in the most feeling way that kindness could suggest, by Colonel Douglas. They, together with my Uncle, V Knox, Sir John Liddell, my brothers, and several other relations and friends, followed my dear Father's remains to their last earthly resting-place on the 29th.

They lie in the cemetery at Widcombe,[1] covered with a simple stone, on which is engraven,

The Beloved Remains of
ROBERT CLEMENT SCONCE,
WHO DIED AUGUST 24TH, 1846,
IN HIS FIFTY-NINTH YEAR.

And in a spot so lovely, that, whenever I visit it, the pleasing idea occurs to me that it is just one he would have fixed upon from which to make one of his most beautiful drawings.

Colonel Douglas, writing to his mother-in-law, Mrs. Duckworth, some time after, from Malta, says:—

"I am now going back to the *Volcano*, as we sail for Corfu this evening; and if I have yet an hour, I am going over to see poor Portelli. It will be a solace to me to see and speak to one who loved and valued our precious Sconce; and he will like to hear from me all I can tell him of his peaceful end."

In another part of the letter, Colonel Douglas, speaking of a brother-in-law, says:—

"It appears to me that the symptoms are very similar to those we witnessed in our beloved friend.[m] May it be my

---

[1] Adjoining Bath.   [m] My Father.

comfort to find my poor brother-in-law in the same beautiful, and calm, and holy frame of mind ! ”

*   *   *   *   *   *

And here I do not think it will be considered out of place if, in memory of both Father and Son, I introduce two letters written to me, when these sad tidings reached Australia, by my dear brother, the “Robert” and “Bob” so often addressed in these volumes, and who, five years later, was also taken from us; when, doubtless, his spirit was reunited to his beloved Father's :—

“ SYDNEY, *Christmas Eve,* 1846.

“ MY DEAREST SISTER,—Join with me in praising God for His great goodness, and praying Him to support us all under the affliction He has sent us. I do praise Him and thank Him with all my heart and soul for taking our own dear Father from a world of which he had had enough,—in which for years he had suffered unceasing pain,—to one of rest and peace.

“ But I need support, and so will you, sweet Sister; for the loss, temporary as it is, of *such* a Father, is hard, very hard, to bear. I have been weeping for hours like a child ; and my soul would refuse to be comforted if I did not know that the best and surest comfort is at hand. Oh, how I loved him !—how he loved me ; and how little did I deserve such love ! God give us both grace to live so that we may be worthy to follow him and be with him !

“ What joy it is, though, Sukey, to think how *surely* he is with the saints at rest,--to think what a humble, devout, earnest Christian he ever was,--to think of all the good he has done, all the poor he has fed and clothed, all the hearts he has won by his gentleness, and sweetness, and kindness,— to think how he loved Christ and trusted in Him,—how he was sustained to the last by continually feeding on the Heavenly food of the blessed Sacrament. My selfish tears scald me with self-reproach when I remember that he is even

now in the joy of his Lord, with our own Mother too, and
with our Fan—bless her sweet heart,—and your Franky and
our Bobby,—a holy family of pure and loving spirits.

"Yesterday evening a note came from Cos. Joseph by the
packet, *alone ;* no other from anybody. It had a deep black
edge, and the post-mark Bath. It is short and hurried, and
tells nothing but that our dear angel Father died on the 24th
of August—St. Bartholomew's Day. His guileless soul fled
on the same day as did that of the Israelite indeed, and kept
the festival above." *   *   *   *   *

" Christmas Day.

" May it be full of blessings to you and lasting happiness,
and of present joy in the midst of our sorrow. This great
day's event it is that has turned death into life. The martyrs
called the day of their death their *birth*-day, and so in keeping the Saviour's birth-day I have been keeping our dear
Father's too, and that guileless Apostle's. I take deep comfort in these providential coincidences.

" We have just returned from our early communion. I
could not do the duty myself; but I never received with
greater hope and love. How thrilling now to us will be
that commemoration of the blessed, when we pray for grace
' so to follow their good examples that with them we may be
partakers of God's heavenly kingdom.'

" The bishop is going to do my morning service for me,
and Bodenham the afternoon; and among them my kind
friends will take my work till I am able to command myself.

" I am not *quite* sure, dearest Sukey, that it will not be
my duty to go to England, and take care of our poor dear
Mother and her eight little ones. It will depend, of course,
upon what I may hear; but how desolate she must be! I
have written a heartily affectionate letter, promising to be to
her all that a son can be, and gladly indeed would I do
anything to cheer her; but England has no charms for me
now our dear Father and sweet Fan are at rest. You are
nearer to me here; my little son lies in the Sydney burial-

ground, and we have warm friends all about us." I could
not go without a bitter pang, and it will only be if the
demands of duty are peremptory. God bless and support
you. I am ever your most affectionate Brother,

"R. K. SCONCE."

After reading his stepmother's narrative of our Father's
last days, he wrote to me as follows :—

"MY DEAREST SUKEY,—After waiting for more than a
month in great anxiety for English letters, I have at last had
the inexpressible satisfaction of receiving the inclosed narrative.° I have copied it all out in a volume, which is now
filled with many memorials of our angel Father, so the
original you may consider as yours. It will, no doubt,
afford you the same thrilling interest it did to me. It is
most admirably written, and tells much for the Christian
strength and energy of mind by which our poor Mother is
sustained in her grief. I have written her a long letter
about it, and I shall continue to write to her regularly as I
did to him, loving her for his sake with all the affection of a
son.   *   *   *   *   *   *

"When you have read the account of our beloved Father's
sufferings and death, I know you will think about it just as I
do, that all was just as we could have wished. I mean, of
course, in his own bearing. His pains and trials were great,
but they were sent by God, and, of course, we are satisfied
that *such* things should be as He wills, not as we will. But,
as far as we can judge by the narrative, *could* he have borne
them more beautifully than he did? Is it possible that
any one could show himself on his deathbed a more thorough

° My dear Brother never returned to England. He died at Sydney in 1852,
in the Roman Catholic faith, which he had embraced two years after his
Father's death. Nothing but the most sincere conviction influenced him in
this step, whereby he sacrificed all his worldly advantages.
    Which I have already given.

Christian? It was, I firmly believe, a most *blessed* death.
See how patient he was through all. See how he *loved*. See
how strong and unwavering was his *faith* in the mercy of
God. See how *meek* and *humble* he was to the last; how
free was his *hope* in Christ from all presumption. You know,
dearest Sukey, I am accustomed to deathbeds, and many a
time have I left a room of one who would have been a *saint*
in the eyes of that unhappy Mr. ——, with a heavy heart.
What would I not give to hear oftener from those I am called
to visit those precious words of our Father's—" I have a
humble hope, a very humble hope." Had I pictured to
myself just what I could have wished my Father's last days
to have been, I should have anticipated all that occurred.
I do not mean I would have had him suffer as he did
(many, many tears have I shed for those sufferings), or that
he should have been tormented and persecuted and *excommunicated*, by that faithless minister of the Church who
attended him. His pains and his trials I said before were
from God; but the rest I would have had just as it was.
His behaviour to Mr. P—— was eminently beautiful. He
calmly and patiently listened to the cant he must have
nauseated, and uttered no word of resentment against him
for the cruel outrage that denied him the bread of life.
Deny it, *indeed*, he could not, for who can doubt that even
then that sweet soul was *full* of his Saviour. The unjust
sentence of a fanatical priest would surely receive no ratifica-
tion in the courts of heaven. He *did* feed on that heavenly
food, and abundant was the blessing he derived from
it. There was much loveliness in the charity that received
Mr. P—— and thankfully used his ministry the following
day. I have prayed for some portion of the same spirit that
influenced him, that I may be able to suppress any undue
indignation. Oh how ardently I do wish that clergymen who
do not '*approve*' of their own Church's commands would
have the honesty to resign their office. Our Father wanted
no Mr. P——, his little finger was worth ten such men—he
wanted a priest—he wanted the ordinances of the Church.

Mr. P—— refused the *ordinances*, and tried to substitute *himself* for them. It was a hard trial, but God's grace in the dear Father's heart was triumphant. Knowing, as you do, what *my* opinions are on such matters, you will not be surprised at any warmth of expression I use in speaking of Mr. P——'s conduct. The truth is, I had set my heart on hearing that the dear man's sufferings had been soothed by that most blessed Sacrament, and my disappointment was great. I could have wished him to have had, as sweet Fan had, a man like Archdeacon Wilberforce[p] to attend him, but God's will be done. All is well, I am assured, and happy in the assurance. God bless you, dearest sister, and Hanmer, and your little ones, and give you health and strength to bear this sad, sad grief.

"We must pray for each other."

And now my labour of love, which has cost me many tears, is over : I close it with a letter from our friend, the Rev. Edward Kitson :—[q]

"MY DEAR MRS. BUNBURY,—I fear you will have thought me unkind in not answering your letter sooner, but really and truly I have not had time to do so, and now I am obliged to write more hurriedly than I could wish.

"I regret much that I have not by me any writing of your Father's, with which to assist you in your praiseworthy purpose of sketching a memoir of his life. If, however, you should be fortunate enough to collect some of his letters, I think your editorial labours will be comparatively easy. Little or no comment would be required. They would only require to be read, in order that the writer's soundness of understanding and goodness of heart should at once be manifest. Indeed, from among men it would be difficult to select one whose life might be so safely held up as an example to those for whose benefit you purpose writing your book.

---

[p] The Bishop of Oxford.   [q] Now of Greenwich Hospital.

"As a gentleman, in the highest sense of the word (no small praise, *I* think), as an elegant classical scholar, and as an accomplished artist, he was an ornament and acquisition to any society in which he might move. But commendable and valuable as such attractions are, there were other features of his character still more worthy of imitation, especially his meekness and unaffected piety.

"Of the many years that I had the pleasure of his acquaintance, I had for three or four the additional gratification of numbering him amongst my congregation at the Dockyard Chapel at Malta. Never absent himself from his place at church on Sundays or festivals, he was also accompanied by Mrs. Sconce and their numerous family, whom, in this respect, as in all others, they took particular pains early to train in the way in which they should go. Certainly amongst that congregation, none, and I doubt if from any other one could be found more attentive to *all* the practical duties of a really good Churchman. All charities, whether of a public or private nature, he was ever ready to sanction and support—and so quietly and unostentatiously, that he seemed literally to fulfil our Lord's injunction on such occasions, 'Let not thy left hand know what thy right hand doeth.' And whilst he acted up to the latter part of the exhortation of the Apostle, 'especially to do good unto those of the household of faith,' he forgot not the former part, which is equally important—'to do good unto *all* men.' I regret that at this distance of time I am unable to specify his numerous acts of kindness and beneficence; I can, however, safely say, that his whole conduct rendered him universally respected and beloved. And although *I* cannot remember his good works, yet he has gone where 'they will assuredly follow.'

"I have, my dear Mrs. Bunbury, thus given a brief and rough sketch of your dear Father's character, so far as I was acquainted with it, and as it is still impressed on my memory. I wish I had time and ability to do proper justice to the subject, but I have neither.   *   *   *   *

" If I can on any future occasion help you with regard to the matter you have in hand I will do so most gladly and willingly.

" Pray remember me kindly to Captain Bunbury, and also to Mrs. Sconce and family, who I believe are still residing in Bath, and believe me to remain, yours very sincerely,

"EDWARD KITSON."

" The just man walketh in his integrity; his children are blessed after him."—*Proverbs,* xx. 7.

May it be so in this case!